"You'd better go below," the pirate said to Sable harshly, refusing to look at her.

"What have I done?"

"I said go below." Morgan seized Sable's arms as if to push her, but it was as if a floodtide burst between them when he touched her. Lifting her into his arms, he carried her below, kicking the cabin door shut. Sable's senses reeled as he kissed her; her lips parted beneath his; she could feel his heart thundering and she trembled with a need as fierce as his own.

Pale moonlight streamed through the unshuttered windows as, unashamedly, she slid her slender arms around his neck, drawing him down. Nothing in all creation, Sable knew then, could rival her love for this man. . . .

Sable

ELLEN TANNER MARSH

A JOVE BOOK

This Jove book contains the complete
text of the original edition.
It has been completely reset in a typeface
designed for easy reading, and was printed
from new film.

SABLE

A Jove Book/published by arrangement with
the author

PRINTING HISTORY
Berkley trade paperback edition/October 1984
Jove edition/October 1985

ISBN: 0-515-08215-5

Jove books are published by The Berkley Publishing Group,
200 Madison Avenue, New York, N.Y. 10016.
The words "A JOVE BOOK" and the "J" with sunburst
are trademarks belonging to Jove Publications, Inc.

PRINTED IN THE UNITED STATES OF AMERICA

For my sister
Gitti

Chapter 1

Pale moonlight filtered through the canopy of gnarled tree branches, illuminating the smooth gray cobblestones that lined the wide, winding street. Dry leaves, whipped by the stiff breeze, scuttled through the gutters while the fragile heads of budding snowdrops bent low in the gardens. On the sidewalk two cloaked pedestrians turned their collars higher against the onslaught of the wind, increasing their strides as they clutched their top hats, eager to get home to the warmth of their hearths.

Sitting on the padded window seat, slim elbows propped against the marble sill, Lady Sable St. Germain sighed deeply as she watched them disappear into the darkness. Was it only yesterday that she had gone riding with her family in Hyde Park, the spring sun warm on her shoulders? With birds singing sweetly in the trees and the crocuses blooming amid the budding green grass, Sable had even ridden out without a cape, the cold of winter held at bay at last.

Yet the following morning had dawned overcast and chilly, the penetrating dampness reminiscent of bleak November afternoons. Sable sighed again, her nose still pressed to the icy glass. Although the weather had cleared later that day, the temperature had not risen, and she found herself thinking now that spring would never come. The winter had seemed endless

1

enough as it was, especially Christmas, which, for the first time in Sable's memory, the St. Germains had spent away from North Head. It wasn't fair, Sable thought passionately.

"It would please me proper, m'lady, if you'd stop moonin' out the window and get ready for the Havertys' party!"

Sable turned to find Lucy Walters standing in the doorway, hands propped on her ample hips as she regarded her young mistress with mock severity. Seeing the look of longing on Sable's face that the young girl was unable to hide, Lucy relented instantly and bustled into the rose-and-gold-decorated bedroom.

"What be it, m'lady?" she asked. "Not thinkin' of Master Derek again, are you?" She sniffed, her tone indicating that the young swain in question was certainly not worth troubling one's head over.

"Goodness, no!" Sable protested, her vehemence satisfying her maid. "If I had my own way I wouldn't even attend that silly party of theirs this evening. Oh, Lucy, I'm sick to death of balls and dinners and theater parties!"

As always, even the slightest show of spirit on Lady Sable's part never failed to bring a brilliance to her eyes that transformed the leaf-green depths to the fire of polished emeralds. She was breathtaking, Lucy Walters decided with a trace of maternal pride as Lady Sable halted before her, slender arms akimbo, a flush creeping to her soft cheeks.

In a wrapper of dark plum shantung silk, her skin took on a rosy glow and her firm young breasts swelled against the plunging, lace-edged neckline. Unbound, her glossy hair spilled in riotous curls below her curving hips, the color neither black nor brunette, but a pleasing shade of both that, when the lamplight fell upon it, reflected dark mysterious highlights of gold.

Tawny brows arched beguilingly over the compelling green eyes which slanted at the corners. These irresistible eyes were set on either side of a small nose that turned up enchantingly at the tip. Yet at the moment there was nothing sweet or childlike about the irate young woman who faced her embattled maid with pouting pink lips and haughtily set shoulders.

"As a matter of fact," Sable was saying in a determined tone of voice, "I believe I'll send my regrets to the Havertys this evening and let Father and Mother endure their company without me."

"You'll do no such thing," Lucy Walters retorted firmly.

Opening the door to the beautiful mahogany clothespress, she began rummaging among the billowing gowns for a suitable one for Sable to wear. "His lordship said you met Master Derek in the park yesterday afternoon and that he personally asked after you to make sure you were coming."

Reference to yesterday's ride reminded Sable of the certainty she had felt then that their return to Cornwall would not be delayed much longer. Her face fell and she turned away, nodding listlessly when Lucy held up a gown for her inspection.

"What be it, lass?"

"Oh, Lucy, when are we ever going to go home?"

So it was North Head the lassie was pining for and not some lovesick suitor, Lucy realized with great relief. She had been afraid all this time that sweet, gentle-hearted Lady Sable was falling for Derek Haverty's pretty speeches and treacly poetry, when actually she'd been nothing more than homesick!

"There, there, my dearie," Lucy soothed, laying the gown across the satin counterpane of Sable's bed and reaching out to embrace her young mistress warmly. "Only a few short weeks, I daresay, and then we can bid London farewell!"

Sable sighed deeply. "I hope you're right."

The older woman's lips twitched. It was the same way with Sable's parents, she knew. Though both the Earl and Countess had a great number of friends and acquaintances in London and were swamped with invitations whenever they came, the couple always strove hard to conceal their impatience to leave the hubbub of city life behind and return to the relative peace and quiet of their isolated Cornwall estate.

"I'll have your bath filled straightaway," Lucy added, her tone indicating that the subject of leaving London was closed for the time being. "Your mother bade me tell you to be certain you're on time tonight, and I intend to see that Her Ladyship's wishes are fulfilled."

"Oh, Lucy, you know I'm never late!" Sable chided, but the tiring woman was already gone, a blast of chilly air blowing through the door she had left open in her haste. Sable's lips curved in an affectionate smile as she shut it firmly behind her, but her sloping green eyes glittered mutinously as she turned and saw the elegant white brocade gown draped amid gauzy layers of petticoats on the coverlet before her. Only a few more weeks, Lucy had said, but in her opinion their return home could not come soon enough, not with Derek Haverty constantly breathing down her neck and making himself an utter nuisance with his repeated requests for her hand.

If only she could speak to her mother about him, Sable thought forlornly, yet knew that she mustn't. After all, it was Lady Raven St. Germain's illness that had brought them here in the first place. Though the winter in London was as bleak as it was in Cornwall, Sable's father had decided that his wife would be better cared for with medical help more available than in their remote duchy. The terrible racking coughs and the chest pains her mother had suffered since the beginning of autumn had thankfully disappeared, but Sable was glad, despite her own troubles, that her father had decided they should remain in London until the advent of warm weather.

Sable's eyes glowed as she thought of North Head. Doubtless her beloved mare waited as impatiently as Sable herself did for the chance to gallop once again across the undulating moors that stretched down to the surging sea. And how many months had it been since she had last seen her brother Edward? Not since he had come to share the Christmas holidays with them, and here it was the beginning of March already!

Sable's heart swelled with pride as she thought of her brother, well aware that running the estates was a great responsibility and that it was a measure of her father's faith in him that Ned, at seventeen, was in charge of North Head in the Earl's absence. Still, she missed him terribly, and only her youngest brother Liam's presence in London had made her separation from him tolerable. Sable suspected that her parents felt the same way, and she was reluctant to increase her mother's homesickness by burdening her with her troubles.

"Are you ready for your bath, m'lady?"

Roused from her musing, Sable nodded and followed Lucy into the sitting room, where the brass hip bath, filled with scented water, stood on the rich burgundy carpet. Deftly she twisted her gleaming hair into a thick coil and pinned it to her head before dropping the Shantung silk robe to the floor and stepping into the tub. Sighing, she closed her eyes and let the warm water caress her body. Although a long evening with Derek Haverty loomed dismally ahead of her, she did not dwell upon it. Instead she thought of North Head and the happy reunion with Ned that awaited all of them. If it were up to her, Sable told herself firmly, she'd never set foot from Cornwall again once they returned!

Lathering a bar of scented soap between her slender fingers, she washed herself, scrubbing her long, tapering calves and silken thighs until her skin glowed pink. Her glossy hair had been washed by a disapproving Lucy earlier that morning to "get the horse smell out of it," and Sable smiled to herself now, thinking how much Lucy objected to the time her young mistress spent in the stables.

"Sometimes I prefer the company of Father's animals to the stuffy people living here!" Sable muttered to herself, reaching for a towel and rubbing herself dry. Actually, she liked most of her parents' acquaintances and had made a number of friends herself, but it was Derek Haverty and his ilk that had annoyed her from the moment she had met them. Sable had made her debut earlier that autumn and since then had known not a moment's peace. Her father had warned her before their arrival in London that she would become the object of ardent pursuit, but Sable had never imagined she'd be descended upon by hordes of admirers at every social gathering she attended.

"Just like a pack of hungry wolves!" she told herself, tossing aside the towel and reaching for the lacy undergarments Lucy had laid out for her earlier. She was in the process of sliding a stocking over one silky thigh when Lucy entered, casting a swift glance at the brass clock that ticked on the carved marble mantel.

"Let me help you with your dressin'," she suggested, pleased that Sable hadn't been lounging in the tub as she had half expected.

Sable patiently submitted to her tiring woman's ministrations, allowing Lucy to fuss longer than was necessary over the proper placement of the yards of petticoats that were to fit over the cumbersome hoops. After straightening the billowing brocade skirts and fastening the countless tiny pearl buttons along Sable's trim back, Lucy stepped back at last and studied her charge with a critical eye.

"Just your hair needs doin', m'lady"—she clucked approvingly—"and then you'll be fair ready to take the evening by storm."

Sable gave a soft, derisive snort. "I'd rather look a little less fetching, thank you! Maybe then I'd be rid of my fawning admirers for a time."

"Even in rags you'd win every heart, m'lady," Lucy answered firmly.

It was true. Without the adornment of jewels, her gleaming coppery-black hair still coiled in a haphazard fashion about her head, Sable St. Germain radiated a natural, enchanting beauty that was breathtaking to behold. The white brocade gown bared her slim shoulders, revealing the satin smoothness of her skin and delicate collarbones. The flounce of frilly Bordeaux lace adorning the scalloped neckline of her ballgown revealed as much of the tantalizing cleavage of her full breasts that convention would allow. A bodice studded with tiny seed pearls tapered down to a waist of narrow proportions, while the tips of tiny satin slippers peeked charmingly from beneath the frothy hem.

Undaunted by her mistress's lack of enthusiasm, Lucy refused to be rushed while doing Sable's hair, and had to admit to herself when the task was complete that her efforts had been well rewarded. She had swept the thick mass of gleaming curls away from Sable's oval face, securing them with the treasured mother-of-pearl combs the Countess had given Sable last year for her seventeenth birthday. The tiny diamonds that glittered within them caught the lamplight as Sable turned dutifully for Lucy's final inspection, giving one the illusion that her dark hair was dusted with precious gemstones.

In addition Lucy had woven a posy of freshly picked snowdrops and white satin ribbon through the glossy curls, the overall effect even more stunning than the tiring woman had anticipated. Snapping open a pearl-studded, ivory-handled fan, she placed it in Sable's hand and gave her an approving nod.

"Fit for an audience with Her Majesty, you be." She sighed, thinking to herself that Lady Sable was no longer the enchanting little girl who had always tugged at everyone's heartstrings.

No, the beautiful creature standing expectantly before her was a woman whose young breasts strained against the bodice of her gown, her magnificent eyes sparkling with the thirst for life that had yet to be awakened by a man to the ripened bloom of passion. Someday, Lucy realized, and not too far in the future, either, Lady Sable St. Germain would be led across the threshold of childhood forever, to experience for the first time the yearnings of love which only a man, the right man, could satisfy.

"I only hope it won't be that milksop Derek Haverty!" Lucy muttered acidly to herself.

"I beg your pardon?" Sable asked innocently.

Unaware that she had spoken aloud, Lucy shrugged her plump shoulders and smiled ruefully. "I must be gettin' senile in my dotage, dearie."

"Oh, go on with you, Lucy!" Sable taunted, an affectionate light glowing in her eyes. "You're still young enough to think about getting married again! How can you possibly consider yourself senile?"

"Here, now, let me put this jewelry on, m'lady," Lucy said hastily, retrieving a slim box of midnight blue velvet from the dressing table in the corner. "His Lordship does so like to see his womenfolk wearing the St. Germain jewels!"

"Stop trying to change the subject, Lucy," Sable teased, a bewitching dimple appearing in her soft cheek. "You promised Reece and Jims both that you'd let them know which one you were going to marry as soon as we returned home." One tawny eyebrow lifted with merry devilment. "Well, which one shall it be? The brawny stablemaster or the sensitive, lovelorn butcher?"

Lucy was unable to keep the color from her cheeks. At forty-two she was a widow of over a dozen years' standing and had long since given up the hope of ever remarrying. Who would have suspected that two appealing offers would arrive nearly atop one another and that she would have the delicious chance of choosing between them?

"Now, Lady Sable, I ain't decided yet," she answered firmly, "and I won't be tellin' nobody before the groom knows himself!"

"Good for you, Lucy," came a soft, amused voice from the doorway. "I know Sable has a way of being persistent, but you mustn't allow her to pry secrets out of you prematurely!"

Raven St. Germain, Countess of Monterrey, smiled as she swept into the room, her petticoats rustling softly. In a gown of port-colored taffeta she looked slim and breathtakingly beautiful. Her lingering illness had only served to enhance the translucent quality of her skin and add a poignant serenity to her lovely features. Her hair was glossy and dark like rare black jade, and it was drawn away from a face as delicate in its oval perfection as her daughter's. Only the startling gold of her eyes distinguished Raven's beauty from Sable's, yet Raven had always been delighted that her daughter's dark emerald eyes and gold-tinted black hair came from her father.

At birth, Sable's hair had been as dark as Raven's own, yet,

as the years passed and Sable spent her days with her father
and brothers in the bright Cornish sun, it had become perma-
nently touched with golden fire. Looking at her daughter now
and seeing, as Lucy Walters had, the rare beauty of a ripening
woman, Raven felt overcome with tenderness for her firstborn
child.

"Are you ready, Sable?" she asked with a gentle smile.
"Your father is waiting downstairs."

"Here, take this with you, dearie," Lucy put in, draping a
shawl of warm Cheviot wool over Sable's shoulders. "It be a
foul night outside, and your cloak may not be warm enough."

Sable accepted it thankfully and slipped her arm through
her mother's as the two of them exited into the corridor. Though
both of her parents were tall, Sable had not inherited height
from either of them. She was small and delicate, her slimness
making her appear deceptively fragile. Yet there was no small
measure of strength in her graceful carriage, and as she descended the winding staircase at her mother's side there was
little to distinguish the womanly fluidness of her movements
from those of the Countess.

Standing in the elegant gilded foyer, Charles St. Germain
allowed a warm smile to curve his lips as he watched his wife
and daughter approach. As always, his eyes went first to Raven,
his wife, and his heart constricted at the sight of her. Though
he himself had helped her dress not a scant hour ago, the process
interrupted more than once by ardent lovemaking, he was unable to drink in enough of her in the beautiful wine-colored
gown that emphasized her girlishly slim figure. About her slender throat she wore the teardrop-shaped diamond pendant he
had given her at Sable's birth almost eighteen years ago, a
symbol of his great love for her and a reminder of the hardships
they had been forced to endure before they could live in peace
together.

Sable, too, was a vision of loveliness, and Charles's broad
chest filled with pride as she stepped down onto the marble
floor of the foyer and gave him a sweeping curtsy, the dimple
in her soft cheek deepening, a teasing light in the emerald eyes
that were so like his own.

"I'm not late am I, Papa?" she asked, standing on tiptoe to
slide her arms about his neck and kiss his lean, scarred cheek
affectionately.

"Promptness is a Barrancourt trait," Lady Raven reminded

her husband as the Earl assured his daughter that he had not been kept waiting. "You must give credit where it's due, Charles."

"Then I take the credit for myself," the Earl told her with a roguish smile, taking her slim hand in his. "After all, since my daughter is so very beautiful she requires little time in primping before the glass."

"Are you suggesting I had no hand in determining Sable's looks?" Raven demanded archly, her tawny eyes glowing as she gazed up into Charles's handsome face.

The twinkling emerald eyes went from Raven's lovely oval face to Sable's smiling one. "In faith, my lady, there is so little of your coloring in my daughter that I'm beginning to wonder where she came from."

"Oh, that's not true, Papa," Sable protested with a giggle. "You've told me often enough that I'm cursed with the stubborn Barrancourt pride."

"That I have," the Earl conceded, "and if I'd known in advance that such a tiresome trait would be passed from my wife to her children, I would have married someone else."

"Would you, m'lord?" Raven purred, and even Sable could see the light of desire that sprang into her father's eyes as he gazed with longing into his wife's beautiful face. She felt no embarrassment at being witness to the great love her parents shared for one another, for that had been something she and her brothers had been exposed to throughout their lives. In truth, it never failed to bring a lump to her throat—and a curious emptiness to her heart of late.

Charles brushed his strong fingers across his wife's cheek in a gentle caress and then turned to his daughter, his eyes lit with deep inner contentment. "Well, ladies, if you're ready? We shouldn't keep the Havertys waiting."

A frown wrinkled Sable's smooth brow as she allowed a hovering footman to lay a fur-trimmed cape across her shoulders. Her father, she knew, wasn't overly fond of the Havertys and had accepted their invitation mainly out of courtesy since George Haverty was one of his business associates. Or was there more to this gathering than met the eye? she wondered as they stepped out into the frosty air where the elegant black evening coach awaited them in the circular drive below. Was her father perhaps aware of Derek Haverty's feelings for her and did he secretly approve of them?

Sable hoped not, yet let none of her doubts show in her small face as her father helped her into the waiting vehicle after solicitously seating her mother inside. She forgot her disturbing thoughts, however, when she caught sight of her brother Liam peeking down at her from his bedroom window. Though he had been put to bed an hour ago, Sable knew that he had waited up to watch them leave, and she waved to him as the coach lurched off down the drive. Instantly Liam's face brightened and he waved back, a mop of dark curls falling in an unruly fashion into his eyes before he disappeared from Sable's view.

The Havertys' townhouse was located only a few short miles from the elegant Mayfair mansion in which the Earl and Countess of Monterrey resided whenever they were in London. With little traffic on the wide, tree-lined streets, the elegant coach bearing the St. Germain coat of arms made excellent time, drawing to a halt before the well-lit entrance, where the coachman jumped down to assist his passengers out.

A Haverty footman in top hat and tails was also there to help, but the Earl ignored both of them, stepping out and turning to personally take Raven's hand in his. For a moment his hold lingered as he lifted her down beside him, and Raven felt as flushed and heady as she had when, as a young girl, she had first fallen in love with the handsome, dashing captain of the *Orient Star*. Dressed in formal black, the Earl of Monterrey looked prepossessingly handsome, his magnificent physique and rugged good looks nearly unchanged by the years that had passed since his marriage to the tempestuous and beautiful Raven Barrancourt.

To Raven's loving eyes he was even more attractive than he had been in his youth. Maturity and rugged good living had etched lines of strength and character into his handsome face, the small scar he carried on one lean cheek emphasizing those qualities and making her heart beat faster as she returned his burning gaze.

Aware that the footman was watching them with a mixture of curiosity and awe, Raven gave him one of her beautiful smiles and then ushered her husband and daughter up the wide flight of steps. As the major-domo announced the arrival of the Earl and Countess of Monterrey and their daughter, Lady Sable St. Germain, Raven leaned down and whispered in her daughter's shell-shaped ear, "Don't let Derek Haverty upset you tonight, love. Your father and I have no intention of accepting his offer for you!"

Sable had just enough time to give her mother a surprised look before they were received by the Havertys themselves. Derek was instantly at her side, impeccably attired and not at all bad-looking with his blond hair combed back from his wide forehead, his eyes devouring her appearance in a shamelessly obvious manner.

"May I say how ravishing you look this evening, Lady Sable!" he informed her in an ardent whisper. Pulling her into a secluded corner, he allowed his hold on her small hand to linger far longer than was deemed appropriate.

"It's kind of you to say so, Mr. Haverty," Sable replied with a forced smile, watching helplessly as her parents were pounced on much as she had been: her father by rouged matrons who batted their fans at him coyly and friends from St. James, his favorite club, her mother by acquaintances and admirers who complimented her appearance and begged to know how she was feeling.

There would be no help for her from that quarter, Sable decided with a rueful smile. She'd have to extricate herself from Derek's presence as best she knew how and hope that he wouldn't prove as persistent as he had in the past.

"There's Lydia Cromwell," she informed him, catching sight of one of her dearest friends, who was sipping champagne in an alcove across the sparkling ballroom. "I haven't seen her for days." Her leaf-green eyes were filled with apology as she gazed up into Derek Haverty's flushed face. "Would you mind very much if I went to speak with her?"

"In just a moment, please!" Derek begged. Tugging at his high collar with a long finger, he reddened suddenly and gave her a self-conscious smile. "You see, I stayed up all night composing a poem for you. I simply had to have it finished for you tonight, and I think, Lady Sable," he added huskily, "that it demonstrates quite aptly the feelings I have for you."

"I don't think——" Sable began hurriedly, but Derek ignored her, clearing his throat noisily and reciting in a passionate voice:

"Her lips are red as coral, my lady fair, my lady fair, her breasts as——"

"Mr. Haverty!"

"Yes, what is it?" Derek inquired politely, gazing expectantly into her rose-flushed face.

"I can't possibly listen to such—"

"But I wasn't finished yet!" he protested. "I think you'll like it very much. Where was I? Ah, of course. Her breasts as smooth as—"

"Oh, Sable, there you are! I saw your mother talking with Mama and knew you had to be here somewhere."

Sable breathed a sigh of relief as Lydia Cromwell appeared in their midst, pale and pretty, a gown of ivory satin clinging to her girlish figure.

"You wouldn't mind, would you, Derek," Lydia added with the familiarity of long years' acquaintance, "if I spirited Sable away for some gossip?" She gave the disappointed young man a charming smile before hurrying off with Sable beside her.

"I owe you for that one, Lyddie," Sable breathed when they were out of earshot.

"Was Derek planning to regale you with another of his creations?" Lydia asked shrewdly.

"Judas, yes! Another minute and I would have been forced to listen to an embarrassing poetical description of every part of my anatomy."

Lydia Cromwell gave her beautiful friend an appreciative glance. "I can well see why you stir Derek's muses the way you do, Sable. Is that a new gown? You look positively lovely in it." She sighed without a trace of rancor, thinking to herself that she was fortunate indeed to number among her closest friends someone as extraordinarily pretty, warm-hearted, and fun-loving as Lady Sable St. Germain.

"I daresay I won't be able to avoid him forever," Sable was saying, glancing back at Derek, who continued to stare forlornly after her.

"Don't worry," Lydia told her practically. "The dancing should start any moment, and then you'll not be lacking partners to monopolize your time." She giggled. "Poor Derek will have a devil of a time stealing you back!"

Sable was forced to agree as she looked about her at the assembled guests and recognized a great many of them as young men who had made it a habit to vie for her attention in the past. She groaned inwardly, finding her patience with such gatherings sorely tried and wishing she had made good her threat to Lucy to remain home that evening.

Accepting a glass of champagne from a liveried footman, Sable stood with Lydia beneath the tall French windows studying the rest of the Havertys' guests. The usual crowd of partygoers was present, the women wearing brightly colored gowns, the young girls in white or pastel blue and pink, while the men looked resplendent in formal black or gray.

Sable's indifferent gaze swept past a small knot of matrons gossiping in a corner and paused briefly upon a lone figure reclining in one of the doorways. Her attention was caught by a silk vest of dark crimson, the color far brighter than the somber clothes worn by most of the gentlemen present that evening. It covered a chest of extremely wide proportions and ended, Sable saw as her gaze traveled higher, at a sun-bronzed throat around which was knotted a cravat of dark gray silk. Her gaze traveled farther, and suddenly she found herself staring straight into the most disconcerting pair of blue eyes she had ever seen, their glittering depths as hard and translucent as the sapphire necklace Lucy had fastened about her neck earlier.

Sable's breath caught in her throat, and she felt her heart skip a beat, unnerved by the intensity of his slow, lazy look. She had the distinct impression that those same eyes had been watching her ever since her arrival in the ballroom, yet was at a loss to explain why she should feel that way.

Certainly nothing in the strange gentleman's stance indicated that her suspicions were correct. He was slouching almost indifferently against the wall, his arms crossed before his broad, silk-covered chest. His visage, Sable saw as she tore her gaze away from his, was hard and rugged, as though it had been carved from granite. Unlike her father, whose own austere features bore the unmistakable stamp of aristocracy, this man seemed all harsh angles and planes, a face that reflected some inner turmoil which, though long since vanquished, had left its mark upon him.

It was a devastatingly handsome face, sun-browned and lean, the cheekbones high, his lips full and generous, almost carnal, his jaw strong and square. The arresting blue eyes were set below dark, slashing brows, and his nose, as strong and gracefully Roman in character as the rest of him, emphasized the hawkish leanness of his ruthless countenance. He was fully as tall as her father, Sable saw, yet where her father was lean and muscle-hard, this man was broad and powerfully built, his torso wide, bespeaking unsettling strength.

He could not have looked less at home to her than he did

in formal evening attire, although his costume was expertly
tailored. His casual stance was nonetheless that of a man who
could move with ease from one world to the next. Like her
father, he was deeply tanned and wore his dark hair long, unruly
curls falling across his brow, and Sable knew instinctively that
this was a man of the sea, his self-assured expression declaring
that he recognized no other authority than his own.

Aware that his ice-blue eyes were still regarding her with
the same unhurried interest, Sable shivered and looked away.
Something about this man unnerved her, made her heart hammer uncomfortably, like a wild animal that senses danger even
though its origin remains unknown.

"My lady, please, you must have this first dance with me!"

"No, Lady Sable, you promised me I'd be the first next
time we met!"

Sable looked up, blinking in confusion. A sea of expectant
faces surrounded her, all of them jostling each other in their
eagerness to be chosen. It was only then that Sable became
aware of the fact that the musicians had begun playing a lilting
waltz and that couples were already sweeping across the ballroom floor, her mother and father among them.

"I'm sorry," she said, recovering herself and gracing her
admirers with a dimpled smile. "I can't seem to make up my
mind."

"Then allow me, please," Derek Haverty said, stepping
forward and seizing her small hand in his. "My parents are
hosting this party, after all," he added, giving his disappointed
companions a gloating look.

Leading Sable onto the floor, he swept her into his arms,
unable to take his eyes from the perfection of her face, her
gold-tinted hair gleaming in the light of the chandeliers, the
diamonds in the beautiful mother-of-pearl combs winking with
a fire of their own. Sable suffered his tight hold in polite silence
and, turning her head, allowed her gaze to stray briefly to the
mysterious stranger who had been studying her earlier.

Her heart lurched when she found him watching her still,
a mocking smile curving his full lips as though he had been
expecting her to turn her head. Though he had not joined in
the dancing, Sable noticed that many admiring female eyes
were turned his way and that a number of fans were being
batted coyly in his direction.

"Who is that man over there?" she asked, curiosity getting the better of her.

"I haven't the foggiest idea," Derek responded, following her discreetly gesturing hand with an indifferent glance. "One of my father's associates, I imagine."

"You've never seen him before?" Sable persisted.

Derek shook his blond head and intimately tightened his hold about her small waist. "Pray don't trouble yourself over his identity, my lady! Doubtless he made an appearance tonight merely to work himself into Papa's good graces."

Privately Sable thought that he was certainly not the sort of man who would worry about his standing with anyone, then forgot him as the waltz ended and she found herself being fought over by the ardent young males who had lost out to Derek earlier. Unwilling to disappoint any of them, Sable agreed to dance with each and every one of them, the reward for her kindness being a parched throat and aching feet when the musicians finally halted for refreshments.

"A glass of lemonade," she pleaded in response to her current partner's enthusiastic question. "I'm so very thirsty!"

"No champagne for the beautiful Lady Sable?" he demanded, disappointed by her request.

"Thank you, no," Sable replied with spirit, thinking that her head was spinning enough already. No sooner was he gone than Sable was seized by an overwhelming desire to be alone. Casting a guilty glance over her shoulder, she hurried impulsively across the floor and slipped quietly out of the double doors onto the terrace.

It was a chilly night, but after the warmth of the ballroom Sable was grateful for the cold air that fanned her hot cheeks. Leaning against the balustrade, she sighed deeply, thinking how glad she would be once she was home and snug in her bed. These parties were becoming vexingly dull, she decided, suddenly hating the attention that was payed to her, the homage of her admirers sounding so insincere and pretentious to her ears. How she longed to be home at North Head, surrounded by her family and close friends, the stuffy social whirl of London a thousand miles away!

"So you managed to escape at last. Fie on you, mistress. Don't you realize you'll have all your admirers howling with frustration over your absence?"

Even before she whirled about to face him, Sable knew instinctively that that deep, mocking voice could belong to none other than the disconcerting stranger with the icy blue eyes. Though she steeled herself as she turned around, she was not prepared for the shock of finding him towering directly above her, his wide chest blocking her entire field of vision. She tilted back her head only to find her eyes on level with his bronzed throat, the once carefully knotted cravat now undone by a careless hand.

"Have you no heart, mistress?" he went on as she stared up at him without speaking, her emerald eyes wide in her small face. "Surely you must realize how disappointed all of them will be!"

The sound of his deep voice rumbling in his wide chest brought Sable to her senses. His accents were those of an educated man, but she heard only the insolence in his tone, saw the mocking glitter of his unsettling blue eyes.

"That may well be true, sir," she said coolly, "but I don't see why it should be a concern of yours."

"You're a prickly little thing, aren't you?" he asked with a devilish grin that might have disarmed Sable completely if she hadn't been so annoyed by his arrogance. "Not very polite, either, I might add," he went on after a moment.

"I can say the same for you," Sable informed him with a haughty toss of her elegant little head. "After all, it isn't proper for you to follow me out here when we haven't been formally introduced!"

His eyes glittered in the darkness. "Then let me hasten to correct that oversight, mistress." Bowing low in her direction he said politely, "I am Morgan Carey, commander of the *Defiance*, which is currently moored below us in the Thames."

"So I was right," Sable exclaimed, ignoring his cryptic tone, "you are a seafaring man!"

"And how did you guess as much?" Morgan Carey asked, interested despite himself. Up close the young woman before him was far more beautiful than he had originally suspected, her startlingly translucent green eyes reflecting pinpoints of fire from the tapers burning in the ballroom behind him. Up close he could see the satin smoothness of her skin and the dainty perfection of her features. Studded with diamonds and adorned with flowers, her rich dark hair was as sleek and beautiful as the coat of a pampered, well-fed cat.

"My father was a sea captain," Sable explained, her gaze sliding from his, suddenly unnerved by the strange light burning in those glittering blue depths. She was old enough to recognize sexual interest in a man's eyes when she saw it, yet what frightened her was the palpable ferocity of his emotions, the heat of his big body tangible across the distance that separated them. She became uncomfortably aware of the smoldering intensity of this man, of the lean, masculine lines of his jaw as he stared down at her in the darkness.

"I'd better go inside," she murmured, suddenly very flustered and not a little concerned about what might happen if she remained alone with Morgan Carey here on the terrace.

"You were quite eager to quit that madness only a moment ago," he reminded her, gesturing toward the crowded ballroom, the silhouettes of whirling dancers passing beyond the clear panes of glass.

"I just wanted a bit of fresh air," Sable countered stiffly, "and I've had enough now, thank you. If you'll excuse me, please."

She made a move to step by him and gave a small cry of alarm as Morgan Carey's arm shot out, the big hand wrapping itself tightly about her slim wrist. It was not so much fear that had prompted Sable to cry out as the shock that swept through her at his touch, his long, steely fingers seeming to burn her flesh. Staring up into his face, Sable suspected that he had experienced it, too, for his eyes had narrowed suddenly, becoming mere shards of ice.

For a moment he looked down at her in silence, and Sable felt a pulse hammering uncomfortably in her throat. The cool March wind whipped a soft tendril of shining hair against her cheek, and almost absently Morgan reached down to smooth it back. Sable flinched violently as the same odd jolt traveled down her spine at his touch.

Morgan Carey's deep voice taunted her. "What are you afraid of? Surely you don't feel yourself in danger when there's a ballroom packed with people nearby? I'm sure there are at least two dozen young gallants waiting within for a single cry of help from your rosy lips to send them storming out here to subdue me."

"I-I'm not afraid," Sable countered, thinking that she certainly had no reason to be, with her father in such close proximity. And yet Morgan Carey's very size, his disturbing nearness did frighten her, filling her with apprehension and a curious trembling.

"You remind me of a frightened young girl expecting her first kiss," Morgan remarked absently.

"And I imagine you've had quite a bit of experience with their kind," Sable retorted, trying without success to extricate herself from his grasp.

"Indeed I have," he assured her with a maddening grin, his white teeth flashing in his deeply tanned face. "But I'm quite sure you're not one of those innocents, are you?"

"What do you mean?" Sable demanded. Staring up into the ruthless features of Morgan Carey, she was filled with a dreadful certainty that he was toying with her, that it amused him to make sport of frightening young girls.

"I was watching you handle your faithful pack of admirers inside," he explained obligingly. "The clever way in which you played one against the other intrigued me. I told myself that it might well be worth my while to get to know you better, but alas, I found I couldn't get anywhere near you all evening. What an opportunity for me when I saw you slip unnoticed onto the terrace."

"You deliberately followed me here! Why?"

Morgan shrugged his massive shoulders. "Why not? I couldn't think of a better way of improving what has been until now a very boring party."

"Are you suggesting I might offer you diversion?" Sable demanded disbelievingly.

The insolent smile tugged again at his full mouth. "Your powers of observation are astute, mistress."

"How dare you!" Sable breathed.

"Ah, now there's a show of the spirit I felt so sure you possessed," Morgan told her, gazing down into her upturned face, at her green eyes glittering with indignation. "Though your dancing partners handled you as though you were made of fragile china, I had the distinct impression there was a woman of fire and passion beneath that haughtily beautiful exterior. It pleases me to know I wasn't mistaken."

"Well, I'm afraid you were," Sable said frostily, unable to believe the audacity of this man. "I insist you unhand me at once before I am forced to call my father!"

"I've handled irate papas before," Morgan Carey informed

her with maddening indifference. "They've long since ceased to trouble me, my dear."

"Why, you arrogant beast!" Sable breathed. Lifting her hand to slap him, she cried out as Morgan deftly caught her fingers in his. Without warning he pulled her toward him so that she landed against the hard expanse of his silk-covered chest. Before she could struggle, he had encircled her with his powerful arms and she found herself swallowed up in his embrace. With her face pressed against his chest, she could hear the strong, steady beat of his heart and became aware of the exotic scent of some expensive cologne that mingled pleasantly with the clean, male smell of him. Unaccountably, Sable began to shiver.

"You are too beautiful to be wasted on anything but love-making," Morgan Carey told her, his deep voice husky with sensuality, for he, too, had felt the current that had traveled between them. Now that he had Sable, slim and unbelievably soft, in his arms, he tightened his hold about her, causing her to look up at him, unsure of what he intended.

Her leaf-green eyes were wide in her upturned face and her soft lips were parted. With every agitated breath her firm breasts rose and fell against him and Morgan, uttering a low groan, lowered his head until his mouth covered hers. The kiss was electrifying, rocking Sable to the depths of her soul, terrifying her with emotions she had never before experienced. The heat of Morgan's muscular body engulfed her, drawing from her a response she could neither understand nor deny. Her hands, which had been pressed against his chest, now moved to slide about his broad shoulders while her body betrayed her and arched into his.

Sable gasped as she felt an alien hardness press intimately against her through the frothy layers of her petticoats. Her breasts were crushed against his wide chest, the nipples taut beneath the smooth material. Morgan's big hands traveled down her spine, fitting into the curve of her hips and guiding her close between his muscular thighs. Pressing her back against the balustrade, he abruptly lifted his hot lips from hers and bent his dark head, tasting the intoxicating sweetness of the ivory skin at her throat.

Sable moaned softly, her fear replaced by a yearning weakness that flooded her middle and left her wanting something she vaguely sensed only Morgan Carey could satisfy. When his devouring lips found hers again, she yielded to him and felt him shudder, drawing a ragged breath as his seeking tongue was met by the tentative touching of her own.

"By God, mistress, you stir my blood," he groaned, his hands roving possessively over her willing body, seeking to lay bare her full breasts and claim them for his own.

The touch of his hand against her naked skin was like a brand, but as he moved impatiently to unlace her bodice, Sable suddenly struggled to free herself. She mustn't let him proceed further, she told herself, panic beginning to break through the drugging warmth that enveloped her. She'd never be able to hide her dishabille from everyone in the Havertys' ballroom!

"Please, you mustn't," she whispered raggedly, and was startled when Morgan obeyed her plea without argument.

Releasing her instantly, he stepped back, the sensuous lips that had kissed hers so devastatingly only seconds before now curved in a cynical smile. "You're quite the tigress, my dear," he said a trifle breathlessly, his eyes still smoldering with lingering passion. In truth he was himself somewhat shaken by the intensity of his feelings, by the surging tide of desire that had washed over him as soon as he had pressed his lips to those softly yielding ones. He had meant only to dally with her, to test the waters, as it were, and see if he had managed to find himself an engaging diversion for his stay in London.

Now he found himself an unwitting victim of an act that had backfired explosively, the tables turned so that he could think of nothing but how much he desired the proud little beauty before him. Her emerald eyes were burning into his, her lips still moist and inviting, but she moved away as he continued to gaze down at her with heavy-lidded eyes, perhaps sensing his intent, perhaps because she did not quite trust herself either.

"I'd better go inside," Sable said in a small voice, her heart hammering painfully in her ribs as she looked up into Morgan Carey's handsome face, her eyes lingering despite herself on the hard fullness of his mouth. "M-my father may be looking for me."

"You speak of him often," Morgan observed, nonchalantly adjusting his wrinkled cravat, his indifference hurting Sable, who could not see the slight trembling of his strong fingers in the darkness. "You must think highly of him."

"I love him very much," Sable said tremulously, her tone

indicating that Morgan Carey would never receive that precious gift from her.

"He's a fortunate man," Morgan said sharply, stung by her words without really knowing why. "Do I know him?"

"I certainly hope not," Sable said contemptuously. She was beginning to recover, the blood no longer singing like madness in her veins, and all she wanted was to get away from this handsome, enigmatic giant of a man who had kissed her against her will and had aroused such odd, frightening emotions within her. She had willingly responded to him, and the realization shamed and embarrassed her, making her never want to lay eyes on him again.

"His name?" Morgan prompted as Sable remained silent, trying to edge away from him although the proximity of his big body kept her firmly pressed against the balustrade.

"Charles," Sable whispered reluctantly, thinking that perhaps he would let her go if she told him. "Charles St. Germain."

One dark brow rose in genuine surprise. "The Earl of Monterrey?"

Sable nodded. "Please let me go," she implored in the next breath, but Morgan continued to block her path. He was so close that Sable could feel the heat of his body, and she shivered and turned her head away, tears welling in her eyes as she felt the same odd breathlessness come over her.

"The Earl of Monterrey has only one daughter, and she's but a lass of seventeen."

Sable looked up, surprised at the harshness of his tone. "I am Sable St. Germain," she said proudly, "and I'll be eighteen this summer."

Morgan's handsome countenance filled with astonishment. "You are Lady Sable St. Germain?"

"I am," Sable replied with as much dignity as she could muster, considering that this enormous rogue of a man had just kissed her and touched her bare breast with bold familiarity.

"My apologies, your ladyship," Morgan said abruptly, his deep voice filled with contempt. "Had I known that you were such a child I would never have forced my attentions upon you."

Sable stared at him open-mouthed, then struggled to contain the rage that welled up inside of her. "I cannot fathom your bottomless supply of conceit, Morgan Carey!" she flared, her slender form quivering with indignation. Her carefully arranged hair had come loose in the roughness of his embrace, and now one silken curl escaped to brush enticingly across her naked shoulder. "Obviously you're accustomed to having women fall at your feet when you so much as crook a finger, but mark this well, sir, I'm not one of them! As a matter of fact, I hope never to lay eyes on you again as long as I live!"

Furiously she pushed her way past him and he let her go, but as she reached the ballroom doors she heard his mocking laugh behind her. Whirling about, she saw him looming before her in the darkness, his legs planted wide apart, his hands on his narrow hips, looking exactly like a lusty pirate captain aboard the quarterdeck of his ship.

"I hope someday we will meet again, my dear Sable," he told her softly, his deep voice filled with unmistakable promise. "One day you will be old enough to give me a woman's love, and then, my lady, I swear to you I shall return to claim it."

"I'll see you dead first," Sable hissed and stalked through the double doors, but not before she heard his mocking laughter drifting softly through the night air behind her.

"Sable, love, where have you been? I've been looking everywhere for you."

She looked up with a stricken expression to find her mother before her, the Countess's golden eyes dark with weariness. Fear made her heart lurch, but Raven, quick to see it, laid a hand over hers.

"I'm fine," she assured her in a whisper, "just a little tired, but your father and I thought we might use it as an excuse to plead an early departure." She sobered and gazed searchingly into her daughter's flushed face. "Or would you rather stay, Sable?"

"Oh no," Sable assured her quickly. "If you're tired, then of course we should go home! Besides," she added with a sharpness that was uncharacteristic of her, "I've had more than enough of this evening!"

Raven smiled in relief and turned to search for Charles, finding him watching her as he made his excuses to George and Dorothy Haverty. Raven's heart warmed, thinking of the long, cozy night that awaited the two of them, and if her daughter was curiously silent as they collected their wraps and waited for the coach to be brought around, Raven was, for once, unaware of it.

Chapter 2

"Liam! What on earth are you trying to prove?"

Edward Hadrian St. Germain, Viscount Audley, wheeled his long-legged blood bay and bore down on his brother, his handsome face filled with anger. Like his father, he had an awesome temper when aroused, although at sixteen he displayed an admirable amount of self-control and maturity, the stamp of manhood already indelibly marked upon him.

It was his older brother's newfound authority, so like his father's, that brought a guilty look to Liam's face as he trotted his fat little pony toward the rangy hunter on which his brother sat. Sable hovered behind Edward on her mare, an anxious expression on her face.

"I'm sorry, Ned, the jump looked so easy when you did it!" he gulped, gesturing at the stone wall that his brother and sister had just cleared, sweeping over it with the dazzling beauty of dancers and firing his determination to do the same.

"We've hunters, for God's sake!" Ned shouted, emerald eyes blazing with anger and aftershock, the sight of his brother on the small Welsh pony leaping the crumbling stone wall having caused his heart to stop. "You could have broken Lillibet's legs and, what's worse, your own fool neck as well!"

Liam's small face crumpled beneath his brother's wrath. "I'm sorry," he murmured dejectedly.

Edward's harsh visage softened instantly and he reached down to squeeze Liam's thin shoulder. Christ, he reminded himself, the laddie was only eight, and he himself had been guilty of poor judgments often enough at that age! "It's all right, you little idiot. I know it's hard to be forced to ride a pony when you're wanting a hunter of your own, but you'll just have to be patient."

"I didn't know Lillibet could jump so well," Sable added encouragingly, guiding her mare closer and smiling down into Liam's tearful expression. "I think you'll be as good a rider as Father someday."

"Do you honestly?" Liam breathed, his face glowing at the prospect.

Sable and Edward exchanged smiles.

"If you live long enough," Ned put in with mock severity. "No more daredevil stunts, Liam, do you promise?"

"Aye," the dark-headed lad swore solemnly.

With Ned in the lead, the three of them started down the winding cart trail that meandered toward the fishing village of St. Ives. Spring had taken tentative hold on the Cornish land, turning the hillsides green, the sun warm as it touched the savage sea and the wind-honed cliffs.

They were undeniably handsome children, the young St. Germains, Ned and Liam possessing their mother's midnight hair, their features sharply chiseled and masculine, though Liam's boyishness was emphasized by his turned-up nose and a smattering of freckles. Dressed in tall black boots and scarlet jackets, they made a dashing pair, offsetting quite charmingly the delicate beauty of their sister. Sable, her cheeks rosy from the wind and crisp, salty air, was radiant in a berry-colored habit with tufted shoulders and lemon piping, her glossy hair dazzling in the sunlight. The bloom of youth added a vibrancy to her looks that was breathtaking, and Ned, turning in the saddle, grinned at her, green eyes meeting green eyes.

"I daresay if you could purr like a cat, Sable, you'd be doing so now."

"I'm just so happy to be home!" Lifting her small face to the sun, Sable breathed deeply. "I can't believe we've only been here a week. I feel as though we've never left."

"North Head is where we belong, isn't it?" he asked, a note

of wonder creeping into his voice, which was almost as deep and richly resonant as his father's. "I've noticed it in Mother, too. She seems to have blossomed since she returned."

"She has, hasn't she?" Sable agreed happily. "Even Father admits he should have brought her back long before this."

"What about you, Liam?" Ned asked, regarding his younger brother with twitching lips as Liam strove valiantly to keep his laboring pony close behind the bigger horses' heels. "Are you glad to be home?"

Liam's dark head bobbed vigorously. "Oh yes! Especially since Perry came back with us!"

Sable and Ned laughed heartily at this, knowing how much Liam worshiped the St. Germain chef and his repertoire of luscious pastries.

At the far end of the cart road they reluctantly agreed that it was time to turn back and leave the whitewashed cottages and twisting lanes of Zennor and St. Ives to be visited some other time. The sun was already high in the sky, and neither Sable nor Edward needed Liam's complaints of hunger to remind them that luncheon would soon be served. With Lillibet puffing valiantly behind, the two big hunters trotted back toward North Head, the tiered fields surrounding them being prepared for planting. Stocky Cornish farmers paused in their work to politely greet the young heir of Monterrey and gaze admiringly at Lady Sable, who seemed to them to have grown even more beautiful in her absence.

"We'll have a long growing season this year," Ned remarked with quiet satisfaction.

Sable's gaze followed his to the granite walls that separated the plowed fields, the enduring stone hedges built by Celtic farmers centuries ago under the guidance of Barrancourt ancestors. Beyond them lay the rocky moors, their heather-covered slopes reaching toward Gunard's Head, where the twisting coastal road had been pummeled by centuries of rain and wind into a narrow, tunnellike lane flanked high on either side by the land.

"It's going to be a grand summer, isn't it?" Sable agreed, a lump rising in her throat as the savage beauty of Cornwall overwhelmed her.

The horses were now heading directly over the cliffs, and the wind, which had been balmy and sweet in Zennor's protected harbor, now buffeted the rocky coastline relentlessly.

Sable lifted her small face to the warmth of the sun and gazed out across the clarity of the whitecapped Atlantic. Though the southern coast of Cornwall was beautiful with its sparkling blue waters, white beaches, and lush vegetation, she preferred above anything the rugged North where, open and unprotected, the cliffs lay exposed to lashing gales and endless, bone-chilling fogs.

In the distance North Head rose above the moors, clinging precariously to its promontory on the cliffs, its twin towers of gold-colored stone reaching stalwart toward the vast blue sky. On the ocean beyond fled a pair of fishing boats, skirting the treacherous reefs beneath a press of stiff white sails, a bounty of mackerel and pilchard luring them toward Land's End. Shunning the sheltered coves where smugglers had once laid by to unload a wealth of perfume and spirits, they ventured with the tenacity of their fearless Cornish captains into waters even Sable had no desire to sail.

"Oyster season's just about ended," Ned remarked, following her gaze to the turbulent water. "You'll not be eating any until next year, I'm afraid."

"It doesn't matter," Sable replied. "There'll be crabs and lobsters to keep us satisfied."

"Don't forget the pasties!" Liam added, licking his lips as he thought of the stuffed herring wrapped in delicate pastry crusts that were among Perry's specialties. Both he and Sable had missed stout Cornish fare while in London, where too-rich sauces and cloyingly sweet desserts had been staples of the diet.

"I'm willing to wager Perry has outdone himself today," Ned informed his younger brother slyly. "I heard Kewie Stephen's fish cart coming up the drive to make a delivery just after dawn."

The possibility of finding fresh pastry waiting for him at home proved too much for Liam. Kicking Lillibet into a canter, he sent the fat little pony down the lane in a cloud of dust, a laughing Sable and Ned following behind.

Though Sable had been born and raised at North Head, she could never approach the noble edifice without being overwhelmed by its sheer magnificence. It had been built by a sea captain named Sir Reginald Barrancourt, who had made a career of plundering the Spanish Main with a letter of marque granted him by his sovereign Charles II. Though old age might

have bowed this great naval warrior, whose exploits had made
their mark on English history along with the likes of Sir Francis
Drake and Walter Raleigh, his love for the sea remained unchanged.

North Head had been a testimony of Sir Reginald's devotion
to that turbulent and most fickle of lovers, and in its brooding
grandeur he had captured the essence of its savage beauty in
a way that haunted the Barrancourt spirit for centuries to come.
Flanked on both sides by stately, corniced wings, the main
block of the house faced the onslaught of the winds, the ocean
pounding relentlessly against the massive boulders directly below. Savage and uncompromising as its location might be, there
were times when the winds were calm and the sunshine flooded
the high-ceilinged rooms and seemed to draw the house into
an extension of the elements themselves. The effect was dazzling when one stepped into the galleries and salons lining the
northern facade of the building to find the sea dancing in silver
waves of light across the wainscoted walls, the salty tang mingling with the sweet fragrance of roses and honeysuckle planted
in the gardens outside.

The fishing boats had vanished when Sable and her brothers
drew their mounts to a halt in the cobbled courtyard before the
stables, but the sweeping vista of water and sky was breathtaking in its solitary grandeur. A lone cormorant battled the
strong winds overhead, its haunting cry lost in the booming of
the breakers that rumbled like thunder around them.

"Had a good ride, did ye?" the head groom inquired as he
lumbered through the Dutch door from the tackroom. "The
mare gave ye trouble, Lady Sable?"

"Not at all, Sam." Sable reached up to stroke Amourette's
velvety nose before one of the lads hurried up to lead her away.
"She remembered me."

"Aye, and there's few'd forget ye, Lady Sable," the grizzled
groom remarked with a grin. Already old and leather-faced in
their mother's time, Sam had weathered the ensuing years without change, as permanent as the cedars that grew straight and
true in the fertile Cornish soil. His strength and skill with the
horses had remained undiminished over the years.

"We've come back to eat pasties, Sam," Liam announced,
sliding from Lillibet's back and coming to a halt before the
thick-barreled man.

"Have ye, now?" Sam twinkled, thinking to himself that

the youngest son of the Earl and Countess of Monterrey was growing into a fine lad indeed, his smart scarlet coat and tall black boots giving him an aura of authority. Of course, he'd always be wee, mischievous Lord Liam to the household of North Head, but there was no denying the laddie had done some growing up during his absence.

"Kewie Stephen brought fresh herring this morning," Ned explained, laying an affectionate hand on his brother's shoulder. "I only hope Perry made enough to feed all of us."

"I'm afraid ye'll be havin' to share your meal," Sam informed him, his bushy white brows suddenly drawing together.

"What do you mean, Sam?" Sable demanded, seeing the big man's hand clench about the dripping sponge he had carried from the tackroom with him.

"It be that good-for-nothing from Blackburn Hall," Sam replied candidly. "Arrived not ten minutes ago, and I know Her Ladyship'll be askin' him to stay. Ran that decent gelding of his too hard across the fields again," he added, his gravelly voice filled with disapproval, for Sam judged a man's worth by the way he handled his horseflesh.

"Wyecliffe Blackburn?" Sable asked.

"Aye, the young master himself."

Sable and Ned exchanged dismayed glances.

"I imagine we'd better change for lunch," Ned said finally. "Liam, you'd best scrub your face before you come down, too. You look as if you've been sharing Nat Clowance's byre with his hogs."

Liam scampered off without argument, deciding to heed his brother's advice rather than risk being chastised later by his mother for appearing dusty and disheveled at the table. Sable and Ned followed more slowly, Sable's berry skirts rustling softly as they entered the house through the arched servants' entrance in the rear of the West Wing.

"You needn't look as though the world's come to an end," Ned reproved, grinning down into Sable's face in a disarming display of the fabled St. Germain charm.

He managed to catch a glimpse of her dimpled smile before she sighed deeply and looked away, her eyes scanning the restless sea as though seeking refuge there. "In London I was never free of Derek Haverty's attentions, and yet I'd cheerfully welcome his suit any time over that of Wyecliffe Blackburn!" She shuddered, and Ned quickly laid his hand over hers.

"You know Mother and Father have no intention of accepting a marriage proposal from him. Besides, he hasn't made it clear yet that that is what he wishes to do."

"Maybe you're right," Sable conceded, yet deep inside she knew that Wyecliffe wanted her, had sensed it even with her inexperience where men were concerned, by the way he looked at her, in the manner he allowed his hold to linger when he took her hand in his. She shivered, finding the stepson of the late Squire Blackburn more odious than a dozen Derek Havertys. At least Derek had been harmless and even amusing, his horrible poetry sincere and somehow endearing, yet Wyecliffe Blackburn, with his brooding eyes and sallow, unhealthy complexion, had always made her decidedly uncomfortable.

In truth Sable had forgotten him during the long winter months in London, and his unexpected appearance at North Head today made her especially unhappy. Perhaps Mother wouldn't invite him to join them, Sable decided hopefully as she and Ned parted on the landing.

Inside her bedroom the heavy drapes had been drawn back to allow the sunlight to pour into the room. The ocean was a deep blue as it rolled toward the horizon. Wyecliffe's presence forgotten, Sable slipped to the window and stood with her slim nose pressed to the glass, drinking in the view that never failed to delight her whatever the season. Autumn's mist and southwesterly gales, the dark shroud of winter, the brilliance of the Cornish summer—it made no difference to Sable what elements raged beyond North Head's thick stone walls, for each of them cast a spell so unique that she found enchantment in all of them.

"Aha, I knew it!"

Sable turned with a start to find Lucy Walters tapping her foot impatiently on the polished hardwood floor behind her.

"Whether it be London lanes or wild Cornish coasts you be lookin' at, Lady Sable, I vow you spend your life with your eyes out the window! Come down to earth now, lass, and get out of them reekin' clothes. Supper's being served downstairs and you've a visitor."

"I know," Sable replied glumly. "Sam already warned me."

"Then you might as well not spend your time complainin'," Lucy advised, making a face as she pulled off Sable's dusty boots. "Your parents be at the table already, and Hannah, bless her heart, be there as well."

Sable's eyes widened, for it wasn't often that Hannah Daniels, her mother's former governess, made an appearance downstairs. "Danny's joining us?"

Lucy snorted. "You know very well the old termagant won't permit a Blackburn inside this house without her bein' present to defend it!"

Sable laughed, well aware that Lucy's tart comment had been affectionately uttered. Though she was well over eighty by now, Hannah Daniels was a beloved member of the St. Germain household. Sable and her brothers had been weaned on the exciting account of how she had accompanied young Raven Barrancourt to India nearly twenty years ago, a story more fraught with adventure than even Liam's favorite tale of King Arthur and the Knights of the Round Table.

It was Squire Josiah Blackburn who had forced their mother, orphaned after her father's death in a hunting accident, to leave England for the faraway Punjab. Before his death, James Barrancourt had borrowed large sums of money from the Squire only to see his investments turn sour and the loan grow to a staggering sum. After he died, the greedy Squire had been quick to seize the opportunity of making North Head his and had informed Raven that she must either pay back the loan or accept his hand in marriage.

Raven, determined not to lose her beloved home or marry the odious Squire, had set off with Danny for the wilds of India, a journey that had nearly cost her life. But for the timely intervention of Charles St. Germain, captain of the rogue clipper *Orient Star,* Raven might have been forced to yield to the Squire's bidding. Though he had died several years ago, Danny had never forgiven him for the hell he had forced her beloved mistress to endure, and she now lived for the pleasure of tormenting his stepson whenever he came to North Head.

"Cliffe isn't really a Blackburn," Sable remarked, shaking her long hair free of the confining pins that bound it while Lucy pulled a flounced muslin gown from the clothespress. "He's Josiah's stepson."

Lucy snorted. "The way that boy handles himself, I'd say there be quite a bit o' the old Squire's blood in his veins! When he came into his inheritance two years ago, I thought for sure he'd turn that terrible place around." She shook her graying head sorrowfully. "Splendid house, Blackburn Hall, and he doesn't care any more than the Squire did about its upkeep.

Lets his farmers starve, too. Never saw tenants so poorly treated."

"It's a shame," Sable agreed, allowing Lucy to slip the bottle-green gown over her head, the muslin cool against her skin. "Mother says it was once a beautiful house, but you can't really tell with all the neglect it's suffered."

Blackburn Hall, situated some three miles beyond North Head's southern boundary, had once been the hunting lodge of Henry VIII, who had retired there while his castle on Pendennis Point near Falmouth was being completed. Built of enduring native gray stone and overgrown with ivy, the enormous house, rebuilt twice over the past three hundred years, had a dignified charm that endeared it to anyone who saw it. Cornish folklore held that King Arthur had originally selected the site upon which it stood to build his own castle but had decided for strategic purposes to erect it at Tintagel instead. Its once fertile fields, which had grown early vegetables and grain for Hampton Court, lay fallow now, and the lovely rose gardens were choked with weeds.

"Best be polite to Master Wyecliffe, m'lady," Lucy admonished as she put the finishing touches to Sable's hair and stepped back to admire the results. Inwardly she knew that Sable would never treat Wyecliffe Blackburn cruelly. She was far too tender-hearted and soft-spoken for that, more was the pity.

"Oh, don't worry, Lucy," Sable replied with a glint in her eyes. "I wouldn't dream of horning in on Danny's fun!"

With a swish of flounced skirts she fled from the room, the thought of fresh pasties and her family's company appealing to her sufficiently to overshadow Wyecliffe's unwanted presence. Her jaunty step faltered in the massive stone-floored entrance hall, however, when she heard that high, grating laugh of his she loathed. A vision of his sallow face with its thin features and glowing eyes followed her into the comfortable, glass-plated Conservatory, where the St. Germains took all their meals save dinner—a vision that was quickly dispelled by a reality far less appealing.

Wyecliffe Blackburn seemed to have grown more pale and gaunt since her absence, his frock coat and tight-fitting trousers failing miserably in their purpose of making him look like the gentrified country dandy. Lank brown hair fell across his wide brow into his eyes, and his wide mouth curved in an avaricious smile as Sable appeared on the threshold.

Rising to his feet, he hurried toward her and brought her hand to his lips, his gaze darting from her eyes, their color deepened by the bottle-green gown she wore, to the alabaster smoothness of her throat and bared shoulders. "I can see that a season in London hasn't done you ill, Lady Sable," he murmured in that husky voice she hated.

Resisting the urge to pull her hand free from the smooth, cold fingers that clasped hers, she said haltingly, "It was kind of you to visit us so soon after our return."

"Someone had to welcome the St. Germains back to Cornwall," Cliffe reminded her as he led her to her seat. "With my father gone, I considered it my duty."

"Never was much of a welcome seein' that insipid face of his!" came a tart voice from the far end of the table.

"Danny, please, you mustn't speak that way about the Squire," the Countess chided. "Especially when he isn't here to defend himself."

"It's quite all right, your ladyship," Wyecliffe assured her gallantly, unaware that Raven's lips were twitching as she met Danny's mutinous look across the board. "I'm well aware that there was little love lost between my stepfather and Mrs. Daniels. I, however, intend to see that the relationship between the Blackburns and the St. Germains becomes closely knit from this point on." As he spoke he smiled down at Sable's bowed head, missing as he did so the slight tightening of the Earl's lean jaw.

Sitting at the head of the polished oak table, Charles St. Germain presided over all of the family meals, the mischievous and difficult-to-discipline Liam at his left, the Countess, as always, on his right. At the far end sat Ned, watching with equally drawn brows the covetous look in Wyecliffe Blackburn's eyes as he gazed longingly at Sable.

"Bah!" came Danny's explosive reply to Cliffe's optimistic comment. She looked tiny and deceptively frail sitting in the high-backed oak chair, but her faded brown eyes were flashing. Her hair, which had been an unruly crop of straw-colored fluff years ago, was now pure white. Her plump hands were gaunt and lined with blue veins, but Danny valiantly continued to reap her revenge on the Blackburn clan.

It had saddened her when the Squire had died, for she had greatly enjoyed their verbal sparring matches. At eighty years of age a woman could damned well say what she pleased, even to her betters, and Danny had developed an acid tongue. It had always delighted her to needle the Squire whenever he came to North Head.

Sometimes she was sure she had goaded him too far and that he'd never return, and yet he always had. His lust for Raven St. Germain hadn't diminished one bit even after so many years.

It was true the Squire was dead and buried, and his mousy wife—who had hated the fog and gales of the Cornish coast— had returned to Devon, but Wyecliffe Blackburn still afforded Danny considerable pleasure. Taunting the Squire's stepson was not as satisfying, for he was such a brainless idiot that he scarcely realized he was being insulted, but Danny persevered nonetheless. Her determination to keep him in his place had only increased of late when she had come to see that Wyecliffe had developed an unhealthy interest in Lady Sable.

"Aye, you've stepped right into your stepfather's shoes, Master Blackburn," she remarked, watching with thinned lips as Cliffe's gaze came to rest on Sable's rosebud mouth.

"Herrumph." An uncomfortable Parris cleared his throat in the doorway. "Shall I serve now, your lordship?"

"Please do," the Earl replied with mock exasperation, although in truth he enjoyed Danny's performance immensely. He had made a halfhearted attempt to tell his wife years ago that it was her responsibility to improve her former governess's table manners when visitors were present, but Raven had heartlessly charged him to bring up the matter himself. Though Charles St. Germain had braved attacks by Afridi river pirates, battled mutinous Sikhs, and weathered ferocious gales aboard his ship, he somehow found his courage failing when it came to disciplining a shrunken old woman with a viper's tongue and a heart of solid gold.

The pasties, to Liam's delight, were delicious, stuffed as anticipated with fresh herring in a piquant sauce. For the time being, silence reigned at the table, even Wyecliffe forgetting his infatuation with Lady Sable long enough to wolf down four of them.

"You never told me, Sable," Edward began unexpectedly as their plates were being cleared, "whether or not you met anyone in London who stole your heart away."

He had intended the question to be a pointed barb for Wyecliffe and was startled when Sable's face flamed with color and her beautiful green eyes dropped to her lap.

"No one," she whispered.

"But not for lack of interest on the part of the London blades," the Countess teased, unable to see her daughter's face from where she sat. She tossed her elegant head dramatically. "Still, Sable's not to blame. I can assure you, Ned, that if you discount the Prime Minister, London's upper circles boast no one worthy of note."

"I'm glad to hear that, madame," the Earl drawled, his green eyes glittering as he regarded his wife over his wine glass. "I wouldn't want your affections to stray."

The Countess gazed at him archly. "In truth there was one man I found quite fascinating, m'lord. He reminded me a bit of you when you were younger. Such dangerous good looks, such brooding arrogance. La, I didn't know what to make of him!"

"And who was that?" the Earl inquired casually.

"Sir Morgan Carey. If you'll remember, he was at the Havertys' party."

Charles nodded his dark head. "Aye, I remember him. Surly fellow. Can't think what he was doing at a gathering like that."

"Do you know him?" Raven asked curiously.

With eyes still glued to her plate, Sable listened, her throat tight.

"Not personally, no. As a matter of fact, the first person who ever mentioned his name to me was the Queen, and that was during my visit to Windsor just before Liam was born. She'd just made Carey a Knight of the Order of the Bath."

"What's a Knight of the Bath, Papa?" Liam asked expectantly, envisioning a group of fiercely armored men with glinting broadswords whose sworn duty lay in guarding Queen Victoria while she bathed.

"It's a military order," the Earl explained. "Apparently Carey distinguished himself in the Crimean War and was duly rewarded for his bravery. I believe Roger Tensing told me that night at the Havertys' that he'd also been a blockade runner during the American war."

"A blockade runner!" Liam echoed, his eyes wide. He had heard of their daredevil feats from the men in the St. Germain warehouses in Falmouth and had been firmly convinced that he wanted to be nothing else when he grew up. Though the

American civil war had hurt his father's business to a certain extent, Liam had been genuinely sorry when it had ended and his chances of joining the exciting ranks of runners had dwindled to nothing.

"He owns a clipper by the name of *Defiance*," the Earl added. "It's rumored she's unbeatable."

Raven couldn't help smiling when she saw the faraway glint in Charles's eyes. "I imagine you'd give anything to test the *Orient Star* against her."

To her surprise, Charles shook his head. "No, madame. I've left the sea and its conquest to younger men of Carey's mettle. There's no need to seek my fortune anywhere else but here."

Raven's breath caught in her throat at the undercurrent of sensuality in his voice. Her children, accustomed to it, paid no attention, but Wyecliffe Blackburn was acutely embarrassed. Good Lord, he thought to himself, did the elder St. Germains always behave like infatuated lovers? Here they were married twenty-odd years and still carrying on like newlyweds! It would be different when he married Lady Sable, he vowed, casting a surreptitious glance in her direction, his gaze lingering on her sweet profile. There'd be no demonstrations of affection beyond the bedroom door!

Wyecliffe's heartbeat quickened. By God, he was near-mad with want for the seductive Lady Sable! How long must he continue to play the genial suitor before the Earl came to trust him and he dared ask for Sable's dainty hand? If not for the blight of the Blackburn name he carried upon him, he was convinced that the Earl would have looked at him more favorably as a suitable mate for his only daughter. No matter, Wyecliffe decided confidently. He'd win the St. Germains over soon enough. He was far too clever to let North Head—and a luscious lady—slip through his fingers as had his poor, foolish stepfather.

"Glad to see the last of him!" Danny snorted when the meal was over and Wyecliffe took his leave. The family had lingered at the table, the Earl to enjoy his brandy and soda, the others to spend a little more time together before afternoon pursuits separated them until evening. "I vow he irks me as much as the Squire did!"

"It's just that you loathe anyone bearing the Blackburn name," Edward chided, bending over to pinch her withered cheek affectionately.

"Blackburns! They all reek of corruption," Danny stated angrily, though she twinkled at him fondly. Ned, possessing the same dashing good looks as his father, had managed to charm his way into her heart long ago.

"I must admit I gave Cliffe every chance to prove himself when he first inherited the Hall," the Earl said seriously, leaning his big frame back in the chair. "Yet I see no difference between Josiah's negligent habits and Cliffe's."

"It's a shame," Raven agreed, allowing a hovering footman to refill her china cup with fragrant green tea. "With proper management his arable acreage could yield almost as much as North Head does."

Ned gave a low laugh. "Now you sound exactly like Father or the steward! Farming should be left to the menfolk, madame. Speaking of which," he added, rising and coming around the table to kiss his mother's cheek, "I wanted to ride down to the pastures and see how the grazing grounds are—"

"Wait just a minute before you go, Ned," his father interrupted. "I've an announcement to make."

Five expectant faces were suddenly upon him, and Charles felt an odd tightening in his chest as he regarded them, each of them dearer than life to him—even Danny, who had sacrificed so much on his beloved Raven's behalf.

"I know all of you were disappointed when we had to cancel the harvest ball this year because of your mother's illness," he began, enjoying the looks of bewilderment his comment aroused. "We all know it's North Head's oldest tradition and that you, Sable, should have made your debut there and not in some stuffy London assembly room."

"I didn't mind, Papa—" Sable began, but he lifted a hand to silence her.

"I know you didn't, my sweet, but to repay you for not complaining, and to announce to all of Cornwall that the St. Germains have returned home intact, I intend to hold the ball a week from tomorrow."

"A harvest ball?" Raven inquired doubtfully, her golden eyes searching Charles's face as though he had taken leave of his senses. "The fields were harvested a half a year ago!"

"Not a harvest ball," he said gently, enjoying himself thoroughly. "A planting ball. We'll celebrate the growing season instead of the yield, and instead of the customary hunt the morning after, we'll have horse races."

"Oh, Father, what a grand idea!" Sable cried while everyone else began talking at once.

"Will you invite the farmers and villagers, too?" Liam piped above the din.

"It'll be no different from the harvest ball, lad," his father promised.

Liam's eyes glowed as he remembered past events when he and a handful of friends off the St. Germain farms had raided the kitchens to sample every one of Perry's painstakingly prepared dishes.

"Gracious me, we'll need new gowns!" Raven exclaimed and turned to Danny, who was clapping her hands in delight.

"Aye, Miss Raven, aye," the old woman agreed enthusiastically. "I'll get out my pattern books first thing. Ooh, think of the materials we'll be able to choose from! No heavy autumn fabrics, but silks and satins, taffeta—"

Under cover of the commotion Ned leaned over and whispered conspiratorially in Sable's ear, "Maybe you'll even meet your Prince Charming at the ball, or at least someone who will make you forget the handsome swain who swept you off your feet in London."

He had expected her to laugh at this, but Sable's expression grew troubled instead, and she regarded him with a grim tightening of her rosy lips. "Judas, I hope you're right, Ned," she murmured and fled from the room, leaving him to gape after her in utter confusion.

Chapter 3

A blaze with lights, North Head's Great Hall was sufficiently dazzling to rival even the immense receiving rooms of Buckingham Palace. Hundreds of hand-dipped tapers burned in gleaming brass sconces along the walls, and the crystal chandeliers glowed warmly, throwing a rich light on the priceless tapestries and reflecting the soft patina of the flagstone floor. In the minstrel's gallery black-coated musicians played softly, the mellow tones of the violins swelling with the effervescent chatter of the guests to the raftered ceiling above.

Most of those present were local gentry, members of Cornwall's most prominent families, while others had traveled great distances to attend the St. Germains' planting ball, their wardrobes and retinues filling the West Wing of the great house to capacity. Champagne flowed in gold ribbands from long-necked bottles into delicate fluted glasses as servants in traditional braided livery passed among the revelers brandishing silver trays.

Women in festive gowns as colorful as the wildflowers blooming within the garden walls fluttered oversized fans and chatted gaily with their escorts. Unlike a formal London soirée,

the St. Germain planting ball projected an aura of rustic gentility, a dismissal of stuffy Victorian convention that promised
an evening of uninhibited enjoyment for everyone present.

In keeping with the country theme of the event, the Great
Hall had been decorated with greens from the gardens, the
tables groaning beneath enormous arrangements of flowers and
heather gathered from the moors earlier that day. Mulled wine
and cider flowed as freely as champagne, and hearty Cornish
fare was as much in evidence on the dining tables as the more
traditional offerings of haute cuisine. Boisterous voices and
smiling faces were in evidence wherever one looked, and all
agreed that the event had been a master stroke on the part of
the Earl and Countess of Monterrey.

A hush fell over the milling crowd as the musicians in the
galley ended a lilting Mozart sonata and immediately struck
up a gay tune that caused toes to tap with anticipation. This,
most of the assembly knew, was the melody of the famed
Barrancourt country dance which was always performed at the
commencement of North Head festivities.

Tonight's anticipation was especially keen, for everyone
knew that the Earl himself would be opening the dancing with
his daughter, Lady Sable, who held a soft spot in the hearts of
all present that evening. Jostling each other for room, the guests
craned their necks for their first glimpse of Lady Sable, whose
appearance, like the bride at a wedding, was impatiently awaited.

Sable's entrance disappointed no one. Floating into the Great
Hall on her father's arm, she seemed oblivious to the collective
sigh of admiration, her eyes on her father's rugged face. The
fact that she was taking part in a centuries-old Barrancourt
tradition brought a tightness to her throat, the pride in her
father's eyes only underscoring the importance of the occasion.
No debut in London could have meant as much to Sable at the
moment.

The gown she wore was of pure white silk that rustled softly
as she took her place at the Earl's side on the empty dance
floor. Because there had been no time for elaborate embroidery,
the seamstress, with a discerning eye and a skillful needle, had
sewn the full skirts in panels, each separated by strips of dazzling white satin ribbon edged with fragile lace. In the candle-
light her hair gleamed softly, the color of rich, warm ebony,
and her large eyes glittered more brilliantly than the fabulous
gems she wore about her throat.

Sable had learned the difficult steps of the Barrancourt dance years ago, and with the rehearsals her mother had held throughout the last week, she felt supremely confident as she laid her gloved hand into her father's and waited for him to take the lead. Muted but enthusiastic applause broke out in the ballroom as Charles guided her across the floor, the resemblance between the handsome nobleman and his graceful daughter so pronounced that admiring whispers and approving nods were exchanged.

When the dance was finally over, the guests crowded the floor to congratulate a flushed and elated Sable while the Earl, relinquishing her hand with a flourishing bow, sought out his Countess for the next dance. Sable had not expected him to openly praise her performance, but the approval in his emerald eyes as he took his leave of her warmed her more than words ever could.

It was an ebullient Ned who seized her small hands in his and waltzed off with her before anyone else could claim her. Though only eleven months separated the two of them, Ned towered above his sister, and there was a protective glint in his eyes as he glared at the young men who had rushed forward to partner her.

"Did I do well?" Sable asked a trifle breathlessly.

"You were grand!" Ned cried with unbridled enthusiasm. "Mrs. Fallows would have been proud to see you tonight!"

Sable giggled as she thought of their former dance tutor. Tall, prim and totally humorless, Mrs. Fallows had despaired of ever teaching the young St. Germain heir and his sister the simplest rudiments of ballroom dancing.

"We must have shortened her life span by a dozen years," Sable remarked with another giggle.

"That's only because she tried to make a proper gentleman and lady of us," Ned replied with a grin. "I think we St. Germains are far too wild for that."

"Especially Liam," Sable put in.

Ned cocked his eyebrow at her quizzically, and she gestured discreetly toward the open double doors, where Liam's freckled face peeked curiously inside. Catching sight of them, he waved brightly before vanishing again, his cheeks smeared with traces of Devonshire cream.

"He's been in the kitchen again," Ned observed. "I imagine he'll be complaining of a bellyache in the morning."

"It's all part of the fun," Sable said. "What would a harvest ball . . . a planting ball, I mean, be without Liam overeating?"

Ned threw back his dark head and laughed at this, and when the musicians ceased their playing, he led her to the chairs set out beneath the tall windows. "I'm afraid I'll have to leave you to your own devices," he informed her regretfully. "Mother warned me that I'd better be an amiable host."

"You've my sympathy," Sable remarked, seeing the yearning in the eyes of the young girls who had followed Ned's progress from the floor. Her dimpled smile grew wicked. "But that's the price you St. Germain men must pay for being so handsome."

"Heartless wench," Ned muttered and made his way to a knot of brightly attired girls gossiping in the far corner, the frantic fluttering of their fans informing Sable that they were not oblivious to his approach.

"You are amused by something, Lady Sable?"

She groaned inwardly as she recognized Wyecliffe Blackburn's voice above her. Glancing up, she found him hovering over her, dressed in a serge suit, his sallow cheeks and long neck rising above an impossibly stiff white collar.

"You wouldn't deny an old friend a dance?" he pressed when she remained silent.

Not wanting to be rude, even to someone as odious as Wyecliffe, Sable rose reluctantly and took his arm.

"You looked so very fragile dancing with your father," he murmured as they joined the other couples on the floor. "Sometimes I worry about his ability to care for you properly."

"What do you mean?" Sable inquired frostily. If this was Cliffe's latest strategy for endearing himself to her, he was certainly making a grave mistake, for Sable would tolerate no criticism of her parents.

"I've always sensed so much violence beneath that polished surface of his," Wyecliffe continued, oblivious to the fact that Sable's eyes had begun to flash. "How, by the way, did he get that disfiguring scar? No one in your family has ever told me."

Privately Sable had always thought her father's scar gave him a rakish look, and deeply resented Wyecliffe's disparaging remark. "It's probably the single greatest tribute of the love my father feels for my mother," she said pointedly. "While trying to save my mother's life he was cut by a Turk, who happened to be aiming his knife at my father's heart." The fire in her eyes deepened. "The man died for what he did."

Wyecliffe thought this a most bloodthirsty statement and was reminded again of how wild and unmanageable the St. Germains were beneath that unscrutable facade of refinement and wealth. Lady Sable, for all her astounding beauty and gentleness, was, he suspected, as barbaric and untamable as the rest of her family. Somehow the thought excited him and he tightened his arm about her small waist, missing the look of displeasure that flashed across her face.

Mercifully the dance was over soon enough and Sable was able to flee Cliffe's presence. The press of young men who demanded her attention was infinitely more welcome, most of them sons of her parents' closest friends, boys Sable had rough-housed with as a little girl. She found herself enjoying the evening immensely, laughing and dancing and drinking far more mulled wine than she should have.

It was a welcome relief when the musicians took a short break around midnight and Sable was able to slip away from her admirers. Unnoticed by anyone, she escaped into the garden, lifting her trailing skirts to wander slowly down the carefully edged walks bordered by budding flowers and hedges. The night was cool, but the garden was sheltered from the relentless winds, and Sable enjoyed the fresh, salt-scented breeze on her naked shoulders. Turning her head, she glanced back at the house where lights glowed warmly from the tall windows. The sound of laughter and gay conversation drifted to her on the night air, giving evidence that the guests were enjoying themselves immensely. She sighed deeply, happy that her father's planting ball was such a huge success.

"Surely you're not running away from your own debut, Lady St. Germain? What an unforgivable breach of conduct!"

Sable gasped as a tall form stepped directly in front of her, effectively blocking her path. The faint light glowing from the house behind her fell full on his face and revealed his dark, aristocratic features. It was impossible not to recognize the mocking glitter of his steel blue eyes, and Sable's hands flew to her cheeks.

"You!" Dismayed, she stared up at him, noting the wide span of his shoulders and the elegant cut of his dark coat. She must be dreaming, she told herself in confusion.

The lips that had kissed hers so devastatingly not two weeks ago on a darkened balcony in London curled into a cryptic smile. "I can see you're overjoyed to see me again."

"What are you doing here?" she demanded. The shock of seeing him was by no means diminished, his very size and nearness wreaking havoc on her self-control.

"Believe it or not, I was invited," Morgan Carey informed her impudently. "I arrived late, but your mother was gracious enough to accept my apologies. Afterward she wanted to present you to me, but you had disappeared and no one seemed to know where you had gone. Guided by past experience, I came out here thinking perhaps you might make it a habit of sneaking outdoors between sets. I see now I wasn't mistaken."

Sable did not know how to react to his sarcasm. The fact that Sir Morgan Carey was standing here before her, boasting an invitation, no less, disconcerted her so that she could scarcely gather her wits about her.

"My father invited you?" she asked at last, daring him to acknowledge it a second time.

Sir Morgan chuckled, the sound rumbling not unpleasantly in his chest. "It seems hard to comprehend, doesn't it? Perhaps it might restore your father's credibility in your eyes if I explain that I requested an audience with him and that he suggested I come to North Head. The fact that I arrived on the eve of your coming out is mere coincidence."

"You came to Cornwall to see my father? Why?"

Sir Morgan regarded her darkly. "You are far too curious for your own good, your ladyship. Rest assured that I have legitimate business to discuss with Lord Monterrey."

He could see the growing mistrust in Sable's eyes, which appeared almost black in the darkness. In contrast her white silk ballgown shimmered like silver, and he could not ignore her bare, sloping shoulders or the rounded firmness of her breasts as they rose and fell in rhythm with her agitated breathing.

"Doubtless you are asking yourself what business a man like myself might have with your father," he went on, but found that he was no longer interested in making sport of her. He was reminded instead of the fierce desire that had swept through him when he had held Sable St. Germain in his arms, a desire he had not been able to satisfy despite the number of women he had taken to his bed since then. Looking down into Sable's questioning face, he was seized with sudden anger. She was just a girl, he told himself sharply, despite the fact that she was so damnably beautiful. Her untutored body and unwilling lips would never satisfy his needs, despite what outward appearances might indicate. What, then, did he find so intriguing about her?

"I really don't care what sort of business you might have with my father," Sable informed him, her voice trembling despite her best efforts to appear unconcerned. "If he chose to welcome you into our home, then I will not shame him by doing otherwise. Now, if you'll excuse me, please, I should return to my guests."

Without another word she turned her slim back on him and vanished into the darkness, leaving Morgan to stare after her with grudging admiration. He shook his head, a rueful smile playing on his lips. She was nothing but a spoiled, high-spirited child with looks too alluring for her own good.

Back in the crowded ballroom Sable accepted with alacrity an invitation to dance. Sweeping around the polished floor with her proud partner, she deliberately ignored Morgan Carey, who had wandered back inside and was deep in conversation with the Earl. He seemed to have forgotten her completely, and Sable burned angrily at the snub while inwardly her curiosity was aroused. Her father had said nothing of the fact that Sir Morgan Carey, Knight of the Bath, would be attending North Head's planting ball. What business could such an arrogant, devil-may-care sea captain have with Charles St. Germain?

She watched as Sir Morgan led her mother onto the floor, the Countess smiling up at him as they performed a stately waltz that caused all heads to turn. Her mother seemed to be enjoying herself immensely, Sable realized, and recalled that the Countess had admitted finding Morgan Carey a fascinating man the night he had first stepped into their lives. She wondered grimly what her parents would have to say if they learned what he had said and done to her on the Havertys' balcony that night. She doubted sincerely that he would be so welcome here at North Head if they knew the truth.

"You look as if you'd just eaten sour grapes," Edward teased when Sable escaped from the dance floor and joined him near the door. "Gallant Cliffe hasn't been pestering you again, has he?"

Sable's eyes narrowed as she watched Morgan Carey take

the Countess's dainty hand in his big one and lead her back to a smiling, benevolent Earl. "No," she said shortly, "I'm afraid it's worse than that."

Ned gave her a quizzical glance, but she merely shook her head and heaved an exasperated sigh. "Never mind. It's just that I wish the St. Germains weren't always so eager to extend their hospitality to every bit of riffraff that knocks on North Head's door!"

She was gone before he could question her further, swept away by another lovesick young man, leaving Ned puzzling over a comment which was, for Sable, totally uncharacteristic.

By the time the revelers withdrew to their rooms it was long after midnight. Peering out of the darkened windows of the Great Hall, Sable could see the faint brightening of the horizon as the early Cornish dawn took tentative hold of the land. She was exhausted and no longer interested in learning why Morgan Carey was here. Why, the man hadn't even asked her to dance as protocol prescribed! Hopefully he would be gone by morning, Sable thought to herself as she bid her parents a tired good night.

Up in her room she did not ring for Lucy, whom she had last seen in the withdrawing room where the servants and villagers mingled, dancing with Blackburn Hall's burly groom, Jims. Lucy had waved to her, her face flushed, and Sable guessed that she had finally managed to make up her mind which husband she would choose.

Yawning widely, Sable struggled alone out of the magnificent ballgown. A single candle glowed on the dressing table, illuminating the warm, rich colors of her bedcurtains. She settled herself for a moment on the padded window seat, her arms about her silken knees. Tired as she was, the wine and music still coursed through her veins, and she didn't really feel like sleeping. It was obvious that the planting ball had been a success. She had seen as much in the flushed faces of the guests as they withdrew to their rooms or called for their carriages, and in the smiling faces of her parents as they stood side by side to bid them all good night, her father's arm about her mother's waist.

A frown knitted Sable's arching brows as memories of Morgan Carey's commanding presence rose unbidden to her mind. She had found herself unconsciously comparing his rugged visage to the youthful faces that had smiled down at her on the dance floor, and was annoyed at herself because of it.

Why, she asked herself, was she so obsessed with a man who had been rude to her, had mocked and insulted her? Just as infuriating was her inability to forget the overwhelming passion of his kisses the first time they had met and the awakening fire he had ignited within her. The fact that she had never experienced anything like it with any other man mystified her, and she told herself now that her inability to forget was mainly born of curiosity. Besides, what did it matter that Morgan Carey's kisses had made her feel so odd? She considered him to be the most conceited, insufferable man she had ever met, and she only hoped she'd be able to convince him thereof quickly enough without appearing rude!

Sable was awakened early the following morning by Liam's giggling tugs on her blanket. Opening her eyes, she found her younger brother hopping impatiently from one foot to the other as he grinned down at her. Dressed in short pants and a white shirt, his dark curls tousled, he looked deceptively innocent.

"Oh, Liam," Sable groaned, turning her face into the pillow. "What do you want?"

"Lucy sent me in to wake you up. She says I'm ever so much better at it than she is."

She was probably right, Sable reflected. It was obvious Liam was bursting with excitement, an incentive for her to rise that was far more compelling than Lucy Walters's impatient prodding. Sable was normally an early riser, but she had gone to bed so late last night that the prospect of another half-hour of sleep appealed to her enormously.

"Please hurry, Sable," Liam begged when his sister made no attempt to rise. "The race is this afternoon and Papa's already gone out to exercise De Coeur. If we hurry we can catch him."

Sable lay still for a moment imagining the salty spindrift in her face as she galloped Amourette across the moors. After a night of too much dancing and drinking, she could think of nothing she'd like to do better.

"Is Ned up?" she asked, slipping barefoot from the bed and splashing water from the fragile porcelain basin on her face.

"He's been waiting in the stable for hours!" Liam informed her. "Please hurry, Sable!"

She gave him an indulgent smile, already busy with the hairbrush, the long tresses crackling beneath her slim fingers. "Send Lucy in to help me with my habit," she suggested, "and

I'll be down in just a few minutes."

Liam sped away and Sable laid down the brush. Moving to the tall windows, she drew back the heavy drapes. Bright sunshine poured through the mullioned panes and her eyes began to sparkle with anticipation as she saw the deep green color of the moors and ocean before her. Tradition called for North Head's guests to be served a sumptuous breakfast in their rooms, which meant she was free to do as she pleased until noon.

She listened with half an ear to Lucy's chatter, submitting impatiently to the customary routine of her morning toilette while munching scones and sipping tea from a small lacquered tray. Ten minutes later she appeared downstairs in her berry-colored habit, the tailored jacket fitting snugly over her hips, a small plumed hat perched jauntily on her head. Her dark hair was swept away from her face and arranged in a smooth coronet. In her gloved hand she carried a leather whip, and old Sam beamed as he saw her coming across the courtyard.

"Mornin' to ye, Lady Sable. Lord Liam be waitin' inside. I've the wee mare groomed and saddled."

Sable's bewitching dimples appeared. "Thank you, Sam. Where's Edward?"

"Already ridden out wi' His Lordship." The grizzled old groom gave his young mistress a keen glance. "'Tisna like ye to miss the chance of ridin' out wi' the two of 'em."

"I know," Sable agreed sheepishly. "I slept late this morning."

Sam nodded knowingly. There was no doubt in his mind that Lady Sable had charmed the very soul from every man present at the planting ball last night. Even the Countess had declined to ride out with the Earl this morning, choosing instead to receive guests in her apartments, and Lady Sable could be excused this once for idling away such precious hours.

He watched with a satisfied grin as the leggy mare and fat little pony started off at a brisk trot down the winding lane away from the house. Lady Sable's dark velvet skirts billowed in the breeze, revealing her slim ankles encased in tailored leather boots. Her seat was faultless, her shoulders squared, and the sight of the young St. Germains sitting with such natural grace in the saddle brought tears to the old groom's eyes. Aye, they were equestrians to be proud of!

"How far did Father say he was going?" Sable asked as the imposing stone walls of North Head fell from view behind them and the jagged, wind-swept cliffs appeared ahead.

"To Gunard's Head and back," Liam piped. "We'll meet them if we hurry, won't we?"

Sable's lips curved as she looked down into his expectant face. "It depends on how far you can coax Lillibet to run."

"She'll run for as long as I tell her to," Liam stated confidently, though he knew perfectly well that the little Welsh pony's laziness was a source of constant amusement to the rest of his family. "I've been schooling her, and Papa says she listens much better now."

To prove his point he dug his heels into Lillibet's sides, and to Sable's surprise the little creature responded. She was forced to urge Amourette into a gallop to catch up with her brother, and side by side the two of them swept across the moors, clods of turf flying from beneath the pounding hoofs.

Further north, where the undulating grass ended abruptly at the rocky shoreline, Charles St. Germain spied the two of them approaching. Reining his stamping stallion to a halt, he watched silently as the fleet-footed mare swept gracefully toward him, his daughter leaning low over the crested neck, while Liam did his best to keep Lillibet beside her. What sight could please him more than this? he asked himself proudly, and turned to say as much to the broad-shouldered man who had ridden up behind him.

Though a man of the sea, Sir Morgan Carey had spent his youth as a soldier, and the Earl of Monterrey could find no fault in the way he handled his horseflesh. His admiration increased when he considered the nature of the beast Carey had been given to ride. Sam, who had taken bristling offense at Sir Morgan's arrogant demeanor, had saddled Falstaff for him before Charles became aware of his intent.

Sable had purchased the mulish gelding in Truro on market day several years ago after having been horrified witness to the poor creature's treatment at the hands of an indifferent farmer. The young animal had been wasted away with hunger and parasites, and only Sable had been able to see his potential. Charles himself had doubted anything would ever become of him, but had given Sam and the children permission to rehabilitate the ugly brown gelding.

To his surprise Falstaff had emerged after months of pampering and training as an animal of grace and unsettling strength. Both Raven and Charles wondered if there was drafter blood in him, for Falstaff never ceased to grow. Yet as his size increased, so had the foulness of his temper, and only Sable and Raven would ride him, for Falstaff would permit no one but a woman on his back without putting up a terrific struggle.

The fact that Sam had saddled him for Charles's guest had gone unnoticed until Morgan had actually led the enormous animal to the mounting block. Falstaff had laid back his ears and showed his long, ugly teeth, but to Charles's and Edward's surprise had done little more than kick up his heels in a show of defiance when Morgan mounted him. He had circled the restless beast about the courtyard several times, and apparently the two of them had struck up some sort of agreement, for the gelding had been docile enough as the three of them started off across the moors, an astonished Sam scratching his head as he watched them go.

As Amourette drew closer, Sable had no trouble recognizing the broad shoulders and sun-streaked hair of Captain Sir Morgan Carey. The fact that he had ridden out with her father and brother surprised her, for she would never have imagined him as a horseman. What amazed her even more was the fact that he was sitting almost negligently in the saddle while Falstaff, that most foul-tempered and intractable of creatures, stood quietly at his command. She forgot her dislike of him long enough to consider this phenomenon. Sam had said nothing to her about Sir Morgan accompanying Ned and her father riding. Had he secretly been hoping that Falstaff might rid North Head of this disagreeable guest for them?

"Good morning, my love," the Earl greeted her as she halted before him. Leaning over, he took Amourette's reins and guided her close to De Coeur's side so that he could drop a kiss on Sable's rose-petal cheek. His eyes lingered with approval on her flushed face, noting the graceful arrangement of her hair and the sparkle in her leaf-green eyes. The mulberry habit became her well, and he felt his heart constrict with pride for his only daughter, whose beauty reminded him so much of Raven in her youth.

"You met my daughter last night, didn't you?" he inquired, turning to Sir Morgan, who had watched their exchange with a cool, impenetrable look.

Sir Morgan inclined his head. "Indeed I did. I trust you slept well, your ladyship?"

Sable tried to keep the heat from her cheeks, conscious of

the mockery behind that formal tone. Tilting back her head, she peered at him haughtily from beneath the arching plume of her hat. "Thank you, I did." Her eyes traveled to his hands, which were wrapped loosely about the reins, and she couldn't help but notice how strong they looked. "I'm surprised that Falstaff permitted you to ride him."

Morgan's brow rose and his glittering blue eyes met hers steadily. "When the proper technique is used, it's possible to tame anything," he told her, adding pointedly, "or anyone."

Sable dropped her gaze from his, outraged that he should speak so rudely to her with her father present. It was obvious that the Earl had missed Sir Morgan's deliberate taunt, however, for he suggested pleasantly that they return to the house.

"Will you have enough time to set up the race course?" Sable asked curiously, deliberately placing herself between Ned and her father and as far away from Morgan Carey as she could get.

"The lads should have it measured by the time we return." Charles patted De Coeur's glossy neck, eager for the chance to pit the muscular thoroughbred against the contenders that had arrived with their owners yesterday.

"Will you be racing, too, Captain Carey?" Liam asked eagerly.

Sable was surprised to see how much the rugged visage softened as Sir Morgan glanced down into her brother's expectant face. "I'm afraid I haven't got a horse, lad."

"Why don't you ride Falstaff?" Liam suggested.

Both the Earl and Sir Morgan laughed heartily at this, and Sable felt a stab of uncharacteristic resentment. It was obvious that her father liked the younger man, and she didn't need to be told that Liam, especially, held the broad-shouldered sea captain in highest regard. Her resentment grew into anger as she contemplated this intrusion on her private life, and she found herself wondering how Sir Morgan had managed to establish himself so quickly in her father's and brothers' good graces.

When they returned to the stable, Sir Morgan was the first to dismount. Turning Falstaff over to a sheepish-looking Sam, he turned to Amourette and made as if to help Sable down. She deliberately ignored him, slipping her small boot from the stirrup and sliding gracefully to the cobblestones without assistance. A haughty glance from sea-green eyes was Morgan's

only reward for his offer, but to her annoyance he merely
inclined his head politely and turned away.

"I say, Sable, you don't seem to like him very much,"
Edward remarked as the Earl and Sir Morgan crossed the lawn
toward the house, Liam tripping happily alongside.

Sable slipped her arm about Amourette's sleek neck and
hugged her possessively. "I don't," she confessed, resentful of
the fact that Morgan Carey was as tall and broad-shouldered
as her father and that he cut an undeniably dashing figure in
his tailored coat and calfskin riding breeches. "What is he doing
here?" she demanded, eyeing her brother distrustfully. "How
did he happen to be out riding with you and Father?"

"Father asked him to come," Ned replied with a shrug. "He
seems a decent sort and Father certainly likes him." An appreciative grin lit his handsome face. "Never seen Falstaff
behave so contrarily with someone who isn't a member of the
family."

Sam, who had returned from unsaddling the unruly gelding
in time to overhear this, vigorously bobbed his graying head.
"Aye, Lord Edward, I'll agree to that! Never expected to see
the cap'n returnin' on the ill-tempered beastie's back."

Sable chewed her lip in vexation. Even Sam seemed to have
developed respect for their unwanted visitor, and she was growing heartily tired of hearing his praises sung! Had she known
this would happen she would have insisted that her father forbid
Morgan Carey to come to Cornwall. If only she had told him
how improperly the arrogant sea captain had treated her in
London, her father would have reacted quite differently to
Morgan Carey's presence at North Head!

"I've no idea why he's here," Ned went on as he and Sable
started across the lawn toward the house. "I think it has something to do with some unfinished business he and Father started
in London."

"Not company business?" Sable exclaimed. "Don't tell me
Captain Carey's become involved with Barrancourt's!"

Edward shook his head. "I don't think so, though perhaps
Sir Morgan's ship is the one Father plans to take when he goes
to Morocco next week."

It was on the tip of Sable's tongue to comment scathingly
that Sir Morgan didn't seem the sort of man to accept assign-
ments as tame as chauffeuring passengers to and fro, but she
forced herself to remain silent. It was not her way to say unkind

things about others or to complain to her family, especially when she was unwilling to tell them exactly why she disliked Morgan Carey so much.

Sable's eyes began to flash. Small wonder Sir Morgan had enjoyed mocking her earlier. He knew perfectly well she would say nothing of their first encounter to her father, not after the Earl had officially welcomed him into his home. Sable knew it would only cause her parents unnecessary embarrassment if it was learned that Sir Morgan Carey had attempted to seduce their only daughter under their very noses. It was something of which Sable herself didn't care to be reminded, either, and she prayed heartily that Sir Morgan would be leaving soon. She didn't know how much longer she could maintain a polite facade as far as he was concerned!

By noon North Head's guests, well sated from an opulent meal taken on the lawn beneath a colorful awning, had assembled at the starting line of the makeshift race course. With an array of colorful parasols and gowns, gray top hats and cutaway coats, the eastern end of the park resembled Epsom Downs on Derby Day. Indeed, an air of gala excitement prevailed, and even the most conservative of matrons had not been able to resist wagering a few coins on the outcome.

A field of ten horses had been organized, some of them brought with their owners from as far away as Suffolk and Lincoln. It wasn't often that the Earl of Monterrey raced his horses merely for sport, and his invitation to compete had been pounced on by friends and acquaintances eager to pit their mounts against the respected Monterrey stable.

"Capital idea, this," Sable overheard one bewhiskered gentleman in an elegantly braided frock coat remark to his wife. "Never thought I'd ever have the chance to run my Imperion against St. Germain's De Coeur."

His wife nodded vague agreement, but Sable could see that her gaze was riveted to the Earl himself, who was standing near the starting line holding De Coeur's head while Sam placed a light racing saddle on the stallion's broad back. A smile curved Sable's lips, seeing the studious expression on her brother Edward's face as he assisted Sam in tightening the girth, an impatient Liam squirming between them to watch.

The other horses were also being readied, and the grounds were noisy with their neighing and the eager buzz of the collected guests. The mile-long course, which had been mapped out by the Earl and his assistants earlier that morning, was lined now with people, a great number of farmers, villagers, and locals having turned out to watch the fun. Their mood was boisterous, and Sable could feel her own excitement growing.

"What a pleasant day for a race, eh, Lady Sable?"

She tilted back her head to see beyond the brim of her Florentine hat and smiled at Lord Gerald Spender, director of the Falmouth bank where her father did most of his local banking. She had known the tall, balding gentleman since she was a little girl and was as fond of him as he was of her.

"It couldn't have been better," she agreed, peering up at the cloudless blue sky, the salty wind cool against her cheek.

"Have you placed your wager yet?" Lord Spender inquired with a wink, thinking to himself that the Earl's only daughter was a picture of youthful innocence in her little hat and pale blue cotton gown. Pinned to the nape of her neck in a becoming chignon, Lady Sable's dark hair reflected highlights of burnished copper. She had grown into an uncommonly lovely young woman, his lordship decided, yet he should have expected as much, with the Earl and Countess of Monterrey for her parents.

"I've not wagered a penny," Sable informed him, her eyes sparkling mischievously. "It wouldn't be fair."

Lord Spender's brows rose inquiringly. "Oh?"

The charming dimples deepened. "Of course not. I know De Coeur will win."

The tall banker followed her gaze to the big chestnut stallion, which had quieted beneath the Earl's experienced hand. "You're probably right, young lady," he agreed, "and I believe I'll put my money exactly where your convictions lie."

"Sable! Sable, where are you? The race is about to start!"

It was Liam, calling for her in a piping voice, and Sable excused herself from Lord Spender to take her place beside her mother and brother amid the crush of spectators near the starting line. The jockeys were mounted now, some of them exercise boys wearing the colors of their owners' stables, though for the most part the horses were being ridden by the owners themselves, who saw the race as an opportunity not to be missed.

Sable's heart plummeted as she saw Wyecliffe Blackburn

riding toward the starting line on his big black colt, his pale eyes searching the crowd. She made an involuntary movement to step away from the front, but Wyecliffe had seen her. Sweeping his hat off his head, he bowed to her, the exaggerated gesture bringing an embarrassed flush to Sable's cheeks.

"I wished Father good luck for you, Sable," Liam said, tugging at her sleeve.

"That was sweet of you. Where's Ned?" Sable asked, glad for the distraction.

"Down at the finish line with Captain Carey." Liam's eyes were filled with pleading. "Can I go down and join them, Mama?"

"Certainly not," the Countess replied immediately, breaking off her conversation with the people around her to answer her son. "You'll only get in trouble with no one but Ned to watch you. Besides," she added more gently, seeing his disappointed look, "the race will be over before you even get down there."

"Look, Liam, they're in position!" Sable added.

The little boy's attention was immediately diverted to the impressive row of Thoroughbreds before him. De Coeur, with the imposing figure of the Earl on his back, was standing closest to them. With the Earl's visage shadowed by his cap, Sable couldn't see the expression on his face, but she guessed that he was thinking of the start and how he intended to come away clean although he had drawn the outside, the most difficult of all positions.

"Are we ready, gentlemen?"

It was Lord Gerald Spender standing on a small box decorated with colorful bunting, an out-of-breath Sam at his elbow clutching the Earl's tooled leather case of dueling pistols in his big hands. The Earl had invited Lord Spender to start the race, and, without preamble, the elderly banker lifted one of the beautiful German pistols from its velvet resting place. The Earl turned his head at that moment, his eyes going briefly to his wife, who stood expectantly before him, one arm about each of her children. A smile curved his sensual lips and he winked.

Before Sable could wave back at him the pistol was fired, bringing squeals from the watching women. Amid a thunder of hoofs the ten horses took off, the attendants and grooms scrambling to get out of their way, the spectators roaring with approval.

"De Coeur's in the lead!" Sable cried, recognizing the streaming banner tail and the dark head of her father as the horses pounded off across the turf.

The cheers about her were deafening, and she craned her neck to see over the spectators in front of her. Liam, hopelessly undersized, hopped from one foot to the other and tugged at her skirts, demanding to know what was happening. Lord Spender, hearing the boy's plaintive cries, reached down from the box and lifted him into his arms.

"Your father's in the lead, lad! By God, I'm glad I bet on him!"

Liam beamed proudly. Before he could speak, however, a shout of alarm went up from the spectators further down the field.

"What is it?" Sable and Raven cried in unison, unable to see.

"I believe there's a horse down on the track," Lord Spender replied, the sudden concern in his voice chilling them.

"A horse?" Raven repeated, pushing her way onto the stand beside him, her skirts swirling about her. She could see nothing on the slope where the horses had vanished save people rushing forward gesticulating wildly.

"What is it, Mother?" Sable asked, her heart thumping as she sensed her mother's fear.

Lord Spender had gotten hold of a set of opera glasses from someone and was now training it on the field below them. "It's true, m'lady," he said grimly. "There seems to be a horse down."

"Which one?" Raven demanded desperately.

"I can't tell. . . . Good God, it seems to be more than one! I believe we'd better go investigate."

Sable's breath came in gasps as she followed her mother and Lord Spender across the lawn, Liam clinging to the Countess's skirts. Most of the guests had started forward by now, asking questions, but no one seemed to know what had happened. Only as Sable came closer did she hear the comments around her from those who had been far enough downfield to witness the accident.

". . . Jostled him, he did. Boxed him up neat as day."

"Couldn't be helped, not with that tight a field."

"How bad is he hurt?"

Sable heard no more, for suddenly the tide of people before

her seemed to part, and she was staring down at her father's still form lying in the grass. De Coeur, limping painfully, was being cared for nearby while a second horse lay unmoving farther downfield. Dully Sable's mind registered the fact that it was Wyecliffe Blackburn's colt, but she didn't care about anything save the fact that her father lay so still.

"Papa!" Liam wailed, having caught sight of his father by now. Bursting into tears, he buried his face in Sable's skirts and clung to her with all his might.

It was then that Morgan Carey appeared before them, his wide chest blocking the Earl's crumpled form from Sable's frightened line of vision. He cast a swift glance into her pale face and said something to Edward, who was beside him. Immediately the young heir of Monterrey hurried forward to take his sister into his arms.

"Oh, Ned! Is he—?" Sable choked and couldn't go on.

"He's going to be fine," Edward assured her, and in his boyish voice there was an undercurrent of authority that calmed her.

Sir Morgan, meanwhile, had placed his hand beneath the Countess's elbow and led her to Charles's side. Sable did not miss the grateful glance her mother gave the blue-eyed sea captain or the protective stance with which Sir Morgan hovered over her.

"Why won't he get up?" Sable demanded, staring at him accusingly. "Ned says he's not badly hurt. Why is he lying there like that?"

Morgan's expression was far more kind than Sable would ever have given him credit for. "He's injured his back," he told her softly. "It's wisest he isn't moved until the doctor arrives."

"Oh, Judas, no!" Sable whispered, tears springing to her eyes.

"He's going to be all right," Sir Morgan assured her and, looking up into his commanding visage, Sable could not help believing him. She felt her dislike for him being replaced by a feeling of profound relief that he was there and taking command.

"Why don't you take your sister and brother back to the house?" Morgan suggested earnestly to Edward. "Dr. Pengelly should be here any moment. I'll see to it your father's horse is cared for and the other one disposed of."

Sable shook her head, her eyes wide in her pale face. "No,

I don't want to leave him. Please, Ned, let me see Father."

She felt a hand close firmly about her wrist and looked up quickly into Morgan's face, where the understanding had been underscored by determination. "You'd be better off waiting inside," he told her in a tone that brooked no argument.

"He's right, Sable." Ned was at her side, gently pulling her away. "Come on."

Sable followed unwillingly, feeling as though everything were passing in a blur before her. She took little notice of the sharp crack of a pistol as Wyecliffe's colt was put out of its misery. Faces and voices surrounded her, pressed in on her, but she could make no sense out of the reassuring words and kind smiles. Clutching a tearful Liam with one arm and clinging to Edward with the other, she watched as a group of men including Morgan Carey lifted her father gently onto a stretcher under Dr. Pengelly's direction. Fighting back her tears, she followed numbly behind as it was taken to the house.

Lucy, competent and bustling, was there to take her three charges into her arms while the door to the master suite closed behind the Earl above them. Afterward Sable could not remember how long the vigil lasted. Lucy begged her to eat, but she refused food, and retreated with Liam into the Yellow Salon to wait. Feeling it was his duty, Ned went outside to be with the guests, leaving Sable alone with her little brother. Closing the door to the Salon behind her, she turned to find him stretched out on the sofa, face buried in the satin cushions, his small body racked with sobs.

"Here, what's this?" she asked with forced cheerfulness, seating herself beside him. "You'll ruin that cover, and you know how Mother treasures everything in this room."

The tear-streaked little face that was raised to hers was heartbreaking to behold, and Sable's smile faded. Drawing Liam onto her lap, she whispered gently, "Don't cry, love. Ned said Father wasn't badly hurt, and you know he wouldn't lie about that."

"Then why did Dr. Pengelly make them carry him home?" Liam choked.

Sable understood the cause of his fears, for never in their lives had they seen their father rendered so vulnerable. How utterly frightening it must be for Liam, especially, who was accustomed to seeing his father in the prime of health, strong, dependable, and without weakness! She choked down her own fears, seeing again in her mind's eye his terribly pale face, her mother's expression drawn as she silently followed the stretcher upstairs.

The door opened quietly behind her and Sable jerked about, stiffening reflexively as she met Morgan Carey's blue eyes. He hesitated when he saw her sitting on the sofa with Liam's curly head on her shoulder, and an unfathomable expression crossed his aristocratic countenance.

"My apologies, your ladyship," he said coolly. "I didn't mean to intrude."

"No, wait, please." Sable rose to her feet, Liam's small hand in hers. "Do you know how he is?"

"Dr. Pengelly is still with him." Sir Morgan came slowly inside and paused on the opposite side of the richly upholstered sofa. It was obvious to him that Sable was terribly frightened but that she was doing her best to hide it from him. He couldn't help admiring her, thinking there was a great deal of the Barrancourt courage in this slip of a girl who returned his gaze so bravely. She was more like her mother than the Countess realized, Morgan thought to himself, recalling how Lady Monterrey had smilingly complained to him on the dance floor last night how exasperatingly like her stubborn father her only daughter was.

"Perhaps you should drink something," Morgan suggested, not caring for Sable's lingering paleness. "Brandy or claret might help."

"Thank you, no," Sable murmured distractedly.

Morgan came around the sofa, his concern growing. "Sable, are you sure you're all right?"

She blinked as she looked up into his handsome face. The urge to lay her head against that wide chest and weep overwhelmed her, for she sensed instinctively that she would find comfort in those powerful arms. But she stepped away from him, an expression of loathing crossing her delicate features.

"I'm fine," she assured him coldly. "Liam and I need nothing from you."

Morgan's brow darkened, but Sable did not notice. Cocking her head, she caught her breath, and Morgan, listening, heard what she did: the sound of footsteps on the landing above. Quickly Sable lifted Liam into her arms and hurried into the hall with Morgan close behind her.

It was North Head's elderly butler Parris thumping down

the stairs. Finding himself confronted by Sable's upturned, frightened face, he halted abruptly, one hand on the carved wooden banister for support.

"Your father's fine, Lady Sable, Lord Liam," he informed them in his most proper tones, although his faded eyes twinkled. "No broken bones. Her ladyship sent me down to inform you that you may come up to see him."

"Oh, thank God! Will you tell Ned, please?" Sable asked, starting eagerly up the stairs with Liam behind her, Morgan Carey all but forgotten.

The private suite of the Earl and Countess of Monterrey had never failed to daunt the St. Germain children no matter how welcome they had always been within its imposing rooms. All three of them had been born in the very bed in which the Earl now lay, and Sable and Liam hesitated briefly on the threshold as they heard the murmur of voices from within. It had always seemed a grownup's room to them, a private domain reserved for their parents alone, and Sable, even though she was no longer a child, could never step inside without experiencing some of the awe that had always overwhelmed her as a little girl.

Yet today she saw nothing of the magnificent mahogany woodwork or the hand-painted Chinese wallpaper her father had personally brought back with him from Hong Kong. Instead her eyes flew to the big four-poster bed where the heavy curtains had been drawn back, the doctor, her mother, and several of her father's friends gathered about it.

The Countess, sensing their presence, turned, and her worried expression softened as she saw her children standing uncertainly in the doorway. Noticing the trembling of Liam's lower lip she opened her arms and the little boy flew to her.

Sable approached more slowly and paused uncertainly at the foot of the bed.

"Come over here, lass!" her father's deep voice ordered sternly. "I'm not on my deathbed yet!"

His dire tone might have unsettled anyone else, but Sable obeyed gladly, bending to kiss his lean cheek. "Oh, Father," she whispered, unable to keep the catch from her voice, "we were so afraid you'd been hurt!"

"I'm all right," Charles growled, touched by the tears he saw glistening in his daughter's eyes.

"You are not all right," the Countess informed him severely, peering at him warningly from above Liam's tousled head. "Dr. Pengelly said you were to stay in bed for at least a fortnight, and I intend to see that you do."

"Quite right, your lordship," the physician agreed, coming closer, his approving gaze resting on Raven, who sat beside her husband on the bed, her son in her lap. "You've injured some nerves in your back, and we must be quite certain they've mended before you get back on your feet."

Sable felt relief course through her at the intimidating scowl her father gave the doctor. The knot of fear she had felt since the accident was beginning to unwind. Surely he couldn't be bad off if his spirits remained unchanged!

"Father!"

Ned's youthful countenance was filled with undisguised relief as he pushed his way to the bedside. "Parris told me you were fine."

"Only if he follows Dr. Pengelly's orders," the Countess said in her most reproving tones. Sable noticed that her mother still looked pale and realized how badly frightened all of them had been by the Earl's accident.

"Excuse me, m'lady."

A disapproving Parris was standing in the doorway. "Master Blackburn is without, requesting an opportunity to extend his apologies for the mishap."

"I'll speak to him, Parris," Raven replied, rising to her feet with Liam in her arms. Her eyes went to her husband's face where the weariness and pain still lingered. "You must sleep now, m'lord," she added in a tone that commanded everyone save Dr. Pengelly to accompany her out.

"Did you find out what happened?" Sable asked her brother in low tones as they started for the stairs.

"Apparently Wyecliffe was trying to pass Father on the stretch and cut in front of him, jostling him as he did. De Coeur went down, taking Wyecliffe's horse with him."

Sable gave him a penetrating glance. "Do you think it was deliberate?"

Ned shook his head, having anticipated her blunt question. "Everyone I spoke to seems to think not, and Wyecliffe was devastated that his colt had to be put down. I don't think so."

But he wasn't sure. Sable could see as much in his uneasy expression, hear it in his subdued tone. She herself found it hard to believe. Wyecliffe Blackburn might be a loathsome, unwanted suitor, but she would never suspect him of deliberately trying to hurt her father. To what end? she asked herself. What could Wyecliffe possibly hope to gain from hurting the Earl? Knowing that she tended too often to overlook the evil in a person, Sable tried to view the matter objectively and still could not find it in her heart to believe the accident had been deliberate. Wyecliffe was a fierce competitor; doubtless he had thrown caution to the winds in his determination to be first across the finish line.

Her thoughts still in a turmoil, Sable accompanied Ned and Liam across the cobblestone courtyard to the stables, where Sam, his face beaded with perspiration, was applying a steaming poultice to De Coeur's front leg. The skittish stallion was being subdued by two red-faced grooms, and Sable hurried forward to lay a soothing hand on his neck.

"How bad is it?" Ned asked worriedly.

"Nothin' what canna be fixed, laddie." The big, blunt fingers expertly smoothed down the thick bandage. "A good soakin', lots of rest, and a hot bran mash'll put him right in a week. How be His Lordship?"

"Lots of rest and some of Perry's hot soup and he'll be fine in a week, too."

Sam's eyes twinkled. "I be glad to hear it."

"It's a shame about Wyecliffe's horse," Sable added quietly, stroking De Coeur's glossy neck until the big animal stood calmly, his ears flicking back and forth.

Sam's lips tightened. "No excuse for reckless ridin'," he said simply, but it was obvious that he was deeply angry over what had happened.

Returning to the house while her brothers remained behind to help Sam, Sable saw that most of the guests were gathered in the courtyard making preparations to depart. Not wanting to speak to anyone, she slipped unnoticed through the servants' entrance, hoping to avoid the activity in the main wing of the house.

"Sable, Lady Sable, wait!"

Her heart plummeted as she recognized Wyecliffe Blackburn's call behind her in the corridor. Of all people, Cliffe was the last one she wanted to see. Turning reluctantly, she couldn't help feeling guilty when she saw the sorrowful look on his face. There was a nasty cut above his eye, and his clothes were smeared with mud and grass. He certainly didn't look like a man who had just deliberately sabotaged a horse race, Sable decided.

"I was hoping to sneak out this way," he confessed, coming to a halt before her. "I'm not exactly popular with your father's friends at the moment."

"Oh, Cliffe, it wasn't your fault!" Sable cried impulsively. "Everyone knows it was an accident."

The thin features relaxed. "I can't tell you how glad I am you believe that! Lady Monterrey was gracious to me when I apologized, but I could sense her distance." His jaw worked. "I swear to you, Sable, I never—"

"It's all right, Cliffe," Sable said quickly, her heart filling with pity for him.

Overcome with emotion at the softening of those lovely features, Wyecliffe uttered a hoarse groan and, without warning, pulled Sable into his arms. Stunned, she could not resist as his lips came down on hers in a hard, wet kiss that was filled, not with relief or remorse, but an all-consuming passion. It was obvious that Wyecliffe desired her fiercely, but Sable felt none of the unexpected heat that Morgan Carey's lips on hers had caused. Instead, when the shock faded, she found herself overwhelmed with disgust, his slobbering mouth and probing tongue revolting her.

"Cliffe, don't," she panted.

"Don't fight me, Sable," he murmured, his breath hot against her cheek.

She tried to struggle free of his hold but he was surprisingly strong. Wrapping his arms tightly about her he forced her closer against his body, his mouth continuing to assault hers.

"Mr. Blackburn, I suggest you let the lady go."

Though the words were softly uttered, they rang with such silken menace that Wyecliffe released Sable as though he had been burned. Whirling about he found himself bumping into a chest of unsettlingly wide proportions. His mouth dropped open as he raised his vision higher to find himself gazing into a pair of blue eyes filled with something he didn't much care for. Who was he? Wyecliffe racked his brains, trying to place the retroussé nose and lean, sun-bronzed cheeks. Carey, that was it, Sir Morgan Carey, the sea captain who had attended the planting ball at Lord Monterrey's invitation.

Aye, he remembered now how heartily sick he'd gotten of the gossip concerning the fellow last night, recalling that everyone seemed to consider Captain Carey some sort of hero. Knighted by the Queen after Crimea, a blockade runner or some such bloody nonsense in the American conflict. . . . What other stories had circulated about him? Wyecliffe couldn't remember, but one thing remained clear. He was only a mere acquaintance of the Earl of Monterrey's, not a neighbor of long years' standing like the Blackburns, and he had no right to intervene on Sable's behalf.

It was none of his sodding business, Wyecliffe decided uncharitably and turned to Sable, prepared to say as much, but the words died in his throat when he saw her furiously rubbing the back of her hand across her lips as though to erase the repulsive touch of his own. A surge of utter rage went through him. By God, he'd not take such an insult, not from her!

"Do you wish to say something to the lady, Mr. Blackburn?"

Looking up into the rugged countenance, Wyecliffe realized that the older man was perfectly aware of his feelings. He knew a moment of real fear, recognizing the warning glint in those cold blue eyes.

"My apologies, Lady Sable," he muttered, still seething inwardly. "The shock of what happened, your kindness in forgiving me . . . I'm afraid I lost my head."

"It—it's all right, Cliffe," Sable murmured though she was unable to meet his gaze. She glanced instead at Morgan Carey, glad for once of his presence, but her relief changed to fury when she saw that he appeared to be deriving amusement from the entire situation. His earlier show of anger had vanished and now he leaned against the newel post, his arms folded across his chest, his lips twitching.

Wyecliffe, becoming aware that he, too, was now the target of the broad-shouldered sea captain's mockery, flushed dark red. He'd had enough of both of them, he decided sullenly. "Excuse me, please," he said brusquely, "I'd better be going. Lady Sable, my apologies again."

The arched door slammed behind him, leaving a tangible silence in his wake. Sable steeled herself, well aware that Sir Morgan was going to make some sort of derisive comment. She glared at him defiantly and was relieved when she heard Lucy Walters's familiar voice from the staircase above them.

"Lord 'a' mercy, what is it, child?" the tiring woman exclaimed, catching sight of Sable's flushed face in the hall below. Her gaze moved suspiciously to Morgan Carey as she descended the steps. "What's happened here?" she demanded threateningly, planting her hands on her ample hips.

"I'd rather not talk about it, Lucy," Sable replied with as much dignity as she could muster. "Perhaps Captain Carey would be kind enough to explain." Avoiding those mocking blue eyes, she gathered up her skirts and fled, wanting to be alone to sort out her confused thoughts. Her father's accident had upset her too much, she told herself as she hurried to the welcoming privacy of her bedroom, otherwise she would never have reacted quite so strongly to Wyecliffe's kiss. Never in her life had she felt so repelled, so violated. Most disturbing of all, she could not explain why Wyecliffe's advances should have made her feel that way when Morgan Carey's impassioned kisses had left her undeniably yearning for more.

What could it mean? Sable asked herself as she curled up on her bed with her chin in her hand. She knew she had no answers and, furthermore, she resented the fact that he had found such amusement at her expense. Her embarrassment grew as she pictured him laughing openly at her now for her inability to handle herself with someone as insignificant as Wyecliffe Blackburn. Ooh! She couldn't wait until the long-legged scoundrel was gone, and she hoped he'd have enough sense to take his leave now that her father was ill!

Chapter 4

With the coming of night quiet descended upon the great house of North Head. The footmen and maids who had worked feverishly to restore the multitude of bedrooms, sitting rooms, and parlors used by the St. Germains' guests were yawning sleepily as they finished. In the kitchen all was spotless, the rows of copper pots gleaming as they were returned to the walls, and a satisfied Perry dismissed his staff at last. Parris and Timms, who were always the last to retire, exchanged pleasant good nights and comments of relief concerning their master's health as they extinguished the lights and turned down the gas before retreating to their rooms.

In the upper hall of the East Wing, Raven St. Germain sighed tiredly as she closed the door to her daughter's bedroom and quietly started back toward the master suite. Though she hadn't looked in on her oldest children at night for many years, she had been seized with the need to do so as she herself was preparing for bed.

Like Ned, Sable had been sleeping when the Countess had quietly entered her room, but the drawn expression on her daughter's delicate face gave Raven reason to believe that Sable was in for a restless night. She stood for a moment looking down into the oval face, which appeared even lovelier in repose, and felt her heart turn over with a fierce, protective rush of love. Reaching down, she caressed the silky curls that spilled onto the pillow before quietly leaving the room.

Earlier Dr. Pengelly had suggested to her without a trace of embarrassment that she sleep in another room during the Earl's convalescence, but Raven, after leaving Sable, could not resist looking in on Charles as well. Expecting to find him asleep, she was startled to hear the low murmur of masculine voices coming from behind the master bedroom door. Her eyes widened disbelievingly when she entered to find Sir Morgan Carey lounging in a chair near the bed, a half-empty glass in one long-fingered hand. He rose politely at the sight of her, but Raven had eyes only for her husband, who sat propped against the pillows sipping wine as though he had never come close to breaking his neck only a few hours earlier.

"Good evening, my dear," Charles greeted her, his eyes twinkling devilishly as he became aware of her anger. "Sir Morgan and I were talking business. The *Defiance* is due to sail with tomorrow's tide, and I didn't want to see him delay his journey by waiting attendance on me."

"You what?" Raven exclaimed, gazing helplessly from one bronzed face to the other. "Captain Carey—" she began warningly.

"No, Raven, the fault is entirely mine," Charles told her quickly. Sobering, he reached for her hand. "I insisted he see me."

"I couldn't refuse a direct order from my host, madame," Morgan added helpfully, though Raven was quite sure that he was a man who never did anything against his will. She shook her head in exasperation, knowing that Charles wouldn't rest until he had finished what he intended to say. It might therefore be wiser to turn to Morgan Carey for help, she decided, and she lifted her chin to gaze at the insolent young man before her.

"Captain, will you please see to it that you conclude your business with my husband shortly?"

Confronted by an oval face as perfect in its patrician beauty as Sable St. Germain's, Morgan found himself softening unexpectedly toward this proud, black-haired woman who was but a few years older than himself. An uncharacteristically gentle smile curved his lips, and his blue eyes twinkled although he spoke gravely.

"I give you my word not to fatigue him."

Raven's answering smile was easily as dimpled and beguiling as her daughter's. "Thank you." To Charles she added warningly, "I'll be waiting outside until you're finished."

"That's kind of you, dear," Charles responded with a long-suffering sigh, but his harsh visage softened as she smiled at him before vanishing through the door.

Morgan, seeing the look they exchanged, felt as though he were intruding on something private and very special, and he returned to his seat with a thoughtful look on his face. Until now he had always believed such love did not exist, but now he was forced to admit that perhaps it was possible to feel so deeply for another person. His lips twisted cynically. Much as he admired the Earl of Monterrey and respected his love for his Countess, he was relieved that such constricting emotions had never tormented him. And if he continued to be lucky they never would, making it possible for him to escape the trappings of marriage for the rest of his life. God forbid it should ever happen otherwise!

Raven St. Germain sat quietly by the fire in the adjoining room, idly turning the pages of a book as she listened to the rise and fall of the deep voices in the other room. Earlier that week Charles had consulted her briefly concerning Morgan Carey's request, and she had agreed that they should welcome him to their home when the *Defiance* arrived in Falmouth. She knew that Charles was favorably impressed with the blue-eyed captain and trusted him to make the right decision with respect to whatever business was currently under discussion.

Still, she could not help feeling impatient, well aware that her husband needed rest and that, despite his jovial mood, he had been in a great deal of pain when she had looked in on him. One small slippered foot tapped impatiently on the thick carpet until at last she heard the outer door to the bedroom close. Footsteps sounded in the corridor outside and she waited until they had receded before peeking in on Charles.

He was lying in bed with his eyes closed when she entered, and she hesitated on the threshold, her throat constricting when she saw how pale he appeared. But then he opened his eyes and smiled, and she came to him gladly, taking his outstretched hand in hers.

"I want you to sleep now," she admonished, setting down her small lamp on the nearby nightstand.

Charles's green eyes glinted. "How can I, knowing you'll be lying all alone beyond the door?"

Raven's lips curved, although his light-heartedness hadn't fooled her. She sensed that he was still in pain, though she knew he would never admit as much. "You'd better get used to it, m'lord, because I intend to abide by Dr. Pengelly's orders."

"The man's a quack," Charles grumbled.

"I don't care," Raven responded crisply. "You're to do as he says, which means you're not to set foot from this bed for at least ten more days."

Charles made a face. "Since when has my beautiful, soft-spoken wife become such a martinet?"

"Since I am determined to have you get well quickly. I mean it, Charles! You've spent your life refusing to take orders from anyone, but in this instance I insist you do as Dr. Pengelly tells you."

Charles chuckled ruefully. "Damn, I'm beginning to regret this very badly! I'd hoped to spend my convalescence being cosseted by my adoring wife and family."

Raven dimpled despite herself. "Oh, I promise that will happen, but only if you do as you're told." She bent down and planted a gentle kiss on his lips. "Now," she added, straightening, "why don't you tell me what you and Sir Morgan have decided to do?"

"It can wait until tomorrow," the Earl replied, waving the subject away with a languid movement of his hand. "First I want to discuss two other things with you."

"And what are they?" Raven asked with a frown. Charles needed sleep, not a lengthy conversation with her!

"Lucy told me earlier what transpired backstairs between Sable and Wyecliffe Blackburn this afternoon," Charles began bluntly. "Have you talked to Sable about it?"

Raven's eyes widened. "Oh, Charles, why should I? I'm certain it was harmless enough, though I don't blame Lucy for getting angry over it. Sable didn't appear overly upset when I saw her later, so I felt there was no sense in mentioning it."

"But you said she had a tray sent up to her room," Charles reminded her darkly, "that she didn't eat dinner downstairs."

Raven gave a tinkling little laugh, touched by Charles's

reaction to such an insignificant thing. How typically fatherly he was being in trying to protect his daughter! She felt overcome with a warm rush of love for him and ran her finger teasingly over his scarred cheek. "No one ate dinner downstairs tonight, Charles, don't you remember? I joined you here and the boys ate in the Conservatory with Danny, and Sir Morgan spent the evening on his ship."

Charles had the good grace to look sheepish. "If you insist there's nothing more to be said—"

"I do," Raven interrupted. The last thing she wanted was for Charles to confront Wyecliffe now when he should be resting in bed.

"What's really troubling me is Wyecliffe himself," Charles said after a moment, a thoughtful look on his handsome face. "I've never trusted him, and I'm afraid that he may try to force his hand with Sable while I'm confined to this blasted bed."

"Sable would never permit such a thing to happen," Raven assured him, shocked at the prospect.

"I'm not so sure," the Earl grumbled, feeling more impotent than ever before in his life. How was he supposed to look after his family laid up like this? "You know how gentle-hearted Sable is. She's so much more innocent and trusting than you were at her age and she might not be able to refuse him."

"It won't happen," Raven assured him gently, afraid that his temper was beginning to rise. "And if it does," she added, her eyes twinkling, "I'll have Timms or another of the footmen haul him up here where he can confront your wrath face to face. Knowing Wyecliffe as I do, it ought to curtail his enthusiasm until you're completely well."

Charles let his hand stray through Raven's shining hair, marveling to himself how easily she could coax him out of any foul mood. She smiled at him in response, her eyes soft with understanding.

"Why don't you tell me what else is on your mind?"

Charles's lips twitched. "If you insist. I've decided to send Edward to Morocco." His eyes glinted devilishly at Raven's blank expression. "You seem surprised, my love. Didn't I tell you I'd been thinking about it earlier?"

"Charles—" Raven began warningly.

"I'm being serious," he told her. "You do remember that Telleborough finally managed to arrange a meeting with the Sultan for me in Fez."

Raven sighed unhappily. "I do, and I've been worrying about that off and on all day," she confessed. "I know how long you've been waiting for that invitation, and I was afraid you'd insist on keeping the appointment."

"I'm not as young and rash as I once was," he told her. "That's why I've been lying here thinking about sending Ned in my place. It's an idea I was toying with in London when it appeared as if your illness might further delay our return home."

"He's just a boy!" Raven protested.

"Not anymore," Charles said with a hint of pride in his deep voice. "The way he ran the estate while we were in London proved to me that our son is quite capable of taking over the family holdings when the time comes."

"But sending him to Tangier as your representative!" Raven cried. "It's pointless! Ned knows nothing of diplomacy or politics! You've told me yourself Morocco is an isolated, unchanging country. Ned doesn't have the negotiating skills required to establish a commercial firm there!"

"But Dmitri will be there to take care of that," Charles reminded her gently, "and I'm certain the Sultan will take no offense at receiving my son and heir in my place."

The mention of Dmitri's name erased some of the doubt from Raven's face, as Charles knew it would. Years ago Dmitri Zergeyev had been the *Orient Star*'s first mate and Charles's closest friend. During her fateful journey to India, Raven had grown to love the ebullient, faithful Russian as much as Charles did, and Dmitri had adored her in return, calling her his "little princess" and vowing his eternal devotion to her.

After his marriage and their return to North Head, Charles had given control of the *Orient Star* to Dmitri and had gone into business with Raven's great-uncle, Sir Hadrian Barrancourt, a retired director of one of London's largest silk and tea emporiums. With Sir Hadrian's skill at marketing and Charles's numerous contacts around the world, Barrancourt Ltd. had become an export and import firm of considerable size with a name that commanded instant respect.

Sir Hadrian had died almost ten years ago, and Dmitri, living a life of semiretirement on Barbados with his beautiful native wife and numerous offspring, had leaped to accept Charles's offer to enter into the business. Just as much a goodwill ambassador as a quick-thinking businessman and sea captain, Dmitri had proven himself a valuable addition to the firm.

For months now, Charles had been attempting to open a commercial branch of Barrancourt's in Morocco to compete with the few French companies the Sultan had given his permission to establish there. Sir Harry Telleborough, a British attaché and one of the few Europeans at the time to have access to the Sultan's palace in Fez, had managed to obtain an audience for Dmitri and Charles. It was a meeting that Charles had resigned himself to missing now that he had been forced to take to his bed. Though Dmitri could doubtless have handled the negotiations alone, Charles was certain that the Sultan would view his own absence as a slight, and the idea of sending Edward had seemed the perfect solution.

"Our son is almost a man, Raven," he said now, gazing up into his wife's pale face. "The Sultan has sons of his own and will understand the honor I'm bestowing him in sending him mine."

Raven was silent for a moment, and Charles could understand her misgivings and the conflicting emotions a woman experiences when she is forced to acknowledge for the first time that her son is becoming a man. He smiled to himself, recalling that he had experienced similar feelings when he had discovered from Lucy Walters that only that very afternoon his own daughter had become the target of sexual attention.

Charles's lean jaw tightened ominously. Regardless of what Raven had said, he intended to come to a reckoning with Wyecliffe Blackburn over that very episode as soon as he was able to leave his bed. How dare the young pup accost his daughter in her own home!

"Do you think we can talk about this tomorrow?" Raven's question brought Charles's thoughts back to the present. "I really need to think about it, and of course there are Edward's feelings to be considered."

Charles laid a gentle hand over hers. "Don't trouble yourself too much over it tonight," he suggested. "You need sleep as much as I do. I'm sorry to bring all of this up now."

Raven rose to her feet and smoothed down the sheets that covered him. "It doesn't matter. Is Captain Carey sailing tomorrow?"

The Earl nodded, his lips twitching. "Much as I like the fellow, I must admit I'll be relieved to see him go. He reminds me far too much of myself when I was his age. Nor can I forget how vulnerable you Barrancourt women are to a seaman's charms. After all, look what happened when you met me."

"It was the most unfortunate event of my life," Raven agreed, the uncertainty on her face replaced by a mischievous look, as Charles had hoped. They smiled at one another, thinking of the past and remembering the journey across India that had changed the course of their lives forever.

"Would it be so terrible if Sable were to fall in love with a dashing sea captain?" Raven teased.

Charles's emerald eyes glittered. "That will never happen, my dear, because our daughter needs someone responsible, level-headed, and totally devoted to her happiness."

"Qualities one cannot find in a man of the sea," Raven added meaningfully, her golden eyes dancing as she looked at him.

"Certainly not," Charles agreed and forgot his pain as he pulled her to him to deposit a warm, loving kiss on her lips.

When Sable arose the following morning she was delighted to find that yesterday's mild, sunny weather remained. The sight of the sea sparkling beneath her window was enough to prompt her to pull her riding habit from the wardrobe. Brushing her dark hair and securing it in a sleek chignon, she reached for her gloves. On the landing she turned with a rustle of skirts toward the opposite wing where her parents' apartments lay. She'd look in on her father first, she decided, and see how he was doing. Knocking on the sitting room door, she was surprised to be admitted by Edward, who seized her hands in his and impatiently pulled her inside.

"I've come to see how Father is," Sable began, but Edward breathlessly interrupted her.

"He's better, Sable, but I was just coming to tell you the news!"

"What news?" She had never seen Edward this excited.

"Father is sending me to Tangier! Believe it or not I'm leaving the day after tomorrow for Morocco!"

Sable cast an astonished glance at her parents, who were smiling at Edward's enthusiasm. A breakfast tray lay propped on the coverlet at her father's side, and he set down his fork long enough to reach for Raven's hand.

"It's true, my love. Since I obviously cannot keep my appointment with the Sultan, I've decided that Edward should go in my place."

"I'm to meet Dmitri in Tangier," Edward added, twirling Sable about in his excitement, "and then we'll leave for Fez via land. We might even have to ride camels, Sable, imagine that!"

"Is it really true?" Sable asked, eyeing her father disbelievingly. She couldn't believe the fact that he intended to obey Dr. Pengelly's orders when something as important as this lay before him.

"Indeed it is," the Countess responded, correctly reading her daughter's mind. "Dr. Pengelly gave me permission to bind your father to the bedposts to prevent him from going."

"Does Liam know?" Sable inquired, beginning to envy Edward now that she had been assured of the validity of his claim.

"He's still at lessons, but I'm going to tell him as soon as he's done." Edward sobered suddenly and glanced at the bed. The similarity between himself and the Earl was suddenly strikingly obvious. Raven was forced to catch her breath, seeing for the first time how much her son had changed in the past year and how closely he had begun to resemble his father.

"I promise to make you proud of me," Edward said soberly.

Charles's eyes twinkled. "I already am, son."

"Excuse me, sir, madame."

Raven lifted her head to regard the iron-haired servant who stood stiffly in the doorway. "What is it, Parris?"

"I bet Cliffe Blackburn is here," Ned interrupted, catching sight of the elderly butler's distasteful expression. "Either that or Perry has burned our lunch."

Sable giggled and even the proper Parris permitted himself the liberty of a brief smile. Squaring his thin shoulders, he tried to look enthusiastic as he announced formally, "Master Wyecliffe Blackburn is downstairs. I've shown him into the Yellow Salon."

Raven couldn't keep the dismay from her voice. "Oh dear! Did he say what he wanted?"

"I believe he wishes to inquire after His Lordship's health."

"I'll go down and speak to him," Sable volunteered with a sigh. She wasn't overly eager to see him so soon after his shocking behavior yesterday, but she knew that her parents wished to be alone and that Ned, in his excitement over the forthcoming trip, might not be inclined to be civil to their guest. Poor Wyecliffe, he probably felt awful about what he had done, and this certainly wasn't the time to alienate him!

"I'd like to suggest you hurry, then, Lady Sable," Parris added in his most proper tones. "With all due respect, Mrs. Daniels is currently with him."

"Not alone?" Edward exclaimed while the others burst into helpless laughter.

"Why don't you go with her, Edward?" the Earl suggested smoothly.

Sable's eyes danced. "Oh, I can handle him alone, Papa, thank you. You ought to go tell Liam your news, Ned."

Edward's chest swelled importantly. "I should, shouldn't I?"

"He'll be so envious," Sable added, and gave him a hug. "I'm so happy for you!"

A pleased flush crept to his cheeks and he excused himself hurriedly while Sable lingered to kiss her parents lovingly before going down to rescue Wyecliffe from Danny. Her eyes began to twinkle in amusement as she neared the Salon door and heard Danny's stentorian tones coming from within. Obviously the elderly woman was engaged in another tirade against their visitor, whose only real crime lay in bearing the Blackburn name.

Preparing to sweep inside and put an end to Cliffe's suffering, Sable came to a halt on the threshold as she heard Sir Morgan Carey's name fall from Danny's lips. Thinking she had misunderstood, she listened without acknowledging her presence to what the old woman had to say. What she heard made her go cold inside.

"Aye, indeed, Master Blackburn!" Danny was saying smugly, and it was obvious that she was enjoying herself immensely. "Ye've no reason to be pantin' about Lady Sable's skirts no more, for His Lordship the Earl has gone and betrothed the child to Captain Sir Morgan Carey!"

If Wyecliffe was shocked by Hannah Daniel's blunt disclosure, he did his best to hide it. "I find that hard to believe, Mrs. Daniels, seeing as I spoke with the Countess and Lady Sable myself yesterday and neither of them acknowledged such a thing!"

"Bah! Why should you be privy to such special information? 'Twas only decided yesterday, it was, between the Earl and Sir Morgan in private! I don't think Lady Sable be aware of it yet, and I only be tellin' ye now to warn ye to keep away from the child and from North Head altogether!" Her quavering voice grew haughty. "Ye'd be wise to watch yourself, sirrah, for I'm sure ye be rememberin' how tall and well muscled Captain Carey be! I don't think he'd take it too kindly if ye continued your attentions toward his future wife!"

"This is an outrage! How dare you speak that way to me?" Cliffe demanded, although he sounded uncertain. It was entirely possible that the Earl had gone and betrothed his daughter behind everyone's back, especially if he was feeling old and vulnerable now that he was confined to his bed. Damn him to hell! Wyecliffe swore silently. This ancient crone might well be telling the truth!

The same thought had occurred to Sable, who stood rooted with shock to the floor outside the Salon entrance. At first she had thought Danny was merely fabricating wild tales to get rid of Wyecliffe, but she remembered suddenly that Morgan's reason for being here had never been explained to her. Moreover, it was entirely possible that her parents had neglected to say anything to her because of Ned's pending journey to Tangier. She herself had spent yesterday evening in her room, supping from a tray and retiring early, yet she had been aware of the fact that Sir Morgan hadn't left the house until later that night. Had he sequestered himself in her father's room, where the two of them had arranged her marriage while she innocently slept?

No! Sable would never believe such a thing! Her parents would never betroth her to anyone before asking her how she felt about it! There must be some mistake, or Danny, in her old age, had gotten everything wrong. Yet why had Sir Morgan come to North Head? What was the reason?

"I refuse to believe that Lord Monterrey would arrange a marriage for his daughter without consulting her first!" Wyecliffe's voice sounded agitated, as though he were fighting against overwhelming evidence to the contrary.

"It was Sir Morgan who offered for her hand and Lord Monterrey who said he'd think on it," Danny announced gleefully. "Of course, Lady Sable will have her say one way or t'other, but she'll not be whistlin' such a grand catch down the wind, I promise ye that!"

Without a word to the two antagonists in the Salon, Sable whirled and escaped through the front door. Lifting her skirts, she raced across the lawn to the stable, issuing Sam a curt order to have her mare saddled. The grizzled groom glanced quizzically at her pale face but said nothing as he brought Amourette from her stall. Sable stood tapping her small boot impatiently on the stone floor, her emotions in a turmoil. She couldn't bear to confront her parents now, not when she was so upset. First she would ride and muster her thoughts, and then, later, when she felt better, she would find out if it was true.

Unmindful of Sam's shocked expression, she clattered the leggy mare across the courtyard and vanished beyond a gentle rise of lawn that led to the open moors. With the wind in her face, loose tendrils of hair clinging to her cheek, Sable rode like a demon possessed. Amourette, unaccustomed to such reckless riding, responded as best she could to her mistress's signals, clearing low stone walls and icy brooks like a hunter after hounds. Only when the little mare was in a lather did Sable become aware of how hard she had run her, and she immediately slowed to a trot, filled with remorse.

Leaning forward, she patted Amourette's sleek neck by way of apology, thinking to herself in the meantime that Danny must have been lying to Wyecliffe in the hopes that her words would drive him off. Marriage to Morgan Carey! Sable's rosy lips thinned and her leaf-green eyes grew hard. She'd rather die than be wed to that arrogant, self-centered, impossible boor!

No, she wouldn't believe for a moment that her father hadn't given Morgan Carey a point-blank refusal, and the more convinced of that she became, the more the certainty grew that Danny had been pulling Wyecliffe's leg. She threw back her head, the sun full on her face, and laughed at herself for being so gullible.

Yet the laughter died on her lips as Sable recalled the tone of Danny's voice as the old woman had uttered her startling disclosure. Danny had sounded so sure, so delighted by the prospect, as though she deeply believed she was telling Wyecliffe the truth. Where had she come by such information?

Sable's eyes narrowed as she clenched her gloved hands about the plaited reins. Was it possible that Morgan had really come to North Head to ask her hand and that Danny, hearing of it, had convinced herself that Sable would accept?

"Preposterous!" Sable snapped aloud, but she knew she wasn't entirely sure. She recalled the gleam in Morgan's eye when he had told her at the Havertys' that someday he would claim her for his own. A sense of dread rose within her. He

couldn't have come to Cornwall to ask her father for her hand!
Morgan Carey was not such a man, and Sable sensed instinctively, as only a woman could, that he was not the marrying
kind and that what he wanted from her was something entirely
different.

Amourette tossed her head, and the restless jangle of her
trappings startled Sable from her thoughts. She became aware
of the fact that she had reined the mare in and was staring with
unseeing eyes across the fertile fields and grazing land that led
south toward Penzance and Falmouth. Sable's green eyes narrowed. Falmouth . . . Hadn't Morgan told her the *Defiance* lay
anchored there? It was possible that she had already sailed with
the tide, but then again he might have delayed his departure—
perhaps because he was waiting for an answer from the Earl?

Making a decision, Sable urged Amourette across the moor
toward the winding cart trail that for centuries had linked the
western tip of Cornwall with the rest of England. If the *Defiance*
was still there, she'd find out for herself what utter nonsense
Morgan Carey had tried to pull on them!

The clipper ship *Defiance* had indeed delayed her departure
until a later tide. Upon returning from North Head late last
night Sir Morgan had been annoyed to find that the surgeon
he had hired in London had disappeared. A systematic search
by the crew had turned him up cold drunk beneath a table in
a waterfront rooming house, and by the time he had been carried
aboard the tide had turned too far.

Chafing at the delay, Morgan had issued curt orders that the
Defiance was to cast her lines as soon as possible and had
retreated to his cabin, much to the relief of the men on watch.
It was Daniel Hayes, a junior officer, who first spotted the
jolly boat rowing toward the anchored ship later that morning.
Normally the sight would not have made him curious since
most of the men were just returning from the newly extended
leave Dr. Pierson's drunken absence had made possible, but
for the fact that the tiny craft's single passenger appeared to
be a woman.

Taking out his spyglass, he trained it across the shimmering
water. His jaw dropped in disbelief when he found the circular
viewing field taken up by a most charming picture of mulberry
velvet trimmed with yellow satin ribbon and a profile of rare
beauty. Dark hair, swept gracefully in a chignon, caught the
rays of the sun and turned it a breathtaking gold. He stared,

certain he had never seen anything quite so lovely.

The crewman whom Daniel handed the glass to whistled softly as he stared through it at the approaching vision. "Lord 'a' mercy! Which of our mates is lucky enough to get a visit from *her?*"

Daniel frowned uncertainly. Whatever the beauty's business, he hoped it wouldn't take long, well aware that Captain Sir Morgan had left strict orders to cast off the moment they could. Several crewmen had gathered at the rail beside him and were now watching appreciatively as the jolly boat drew alongside and permission was granted for its passenger to come aboard. They gaped admiringly as the young woman negotiated the nets without difficulty, and whistled as the wind caught her skirts and lifted them, revealing the shapeliest pair of ankles any of them had ever seen.

Then she was standing on the deck by the entry port, and the *Defiance*'s loyal men gathered in a semicircle around her. She lifted her small chin imperiously, and not one of them could find fault with the sweetness of her delicate features or remain immune to the haunting emerald color of her eyes and the rosebud perfection of her lips.

Daniel Hayes came hurrying forward, elbowing his men aside. "I'm officer of the watch, miss," he said politely. "May I be of service to you?"

The voice that addressed him was enchantingly soft and clear yet filled with unmistakable purpose. "I should like to see Captain Sir Morgan Carey. Is he aboard?"

Daniel hesitated. Should he lie and spare the captain what seemed certain to be an unpleasant encounter? He could tell the young lady had something on her mind, and knowing the captain's current mood he was reluctant to expose such a fragile thing to Sir Morgan's foul temper and ungoverned tongue. On the other hand, she had come all the way out here to see him, and from the haughty look in her eye she didn't seem ready to take no for an answer.

How long Daniel would have pondered this dilemma would never be known, for the men gathered about him stirred suddenly, and he heard Morgan Carey's deep, antagonistic voice behind him.

"What's the meaning of this, Mr. Hayes?"

Daniel whirled about, flushing uncomfortably as he met the

dark visage of his captain. "Someone here to see you, sir. I didn't catch her name, but—"

"Thank you, sir, but I can speak for myself," Sable informed him crisply, stepping around him with a swish of her skirts. She tilted back her head to gaze fully into Morgan Carey's face and was quick enough to catch his start of surprise before his expression went smoothly blank.

"You wished to see me, madame?" he inquired and his brows rose in mock astonishment when he gazed past her at the empty entry port. "Without an escort? Tsk, tsk, I hope your father isn't aware of this."

"I'd like to speak to you, captain," Sable responded coolly. "Before your men or privately, it makes no difference to me."

The watching crewmen exchanged admiring glances. How bravely the little beauty was standing up to their captain, and Christ, wasn't she the rarest flower that had ever graced these decks? A true lady from the look and sound of her, no less. Where had the captain come by such a find?

Morgan's cold eye mustered each man in turn and slowly, discreetly, they slipped away, well recognizing the warning in that silent glance. Left alone on the deck with Morgan, Sable steeled herself against the momentary fear she felt in confronting him here on his ship, surrounded by his loyal men. She hadn't really forgotten how tall and forbidding he was, but somehow here on his ship he seemed to loom larger and more menacing than ever. She felt out of place and undeniably helpless, and the way he was looking at her informed her that he was aware of her feelings. She forced herself to remember why she was here.

"I want to talk to you about your reason for coming to North Head," she began, her leaf-green eyes boldly meeting his. "I would like to know exactly what you said to my father and how you dared to make such a request of him!"

Morgan regarded her disbelievingly. "What the devil are you getting at? Does your father know you're here?" he demanded.

"Of course not!"

Morgan's lips curved into a smile, but it held no amusement, and to Sable it appeared totally unnerving. "Then I'd suggest that you ride home and ask him first if you have a right to interfere in something that is not at all your business."

"Oh!" Sable stepped back as though he had struck her. "How dare you!"

Morgan reached out and seized her by the arms, moving so fast that she didn't have time to react. Brutally he jerked her against him, his glittering blue eyes inches from hers. "I've just about had it with your missish airs and affronted dignity, my dear. Lady Monterrey warned me that you were stubborn, and I'm inclined to believe she views you with a mother's loving and not at all objective eye. It would be a pleasure to make you mine even for a short space of time and show you what it means to behave in a manner consistent with your station."

The heat of his anger enveloped her and Sable swallowed painfully, aware of the hard length of Morgan Carey's body that was pressed against hers and the strength of the long fingers biting into her flesh.

"Furthermore, you should learn," Morgan went on roughly, "that it doesn't pay to stick your pretty nose where it has no business being."

"Y-you'll never get what you want, no matter what my father might have told you," Sable whispered.

Morgan's laugh was harsh. "I won't? I have half a mind to take you with me now, just to prove to you how wrong you are."

"You wouldn't!" Sable gasped, but her uncertainty and fear were reflected in her eyes.

Morgan released her abruptly, unable to tolerate any longer the feel of her soft, curving body against his. Desire had insinuated itself where anger had been, and he cursed himself for wanting her when she was little more than a spoiled child in need of a sound thrashing.

"I'm afraid you have yet to learn the extremes I'm capable of going to in order to get what I want. And when I return," Morgan promised in a voice that made her heart hammer, "you'll see exactly what I mean."

It was obvious to Sable that he had already made up his mind to have her regardless of what she might have to say to the contrary. Tears sprung to her eyes. "I just don't understand why my father didn't say something to me first!"

Morgan was moved to unexpected anger. "Perhaps he feels you needn't have a say in this," he told her, and his voice was little more than a mocking sneer.

Sable uttered a strangled cry and ran from him, and he watched without moving as she climbed back into the waiting jolly boat. A moment later it vanished beyond the stern, Sable's dark head bent, her hands clenched in her lap. Morgan waited until he saw it draw alongside the wooden wharf, then turned away. Curious as his crewmen might be, they didn't dare address him as he disappeared below, recognizing that savage look on his face far too well. To speak to him now would be risking his wrath, yet none of them could help speculating about the beautiful girl and what her purpose in seeking Morgan Carey had been.

Sable's tears were spent by the time the turrets of North Head thrust into view before her. Though she knew that her parents would never force her to accept Morgan Carey's hand if she didn't wish to, she was afraid that he was manipulative enough to get what he wanted. For the first time in her life Sable felt her safe and sheltered existence threatened, feeling the insidious presence of something over which she had no control.

Yet regardless of her misgivings she was determined at all costs to avoid becoming betrothed to Sir Morgan Carey. Recalling the hands that had roved so boldly over her body, the lips that had so weakened her when they clung to her own, Sable's tears began to fall anew. She didn't want to become Morgan Carey's plaything, to be forced to submit to the desires he had intentionally, she now felt certain, aroused within her in London. Her lips tightened grimly. Doubtless he had been certain that when he came to Cornwall he would find her swooning with desire for him and ready to welcome his suit!

"It won't work, Morgan Carey!" Sable swore, though no one but Amourette was there to hear her. He had said he would come back for her after this voyage—but she intended to show her parents by then that she would sooner throw herself into the sea than marry that hateful, despicable cad!

Sable almost laughed aloud as she envisioned Morgan's impotent anger at being so thwarted, but inwardly she felt no triumph, only an odd, gnawing emptiness. For the first time in her life she felt herself at odds with her parents and governed by feelings that were beyond her ken. She could not deny that Morgan Carey had managed with a simple kiss to bend her will to his once before. It was this loss of control that frightened her now, and she vowed that, whatever the cost, she would never allow it to happen again.

"Why, Liam, what are you doing here?" she asked in surprise, leading her mare into the cool, stone-floored stable building to find her brother sitting on a stall door, his feet swinging idly.

Brightening at the sight of her, he sprang down to the floor. "I wanted to be the first one to find you! Everyone's been looking for you, Sable! Where did you go?"

Sable's heart sank. "I must have ridden farther than I intended," she murmured, then asked hesitantly, "What's the matter? Why. is everyone looking for me?"

Liam's expression was puzzled. "Didn't you know that Ned's supposed to go to Morocco in Papa's place?"

Sable handed Amourette's reins to one of the grooms and began pulling off her gloves. "Of course I knew. He told me this morning. But what does that have to do with me?"

Liam hopped excitedly beside her as she swept across the lawn, delighted that his patient vigil had been rewarded and that he would be the first to tell her. "It's because Mama and Papa have decided you should go with him!"

Sable stopped in her tracks and stared down at him disbelievingly. "Me? What for?"

"Because I overheard Mama telling Lucy it might be a good idea if you went away as long as Papa has to stay in bed." His brow furrowed in concentration. "I think it has something to do with Wyecliffe coming here so much or maybe even because of Captain Carey, but he's gone, isn't he, Sable?" he asked, unable to hide his disappointment. He had grown very fond of the tall sea captain, especially after discovering that both of them shared a great passion for pasties.

"Thank goodness he is," Sable acknowledged grimly, but Liam's words had relieved her greatly. This meant she wouldn't have to confront her parents while her father lay injured and in pain in bed, something that had been troubling her during the ride back from Falmouth. This way she could wait until she returned and he was fully recovered before she told them precisely what she thought of Morgan Carey, provided they didn't bring up the matter before she and Ned departed.

She looked down, aware that Liam was tugging impatiently

at the hem of her riding jacket. "What is it, love?" she asked softly, her spirits rising once again.

"Are you going?" he demanded eagerly. "Papa said it was up to you. Well?"

She laughed and scooped him up in her arms, kissing him until he began to squirm in protest. "I wouldn't dream of saying no!"

The unpleasant encounter with Morgan Carey was beginning to fade from her mind. What did she care that he considered her his already? He was gone, and though she had no idea where or when he might come back, it no longer mattered. Let him return expecting her to greet him with eager assurances that she wished to become his wife. She'd not only laugh in his face, but she'd also take great pleasure in informing him that he was no longer welcome at North Head and that he'd better take himself off before the Earl himself sent him packing!

Chapter 5

On a warm, sunny afternoon in late May 1867, the steam packet *Eliza*, owned by the Earl of Monterrey, docked along the wide wooden pier in Tangier's sheltered bay west of the headland where the Atlantic Ocean met the Mediterranean Sea. The packet's passengers, having come up from their cabins to watch the docking, found themselves dazzled by the emerald hills and stretches of blinding white beaches.

Sable St. Germain, wearing a bright blue cotton frock and a wide-brimmed straw hat to protect her from the sun, leaned on the rail at her brother's side, her green eyes sparkling with excitement. "Can you see the Casbah?" she asked, tugging at his sleeve.

Ned lowered the field glasses he had been using and grinned at her with mock exasperation. "For God's sake, Sable, I'm not an authority on Morocco! There are several fortresses and palace ruins up there, but I've no idea what they are. See for yourself or go ask Captain Joudy."

"He's far too busy to trouble himself with me," Sable retorted, taking the glass from him.

"Are you sure? Since Father charged him with your welfare,

he's been damned protective of you, I will say that."

"Oh, go on," Sable chided, studying the beautiful shoreline herself. "He feels responsible for us, that's all."

"Mostly for you," Ned observed.

The *Eliza*'s handsome young captain had certainly gone out of his way during the voyage from England to assure himself that the Earl of Monterrey's daughter was lacking nothing in the way of comforts. More often than not he could be found hovering at her elbow, explaining to her the running of the ship or the sights they passed as the *Eliza* skirted the coast of Portugal on her journey south. Sable had welcomed his attentions, for his pleasant manner and ready laugh eased the homesickness that had assailed her when the *Eliza* had put out of Falmouth, leaving North Head far behind.

Sable had never imagined that she could miss her home and family so much. Was it perhaps a guilty conscience that kept her wishing she hadn't agreed to come on this voyage? She remembered how restrained she had behaved toward her parents before the *Eliza*'s departure, waiting with bated breath for one of them to mention Morgan Carey and his offer for her hand. She had been relieved, yet puzzled, when nothing had been said, and she winced whenever she recalled that she had made no effort to hide the fact that she was eager to be gone.

A lump rose in her throat as she thought of her mother standing on the wharf as the *Eliza* put out to sea, the faithful Timms by her side. Raven had waved to them as they stood by the rail, and as she grew smaller and smaller she continued to wave, no doubt doing so until the packet had been well out of sight.

Oh, why hadn't she said anything to them? Sable had asked herself countless times in the long days that followed. Now that the shock and anger had worn off, she realized how foolish she had been not to go to them immediately. Never in her life had she hidden anything from them. She berated herself for having let her heart govern her thoughts, even when something as odious as marriage to Sir Morgan Carey was the cause!

She would write them a letter as soon as she arrived at the Telleboroughs', Sable decided at last. Captain Joudy could take it back for her, and in it she would explain exactly why she had been so distant with them prior to her departure. She would tell them how grateful she was that they hadn't burdened her with making a decision when so much else had been on her mind, but that it didn't really matter because she disliked Morgan Carey too much to ever contemplate marrying him. Surely on paper it would be much easier to put down her emotions and thoughts in a clear, forthright manner!

Yes, that was what she'd do, Sable decided, watching from the deck as the packet's mooring lines were made fast. She'd write a letter, and by the time she and Ned returned, the misunderstanding that had prompted her to flee in the first place would be long since resolved!

"Excuse me, Lady Sable, your lordship."

Sable turned to find Captain Joudy before them, looking handsome and quite important in his neat blue uniform. Beside him stood a smaller man with graying hair and a nervous manner who bobbed his head when they were introduced. His name was Edmund Proust and he was Sir Harry Telleborough's secretary.

"I've come to take you to Sir Harry's residence," he explained, steadfastedly avoiding the expectant gazes of the St. Germains and tugging shyly at his high collar. "Sir Harry sends his regrets. He is currently engaged in business matters, and Lady Telleborough is indisposed with a headache."

"Oh dear, I hope our presence won't be an inconvenience," Sable exclaimed worriedly. Beneath the brim of her straw hat her clear green eyes met Mr. Proust's for confirmation.

"Not at all," he assured her quickly. "Naturally we were shocked to learn of Lord Monterrey's accident, but as he was kind enough to cable us of the change in plans, there was plenty of time to make the proper arrangements for you. Lady Telleborough's maladies are quite frequent, I'm afraid, but have nothing to do with your arrival."

Looking at her at last, he felt the heat flooding his cheeks, confronted by what he felt certain was one of the most ravishing creatures he had ever seen. "Please don't believe for a moment that you are unwanted, Lady St. Germain," he added hastily. "I'm certain we'll find your hostess quite recovered by the time we arrive."

Sable smiled at him, thinking he was a dear little man to go to so much trouble to make her and Edward feel at ease. Mr. Proust, finding himself the recipient of that charming smile and its accompanying dimples, felt the heat rise even higher in his wan cheeks. His heart began to flutter uncomfortably, and he quickly pulled a handkerchief from his waistcoat pocket with which to mop his brow.

Accustomed to the furor his sister was wont to cause among members of his own gender, the watching Ned fought down an amused laugh. As usual Sable had unknowingly made a conquest, and judging by the scowl that Captain Joudy gave the oblivious Mr. Proust, the *Eliza*'s captain seemed perfectly aware of it.

"I'll have your bags brought up, Lady Sable," Captain Joudy said, deliberately stepping forward to block her slim form from Mr. Proust's admiring view.

"Please have someone inform Katie and Hugh that we're ready to disembark," Ned added, referring to his valet and the girl who had replaced the soon-to-be-married Lucy as Sable's maid on the trip.

Edmund Proust had arrived in a carriage fully as roomy and well sprung as any hansom that traversed the London thoroughfares. Once their baggage was safely stowed away and they had been helped inside, he gave the Arab driver the order to take them home.

"I've been wondering why Sir Harry chose to settle in Tangier and not in Rabat or Casablanca," Ned remarked. "Surely they are closer to Fez, or does the Sultan not receive him there every time?"

"We've a small but pleasant European community here, your lordship," Edmund Proust began, but Sable wasn't listening. Through the small carriage window she had caught sight of the massive seventeenth-century fortress on the summit of the hill before them that had once housed the English governors. The Casbah, with its royal palace and sprawling gardens, sat nearby, and for the first time Sable began to feel that they had really entered a foreign country.

Nothing at home even remotely resembled any of this, she thought to herself, studying the adobe huts that cluttered the slopes of the tiny medina. The streets were narrow and the market was filled with women and men in ankle-length cotton shirts or flowing, hooded capes of colorful stripes. Donkeys appeared to be the main form of transportation, though she did spot a camel or two wearing curious saddles hung with bells.

All too soon the carriage drew to a halt, and Sable, assisted to the ground by Mr. Proust himself, was surprised by the splendor of the bungalow before which they had stopped. Exotic vegetation was in evidence throughout the garden, and flowers of every imaginable color bloomed along the walks and in containers flanking the steps.

"Is Lady Telleborough still resting?" Edmund Proust asked as the front door was opened by an imposing Moorish servant in flowing robes.

Fascinated, Sable listened to the rapid rise and fall of the Arabic tongue as the Moor gave an affirmative reply. Under Mr. Proust's direction she and Ned removed their shoes while the servant supplied them with soft embroidered slippers. The Telleboroughs' home was small and almost entirely without windows, but the decor gave one the impression of openness and grandeur. Beautiful antiques and fine Oriental carpets were scattered through the rooms, and the whitewashed adobe walls were lined with an eclectic mix of European portraits and African treasures.

Sable and Katie were taken to a small bedroom that opened onto a patio containing a bubbling fountain and lush greenery. Beyond the intricate wrought-iron railing was a breathtaking view of Tangier and the Strait of Gibraltar behind it. Because the day was clear Sable could even see Tarifa, the southernmost tip of Europe.

"Oh, Katie," she said with a sigh, coming back into the room, "isn't it beautiful?"

"If 'ee say so, m'lady," Katie responded without enthusiasm. She had proved to be a poor sailor, and even now she was pale, her freckled face wan and pinched.

Sable laid her arm about the younger girl's shoulders and led her to the small bed in the adjoining room. "Why don't you lie down for a bit?" she invited. "The luggage can wait awhile before it's unpacked, and I won't be needing a bath or a change of clothes until the Telleboroughs receive us."

"Oh, m'lady, I can't do that!" Katie protested.

"You can and you will," Sable answered firmly.

Not having the strength to argue with her mistress, Katie stretched out on the bed and drifted off to sleep almost immediately. Sable covered her legs with the woven caftan lying on a nearby trunk. Exiting quietly, she found Ned and Mr. Proust in a sitting room cluttered with objects of African and Asian art, which the Telleboroughs apparently collected quite avidly.

"Sable, Mr. Proust tells me the *Orient Star* is due in some-time tomorrow or the day after," Ned informed her as she swept gracefully into the room. His boyish face glowed with antici-pation. "We'll probably be leaving for Fez right after that, and we'll be under the care of a Moorish escort. It looks as if we'll definitely have to ride camels!"

Sable suppressed a smile, thinking there was still a good bit of the mischievous boy lurking beneath Edward's grown-up facade. To her, the thought of riding a smelly, flea-bitten camel was less than appealing, and she was glad that she would be remaining behind in Tangier, a city she was eager to explore. She had promised a tearful Liam that she would bring him back a present, and she couldn't wait to barter for one of the beau-tifully wrought daggers she had spotted in the market on the way over from the docks. In fact, she had promised presents for nearly everyone at North Head, she recalled. She hoped to find something especially nice for her parents and felt certain that there were enough bangles, baubles, cloths, brassworks, and djellabas on display in the crowded shops of Tangier to satisfy them and every last maid and footman back home.

"Mr. Proust also says," Ned continued excitedly, "that we're to dine this evening aboard the Agent-General's yacht, Sable! Don't you think that's going to be grand?"

"Perhaps Lady St. Germain has had enough of ships for the time being?" Mr. Proust asked. She appeared so young and fragile as she stood in the doorway regarding him, a vision in cornflower blue, her dark hair loosely looped to her head. "I could suggest to Lady Telleborough that we dine at home to-night."

"Oh no, I'd love to go sailing!"

"You have no aversion to water?" Mr. Proust asked her doubtfully. As large and wide-hulled as the Agent-General's *Aloysius* might be, she was no steamer, and on occasion he himself had been known to display poor seamanship while sailing across the bay. He hated to think of Lady Sable in the same position.

"My sister is an excellent sailor," Ned assured the worried Mr. Proust. "You forget, sir, that we were raised in Cornwall. There's a bit of the sea running in all our veins."

"Will you be accompanying us this evening, Mr. Proust?" Sable added as the nervous little man continued to look doubt-ful.

"Sir Harry has asked me to come."

"Then I wouldn't think of refusing!" Sable stated.

Edmund Proust flushed to the roots of his thin gray hair. What an enchantress the Earl's lovely daughter had turned out to be! Hearing Sir Harry's loud voice in the hall, he rose quickly, a defensive thrust to his jaw. His employer, as Edmund well knew, was a notorious womanizer and must at all costs be kept from spoiling Lady Sable's natural innocence. After all, Sir Harry had been known to dally with women even younger and far less beautiful!

Upon hearing from his servant that the St. Germains were in the receiving room, Sir Harry hurried inside, only to draw up quickly at the sight of Sable standing in the doorway before him. In the first moment that his eyes locked with hers he knew that he was looking at a young woman of rare, unspoiled beauty, a child-woman of the sort he dreamed of possessing yet never had. In the next moment, however, he remembered that she was the daughter—the only daughter, at that—of the notorious Earl of Monterrey.

Sir Harry had known the Earl for a number of years. They had met many times in London and during international trade symposiums in Geneva. Beneath Charles St. Germain's facade of refinement, Sir Harry knew, lay a man with almost savage convictions of right and wrong, a man who wouldn't hesitate to strike swiftly and brutally if his daughter was in any way compromised. No, Sir Harry decided with a shudder, the risks were far too great, and, in truth, he respected the Earl far too much to attempt wooing his daughter into bed. Better to let that one go, he warned himself, but not without considerable regret.

"My dear, dear Lady Sable!" he exclaimed in a warm baritone. "May I be so forward as to address you thusly? I feel I know you well, what with the many tales your father has told me about you in the past."

Bringing Sable's hand to his lips he bowed formally and Sable, looking into the twinkling brown eyes, was immediately taken in by his charm. Her father had mentioned to her that Sir Harry was something of a rake but that he was also totally harmless, and she found herself beginning to like him. He was tall and decidedly handsome, his graying temples giving him a distinguished air. In a dark suit and polished shoes he certainly fit his role of wealthy banker, financier, and personal attaché to Great Britain's ambassador in the Sultan's court.

"And this, of course, is Viscount Audley," he added, shaking hands with a solemn Ned. There was approval in his tone as he looked the young heir of Monterrey over, deciding that for all his youth, Edward St. Germain was unquestionably made of the same fiber as his father.

"I apologize for not being here to receive you," he went on, leading Sable to the cushion-covered bench lining one wall. "Business, you know. One can never get out from under it. Did you wish to discuss anything with me, Edmund?" he asked, glancing sharply at his secretary, who was standing nearby with a miserable expression on his thin face.

"No sir. The paperwork can wait, I imagine."

"Indeed it can," Sir Harry agreed in a tone of dismissal. "Ask Ovid to bring refreshments, and have someone inform my wife that our guests have arrived."

"Lady Telleborough is currently indisposed," Edmund informed him regretfully.

Sir Harry made an impatient gesture. "Not another of her headaches again?"

"I'm afraid so, sir."

"Well, then, leave her be. I'd rather she got over it so she'll feel up to joining us on the *Aloysius* later this evening."

"I hope we haven't come at a bad time," Sable said.

Sir Harry patted her small hand, finding her skin as soft as silk. Damned shame! he lamented silently. "Not at all. Marianne hates Morocco, and her bouts of illness are merely her way of punishing me for bringing her here."

"I see," Sable said politely. Small wonder Sir Harry chose to stray as much as her father intimated he did! Why did some marriages fester with bitterness while others, like her parents', were so blissfully happy?

No sooner had Edmund Proust been excused than Sir Harry launched into a lengthy narrative concerning the Agent-General's yacht. Ned and Sable listened politely as they sipped cool beverages, though it was obvious to Sable that her brother had many questions concerning the upcoming trip to Fez.

"Don't worry," she whispered to him as they withdrew to their rooms an hour later to prepare for their outing. "You'll have plenty of time to ask him about the Sultan tonight."

"He seems more concerned with the *Aloysius*'s tonnage and

keel displacement than Father's business," Edward remarked glumly.

Sable stood on tiptoe to kiss his cheek. "Never mind. Sir Harry seems far too competent and capable for me to believe there's a chance the Sultan will turn down Father's request."

Despite Ned's enthusiasm for the trip, Sable knew that he was concerned about his lack of experience in diplomatic circles and his ability to woo Sultan Moulay as well as his father might have done. After all, despite his newly attained maturity, Edward was still seventeen.

"You've nothing to be worried about," Sable repeated. "Sir Harry will take you under his wing and won't let you commit a single faux pas."

"I hope you're right," Ned murmured uncertainly. The adventure upon which he had embarked so eagerly was looking a bit less grand to him now that his responsibilities had settled with unavoidable reality upon his shoulders. For the first time since leaving home he found himself wishing that his father had come in his stead.

"Let's have fun tonight," Sable suggested, slipping her arm through his, "and tomorrow we can worry about the Sultan and Fez."

Edward found himself beginning to relax. Preoccupied with his own worries as he had been on the voyage over, he had not been unaware of the fact that something seemed to have been troubling Sable as well. He had wanted to ask her about it, but looking at her now he saw that she seemed to have resolved it herself, for she was behaving like the Sable of old, laughing and smiling and displaying all of her charms. Her high spirits infected him, making him feel certain that the confidence his father had placed in him would not be unjustified.

"Oh, Sable," he exclaimed, squeezing her hand, "I'm so glad we came! I've a feeling everything is going to work out for the best because of it."

The smile his sister gave him was warm and filled with confidence. "You know, I've a feeling you're right," she said, and gave him a quick hug before vanishing into her room to write her letter home and change into a more appropriate gown for the coming festivities.

* * *

The *Aloysius* was indeed as impressive as Sir Harry had boasted. Almost sixty feet in length, she listed beneath the press of clean white canvas strung from two soaring masts. Her decks were of polished wooden planks, lovingly tended over the years, and Sable caught her breath excitedly as she stepped aboard.

"Isn't it grand?" Sir Harry asked, escorting his wife up the gangplank behind her.

Sable nodded, her green eyes sparkling with anticipation.

"I hope the bay won't be too windy," Lady Telleborough complained. "You know I can't stomach rough seas, Harry."

Lady Marianne Telleborough was a pale woman given to numerous ailments, both real and imagined. She had shaken Sable's hand with a limp grasp upon being introduced and had murmured something about what a beautiful child she was before suddenly collapsing on the sofa and calling for her smelling salts. Alarmed, Sable had summoned Sir Harry, who had assured her that his wife's bouts of dizziness were nothing to be concerned about or, for that matter, to be taken seriously.

Observing how stiff and silent husband and wife sat beside one another in the phaeton on the way to the marina, Sable could see that there was little love lost between them. Her heart had grown heavy with sympathy, unable to fathom how one could endure such a loveless marriage. How glad she was that no such future lay before her!

She had forgotten her musing when they alighted from the vehicle and were helped aboard the *Aloysius* by a young Moorish deckhand in striped shirt and white cotton trousers. The Agent-General, who had generously offered Sir Harry the use of his yacht, was not present that evening, but several European couples had accepted the Englishman's invitation. After introductions had been made, the small group moved aft to enjoy the sunset.

Ned, Sable noticed with secret amusement, seemed to have overcome his earlier nervousness and was avidly discussing Barrancourt Ltd.'s share of the Indochina market with Sir Harry and the other gentlemen. She, in turn, was soon drawn into a conversation with the wives concerning fashions, a topic inspired by Sable's gown, which had all of them exclaiming in envy.

Katie had insisted that her mistress wear a heavy gold chiffon which the Countess had ordered packed for her daughter in the event that Sable would be attending a state dinner while in Morocco. Sable had scoffed at Katie's suggestion to dress so formally for a cruise around the bay, but Katie had been adamant. Looking at the other women—Lady Telleborough in particular, who had donned a gown of azure silk and strings of pearls with matching earbobs—Sable had to admit that her young maid had been right after all in dressing her so finely.

The neckline of her gown was cut low and draped in a manner that revealed the smooth roundness of Sable's breasts. Unlike most other gowns that Sable owned, it was fitted only slightly at the waist, although a sash of silver crepe had been tied about it to emphasize the slimness of her hips. She was truly a vision that night, her dark hair glowing with pinpoints of gold, her brilliant emerald eyes flecked with it, and in the light of the oil lamps that bobbed along the rails she seemed to radiate some mysterious inner fire.

The sun was beginning to set as the *Aloysius* slipped silently from her berth, and it hung brooding on the horizon, painting the bay and the emerald hills in gentle washes of orange and rose.

"We'll have dinner as soon as the port's been cleared," Sir Harry informed them with a smile. One of the deckhands was passing out fluted glasses of champagne, and Sable, sipping hers, leaned back against the cushions and let contentment creep over her.

The breeze that fanned her cheeks was warm and her eyes traveled upward to the rose-tinted sky and the sails that were shining gold in the fading sunlight. Across the deck she saw Ned speaking with Sir Harry and the other guests, and the familiar St. Germain profile with the retroussé nose and dark, wavy hair warmed her heart. She couldn't explain why she felt so contented all of a sudden, unless the excellent champagne had something to do with it. She felt as though this evening was destined to be something special and that it would somehow change her forever.

What nonsense! she told herself severely. That's simply what becomes of people who sip their drinks too fast on an empty stomach!

"Have you ever seen such a glorious sunset?" Lady Telleborough sighed. The sun, now only a sliver of dull red on the horizon, had burnished the clouds above them. The *Aloysius* was sailing parallel to shore and the first lights twinkled on the hills before them.

"Surely they're nowhere near as beautiful in Cornwall?" Winnifred James inquired of Sable.

"Sometimes they're even more spectacular," Sable replied. "The sun reflects off the cliffs in the winter and turns them to molten gold. It's truly magnificent, but," she added generously, "I can't imagine when I've ever enjoyed a sunset more than tonight."

Lady Telleborough smiled, extremely pleased. "We did so want to show you children a good time. Harry thinks so highly of your father, my dear. Oh, here's Kelrah with our dinner!"

Sable looked up to find one of the deckhands standing patiently before Lady Telleborough with a copper basin and a towel in his hands. She watched as her hostess took the offered cake of soap and washed her hands, then rinsed them with the water Kelrah had supplied. When it was her turn she washed her hands while Lady Telleborough explained that Moroccans ate with their fingers. Although they themselves had never adopted the habit when among themselves, they did try to observe the washing ritual before every meal.

By the time the men had joined them, two large trays covered with elegantly embroidered cloths had been set before them. While the men washed their hands, the servants carried out terra-cotta dishes filled with delicious mutton stew and flaming kebabs of beef sausage served on round pieces of bread. Still other dishes were brought out that contained delicate fish fried in fennel and savory chicken breasts stuffed with dates and raisins.

Afterward they were served a variety of fruits, particularly juicy oranges, which Sable could not resist. Ned, she noticed, was eating as heartily as she was, and blamed the *Eliza*'s lack-luster fare on her voyage from England for their overindulgence. When the table was cleared their hands were rinsed again, and Kelrah returned with an enormous silver teapot that he set down before them.

"Usually our tea is prepared in the galley," Lady Telleborough explained, "but I thought you young visitors might enjoy watching how it's made."

Sable watched with interest as Kelrah placed three silver boxes on the table beside the teapot. From the first he took out the tea leaves and placed them in the pot, pouring the water that had been boiling on a nearby brazier over them. After that he broke off a chunk from the loaf of sugar stored in the second box, then added a sprinkling of fragrant mint from the third. Sipping the contents of her gilded cup, Sable had to admit that even the tea at home had never tasted quite this good.

"It's delicious," Ned agreed, savoring his first sip. "I don't suppose—"

Whatever he had intended to say was never heard, for his words were suddenly drowned out by an Arabic cry from the Moor at the helm.

"What the devil?" Sir Harry sprang to his feet, nearly up-setting his cup as he craned his neck to see what was amiss. "Great God!" he screamed, his eyes bulging.

"What is it, Harry?" Lady Telleborough cried fearfully.

It was nearly dark by now, their meal having been finished beneath the flickering lights of colorful lanterns. Only a faint streak of crimson remained where the sun had set, but the light was sufficient for all of them to see what had caused the *Aloysius*'s captain to raise his cry of alarm.

Afterward Sable could never quite remember what sort of ship it was that bore down on them in the darkness. She had risen at Sir Harry's exclamation, but her curiosity had changed to terror when she had seen the enormous press of sails charging toward them at frightening speed. The ship was many times larger than their own, perhaps a dhow or even a packet, throwing a wake from her battered hull as she fled before the wind.

Sir Harry had rushed to the helm and was bellowing something to the skipper in Arabic. Sable was nearly thrown off her feet when the *Aloysius* jibed sharply in response to his command, and for a moment it seemed as though they had succeeded in clearing the other ship's bow. Sable couldn't really believe that they would actually collide. The *Aloysius* hoisted a number of lanterns in addition to her running lights and it wasn't entirely dark yet. How could such a large ship have crept up behind them without seeing them?

Whatever hand fate had dealt the *Aloysius* that night, luck was not among the playing cards. With her passengers sated with good food and wine, her crew intent on making best use of the wind, no one had noticed the big sailing ship approaching before it was far too late. Sable only vaguely remembered watching the hull loom larger and larger before her terrified eyes and Ned shouting her name just before it hit. The impact itself sounded like an explosion to her ears, and Sable found herself flying weightlessly into the air before landing with a splash in the water.

The shock of the dousing restored her to her senses, and she fought her way back to the surface, kicking at the heavy skirts which threatened to drag her under. When she broke clear she dashed the water from her eyes, but darkness had descended so fast that she could no longer see a thing. Frantically she looked about her, straining to catch a glimpse of the *Aloysius*'s lights.

"Help! Help me, please!" she screamed, and faintly through the darkness she thought she heard an answering shout that sounded like her brother.

"Ned!" she screamed, but this time there was silence. Treading water, Sable fought down her rising panic. How could she have been thrown so far from the boat? She had only been underwater for a matter of seconds. Striking out with her arms, she suddenly realized that she couldn't swim forward at all, for a roaring current was dragging her in the opposite direction.

"Ned!" she screamed again.

It was no use. The current sucked at her mercilessly, and Sable was obliged to turn over on her back and float with it lest the weight of her skirts drag her under completely. It would be useless to waste her energy trying to swim, she reasoned, especially since she had no idea in which direction the *Aloysius* lay. The accident had happened so quickly and unexpectedly that she could scarcely believe even now what had happened.

"I must get to shore," she whispered to herself, feeling the current pulling relentlessly at her hair and heavy skirts. Turning her head, she saw the twinkling lights of Tangier not far away and her heart leaped. Surely it wouldn't be too hard to reach the shore! Her father had taught her to swim as a child, and Sable had never felt the least bit of fear for the water. She knew, too, that it was futile to attempt to swim against the current, especially wearing bulky clothes. Better to float with it until she was free of it, she decided, then strike out for shore.

Sable knew that she would have drowned had the current not buoyed her as it tore her madly along in its flight to the sea. She tried to struggle out of her dress but succeeded only in going under, and when she finally fought her way, coughing and spluttering, back to the surface, she resolved to lie on her back and not move at all.

She had lost all sense of time, and when she felt the tearing pressure of the water recede at last, she had no idea how far she had been carried away from the scene of the accident. The water wasn't very cold, and yet she felt chilled as she struck out at last in the direction of the shore. Sable was a strong swimmer, but the lights remained stubbornly out of reach no matter how valiantly she propelled herself toward them. Tears of anger and frustration welled in her eyes, and she raged against the thought of drowning and the grief it would bring to her parents if she did.

Just a little farther, she kept repeating to herself, but it soon became obvious that her strength was ebbing. Sobbing with fatigue, Sable turned over again on her back, breathing harshly as she tried to rest. How much longer could she keep this up, she asked herself, and what if another current dragged her back out to sea?

Perhaps it was because sounds carried farther across the water at night or perhaps because her ears were so keenly attuned in the depth of her panic—Sable was never quite sure what had brought her attention to the almost inaudible sound she heard, yet she lifted her head out of the water and listened intently. There it was again—the unmistakable clanging of a halyard pulley against wood.

Taking a deep breath, Sable screamed for help. When no one responded to her cries, she screamed again.

"Ahoy!" came an answering shout through the darkness.

"Help me!" Sable cried, unable to believe someone had heard her.

"Where are you?"

"I'm over here!" she shouted back, her voice breaking with relief. "Help me, please!"

A moment later lights sprang to life before her eyes, and though her vision was blurred by the sting of salt, Sable could clearly make out the faint shadow of a ship's hull ahead of her.

"Help me!" she cried again. "I've fallen overboard!"

Orders were shouted through the darkness ahead of her, and Sable could have wept when she heard the unmistakable splash of a boat being lowered into the water. The creaking of oarlocks gave her strength, and she bravely struck out toward it, gritting her teeth against the numbness in her limbs. All of a sudden a dory loomed before her in the darkness with a man standing in the bow holding a lantern on a hook before him.

"There he is!" she heard him cry, but by then Sable's strength had failed her.

A half-dozen arms reached out as she went under, and someone managed to snag her under the armpits, dragging her forward and pulling her over the gunnels. Sable collapsed on the rough wooden bench, her gold chiffon skirts trailing water, her beautiful hair hanging limp and sodden over her breasts.

"Why, it's a lass!" she heard an astonished voice exclaim, but Sable was oblivious to everything, even the heat of the lantern thrust rudely in her face. Numb with shock and shivering uncontrollably, she slipped quietly into unconsciousness.

Chapter 6

Sir Morgan Carey, captain of the clipper ship *Defiance*, watched silently as a small assembly of his men gathered near the rail to hoist the returning launch back aboard. In the bow of the dory he could make out the crouching form of his first mate Jackson Torance, the bobbing lantern light throwing his sharp features into graphic relief.

Feeling the watchful eyes of his captain upon him, Torance looked up. "We've got ourselves a girl, sir! I've no idea how she came to be floating in the bay!"

"Is she dead, Jack?" the captain called down, his deep voice expressionless.

"No sir. Leastaways I don't think so. She's chilled through to the bone, though, poor mite."

Morgan's sensual lips thinned into a grim, impatient line. The last thing he needed at the moment was a girl on board his ship, especially one that required nursing.

"Mr. Hayes!"

A young man in a dark blue watch cap snapped smartly to attention. "Aye, sir!"

"Send someone down for Pierson. If he's not on deck in

thirty seconds I'll have him keel-hauled, is that understood?"

Young Daniel Hayes's eyes dropped to the deck, unable to meet the cold gaze of his captain. "Aye, aye, sir."

Morgan turned back to the rail where the launch was being secured with the aid of pulley hoists and stout rope. Several crewmen had rushed forward to help lower the limp bundle of the girl onto the deck. Running his hand irritably through his thick crop of curls, the *Defiance*'s captain moved closer.

"Are you sure she's alive, Jack?" he demanded dispassionately, halting on the outside of the circle of men.

At his words they parted respectfully, and Morgan had a clear view of sodden skirts and a pale, still face partially obscured by limp black hair.

"Not dead, sir, just fainted," Jack Torance replied. He was a small, hard man in his late fifties, as silent and loyal as a Devon man could be. He had been the first of many skilled sailors who had signed aboard the *Defiance* when she had first been outfitted, and Morgan had never disputed the fact that Jack Torance was one of the few men in this world he trusted with his life.

"Captain! Mr. Hayes tells me you've brought a girl aboard!"

Dr. Aaron Pierson, disheveled and out of breath, had appeared on the deck behind them, his spectacles askew on his long, thin nose. Morgan curbed his irritation, aware that his dislike for the man stemmed merely from the fact that he was a poor sailor. Good seamanship was a trait Morgan valued highly, and when he had hired the tall, gangly physician on this particular voyage, the Scottish-born doctor had assured him that he had no quarrels with the sea.

Unfortunately this had quickly proven to be a lie. As the *Defiance* met with stormy weather on her journey from England, Dr. Pierson had taken to his bed with a wretched case of nausea and vomiting. Moreover, the only cure for seasickness, he had kept insisting, was a bottle or two of the captain's best brandy, which Morgan had made available to him despite his reservations. The hapless Dr. Pierson never knew how close he had come to being put ashore in Lisbon, but Morgan desperately required the offices of a physician on this voyage, and for all his flaws, the Scotsman possessed great skill in the field of medicine.

"Is she bad off?" Daniel Hayes inquired worriedly when Dr. Pierson had finished a brief examination of Sable that included listening to her heart and tapping her chest to gauge her breathing.

"There doesna seem to be water in the lungs," Dr. Pierson replied, addressing Morgan as he straightened his spectacles and let Sable's hand fall limply onto the wooden planking. "Her pulse is regular, and I'm inclined to believe she's merely a victim of exhaustion."

Morgan Carey's harsh features relaxed. "Then she's in no danger of dying."

Dr. Pierson looked startled. As yet he hadn't accustomed himself to the blunt, straightforward manner of the *Defiance*'s captain's speech. In truth the towering Sir Morgan made him extremely nervous, and he always suspected, rather uncomfortably, that the mocking twinkle in those unnerving blue eyes was Sir Morgan's way of letting him know that he was perfectly aware of it.

He turned back to Sable's inert form. "Of course not. She should be regaining consciousness shortly."

Morgan nodded in approval. "Excellent. Jack, as soon as she comes about, give her some brandy and send her back to shore."

Dr. Pierson's eyes widened. "You canna do that!"

Morgan's dark brows drew together. "I can't?"

The men gathered round shifted uncomfortably and the physician realized he had blundered badly. It was obvious that no one questioned the captain's orders. Yet Aaron Pierson, coward and drinker that he might have been, had always placed the welfare of his patients above his own. Drawing himself up he stared boldly back into the cold blue eyes.

"I said she'd be regaining consciousness, sir, but not that she'd be strong enough to be moved."

Morgan's eyes narrowed. "What do you mean?"

"Her body temperature is dangerously low. She needs to be taken to warmer quarters immediately. You'll be risking her life if you expose her to the damp night air on a trip across the bay."

Morgan's lips tightened. "What the hell do you expect me to do, Pierson?" he grated. "I can't nurse her till she's strong enough to be taken back to Tangier! Too much time has already been lost!"

Aaron Pierson stood his ground. Though he was nearly as tall as the *Defiance*'s captain, he was thin and his shoulders were stooped. Even from the short distance that separated them, he could feel Sir Morgan's mounting annoyance emanating from him like heat. His lower lip quivered but he continued to hold the smoldering gaze.

"If you move her now she will fall victim to pleurisy or some other damnation of the lungs!"

"Other lives are at stake here, Dr. Pierson," Morgan said, his voice low and filled with such menace that the physician retreated a step. "Lives that, to me, are worth a great deal more than that of a girl stupid enough to fall over the railing of some ship!"

His head jerked round to take in the immobilized crewmen. "Bring her down to my cabin," he snarled. "When the pilot leaves, she goes with him."

"You'll have her death on your conscience, captain!" Aaron Pierson cried.

Dead silence descended on the darkened deck. Morgan, already halfway toward the helm, turned slowly on his heels, the animal grace of his movements reminding the terrified doctor of an enormous jungle cat tensing to spring. Before anyone could utter a sound, however, Sable uttered a sharp cough and groaned, bringing everyone's attention snapping back to her.

Morgan's handsome face was tight with contained annoyance as he watched the physician bend quickly to examine her. Coming closer, he paused with his polished boots nearly touching Sable's inert body. Dispassionately his eyes swept over the sodden gold skirts that clung to the curves of her hips and breasts. She coughed and moaned again, moving her head feverishly to one side. The limp curls that had been hanging over her face fell back, giving all of the gathered men a clear view of her features.

"Good God!" Morgan exploded.

Aaron Pierson yelped fearfully as he was thrust aside by Morgan's impatient hand. "In the name of God!" he cried in terror. "What are you doing!"

"I'm not going to harm her, you fool!" On bended knee Morgan examined the pale face before him. Sable's lips were bloodless, and she was shivering uncontrollably, but Morgan saw only the unmistakable beauty of her features and the telltale tilt of her upturned nose.

It wasn't possible, he told himself, the indignant doctor

hovering at his elbow. He must be going mad to think even for a moment that this was the same young woman he had kissed on a London terrace months ago, whose shy response to him had unleashed within him a passion he had as yet been unable to satisfy. He recalled the last time he had seen her standing defiantly before him on this very deck, goading him to anger with her haughty words and red, alluring lips.

It can't be, he told himself. His big thumb strayed to the line of her jaw, where her skin felt cold beneath his fingers, not warm and silky as he remembered. Sable's brow furrowed at the barely discernible touch and she moaned fretfully. Morgan's wide chest expanded with a rush of air as Sable's eyes opened and he found her bewildered gaze leveled upon him. She blinked rapidly, straining to focus her blurred vision, but before she could recognize him, the translucent eyelids fluttered shut. Still, the moment had been enough for Morgan to see that her eyes had been the color of a deep green forest, eyes that had stubbornly haunted him since his departure from England.

"Jack!"

The first mate was instantly at his side. "Aye, sir."

Morgan rose to his feet, towering above the smaller man. "Have her taken down to my quarters. Get all the extra blankets you can find." His iron forefinger jabbed into the physician's bony chest. "Pierson, you're responsible for her. If she dies, I'll have your head. Is that understood?"

The Scotsman gawked, unable to believe the change in the angry giant before him. Sir Morgan's eyes glittered and his handsome face glowed with exhilaration not unlike that of a warrior who has captured and taken into his keeping an enemy of great significance.

"I told you she won't survive a trip back to Tangier tonight!" he squeaked.

"She's not leaving this ship," Morgan responded, his harsh words stopping the men carrying Sable in their tracks. "Aye," Morgan went on, his fierce gaze sweeping all of them. "I can't waste my valuable time returning her to port."

"But you can't just keep her like this!" Jack Torance protested, shocked. "That—that'd be kidnapping, sir!"

Morgan's grin was wolfish. "Then so be it."

"But sir—"

The blue eyes blazed and Jack realized that he had pushed his captain too far. He stood his ground, however, his inquiring gaze on Morgan's rugged face.

"What would you have me do?" Morgan inquired calmly. "Pierson says the girl will die if I send her back with the pilot. On the other hand, our voyage cannot be delayed long enough to nurse her until she's stronger, nor do we have the extra hours to lose taking the ship back to port, dropping the girl off, and then weighing anchor again."

"But you don't even know who she is, captain!" Jack persisted, pity stirring his heart as he became aware of the fragility of the girl he carried in his arms. "Her family will think she's drowned!"

Morgan's intimidating gaze swept the faces of his men, whose closed expressions revealed to him that they sided with his first mate. A cynical smile curved his lips. "Ah, but you're mistaken, Jack. I know very well who she is, and I'll see to it that the pilot carries a message back to her loved ones. She'll be returned to them, unharmed, when we get back."

Turning heel he strode off, the blackness swallowing his broad-shouldered frame, and Jack had no choice but to carry the shivering girl down to the captain's spacious quarters. Lowering her onto the bunk while Dr. Pierson fussed around him, he felt his heart grow heavy. He knew that the captain was right, that too many lives depended on the *Defiance*'s haste, but he was an honest, simple man, and something about the girl's wan little face touched him deeply. He hated to think of the grief they'd be causing her by taking her so far away from home against her will.

"What is it?" he asked when Dr. Pierson muttered beneath his breath beside him.

The physician looked up. "The chills are getting worse. I'm afraid she's comin' down with a fever. Mayhap the kindest thing the captain did for her was deciding to bring her along. In this condition she canna be moved for a while. Here, help me get her out of this wet gown, will you?"

"I'll do it, Jack."

Morgan's deep voice was cold, his face expressionless as he strode into the cabin.

"Aye, sir. I'll see if I can find those extra blankets."

Stripping off Sable's soggy clothes, Morgan paid no attention to the sight of her naked body. Instead his mind raced over the reasons for her presence in Morocco. Was it fate, he wondered grimly, that had cast her into the sea to be brought aboard his ship alone, unprotected, so many miles from home?

There would be more time to dwell on these insistent questions later, he told himself, drying her unresistant body vigorously with a towel, becoming aware of her convulsive shivering and the growing heat of her fever. Noticing the concern in Aaron Pierson's eyes as he slipped one of his shirts over her head and covered her with a blanket, Morgan demanded roughly,

"How ill is she?"

"Not very . . . yet," the physician replied ominously. "Time will tell."

"You'll do what you can to save her." It was an undisputable command.

Dr. Pierson spread his thin hands. "She will require constant attention, sir."

Morgan's lips thinned. "Leave that to me, Pierson. I've no intention of losing her." His wolfish grin flashed again, making the physician shift uncomfortably. "Only a fool would toss away what Mother Ocean has so generously bestowed upon him, wouldn't you agree?"

Aaron Pierson swallowed hard. Though Morgan Carey's quarters were spacious, the stern windows standing open to reveal a twinkling canvas of blueblack sky, the towering sea captain seemed to dwarf everything with his intimidating presence, making the room seem hot and close. "I imagine so, sir," he responded wretchedly.

As the doctor had predicted, Sable's health proved too precarious to risk a return by boat to Tangier that night. Though the *Defiance*'s loyal crew murmured among themselves at the captain's odd decision to keep the girl aboard, news that her fever had worsened during the night made them believe that perhaps he had been justified.

"How is she?" a concerned Jack Torance asked Dr. Pierson when the physician appeared on deck early the following morning. A pale sun was rising in a cloudless sky and Morocco lay like a shimmering jewel behind them. Though it was Sir Morgan's custom to leave his quarters shortly after dawn, he hadn't shown himself, and his first mate was curious and not a little anxious.

Dr. Pierson removed his spectacles and cleaned them with

the hankerchief he pulled from his breast pocket. "I'm afraid the young lady is seriously ill," he informed Jack with a regretful shake of his graying head. "Her fever's very high and I'm concerned that delirium may set in."

"And the captain?" Jack asked.

"Spent all night up with her, as far as I ken." Dr. Pierson opened his mouth to add that Morgan Carey was a decidedly odd man, then shut it again. He had discovered quite early on that no one among the *Defiance*'s crew took kindly to criticism concerning their captain. It was possible that Sir Morgan was merely demonstrating the first hint of compassion Aaron Pierson had ever known him to in his decision to keep the girl with them, yet, examining the idea more closely, he thought it highly unlikely. Ever since the captain had made his startling announcement that he knew the identity of the girl, Aaron had wrestled with the preposterous idea that he intended to keep her for some kind of ransom.

Obviously their mysterious patient was a young woman of considerable wealth. Her gown, which the cabin steward had removed last night to wash and repair, had been expensive, and her slim hands and aristocratic features bore the unmistakable stamp of nobility. Did Sir Morgan perhaps plan to extricate payment from her family for her safe return? The entire sad affair was beyond Aaron Pierson's ken, and yet he couldn't find fault with the captain's diligence in caring for the girl during the long night just gone.

He had visited the stern quarters several times to assess the patient's progress and on every occasion had found Sir Morgan lounging in a sea chair, his long legs crossed before him, watching the feverish figure in the bunk with heavy-lidded eyes. Pierson had noticed that the cool compresses on her burning forehead had been patiently changed each time and his orders followed to the letter.

"I'm surprised to admit that Sir Morgan is taking admirable care of her," he confessed to the first mate. "Though for the life of me," he couldn't help adding, "I'll never ken why."

Jack Torance's leathery features were expressionless. "For the first time, doctor," he said in his quiet, direct way, "you and me are in agreement."

With the sun climbing slowly into the sky, the air in the stern cabin began to grow uncomfortably warm. Morgan Carey rose from the chair in which he had spent the previous night and stretched his long limbs. Crossing the floor in two easy strides, he threw open the windows. The metal frames creaked as he did so, and he glanced at the bunk, but Sable showed no sign that she had heard.

Frowning, he stood looking down at her. Her frantic thrashing had stopped for the moment, but she seemed no nearer to regaining consciousness. During the night she had tossed and turned incessantly, throwing the blankets off her burning body. At other times chills had overwhelmed her and Morgan had risen to cover her until she fretfully threw them aside again.

The unpleasant thought occurred to him now that Sable was extremely ill and that his own selfish actions might cost her her life. Abruptly he thrust the thought away. She could get no better care in Tangier than she could aboard his ship, and she was a St. Germain besides. From what he'd learned during his visit with her colorful Cornish family, they were of hearty stock indeed.

Sable moaned softly, bringing Morgan's attention back with a snap. Startled, he looked down to find her beautiful green eyes resting upon him, but he saw at once that she did not know him.

"Sable," he said softly so as not to frighten her. "Lady Sable, can you hear me?"

"I'm thirsty," she whispered, her lips barely moving. "So thirsty."

Morgan reached quickly for the ewer that stood on the nearby dressing table. Filling a glass, he bent down and lifted Sable with an arm beneath her shoulders. Her unbound hair spilled across his chest as she sipped the cool water through parched lips. The effort exhausted her, and when she coughed feebly, Morgan laid her gently back against the pillows. Setting the glass aside, he turned back to her but she had already slipped away from him again.

"Captain?"

He looked up irritably at the steward who hovered uncertainly in the doorway. "What is it, Grayson?"

"I thought you might like some breakfast," Grayson informed him stiffly.

Morgan ran a hand across his eyes, striving to curb his mounting irritation. He was tired, he told himself, and there was no reason to vent his annoyance on his steward. "Bring it here."

It was obvious when Grayson stepped inside that he was a gentleman's gentleman, a valet of such fastidious conviction that one could well wonder what had caused him to trade his fashionable Devonshire existence for the discomforts of life aboard a clipper ship. The answer lay in the fact that Grayson had served as Sir Morgan Carey's personal valet for the past nine years. After nursing his master through the injuries he had received on the battlefields of Crimea, the prospect of becoming a cabin steward hadn't made a single ruffle in Grayson's inflappable demeanor. The sea, he had privately thought at the time, would prove a perfect balm to soothe Sir Morgan's war-ravaged spirit. That blockade running and rescue missions like this one had been on the agenda had not startled him overly either—he was accustomed to that sort of thing from his master by now—but the bringing aboard of the half-drowned girl and the decision to take her with them had caused Grayson's eyebrows to rise in astonishment.

"How is the young lady?" he inquired politely as he ventured inside. In contrast to Morgan's worn breeches and plain cotton shirt, he appeared ludicrously out of place in proper patent shoes, a tightly tailored gray vest, and a high, white collar.

Morgan's eyes flicked back to the still form lying in his bunk. "Very ill, I'm afraid. Pierson was right. It would have been her death to move her."

Grayson made no reply. He did not need to ask why the captain had been too stubborn to sacrifice several hours of their time in returning the girl to shore. Only he alone, and perhaps Jack Torance, knew what this journey meant to Morgan Carey and what any delay might cost them.

"I've cleaned and pressed the young lady's garments," he went on, laying out silverware and china on the small table beneath the stern windows. "I hope she'll be well enough to wear them soon."

A sardonic smile touched the corners of Morgan's mouth. "Are you hoping she'll be out of my cabin soon, Grayson? I gather you don't approve of my keeping her here."

Grayson shrugged his thin shoulders. In his nine years' service under Morgan Carey he had seen enough females taking up occupancy in his bed. "I am only concerned with your welfare, sir. Where do you intend to sleep while she . . . ah . . . recuperates?"

"I'll have a hammock brought down from the main cabin

tonight," Morgan responded. Sitting down at the table, he wearily massaged his temples.

"Begging your pardon, sir," Grayson began hesitantly, pouring him a cup of fragrant coffee. "Mr. Torance claims you know the young lady, and some of the men swear they saw her come aboard this very ship while we were still anchored in Falmouth."

Morgan threw him a mocking glance. "Are you wondering who she is?"

Grayson nodded, as always totally honest. "I don't mean to pry, sir, but I can't help being curious. We all are."

The two men were of roughly the same age, Grayson a bare three years older than his master, and perhaps that was why Morgan Carey tolerated more insolence from him than anyone else.

"All right," he said finally, "I'll tell you. Aye, I know her, and you do as well. At least you've probably heard of her father. She is Lady Sable St. Germain, daughter of the Earl of Monterrey."

Grayson's composure fled and his startled look encompassed with new interest the still form reclining on his master's bunk. "Surely you're not serious, sir!"

Morgan gave a low laugh. "Oh, but I am, Grayson, I am. And what I want to know," he added, sipping his coffee while his eyes traveled to Sable's flushed face, "is how she came to be floating about in the Bay of Tangier when last I saw her at her father's home in Cornwall."

"And what *I* would like to know," Grayson put in quietly, uncovering a basket of freshly baked croissants, "is what you intend to do with her."

"Do?" Morgan repeated. His blue eyes glittered suddenly, and a predatory grin curved his lips. "What does one normally do with a beautiful young woman Lady Luck has been kind enough to throw into your lap?"

Shocked, Grayson almost upset the sugar bowl. "Surely you aren't going to keep her as your—your mistress, sir!" His tone indicated that this was far too cruel an act to contemplate, even from Sir Morgan Carey.

Morgan chuckled, but his eyes held no warmth. "No, I don't believe I've the patience to make her my mistress, Grayson. She's a spoiled, cunning brat who'd drive me instantly mad." Unwittingly his thoughts went back to the Havertys' darkened terrace, and it was almost as if he could feel Sable's willing lips beneath his, her silken flesh yielding to the pressure of his seeking hands. His loins tightened and he gave his steward a ruthless glance.

"On the other hand, I'm not adverse to having a bit of fun with her before I return her to her family."

"Lord Monterrey is rumored to be a most vengeful man," Grayson remarked worriedly. He was unfamiliar with the brooding look on his master's face and had to admit that he didn't care overly for his plans. "Though he may think highly of you now I seriously doubt he'd tolerate something like this."

Morgan shrugged, totally unconcerned. "St. Germain may be a formidable foe, but I'm not especially worried about him."

A groan from the bunk brought him to his feet, and Grayson watched anxiously as Morgan bent over Sable's still form. How small and vulnerable she appeared, the valet thought to himself. As Morgan changed the compress on her forehead, he couldn't help but notice how large and powerful were the hands that touched her, how bronzed the captain's skin in contrast to her own.

A feeling of dread rose in Grayson's heart. Morgan Carey had obviously decided that he would keep Lady Sable for himself, otherwise he would not have spoken as he had. Even with Aaron Pierson aboard, the fact that the captain had decided to tend her personally, alone in his cabin, boded no good either.

Grayson sighed as he refilled the half-empty coffee cup. If Lady Sable St. Germain was anything as spirited as her father, then Sir Morgan was in for one hell of a battle when she recovered. He glanced at the tall form of the captain, who was still standing beside the bunk, his profile harsh and unrelenting. There was going to be trouble, Grayson sensed deep within his heart, and he cursed the fates that had sent Lady Sable here.

When Sable awoke, her head throbbed so miserably that she felt certain it would split in two. Her throat was raw and she found herself too weak to move. Without being consciously aware of it, she knew that the burning fever which had plunged her into fiery hell had finally receded, and she savored the welcome coolness of the air against her skin.

She lay on her back with her eyes closed, not moving, enjoying the freedom from consuming fever and the disappearance of the agonizing pain that had assailed every joint and limb of her body. Presently she grew aware of sounds, the raucous crying of gulls overhead and the scratching of a pen on paper. She was obviously in her bedroom at North Head, she thought, for the gulls always called this plaintively beyond her window, but who was writing at her small desk and rustling paper in such an annoying manner?

Sable opened her eyes to ask whoever it was to stop, and to beg a drink of water. To her total bewilderment she saw above her not the flocked wallpaper and carved crown molding of her bedroom ceiling, but beams, solid and strong, that angled across the roof overhead. Nor was the smell of her room the same. Oh, the salty tang of the sea was there, but the perfumes that sat in the carved glass bottles on her dresser and had always scented the air so sweetly had been replaced by a more masculine odor of leather and some faint but not unpleasant cologne.

Confused, Sable turned her head, but a wave of dizziness made her vision blur. Blinking rapidly, she saw a huge shape rise from a nearby chair and approach her bed, but she had no idea who it might be. She was frightened suddenly, some sixth sense warning her that she was alone in a strange, unsafe place. The feeling was heightened when the towering form spoke, the words like distant thunder.

"So you're awake at last. I've been wondering when you were going to get around to it."

Sable blinked again and a face swam into focus—a face of rugged, angular proportions, brutally handsome and totally terrifying. The stubble of a beard grew along the square, tanned jaw, and above a long, hooked nose a pair of glittering blue eyes regarded her with cynical amusement.

"Who are you?" she asked, but her voice cracked and her words ended in a fit of coughing.

Instantly she felt a pair of arms slide about her, their muscular strength reminding her of her father. Unconsciously Sable relaxed against them, and when the coughing subsided she found a glass of water being held to her lips.

"Drink this," the deep voice commanded, and Sable could hear the words rumble from the massive chest against which she had been leaning.

She obeyed, the sweet, cool liquid bathing her fiery throat. Opening her eyes, she found the same rugged face above hers, so close now that the glittering blue eyes seemed to burn her. Frightened, she tried to struggle away, but the arm that encircled her was like a vise.

"Be still, Sable. I'm not going to hurt you."

The sound of her name soothed her, as did the softness of the deep, familiar voice. She fell back weakly against the strong arm and was asleep before he had the chance to lay her gently against the pillows.

When Sable awoke again it was evening. The stern windows had been tightly shuttered and an oil lamp glowed softly overhead. She felt more clear-headed than she had the last time, and when she looked about her she realized at once that she was in the cabin of a ship.

Which ship? she asked herself. Hadn't she and Ned disembarked from the *Eliza* long ago? Furthermore the *Eliza* had never boasted quarters like this one, with burnished teak paneling, a fine writing desk, and a roomy bunk. Cautiously Sable slid one foot onto the floor and, grasping the thick beam nearest her, was able to haul herself slowly upright. She felt weak and every bone in her body ached. She must get outside, she told herself dazedly, to find Captain Joudy and ask him what had happened to her. Had she been ill? She seemed to recall that she had had a fever. Someone had tended her with gentle, soothing hands, she recalled vaguely, remembering too the deep yet not unpleasant voice that had spoken to her and calmed her when she had cried out in her delirium.

"What the devil are you doing out of bed?"

Sable froze, her wide green eyes meeting the startled blue ones of the man who had strode unannounced into the cabin. He was taller than any man she had ever seen, with the possible exception of her father, and so broad-shouldered and wide of chest that he seemed to fill the entire cabin with his intimidating presence. His thick brown curls were windblown and his white shirt was opened at the throat to reveal a smooth, tanned chest ridged with hard muscle. Worn calfskin breeches hugged his muscular thighs and Sable blinked, confronted, she thought in a moment of madness, by what could only have been a young Greek god.

"Who—who are you?" she stammered, still clutching the beam for support.

A slow smile curved the full, carnal lips, replacing the startled look on Morgan's handsome face. His shock at seeing

Sable out of bed had changed instantly to pure masculine interest, for what man could look at her as she appeared then and not be moved by her unconscious sensuality? Clad only in a thin cotton shirt that reached to her silken thighs, she stood barefoot before him, her unbound hair spilling over her hips in a riot of colors unleashed by the glow of the lamp.

Her skin was translucent as a result of the fever, and her wide green eyes reflected pinpoints of gold from the same lamp that burnished her dark tresses. Its silky thickness reminded Morgan of the priceless Barguzin sables he had seen in Russia during the war, and he wondered fleetingly if her parents had deliberately chosen her name for the same reason.

Leaning against the beam for support, her fingers clutching the smooth wood, Sable's slim body was outlined against the darkness, the tops of her rounded breasts revealed by the unbuttoned shirt collar. She drew herself up defiantly as Morgan approached, her upturned face pale but breathtakingly beautiful.

"Who am I?" he repeated, towering over her, her slim, bare feet almost captured between his booted legs. "Don't tell me you don't remember, my fair Sable."

Her arching brows drew together. "I don't," she confessed helplessly, wishing he'd go away. Her head ached miserably and she was so dizzy and confused that nothing made sense to her at all.

Morgan laughed, the sound rumbling in his wide chest, making her heart beat faster with the sensation of being overwhelmed by his nearness. "Why, I've been your devoted nurse this entire week, my dear. Surely you can't be totally ignorant of the fact that I took care of you."

The look on Sable's face was touching in its confusion and instantly Morgan lost the desire to toy with her. "Get back to bed," he told her roughly, and made a movement toward her to help. Sable shrank away from him, her dark, accusing eyes on his face.

"Yes," she whispered, her mind clearing at last. "Of course I know who you are! Sir Morgan Carey, a charlatan if ever there was one!" She gazed wildly about her. "What are you doing here? Will you tell me what's happened? Where's Ned? I want to see Ned!"

She had begun to tremble uncontrollably, and Morgan, fearing for her sanity given her fragile state of health, gathered her swiftly into his arms. She struggled weakly as he carried her back to his bunk, but by the time he laid her gently down she had given up and lay with her cheek against his shirt, her eyes brimming with tears. She was already fast asleep when he covered her with the blankets, the tears still trembling on her gold-dusted lashes, and Morgan felt a moment of remorse as he gazed down into her young face, its defenselessness touching him oddly.

She had been frightened and confused by his presence, and he had been unkind. He should have talked to her softly, calmed her fears instead of mocking her as he had. Devil take her, he swore to himself, straightening and turning away from the bunk. He'd done what he could to bring Sable St. Germain through her illness, and he'd not start coddling her now.

Sable dreamed, and in her dream the setting sun was warm on her face. Images came to her in fragments of great beauty and color: of the shimmering sea and emerald hills, a sailboat with its white canvas turned to gold. She murmured contentedly and snuggled deeper into the pillow, but the dream abruptly changed. She heard screaming, people shouting, and in the crystal-clear images that nightmares often produce she was reliving again the moment of collision aboard the *Aloysius,* seeing the other ship scuttling nearer and nearer, hearing Ned's frantic cry before she was thrown into the sea. Icy water closed over her head, dragging her lower and lower until there was nothing but murky blackness and the terrifying threat of suffocation—

Sable screamed. Sitting up in bed, she looked about with wide, sightless eyes, but still the blackness pressed in on her. "No!" she whispered, burying her face in her hands.

"Sable!"

Instantly she could discern the presence of someone before her, and she reached out instinctively, her hands sliding about a powerful neck. She pressed closer, burying her head against a warm shoulder. A pair of strong arms came about her, drawing her close. Sable sighed contentedly, the nightmare fading.

Morgan, who had leaped from his hammock at the sound of her cry, settled himself on the bunk, being careful not to jostle Sable, who had fallen asleep with her face pressed against his naked chest. Obviously she had had a nightmare, and he was loath to awaken her a second time. Perhaps she hadn't ever come fully awake at all. No sense in lighting the lamp; it would be better to let Sable continue sleeping. Rest was what she needed above everything.

Morgan was silent as he contemplated the pleasure he experienced while holding the sleeping Sable in his arms. With every breath she drew he could feel her rounded breasts press against him. The long-tailed cotton shirt she wore had tangled about her waist and her bare legs brushed intimately against his. The scent of her hair, which he himself had washed not too long ago, assailed his senses, as did the softness of her skin.

Morgan could feel his desire stirring. He could no longer doubt that he wanted Sable St. Germain and had done so since he had first kissed her in faraway London. Why this beautiful child-woman moved him he could not say, but he was forced to admit to himself that his feelings hadn't diminished even after their last unpleasant encounter in Falmouth.

He had met women before who roused him with little cause into a state of sexual readiness; but it surprised him that such an innocent child could do so as well. Yet the emotion evoked from holding this defenseless girl in his arms, her head heavy against his chest, was not entirely lust; even Morgan would have been a fool to believe so. There seemed to be something innocent and vulnerable about Sable St. Germain that touched within him an instinct, purely male, to protect her.

Morgan almost snorted aloud at his ridiculous thoughts. Innocent Sable was, aye; but vulnerable? He recalled the times she had stood up to him at North Head, refusing to back down until she had had her say. She was no different from her proud, domineering father, and if there was one thing he should have learned during his visit to Cornwall, it was that the St. Germains were a close-knit family he had no business involving himself with.

Yet Morgan knew that he could not overlook this enchanting gift from the sea. Sable was his now, although not by design, and he intended to show her what it meant to respect his authority before he returned her to Tangier.

Morgan lowered his chin against the silken curls and in her sleep Sable murmured. A feeling of peace overcame him unexpectedly, and shortly he, too, slept.

Chapter 7

Sable awoke with her cheek pressed against a rough, scratchy blanket. Kicking it aside, she looked around, puzzled to find herself in the same teak-paneled cabin she had dreamed about in her feverish delirium. The last few days seemed like a hazy blur in her memory, but she had no trouble recalling in vivid detail the terrible accident aboard the *Aloysius*.

Scrambling to her feet, she tottered to the stern windows and pressed her nose to the glass, seeing the gray outline of land in the distance. She had fallen overboard when the *Aloysius* was hit, she remembered, and had obviously been brought aboard this ship before she had drowned.

Sable frowned. During her illness she seemed to recall having seen Morgan Carey, the scoundrel sea captain who had been the cause of so much heartache. Surely that had been a dream! Yet if this ship and its elegant cabin were real, then could it be possible—

"What are you doing out of bed? Do you want to bring on your fever again?"

Sable whirled, her jaw going slack when she saw Morgan Carey himself standing before her. Sun-browned and strong, he loomed not only larger than life, but more real than any product of her feverish imaginings.

"So you *are* real!" she said heatedly, her green eyes flashing. "I was hoping you'd been a mere figment of my imagination!"

Morgan surprised her by throwing back his dark head and laughing. It was a deep, unaffected sound, as lusty with the spirit of life as he seemed to be, his hands on his lean hips, his booted legs apart, his blue eyes glittering.

"So you've wished me away into the dim recesses of your mind," he remarked, sauntering closer. "Obviously you're feeling better. Your tart tongue has made a remarkable comeback."

His gaze roved over her intently, and Sable became aware of the fact that she was clad only in a man's shirt, hopelessly oversized, her fingertips barely visible beyond the cuffed sleeves. Her bare thighs and feet were exposed to Morgan's eyes, and she hastily retreated to the bed, where she wrapped herself up in the blanket, trying to retain as much dignity as she could.

"Your modesty seems restored as well," Morgan observed, crossing his arms casually before his chest.

"Where are my clothes?" Sable demanded, color burning in her cheeks.

"I'll have Grayson bring them to you," Morgan replied obligingly. His wolfish grin widened. "There's no need to be embarrassed, my dear. You required quite strenuous nursing while you were ill, and I assure you"—his blue eyes gleamed— "there was little of your body left unexposed to me during your sponge baths."

Sable said nothing but Morgan could see her throat bob painfully as she swallowed. His own lips tightened grimly, and he wondered what it was about Sable St. Germain that made him take such cruel pleasure in taunting her. True, she annoyed him no end with her defiant ways and haughty manner, but she was the daughter of a man he greatly respected. Shouldn't that be enough to prompt him to treat her well?

Morgan glanced at Sable, whose head was bowed as though in defeat. His unkind words seemed to have hurt her considerably, for he could swear there were tears trembling on her gold-tipped lashes. Overcome with remorse and angered because of it, he said curtly,

"I'll send my steward down to help you."

"Thank you," Sable said stiffly without raising her head to look at him. The light streaming in through the stern windows behind her illuminated her dark hair and caught the golden highlights within it. Now that the fever was gone it shone softly, and from past experience Morgan knew that if he touched it, he would find it as soft and sleek as satin beneath his hand.

Abruptly he left the cabin, slamming the door behind him while Sable fought to check her threatening tears. Of all ships, of all people, she moaned to herself, why did she have to be rescued by the *Defiance* and its conscienceless captain? Better to be dead, she told herself, but in the next moment berated herself fiercely for her thoughts. Her parents would be grief-stricken if she had drowned and Ned—

Sable's breath caught in her throat. Dear God, suppose they did believe her drowned! After all, she hadn't been brought back to Tangier during her illness, and the *Defiance* was under full sail. Sable's heart began to beat faster in alarm. Where were they going? What had happened to Ned?

"Good morning, your ladyship. Sir Morgan informs me you've been asking after your clothes."

Sable, still wrapped in the protective blanket, looked up at the cheerful words to find herself gazing into the pleasant face of a man not much older than Sir Morgan himself. Kindly brown eyes regarded her steadily and the smile on his lips appeared warm and genuine. He was holding her gown and undergarments in his hands, and Sable felt a wave of relief wash over her. Could it be possible that she had found someone who might prove a friend?

"Thank you, sir," she said with a timid smile of her own.

"It's Grayson, your ladyship," he corrected her, laying the gown on a nearby chair. Inwardly he was grappling with his emotions, stunned by Lady Sable's radiant beauty. The few glimpses he had caught of her feverish face during her illness had not prepared him at all for this stunning young woman with eyes the color of summer grass and a voice as sweet as church bells. Small wonder Sir Morgan hadn't wanted to part with her!

"Oh please, don't go!" Sable implored as Grayson bowed and began to back out of the door. There was a note of desperation in her voice and he saw that her lower lip trembled.

"What is it, m'lady?" he asked, his concern bringing fresh tears to Sable's eyes. It indeed appeared as if she had finally found a friend!

"Will you tell me what's happened? I know I've been ill

and that I fell overboard, but I need to know if—"

"Perhaps you'd better let Sir Morgan explain everything," Grayson advised.

Tossing the blanket aside, Sable sprang up and grasped his sleeve. In her upturned face he could see terror and heart-rending appeal. It was a look he could no more resist than the cries of a frightened child.

"Sir Morgan will only torment me with half-truths and riddles," Sable said. "Can't you tell me anything?"

Grayson relented. "I imagine the captain would have no objections." He blushed furiously as he became aware of the fact that she was wearing naught but Sir Morgan's shirt, which ended tantalizingly at midthigh. "Perhaps you wish to dress first, m'lady?" he asked politely.

Sable cringed with embarrassment but made a great show of hiding it as she wrapped herself back in Morgan's blanket. It galled her that she was forced to recline like some well-used paramour in his bed, yet what choice did she have? It didn't matter anyway. She wanted nothing at the moment save answers to her questions.

"Perhaps I should explain everything I know," Grayson said, taking pity on her.

"Oh yes, please," Sable whispered.

He busied himself with shaking out the magnificent skirts of the gold chiffon gown, refusing to look into her anxious eyes. "Sir Morgan learned all about the accident between your sailboat and the other from the things you said while you were—" He broke off, thinking Sable might be insulted if he used the word *delirious*. "You talked quite a bit during your illness," he amended, "so we knew how you'd happened to end up floating in the bay."

"It was the *Defiance* that picked me up," Sable said. "I remember a launch and a face before me, but that's all."

Grayson nodded. "You were chilled to the bone and quite feverish by the time you were brought aboard. Dr. Pierson insisted you wouldn't stand the trip back to Tangier on the pilot launch, so Sir Morgan decided to keep you here."

"Why wasn't I brought back to port when my health began to improve?" Sable demanded.

Grayson looked uncomfortable. "I'm afraid it proved impossible, m'lady. We were under a strict schedule and are so even now. The *Defiance* has been under full sail since we brought you aboard."

Sable paled and regarded him with wide, frightened eyes. "Where in God's name are we going?"

Grayson coughed. "I'm not at liberty to say."

"Do you mean," Sable whispered with dawning understanding, "that the *Defiance* has embarked on some sort of mission and that I've been taken along? Solely because you couldn't spare the time to take me back to Tangier? What sort of nonsense is that? How far was I swept out to sea?"

"Please, your ladyship," Grayson begged. "If you knew the circumstances surrounding our voyage you'd not be so hasty to—"

"I don't give a damn about this voyage or your mission!" Sable flared. "How could anything be more important than your compassion? Surely the few hours sacrificed in returning me to my brother wouldn't have jeopardized your important quest!"

"Sir Morgan sent a message to your family by way of the pilot," Grayson said, attempting to soothe her. He was concerned about Sable's pallid color and the tears that trembled thickly in her voice.

"How good of him," Sable sneered. "I'm sure Ned will be pleased to learn that, though I didn't drown, I've been kidnapped and taken along on some unknown yet, I suspect, highly reprehensible journey!" Her voice shook. "That's provided he even got the message Sir Morgan was kind enough to send. How can you guarantee the pilot will deliver it? How can you know my brother isn't"—she swallowed hard—"isn't lying injured in some hospital bed himself?"

"That's enough, Sable. You'll only make yourself ill again."

The curt voice was that of Sir Morgan, who had entered his quarters in time to hear her impassioned words. Grayson relaxed visibly at the sight of his master, but Sable unexpectedly launched herself at him, her small hands balled into fists, her eyes glittering ferociously.

"You!" she cried. "I hate you! How could you have done this to my brother and my parents?"

Morgan caught her slim wrists in his big hands but was unable to subdue her. She was crying openly by now, attempting to kick at him, but he merely wrapped his arms about her and pulled her against his body, pinning her there.

"No man could be so cruel, so heartless," Sable choked, her green eyes swimming with tears. "I hope you rot in hell!"

Above her bent head Morgan and Grayson exchanged brief glances. For a moment the valet saw the struggle in the blue eyes before they grew as cold as ice, and he turned away, oddly gladdened despite everything. For the first time in his life he had been shown proof, however slim, that Sir Morgan Carey possessed a conscience after all.

In the next moment his belief was sorely tried as Morgan shook Sable cruelly, causing her head to snap back and forth on her slender neck. "Pull yourself together, Sable," he said curtly, his tone totally devoid of warmth. "Sniveling and whining will not alter your fate, nor are they becoming traits for a woman of your station."

Sable struggled to free herself, a murderous look on her face. She wanted to slap the smug smile from his sensual lips. Morgan, reading her intent in the furiously blazing eyes that were only inches from him, laughed and tightened his grip.

"Damning me to hell won't help either, lass, for I fear I've already been allocated a position there long ago. Now go put on your clothes and let Dr. Pierson examine you."

"I won't," Sable retorted mutinously, hating to be ordered about like a child. Her head ached and the world was swimming dizzily before her.

"You will, or I won't allow you to go topside," Morgan informed her harshly. "You're not to leave this cabin until Dr. Pierson proclaims you well enough."

Releasing her, he waited for her to fly at him again, but Sable merely stood with her head bowed, her beautiful hair hanging in her face. Morgan studied her for a moment, then strode out, Grayson following dutifully behind. As soon as the door swung shut behind them, Sable snatched up the empty coffee mug that stood on the nearby table and dashed it with all her might against the thick wood.

Though the mug was too heavy to break, the sound it made and the splinters that flew from the door upon impact satisfied her. For a moment she waited, steeling herself for Sir Morgan's stormy return, but all remained quiet in the corridor outside. Shrugging, she locked herself in and pulled off the oversized shirt, tossing it unceremoniously into the corner. She had lost weight since the onset of her fever, she saw, looking at herself in the pier glass standing near the head. Her ribs protruded and there was an unhealthy pallor to her skin that only the touch of the sun could cure.

Sable sniffled dejectedly as she slipped into her clothes, her murderous rage at Morgan Carey fading into exhaustion. Somehow she must convince his crew to return her to Tangier. No matter what the *Defiance*'s destination, she had no intention of remaining aboard any longer than she had to. Poor Ned must be worried sick about her. Tears sprang afresh to her eyes as she thought of him.

Stop it, she reprimanded herself fiercely. Moping wouldn't help. She must keep her spirits high if she intended to wage war against Captain Morgan Carey. Her lips tightened grimly as she recalled the strength in the iron fingers that had wrapped themselves about her wrists. It wasn't going to be easy to defeat someone like him and find a way off of this ship, but St. Germains were not cowards, and she was determined to fight with every ounce of strength left in her body.

A discreet knock on the door brought her from the mirror where she had been untangling her hair with a silver-handled brush she had found on Sir Morgan's dressing table. The long curls felt clean and silky beneath her hands, and Sable wondered who had washed the salt water out of them and bathed her during her illness. It had to have been Morgan Carey, she thought with a sickening lurch of her heart as she recalled his mocking comments concerning how diligently he had tended her. How like him to take advantage of her helplessness!

"Lady St. Germain?"

It was a strange voice with a faintly discernible Scottish burr.

"Who is it?" she asked suspiciously.

"Dr. Pierson. May I come in?"

Reluctantly she smoothed down her skirts and slid back the bolt. From the startled look on the thin, bespectacled face, Sable guessed that the physician had not expected to find her up and dressed. In truth he was more stunned by her beauty than anything else, for he had never seen Sable dressed in shimmering gold with her hair unbound and floating like a burnished cloud down her back.

"I can see a marked improvement, your ladyship," Dr. Pierson announced, smiling at her enthusiastically, "even without the benefits of a proper examination."

Sable responded with a halfhearted smile of her own. She felt uncomfortable in the doctor's presence, his fidgety manner and high, squeaking voice grating on her raw nerves. Yet he proved competent enough in his examination, declaring her in excellent health when he was finished.

"Rest, plenty of food, and sunshine, your ladyship," he told her, taking her slim hand to help her to her feet, "and you'll be back on the proper track in no time."

The mention of food made Sable's stomach rumble, and she realized all at once that she was ravenous. It was Grayson's good fortune to enter the cabin at that moment bearing a tray from which delicious smells enticed her, and he was rewarded for his foresight with a dazzling smile that nearly smote him.

"Sir Morgan had this sent down to you," he stammered, setting the tray on the table.

Sable was about to retort that she wanted nothing from the *Defiance*'s odious captain, but Grayson had lifted the cloth to reveal a slab of healthy pink roast, a bowl of steaming stew, and a loaf of freshly baked bread giving off the most tantalizing of odors. Sable's mouth began to water in a most unladylike fashion and the steward smiled to himself, recognizing the famished look in her eyes.

"If you're finished, Dr. Pierson," he added, glaring at the physician, who was unabashedly admiring Sable's delicate profile, "the captain requests your presence on the quarterdeck for a report."

Dr. Pierson exited reluctantly, already forgotten by his young patient, who had seated herself before the table and was attacking the stew. Grayson doled out a generous helping of the beef and boiled potatoes, then fetched a bottle of claret from the small glass-fronted cabinet standing against the far wall.

"Is it to your liking, m'lady?" he inquired as Sable took a tentative sip of wine.

"Delicious," she assured him.

He was pleased to see that some of the color had returned to her face, although her beautiful eyes were still red from the tears she had shed earlier.

"You mustn't be so harsh with Sir Morgan, m'lady," he said impulsively. "If you knew the circumstances involving our voyage and the enormous strain he is currently under—"

"Please don't feel compelled to defend your captain, Grayson," Sable told him stonily. "Nothing you or anyone could say will erase the hatred I feel for him in my heart. It's not myself I'm worried about," she added, her eyes on his face as she pleaded for understanding. "It's my brother, you see. This is the first time my parents have ever entrusted him with my care, and he probably thinks I'm dead. He—" She choked, unable to go on, and lowered her eyes to her plate.

Grayson felt utterly helpless knowing he would never find the proper words to comfort her with. "Perhaps if I explained the reason for Sir Morgan's actions," he began, but Sable shook her head.

"It wouldn't matter to me."

The steward refilled her wineglass, which she had drained in one long, desperate swallow. "Perhaps it would, your ladyship."

Sable's green eyes flashed. "Surely you would be incurring the Great One's wrath if you confided in me his secrets."

Grayson bowed his head. "That may well be, but I cannot stand by and watch you torment yourself this way. It may be a matter of weeks before we can return you to Tangier, and your health will only suffer if you continue to live with your hatred and doubts."

Privately Sable intended to see that she was on her way back to Tangier by morning, but she said nothing. Looking up into Grayson's pleasant face, she couldn't help feeling the hardness within her melt just a little. No matter what, he seemed a good and honest man, and she couldn't find it in her heart to hate him as she did his master.

Perhaps some of her thoughts showed in her eyes, for Grayson set the wine bottle down and began earnestly, "This entire affair has to do with events that took place during the Crimean War. Sir Morgan was a mere youth when England entered, but he quickly distinguished himself and had a small command of his own when the battle lines were drawn at Balaklava."

Sable, by no means ignorant of her country's involvement in a war that had taken place when she was but a little girl, felt her eyes widen. "You mean to say that Sir Morgan was present during the attack of the Light Brigade?"

"Present?" Grayson's merry eyes grew clouded by memories the intervening years had been unable to erase. As told by Sir Morgan himself, the bickering of inexperienced regimental of-

ficers, the rivalry of the company commanders, the misman-
agement of an ignorant commissariat were images branded
forever in his soul, for they had all contributed to the terrible
slaughter of the dashing Light Dragoons and the noble 17th
Lancers. To look upon that sort of horror was to be changed
forever, and Grayson above all men knew how deeply the
wounds had cut into Morgan Carey's soul.

"Present?" he repeated again, shaking his head sadly. "Not
only was he present, m'lady, but he also attempted singlehandedly to avert the tragedy, the madness of sending six hundred
British cavalrymen to attack an entire Russian force. Taking
the place of one of the gallopers who carried messages within
the lines and ranks, he rode alone and in full view of the entire
Russian army to attempt to divert the charge."

Sable stared at him, the meal forgotten. Despite her hatred
for Morgan Carey she could not deny his bravery. "He was not
successful," she said after a moment.

Grayson shook his head. "Unfortunately, no. As I'm sure
you know, less than a third of the six hundred survived. Sir
Morgan," he added quietly, "never could accept his failure,
though I believe only God could have stopped the charge that
day. Failure to a man like him is a bitter pill to swallow,
especially when so many lives hung in the balance."

"What happened to him on the battlefield?" Sable asked
breathlessly.

"He was wounded during the fighting and taken prisoner
by the Russians."

"How in the name of God did he survive?" Sable demanded,
remembering the stories her father had told her of the brutality
of Russian soldiers toward their prisoners of war.

"By all counts he should have died at their hands," Grayson
informed her soberly. "Yet he was befriended by a young lieutenant named Sergei Vilyusk, who cared for him until his wounds
healed and then risked his own life to smuggle him out of the
country."

Sable was silent for a moment, toying with her food. Doubtless the horrors of war and the senseless massacre of the British
Lights had impressed the youthful Morgan Carey deeply. In
addition it was entirely possible that war had hardened and
embittered him until he became the cruel, mocking man she
had come to know and despise.

"I fail to see," she said at last, feeling no more warmth for her towering tormentor than before, "what all of that has to do with Sir Morgan now and the fact that he has, for all practical purposes, kidnapped me."

Grayson nodded his head. "I understand your sentiments, m'lady, so allow me to explain." He paced restlessly to the stern windows and stood with his hands clasped behind his back, staring thoughtfully outside. "The war ended two years later. With the cessation of hostilities, Sir Morgan, himself a lieutenant at the time, tried to learn what had happened to Sergei Vilyusk. A debt of gratitude was owed the man who had saved his life, but Vilyusk was reported lost in one of the final skirmishes against the Turks. The debt could not be repaid."

Sable remained silent as the soft-spoken steward paused, aware that she was no nearer enlightenment than before but realizing that he would explain everything in due time. Spearing a piece of meat with her fork, she popped it into her mouth and began to chew, her eyes on Grayson's face.

"Last winter the *Defiance* was returning home from a wool run to Australia," he resumed after a moment. "We encountered a Turkish ship in Dakar and its captain, upon learning Sir Morgan had fought in Crimea, imparted a most startling piece of information. For the past ten years the court of the Sultan in Istanbul has included a pair of Russians who act as political advisers, Russians who had been captured at Eupatoria and have been living in Turkey ever since."

Sable grasped the situation quickly. "Are you saying one of those Russians was Sergei Vilyusk?"

Grayson nodded. "Sir Morgan sailed for London immediately to beg an audience with the Queen. Because Turkey and England had fought on the same side, he felt certain Victoria could obtain amnesty for the pair. She had made the Sultan a Knight of the Order of the Garter, no less, and her request would doubtless have been granted."

"But it was not," Sable guessed.

"No. Her Majesty refused to look officially into the matter. Relationships between Russia and Turkey have been strained, to say the least, and she was reluctant to open old wounds."

"I can't really blame her," Sable added. "The fate of two single men cannot be placed before the alliance of two countries."

"In Queen Victoria's mind, perhaps not. But in Sir Morgan's—" Grayson paused and regarded Sable keenly. She gasped disbelievingly.

"Surely you're not saying that Sir Morgan intends to rescue them himself!" At his nod she burst out, "But that's utter madness! How can the word of a Turkish sea captain be trusted? Furthermore, ten years have passed since then, which is ample time for this Sergei Vilyusk and his companion to have made good an escape!" Her tone grew mocking. "Surely Sir Morgan doesn't intend to storm the Sultan's palace in a heroic rescue mission? I warrant he'll find two wealthy, contented Russians who haven't the faintest inclination of returning to their country and who will resent his intrusion wholeheartedly."

The steward shook his head. "From the stories we've heard both the captain and I are inclined to think not. True, it's odd that so many years have passed, and yet Sir Morgan is unwilling to let the matter lie until he has investigated himself."

Sable picked up her fork again, but she had lost her appetite. Insulting words trembled on her lips, yet it was not in her heart to utter them. She could not censure Morgan Carey for following the dictates of his conscience. Her father, she suspected deep within her heart, would have done the same if his friend Dmitri Zergeyev had been thusly imprisoned, no matter how many years had elapsed. Perhaps Sergei Vilyusk had not been held all these years against his will, but if Morgan Carey was anything as determined as her father—and Sable had already begun to suspect that he was—then he would not rest until his own curiosity had been satisfied.

"Then why so much haste?" she asked bitterly after a moment, her dislike for Morgan Carey driving all kind thoughts from her heart. "If Sergei Vilyusk has been a prisoner for ten years, surely Sir Morgan could have abandoned him to his fate a few hours longer by returning me to Tangier."

Grayson looked apologetic. "Would that this were the case, m'lady, for I'm certain that Sir Morgan would have done so without hesitation. Yet the Turkish captain's tale included the fact that one of the Russians is gravely ill and that the Sultan's physicians have not the means or skill to cure him."

"I see," Sable said, her green eyes cold as she gazed up into the steward's face. "Will you tell me then why, if Sergei Vilyusk's life hangs in the balance, Sir Morgan found it necessary to sail to Cornwall first?"

"I believe Lord Monterrey lent invaluable assistance to him in the matter," Grayson responded evenly. "Though I'm not clear what it was, I do know that it necessitated a trip to Cornwall by the captain himself."

Sable said nothing although her jaw worked as she strove to control her mounting anger. So Morgan had come to North Head to ask her father for help, had he? Did her father know that he had also been conveniently used to further Morgan Carey's desire to take possession of her?

Sable's eyes narrowed suspiciously. It wasn't possible that Morgan had sailed to Tangier to lie in wait for her, was it? For a heart-stopping moment she could almost believe he had arranged the collision between the *Aloysius* and the unknown yacht. Yet as soon as the terrible thought rose to her mind she dismissed it. It was too far-fetched to be believable, and, unscrupulous as he might be, Sable knew Morgan wasn't capable of planning something that violent. Besides, he couldn't have known that she would be traveling to Morocco with her brother, could he? That had been decided only after he'd already left Cornwall.

"Are you feeling unwell, m'lady?" Grayson asked anxiously as she sighed and massaged her aching temples.

"No, I'm fine, but there's still so much I don't understand." She didn't want to admit to him that she was a little bit frightened. She didn't like the thought of being at Sir Morgan's mercy while her home and family were so far away.

Grayson stirred and began to busy himself stacking the empty dishes. "Perhaps you'd better take the matter up with the captain," he suggested, thinking he had told her far too much already. Not only was she a gentle-bred woman of fragile constitution, but she had been gravely ill only recently and he shouldn't have involved her so thoroughly in Captain Sir Morgan's dangerous affairs.

"What does Sir Morgan intend to do once we arrive in Istanbul?" Sable couldn't resist asking. She peered up at him contemptuously. "Not attack the palace singlehandedly, I hope?"

Grayson shrugged, but she could not ignore the concern in his expression. "I imagine that remains to be seen, your ladyship. Whatever the captain's plans are, he appears to be keeping them to himself."

Sable was thoroughly dissatisfied with this, but did not persist in questioning him. It didn't really matter, she told herself firmly, watching as Grayson maneuvered the heavy tray through the door. She wasn't about to accompany the *Defiance* or its half-mad captain to Turkey. The sooner she could persuade him to let her go, the better.

Her course of action decided, Sable took a last look in the mirror. Deftly twisting her thick braid of hair, she pinned it to her head and smoothed the folds of her skirts before starting up the flight of narrow steps leading to the upper decks. She would confront Sir Morgan now, she decided, before any more time had elapsed.

The sunshine blinded her when Sable stepped outside, and she paused for a moment with her hand on the rope banister, blinking until her eyes adjusted. On the voyages she had made years ago aboard the *Orient Star,* Sable had become intimately familiar with sailing ships. The *Defiance,* she saw at once, was fully as fast and well manned as her father's own rake-masted clipper. On a tautly run ship the hands were always busy, and Sable was not at all surprised at the number of men polishing brass, scrubbing the decks, coiling lines, and checking the fittings.

Now and then one of them paused in his task, startled at the sight of the golden beauty standing in the companionway before him. He would touch his watch cap and duck his head politely, and Sable was forced to smile back, causing him to color furiously and turn away. With the warm sun caressing her shoulders, Sable wandered over to a short, wiry sailor stowing gear in a wooden crate, his back turned to her as he worked.

"Excuse me."

He straightened at the sound of her voice, and Sable was startled to find herself looking into the oddest pair of eyes she had ever seen. The left one was blue—as blue as Morgan Carey's, she thought with an ungenerous scowl—while the other was green, a pale, washed-out green like the tarnished bronze of statues.

"Aye, your ladyship?" he inquired politely, recovering himself.

"I'd like to speak to the captain, please."

"I'm afraid that's impossible. He's busy at the helm."

Sable scowled although the man's tone had remained polite. "Then I should like to speak to the first mate."

The small man touched his cap deferentially. "You're speakin' to him now, your ladyship. I'm Jack Torance, first mate of the *Defiance*."

Sable regarded him silently. For all his unimpressiveness he seemed to possess a certain amount of character, a sense of fairness and honesty that had to be genuine. Sable hesitated. Should she ask him for help or would she be wasting her time? From past experience with her father's crew she knew that sailing men were loyal to the death to their captain and would never question his word.

"Would you be wantin' something, m'lady?" Jack inquired as she continued to stand silently before him, a thoughtful look on her small face. She was the bonniest thing he'd ever seen, Jack decided, and could understand now why his captain had been so reluctant to give her up. All of them had been wondering curiously about Sir Morgan's newest acquisition, laying bets on when she'd make her first appearance on deck and wagering how much of a fight Sir Morgan would have on his hands to keep her.

A good one indeed, Jack Torance decided. For all her fragility, Lady Sable had a determined gleam in her bonny eyes and a set to her small chin that warned of coming trouble. The struggle in her face could only mean she was desperate to enlist help from someone, and he felt an uncustomary stab of anger toward his captain at putting her in such a quandary.

"No, thank you, Mr. Torance," Sable said at last, the indecision within her changing to despair. Glancing about at the men who were watching her surreptitiously as they completed their tasks, she knew perfectly well that, while their sympathies might eventually come to lie with her, their duty would always bind them to Morgan Carey. He would be the ultimate victor, Sable realized, and if she was to get free of him, she must think of some other way to fight him.

"We're all glad to see you're finally better, Lady Sable," said another sailor, coming forward to address her with his cap in his hands. "Dr. Pierson said you was doing fine."

"Nat Palmer is the one who pulled you out of the water, your ladyship," Jack Torance informed her.

"Then I owe you my life," Sable said with a rush of gratitude which, for the moment, was free of the bitterness of her current dilemma.

Nat Palmer blushed to the roots of his sandy hair. "'Twasn't nothin', Lady Sable."

"Lady Sable, is it true you was thrown overboard durin' a collision?"

Now that Jack Torance had broken the ice by addressing the fair creature in gold, the men of the *Defiance* gathered about her, eager to be introduced and to gaze into her lovely face. The lilt of her Cornish voice charmed them, as did the smoky emerald color of her eyes, and all of them agreed among themselves that she was far more beautiful than they had imagined when she'd first been carried aboard, a half-drowned, pitiable waif.

From the quarterdeck of his ship, Sir Morgan Carey watched the circle of admirers grow around Sable's slender form. The fact that his men were behaving like lovesick cattle did not surprise him, but Sable's shy, smiling responses did. He wondered if perhaps she wasn't trying to charm them into aiding her escape from the ship, preying on their weakness for wide-eyed, innocent beauties.

Morgan could not know that it was simply not in Sable's gentle nature to be unkind to people who had done her no harm. She was a tender-hearted, loving young girl by nature, and her bitterness and anger were reserved for Morgan alone, who was solely responsible for her kidnapping and therefore fully deserving of the blame. His men, on the other hand, were simple sailors of a sort Sable knew and understood. She could not find it in her heart to treat them aloofly.

To Morgan, ignorant of her true character, her smiling face and warm, shining eyes were deceitful wiles, and he resolved to impose stern punishments on those men who tried to help her in any way. The endless nights he had spent battling Sable's fever, when at times he hadn't been sure whether or not he'd lose her, had proven more of an investment than he had originally intended to make. He would claim return payment—in full—before he let her go.

His eyes narrowed to slits as he watched the warm breeze play with loose strands of her silken hair. The gold chiffon gown with its loosely draped neckline revealed the rounded curves of Sable's hips and breasts, and Morgan felt his desire kindle hot in his loins. How long since he'd last had a woman, and how long since a woman had been able to satisfy him?

Too damned long, he told himself harshly. He had sought relief in many beds since Sable St. Germain had unwittingly unleashed such powerful needs within him. While waiting in

London for his audience with the Queen, he had dallied with numerous women of great beauty and skill, but they had all of them left him wanting more—left him with some undefinable need that seemed to be centered now around the dark-haired girl laughing on the deck below him.

As though feeling his pensive gaze upon her, Sable turned her head and looked up. Their eyes met across the expanse of polished wooden deck, the cool, predatory gaze of the hunter and the uneasy wariness of his prey. Sable glanced away quickly, her slim back turned toward him, but Morgan felt sure she had understood the look they had exchanged. She could not, he told himself grimly, be innocent enough to have misconstrued it.

In truth Sable had, yet even in her ignorance she realized that Morgan Carey meant to have her. The lines of battle had clearly been drawn in that negligibly brief glance. Sable shivered, suddenly more afraid than she had ever been in her young life. If Morgan Carey intended to take her, what could she possibly do to stop him?

"Are you feelin' all right, your ladyship?" Jack Torance asked anxiously, seeing that she had suddenly grown pale. "Shall I call Dr. Pierson or the captain?"

"No!" Sable responded, near panic. Quickly she smiled at him, hoping to reassure him. "I'm fine, thank you. Just a little tired. Perhaps I ought to lie down for a while."

Numerous offers were made to escort her below, but Sable graciously refused, and the men watched with keen disappointment as she vanished down the companionway. She was still shivering when she returned to Morgan's quarters. How to escape a fate she knew to be inevitable? Restlessly she prowled the cabin, searching for a weapon of sorts to defend herself and her precious honor from the man she knew instinctively intended to have both at all costs.

Her eyes fell on her image as she moved past Morgan's large dressing mirror. In the clinging material of her gown her breasts rose tautly, the womanly curves of her body more pronounced than they had ever been.

Dimly she recalled the passion kindling in Morgan Carey's eyes when he had kissed her in the Havertys' garden and again the night she had confronted him at North Head. He had promised to have her, a promise that fate seemed cruelly disposed to grant him. It would be useless to fight him, Sable knew, unless the weapon she used was one powerful enough to subdue him.

In the mirror before her lay the weapon she needed. Why not deceive the arrogant Sir Morgan by playing the role of seductress herself? He had told her father he wished to marry her even though Sable knew that he had lied to the Earl. Morgan didn't want her to be his wife, he wanted her to warm his bed! She might be innocent in the ways of love, but she was not ignorant and could guess well enough what had prompted Morgan not to return her to Tangier when he had had his chance.

Yet innocent she was, and Sable did not realize the experience a woman must gain before she can play so dangerous a game and win. She told herself that it would be simple enough to respond to Morgan as she had done albeit unwittingly in the past.

She felt a twinge of uncertainty and not a small measure of fear as she recalled how strong and forceful Morgan was. Then she thrust those fears away, mocking herself for her cowardice. What else could she do? Remain docile while Morgan Carey compromised her honor and dragged her on a dangerous mission to rescue some unknown Russian soldier from the palace of the Sultan of Turkey? Never! Sable's lips tightened mutinously. She was a St. Germain and a Cornishwoman besides. She was not the kind to turn and cower in the face of adversity!

The decks were dark and nearly deserted when Morgan Carey at last quit his position near the helm. The new watch had been set, and he anticipated no change in status until morning. The *Defiance* was heeling smoothly through the water, the islands of Greece before her, the canvas snapping stiffly overhead. For a moment Morgan paused on the ladder to savor the subtle canting of the enormous ship beneath him. Only here, on the open sea, did he ever come to feel truly alive and know at least a semblance of the peace that had eluded him all his life.

He frowned at his thoughts and forced himself to go below. There were more pressing problems to consider at the moment, not the least of which was what he intended to do with his prickly little captive now that she was well. Dr. Pierson had declared her completely recovered, taking most of the credit onto his own shoulders and conveniently forgetting the long hours Morgan had labored over Sable's burning body, sponging her time and again until the terrible temperature had at last begun to recede.

Preoccupied, Morgan threw open the door to his cabin but drew up abruptly as he stepped inside. Instead of finding Sable lying fast asleep in his bunk as on so many occasions in the past, he found her curled on the seat beneath the stern windows, her arms resting on her knees, her head down. She was wrapped again in one of his shirts, the cuffs trailing to the padded leather cushions.

Morgan uttered her name but she did not stir, and only then did he realize that she was asleep. The moon cast silver beams upon her that danced on her dark hair and he could see the steady rise and fall of her chest as she breathed.

Quietly he came closer and only then did he see the tear tracks that still lingered on her cheeks. She appeared so young, so oddly defenseless at the moment that Morgan was almost ashamed of the lust he could not deny feeling for her. She was so fragile, he thought to himself, that he could easily crush her or break her neck with his bare hands if he chose.

Sable stirred, her sleep made restless by the uncomfortable leather seat. Rolling on her side, she cradled her cheek against the hard wooden frame beneath the windows, her feet tucked beneath her. With her head thrown back, her throat exposed, the moonlight fell upon her slim form and touched the smooth breasts revealed by the deep plunging vee of the open neck of her shirt.

Morgan gazed down at the flawless beauty of the body he had come to know nearly as well as his own. In tending Sable during her illness he had touched her smooth skin so many times that he had become familiar with every curve and shapely line. At the time passion had not stirred him, for he had been concerned only in breaking her ferocious fever and recalling Sable back to life.

Yet now the last vestiges of illness were gone and Sable reclined on the window seat before him like a pampered cat, her body outlined in silver so that she seemed ethereal and wildly desirable. Morgan reached down to run his big hand across the sleek mane of hair that spilled down her shoulders. Sable did not respond and he leaned closer.

"Sable, can you hear me?"

She opened her eyes in response, the green depths flecked with silver, and Morgan forgot instantly that she had cried

herself to sleep only a few minutes before. Her soft lips were
parted and with a groan he bent down, lifting her into his arms
and planting his own upon them.

Sable, still lingering in the gray world between sleep and
wakefulness, found the sensation of being held against a hard,
muscular chest pleasant. The burning mouth covering hers was
pleasant, too, and she moved her lips experimentally beneath
his, liking the contact between them. Morgan's response to this
was to press her even closer to him, pulling her onto his lap
and sliding his powerful arm about her waist.

Almost without being aware of what she did, Sable slipped
her arms about his neck, her slim fingers moving through his
thick chestnut curls. A small sigh escaped her and she nestled
closer, her firm breasts brushing his chest. She had all but
forgotten that she had planned to seduce Morgan that night and
that she had been weeping bitterly over her fate not too long
ago. There was no longer room for anything in her mind save
Morgan, whose big hands were caressing her intimately through
her thin shirt and whose tongue was plundering the softness of
her mouth.

With his hand against her bare skin Morgan found her breast,
his fingers curving about the soft mound of flesh, causing Sable
to arch against him. The tip of her small tongue met his in
tentative exploration and the gentle touch served to unleash
Morgan's passion in a frenzy that startled even him. His features
taut with desire, he lifted Sable into his arms and carried her
to the bunk, laying her roughly across the blankets.

Sable opened her eyes to find his handsome face hovering
close, his blue eyes smoldering. When he lowered his mouth
to hers the searing contact took her breath away.

"My sweet, tempting Sable," he murmured hotly and pressed
himself against the length of her.

Sable gasped when she felt the hardness of his manhood
between her soft thighs. Her shirt was hiked precariously above
her hips and only Morgan's breeches separated their nakedness
from each other. She felt as though he might crush her with
his enormous weight, and when she looked up again into his
eyes, she was taken aback by the dark passions burning there.

Morgan's upper lip was dotted with sweat and there was a
wildness to his breathing, a desperation in his seeking hands
that made her sense instinctively that he was on the verge of
losing control. Untutored as she might have been, Sable's wom-

an's intuition could distinguish the difference between love-making and rape, and she knew that she would never be able to bear the humiliation of being taken by Morgan Carey against her will. Not that she was actually unwilling, for never in her life had she yearned for something more than this, however mysterious the outcome might be. Yet she knew that Morgan Carey was nearing the breaking point and that he would take her fiercely now, with no thought of her own pleasure, his possession of her the only thought in his mind.

"Please, don't," she whispered brokenly, the throbbing of her body mocking her cruelly. "Not like this."

Though her voice was barely audible, Morgan's head snapped up, his nostrils flaring. The urge to tear the shirt from her body and drive deep inside of her, to take her with a vengeance, nearly overwhelmed him and he was forced to struggle with himself as he had never done before.

Sable held her breath, her heart hammering, aware that he was trying to overcome his baser male instincts. Abruptly his great weight lifted from her, the movement so quick and un-expected that Sable was left blinking in confusion.

"If the lady is not willing," Morgan told her in a voice that grated harshly between his teeth, "then I'll not force her."

Though this had been what she wanted, Sable felt a stab of disappointment so deep that it brought real pain. A feeling of rejection and humiliation overwhelmed her, and she turned her face to the wall, swallowing hard to hold back her tears. She could not know that her own rejection had cut him to the quick and that, though every fiber of his being still ached for her, Morgan refused to submit. He knew as he watched her huddle in his bunk that she also still trembled with need, but he could not bring himself to touch her. To do so would mean the utter loss of self-control.

Never in his life had Morgan felt such violent desire to possess something as he yearned to possess Lady Sable St. Germain. The scent of her skin, the softness of her yielding lips had nearly driven him mad with want, and the realization made him uneasy. Emotions that cut so deep were dangerous. He must not let them run away from him like that again.

Savagely he tucked his shirttails back into his breeches and quit the room, slamming the door behind him. Tears welled in Sable's eyes when she realized that she was alone and that she had unwittingly unleashed Morgan's terrible anger against her.

Sitting up in the bunk, she pushed her hair from her eyes, her lower lip trembling. What could she have done? It had been utter madness to believe for a moment that she could control him sexually when the merest touch of his lips against hers made her weak with longing, his captive slave.

She still couldn't believe that he had turned away from her so abruptly, that he had heeded her request and left her alone. But was that the end of it? she asked herself fearfully. She was no nearer escaping the *Defiance* than she had been that morning. Worse still was the realization that she hungered for Morgan Carey, that with a single, burning kiss he had mysteriously been able to rob her of her will to resist him.

Hot tears stung Sable's eyes and she rolled over, but the scent of Morgan Carey lingered in her hair and on the pillow upon which she lay. She sobbed a little, feeling more alone and frightened than ever in her young life. She was a hopeless victim, she realized, not only of the powerful man who could manipulate her however he chose, but of her own, unconquerable woman's longings.

Chapter 8

It was nearly dawn when Sable opened her eyes the following morning. Pale light filtered weakly through the shuttered windows, but it was enough for her to see that the hammock strung between the beams in the center of the cabin was empty. She sat up, pushing her hair back from her face, a relieved sigh escaping her. She couldn't bear to encounter that mocking, blue-eyed stare, not after what had happened between them last night.

Sable felt the color rush to her cheeks, recalling her wanton response to Morgan Carey's impassioned kisses. His bold, seeking hands had left her weak with longing, and even now she could vividly recall the heat and hardness of his manhood as it had insinuated itself between her thighs. Morning hadn't diminished those memories as she had hoped. Instead, they were intensified by the clean, male scent of Morgan that seemed to dominate the cabin even though he wasn't there.

Sable scowled and began to dress with hasty, jerking movements. Perhaps a turn on the deserted decks might clear her mind and drive him from her thoughts. At any rate she was far too restless to wait down here until Grayson brought her breakfast.

Catching sight of herself in the mirror, Sable saw that she was pale and that dark shadows were etched into the smooth skin beneath her eyes. Her lips were still swollen from the bruising pressure of Morgan Carey's mouth, and she uttered a strangled sound of despair and fled the cabin.

On deck she saw that the sea was becalmed and that the stiff canvas sails were fluttering limply overhead. A few stars still shimmered in the west, and the air was heavy with the stillness that always comes before dawn. Sable wandered to the rail, where in the pale, silvery light she could see the darkened shapes of islands in the distance. She breathed deeply, the whisper of a breeze stirring the tendrils of silky hair that brushed across her temples. She had done right to come out here, she thought to herself, a feeling of peace settling over her. Dawn was such a magical, expectant time in which nothing, no troubles or heartache, could intrude.

"What the devil are you doing up so early?"

Sable flinched away from the deep voice and the man it belonged to, whose presence immediately made a mockery of her previous thoughts. Instantly she felt her contentment fleeting, replaced by embarrassment and uncertainty and the despairing realization that Morgan Carey held as much tormenting fascination for her now as he had the night before.

Clad only in worn breeches that molded to his muscular thighs and narrow hips, he stood bare-chested and magnificent before her. In the gathering light she could see the sheen of sweat on his wide chest and the pulse that beat so strong and vital in his throat. His eyes glittered and his sardonic expression taunted her.

"I couldn't sleep," Sable confessed, then set her jaw as she realized how easily he might misconstrue the reason behind her restlessness. "I've been confined aboard this ship too long," she added defensively. "I'm not accustomed to such restricted activity."

"Doubtless you'd prefer the Cornish moors and a good, hard gallop on your blood pony," Morgan agreed darkly. He was thinking, too, of the restless night behind him and the ache in his loins that had not been satisfied. With the rosy caress of dawn upon her, Sable looked exquisite, her large green eyes so expressive that to continue gazing into them was madness.

He longed to tear the beautiful gold gown from her body, to drive away his own torment by taking her now on the deserted deck of his ship.

Morgan's mouth tightened and he turned away from Sable's questioning face. Why didn't he do so? he asked himself contemptuously. He was captain of this ship, he answered to no man, he could easily use his great strength to overpower the defenseless girl before him. Why, then, didn't he? What foolish inhibitions held him back?

He heard Sable's soft voice behind him, thick with unshed tears but trembling bravely. "I'd rather be anywhere but here, Captain Carey, and it's only the memory of Cornwall, my family and, yes, even my 'blood pony' that keeps me from ending my troubles by throwing myself into the sea."

Morgan's head came around and he stared hard into her anguished eyes, his handsome face filled with astonishment. "You would go to such lengths to escape, lady?"

Sable's lower lip trembled dangerously, but she nodded. Morgan could not know that it was not her fear and hatred of him that drove her to contemplate such a violent end. Rather, it was the awakening of her own desires, achieved by his own hands, that frightened her and made her realize she was in danger of losing her will and perhaps even her heart to this cruel, arrogant man.

Captain Sir Morgan was a scoundrel and a rogue, a man no decent society would accept. The thought of what it would do to her father and mother if she succumbed to his attentions haunted Sable, and the guilt of knowing she responded to that passion was too much weight for her slender shoulders to bear.

Looking into her tormented eyes, Morgan was forced to believe her simple threat. Cursing softly beneath his breath, he stared across the placid water to the islands which were clearer now in the gathering light. The breeze ruffled the chestnut curls that lay in an unruly wave across his forehead, and to the girl peering up at his unrelenting profile he seemed intimidatingly handsome and frighteningly forbidden.

Morgan's chest expanded as he took in a great lungful of air. His lips thinned, and when he turned to look down at Sable, she felt her heart skip a beat at the ruthless expression on his hawkish features.

"You have nothing to fear from me, Sable St. Germain," he told her shortly, his words like the lash of a whip. "Not

from me or anyone else among my crew. If your predicament
is so abhorrent that you must contemplate suicide as a means
to escape it, then I cannot allow things to continue as they have
been." His blue eyes bored into her. "I am responsible for
everyone aboard this ship, yourself included, and I already
gave my word that you would be returned to your family unharmed at the end of this voyage. So be it."

Sable swallowed hard and twisted her hands together. She
could feel the heat of Morgan's anger like a physical force and
sensed from the big hands clenched about the rail that he was
controlling his emotions with the utmost of his great strength.
Relief washed over her, yet her victory was bittersweet, tem-
pered by some undefinable pain that pierced her to the soul.
Confused and unsure, she continued to gaze up at him with
wide eyes until Morgan rounded on her, his expression so
forbidding that her heart leaped into her throat.

"Have I made myself clear, m'lady?" His voice grated.

Sable nodded mutely.

"Then go below." He jerked his head in the direction of the
companionway, and Sable, trembling violently, complied.
Watching her slim form vanish below, her unbound hair streaming like a golden banner behind her, Morgan uttered a curse
and returned to the quarterdeck, his expression savage.

By the time Sable managed to muster enough courage to
return topside, the sun was high in the sky and the enchanted
island of Crete lay behind them. She had wept stormy tears
after Morgan had so cruelly sent her below, but when Grayson
had entered the cabin with her breakfast later that morning,
she had smiled at him bravely. Though her beautiful face was
slightly puffy, she had denied with a catch in her soft voice
that something was troubling her.

Grayson hadn't persisted in his questioning, but it didn't
take a clever man to guess that Lady Sable's obvious tears and
Sir Morgan's foul mood were somehow connected.

When Sable finally did return topside she found that Sir
Morgan ignored her completely. With his dark head bent over
the navigation charts, he held counsel with his officers, seemingly oblivious to the beautiful girl gracing the deck below
him. Once or twice his steely eyes fell upon her, but no change
came over his expression.

Sable chafed at the fact that Morgan treated her as though

she wasn't even there. She hated him, it was true, and feared him above all else, but she couldn't bear his indifference and cold, expressionless eyes whenever he looked at her. She was suspicious, too, not trusting him enough to believe he'd keep his promise to return her home unharmed, and wondering if perhaps this wasn't some despicable ploy to catch her off guard. Yet it wasn't like Morgan Carey to hide behind pretenses, she admitted to herself. He was a direct and forceful man who would have taken her unhesitantly if he had really wanted to.

That was what truly bothered her. Sable sensed intuitively that he had wanted to, that he had struggled with his desire when he had confronted her on the deck this morning, grappling with his need just as earnestly as last night when he had lain hard and ready above her. She bit her lip as she stood by the rail, willing herself not to turn and gaze up at his tall figure. That would be a weak, womanly thing to do, and she was determined not to behave like that.

"It won't be long until you can see the coastline of Turkey, m'lady."

It was Nat Palmer, the sandy-haired carpenter and sailmaker, who stood shyly at her side. Though Sable's eyes were bright with unshed tears, she returned his smile kindly, bringing a wave of heat to the young man's face. "I never in my life imagined that some day I'd see it, Mr. Palmer!"

"It's a shame there wasn't time to show you Crete, m'lady," he added. "Greece be a paradise, it be."

Sable suspected he was right. Emerald islands were strung like jewels through the sparkling water, and from the *Defiance*'s decks the blinding white beaches and charming whitewashed houses were clearly visible. It was impossible not to be touched by such beauty, and for the first time since the accident aboard the *Aloysius* Sable began to feel the stirring of life within her. If not for the worry over her family, the gravity of the *Defiance*'s mission, and the disturbing presence of Sir Morgan Carey, Sable might have found herself enjoying the voyage now that her health and strength had returned. She had always loved the sea and the feel of a solid ship beneath her, and the warm Mediterranean sun had cast its beguiling spell upon her.

She cast a swift glance over her shoulder at Sir Morgan, who was standing with his back to her on the quarterdeck, the sun turning his naked torso copper. She shivered and looked quickly away. No, it was impossible to think of this voyage as anything but a terrible nightmare, no matter how seductive the lure of paradise.

"Lady Sable, will you sit with us while we work?"

With a relieved smile Sable accepted Seaman Gilpin's shy invitation. Several crewmen had spread a massive expanse of canvas on the polished planks before the capstan and were squatting around it, their stubby, work-callused fingers busy with needles. Sable had learned all of their names yesterday, and the fact that she remembered them brought delighted smiles to their weatherbeaten faces.

Morgan, watching Sable's glossy head bend close to the grizzled ones of his men, her soft lips curved in a sweet smile, felt his anger mount anew. She was nothing but trouble, this alluring creature from the sea, and he sorely regretted having brought her aboard his ship. No woman was worth the loss of one's peace of mind and Sable St. Germain, with her tantalizing curves and forest green eyes, was guilty of exactly that offense.

Devil take her, Morgan swore silently to himself. He'd washed his hands of her completely and should be relieved that he had. She was a spoiled, tart-tongued brat who happened to be cursed with a body he yearned to possess. Once they returned from Istanbul, he'd turn this difficult handful of young womanhood over to her father and be heartily glad to get rid of her.

When Sable quit the main deck it was late afternoon and she was feeling hungry. Since Sir Morgan was still on the quarterdeck, there would be plenty of time to freshen up before Grayson brought her something to eat. Glancing in the mirror Sable saw that the warm Mediterranean sun had left a rosy blush on her cheeks. She would have to ask Grayson for a hat, she reflected, unpinning her hair and working the thick braid free. If she didn't take precautions she'd return to Cornwall looking as brown as the sailors who spent their days naked to the waist in the rigging.

Sable's heart constricted with sudden pain. She mustn't think of Cornwall or her family, she warned herself, lest Grayson enter the cabin and find her weeping. Sir Morgan had given his word that he'd return her home, and she should be grateful for that much from the heartless blackguard.

"Good afternoon, Lady Sable."

She whirled about. "Oh, hello, Grayson."

"I've brought your lunch. A tasty soup, some baked chicken, and a piece of lemon pie for dessert." If Grayson noticed Sable's troubled expression, he gave no sign. His pleasant features were open and friendly as ever, his reddish hair neatly brushed, and his vest and trousers were fastidiously pressed.

"How can you possibly stand him, Grayson?" Sable demanded impulsively, watching as the steward busied himself with setting a place for her at the table.

He glanced briefly into her flashing green eyes, then looked away, his lips twitching. "Who, m'lady?"

"You know very well who! The Great One, Captain Sir Morgan Carey himself. I vow his arrogance and his airs drive me mad. He's a thoroughly despicable—" Her hands clenched as she sought a fitting epithet, but the proper words failed her.

What had angered her this time? Grayson wondered. Had the lovely Lady Sable and the insolent Sir Morgan been arguing, or was she merely miffed at his callous treatment on deck earlier? No woman, Grayson well knew, liked to be slighted by a man, however much she might dislike him, especially if that man was as maddening as Sir Morgan Carey.

"I've grown accustomed to him, m'lady," he told her mildly, busy with the silverware. "I can assure you, however, that he was far worse in his youth."

"I find that hard to believe," Sable sniffed. The more she thought about Morgan's indifference toward her, the more annoyed she grew. Three hours she had spent out in the sunshine, talking and laughing with his men, and not once had he so much as acknowledged her presence!

Grayson gave her a brief glance, smiling to himself when he saw the fire in her eyes. Hell has no fury like a woman scorned, he thought to himself, though he strove hard to hide his amusement.

"You won't have to put up with that impossible giant very much longer, m'lady," he told her soothingly. "You'll be pleased to know that Sir Morgan has arranged for you to move to your own quarters this very afternoon."

Sable's eyes widened. "He has?"

"Yes, indeed. Mr. Torance kindly agreed to bunk with young Danny Hayes, which has freed a cabin for you right down the corridor."

Sable grappled to come to terms with this startling piece of news. Could this mean that Sir Morgan really intended to keep his word? Sending her out of his cabin would unquestionably assure that nothing untoward happened between them! A wave of relief washed over her, and she felt as if an enormous weight had been lifted from her shoulders. She'd not have to lie sleepless at night anymore, aware that only a few feet of space separated her from Morgan's hammock, nor pretend to be sleeping when he rose before dawn and dressed in the semidarkness, his body naked and glistening as he washed himself at the basin in the corner. Judas, she should be glad all of that was finally over!

"Mr. Torance needn't have made such a sacrifice on my behalf," she said weakly, seating herself at the table, her eyes on Grayson's face.

Grayson coughed delicately. "Now that you are well, m'lady, it seems only . . . er . . . proper that you have a place of your own."

A wave of heat rushed to Sable's cheeks and she averted her face so that the steward wouldn't see. "You're quite right," she murmured.

"After all," Grayson added more firmly, "unhappy circumstance might have brought you here, but you are still a lady of quality, and your honor must not be . . . ahem . . . compromised."

In truth he could scarcely believe himself that Sir Morgan had given the order to move Lady Sable out of his quarters, especially since the captain had been so adamant at first about keeping her for himself. Perhaps he had come to see, as all of them had, that Lady Sable St. Germain was too young and innocent to be so callously abused. Whatever the reason, Grayson was hard pressed to hide his relief.

"I'll have your things brought over and the bunk made up right away," he told her, ladling steaming soup from the tureen into her bowl.

"I haven't any 'things,'" Sable reminded him with a ghost of a smile. "Just the clothes on my back, which are none too well suited for this type of existence."

It was true that Sable's magnificent chiffon gown was more appropriate for a formal dinner party than for daily appearances on the main deck of a clipper ship. She had found it cumbersome, to say the least, to fasten the hooks and eyes herself every morning and undo them alone every night, and more than once she had tripped over the heavy skirts while negotiating the narrow flight of steps leading topside.

"I wish I had other clothes," she said somewhat wistfully, taking up her soup spoon.

"I'm afraid there's none to be had," Grayson quipped, "unless you borrow some mate's breeches and shirt."

His eyes widened when he caught sight of Sable's cunning expression. "Oh no, m'lady, you wouldn't!"

"Why not?" Sable demanded, the thought of getting rid of her hot, heavy gown sounding like heaven to her.

"It—it isn't proper!"

"Sometimes one must make do with what little one has," Sable pointed out practically, "especially in circumstances like these." Her chin tilted obstinately. "You'll find me some new clothes, won't you, Grayson? Daniel Hayes is small. Perhaps he might have an extra pair of breeches he could lend me."

Gazing into her determined eyes, Grayson knew he was lost. How could one argue with such an enchanting creature, whose expression of mingled womanly stubbornness and child-like pleading confounded any attempts to deny her?

"The captain wouldn't approve," he tried, but saw at once that he had taken the wrong tack. The little chin came even higher and the expressive eyes began to flash.

"Captain Carey doesn't have to parade about the quarterdeck all day in bulky skirts and confining undergarments! He'll simply have to be made to understand that I cannot do so either."

Grayson swallowed, aware that it was not a steward's place to argue with a lady. "Aye, your ladyship," he murmured unhappily. "I'll see what I can do."

Perhaps Danny Hayes wouldn't even have a pair of breeches that would fit Lady Sable, he told himself hopefully as he left her under the stern windows eating her meal with a hearty appetite, a complacent look upon her lovely face. Unfortunately for Grayson, Daniel did indeed have an extra pair which had been sitting in the bottom of his seaman's chest for several years. They were dusty and in need of patching but otherwise sound and, to Grayson's dismay, were deemed thoroughly suitable by Lady Sable when he presented them to her later that evening.

"I've taken the liberty of cleaning and repairing them, m'lady," he informed her glumly. "Are you certain you won't change your mind about wearing them?"

"They'll do splendidly," Sable assured him. Standing on

tiptoe she kissed his cheek and, with shining eyes, shut the
cabin door in his face.

Blushing hotly, Grayson turned away only to come face to
face with Sir Morgan, who had rounded the corner in time to
witness Sable's impulsive gesture. A smile curved his lips, but
his steel blue eyes held no warmth, and to Grayson it was more
the baring of teeth by a dangerous predator than the grin of an
amused gentleman.

"Have you decided to try luring the girl to your own bed,
Grayson?" Sir Morgan inquired.

The former valet drew himself up, unafraid. Though Sir
Morgan's awesome temper had been unleashed toward him
before, the two men had lived through so much in the past
nine years that Grayson rarely felt afraid of the towering man
who was his master. At the moment he was embarrassed, however, and Sir Morgan's cutting tone put him on the defensive.

"I would never contemplate so vile an action against anyone
as gentle and innocent as the Lady Sable," he said in a tone
that caused Morgan's brows to rise inquiringly.

"Are you suggesting that my morals are less than sterling
because I, once, intended to do so?" His voice was low and
unthreatening, yet Grayson felt himself beginning to grow uneasy. Where Lady Sable St. Germain was concerned, his master
was an enigma to him, a man whose moods were dangerous
and impossible to fathom. How could a barrier have been erected
between them so quickly, he wondered, and wherein lay the
cause? They had been at cross-purposes over women before,
most notably the "ladies" Sir Morgan had dallied with in the
past who had gone to astonishing lengths to snare him. How
many countless times had Grayson argued that his master was
blind, that he would be entrapped at last, and how many times
had Sir Morgan laughed at his valet's fears and always ended
up extricating himself quite neatly?

Yet this time things were different. Sir Morgan had vowed
to take his green-eyed prize at all costs, only to abruptly abandon the pursuit and set her free, even though, as Grayson could
clearly see, he still hungered to possess her.

The steward shifted uncomfortably. The look in those hard
blue eyes was unnerving, and he knew it would be wiser to
tread softly on such unfamiliar ground. "Lady Sable was thank-
ing me for services I performed for her as a cabin steward,"
he informed his captain stiffly. "As you doubtless know, she

is a sweet and gentle-hearted young woman."

"And obviously not one to hide her affections," Morgan grated, the icy blue eyes going to the closed door before them. "You are fortunate, Grayson, to have earned them." This time there was a mocking twist to the finely carved lips.

"It's probably due to the fact that I have done nothing to make her feel otherwise," he said pointedly.

The steely eyes narrowed and a pulse began to beat strongly in Morgan's tanned throat. Grayson tensed himself, sensing trouble, and was astonished when Sir Morgan threw back his head and laughed abruptly. "You damned impudent swine," he growled. "I should have dismissed you years ago."

Relief washed over the valet, and for the first time he realized that his heart had been hammering uncomfortably in his chest and that a fine film of sweat had broken out over his body. "Shall I bring you some supper, sir?" he asked in his most proper tones.

"Aye," Morgan assented. "Invite Torance and Pierson to dine with me." After a pause he added, "And the fair Lady Sable. I imagine she'll have to take her meals in my quarters from now on. There isn't enough room in hers."

"Very good, sir," Grayson replied and hurried away, relieved that trouble had been successfully diverted for the time being.

When he returned to the spacious aft quarters a half-hour later to set the table for the evening meal, he was pleased to see that the captain's mood had improved even further. Sir Morgan had just stepped from his bath and was shaving himself, a habit Grayson deplored, although in his nine years of service he had never been able to convince Sir Morgan that it was he who should shave his master. Moisture gleamed on Morgan's naked chest, and his breeches hugged his damp thighs and hips as he turned to greet his valet with a curt nod.

"Your guests should be arriving shortly, sir," Grayson said with a faint note of disapproval. "Would you care for assistance?"

Sir Morgan chuckled, rinsing the razor in hot water. "I can cut my own throat, Grayson, thank you. Has Lady Sable been informed that she's to dine here every night?"

"Aye, sir, and relieved she was to hear it."

Morgan gave a start of surprise but his voice was level. "Oh?"

"Aye, sir." If Grayson noticed the captain's hesitation he

gave no indication. Busying himself with a corkscrew, he added, "There's scarcely enough room in Master Jack's cabin to turn around in."

"Small wonder Torance normally eats with the crew," Morgan muttered, drying his jaw with a towel. "Come in," he added in response to a timid knock on his door.

"I hope I'm not late," came Sable's soft voice as she stepped inside, but the apology died on her lips when she saw Morgan standing before her clad only in breeches and polished boots, the lamplight shimmering on his bronzed chest. His dark hair had just been washed, and it curled damply across his forehead and neck. The scent of his cologne was sharp and masculine as it assailed her senses, and Sable felt the heat rise to her cheeks.

"What in God's name have you got on?" Morgan exclaimed at the sight of her.

Grayson's head jerked up at the curt words, and he stifled a groan, his pleasant mood evaporating. Private quarters for Lady Sable, proper meals in the captain's cabin with an officer or two present, surely these were simple enough criteria to avoid tempting the virile Sir Morgan! Why, then, did she have to do something like this?

On any other woman the attributes of masculine garb would have served to mask any feminine allure. On Sable, however, it was more than enhanced, clad as she was in a pair of breeches that molded themselves to her slim thighs and shapely calves. The curves of her hips were displayed to perfection and nothing hid the roundness of her small rear end or the leather patch riding impudently across one buttock. The muslin shirt she wore did not hang on her as Sir Morgan's had, but revealed the fragile collarbones and the swell of her firm breasts. Sable had braided her hair into a proper chignon, although the severity of the style was softened by the silky tendrils that escaped to curl across her forehead and temples.

The expression on her lovely face was one of childlike innocence, yet the alluring curves revealed by the leather breeches were maddeningly impossible to ignore. Grayson cast a swift glance at his captain, and his heart sank when he saw the ice-blue eyes glinting with mounting anger. Sir Morgan's lean jaw clenched and his voice was ominously still.

"What in the name of God are you wearing?" he repeated.

Sable lifted her chin defiantly, although a flicker of fear had passed across her face. "My n-new clothes."

Morgan crossed the distance between them, his big body completely blocking her from Grayson's worried line of vision. Sable's lower lip trembled but she stood her ground. She had anticipated disapproval on the captain's part, but not this steely anger that left her feeling weak. She dropped her gaze from the smoldering blue eyes, only to find herself staring at Morgan's naked chest, the ridges of hard muscle only inches from her face. Unexpectedly she found herself remembering how she had felt when he had pressed her against the heated length of him and she had run her fingers over the smooth, taut skin. A yearning to lean into him overwhelmed her, overriding her fear. Without even being aware of it she lifted her face to his, her soft lips parted, her pupils dilated so that her darkening eyes grew smoky green.

Morgan's hawkish features went rigid, his latent desire for her unleashed with a fury by her unconscious appeal. Every fiber of his being ached to seize Sable into his arms and tear the clothes from her enticing body, to drive deep inside of her and feel her closing about him, her soft, willing lips opened beneath his.

Behind him the cork came free from the bottle Grayson had been holding in his hands, the sound unnaturally loud in the charged atmosphere, startling all of them. Morgan bit back the groan of despair that was torn from him and viciously grabbed Sable's arms, lifting her clear off the deck as he jerked her against him. Even in his anger he could feel the soft, pliant curves of her body and the wild hammering of her heart.

"Take those things off," he grated in a tone that made her blood run cold.

"I won't," she whispered.

"Damn you, you will, or I'll do it myself," he threatened.

Both of them were breathing harshly, their eyes locked, Morgan's ruthless face nearly touching Sable's. To the watching Grayson they appeared to be struggling against much more than their anger, and he hurried forward, afraid of what might happen.

"Please, sir," he said hastily. "I'm to blame for everything. I'm the one who gave Lady Sable those clothes."

The sound of his voice shattered the tension in the air. Morgan set Sable roughly aside, ignoring the tears that sprang to her eyes as she rubbed her arms where his iron fingers had bitten into her flesh. "You, Grayson?" he asked quietly.

The valet nodded. "Since the weather has been growing hot of late, I thought Lady Sable might be more comfortable in breeches."

"That's not true," Sable said, glaring up at Morgan as she continued to rub her aching arms. "I told Grayson my gown was ill-suited for the climate here and he jokingly said I should find myself a pair of breeches to wear."

"A suggestion your devious mind instantly seized upon," Morgan remarked. There was a coldness and reserve to him that frightened her.

"Yes, that's right," she said as bravely as she could. "Grayson found these for me and I've no intention of giving them up."

"M'lady, please—" Grayson implored, but Morgan held up his hand to silence his valet. For a moment he was still as he gazed down into Sable's upturned face, her eyes wide and fearful. Then a mocking smile curved his slashing mouth.

"If I had named my ship *Defiance* with you in mind, little one, it couldn't have been more aptly christened." The mocking tone grew cruel. "By all means keep your attire, if that's what you wish. Apparently there's more of the guttersnipe in you than I'd first imagined."

Sable gave a shriek of outrage, but the warning light in Morgan's eyes made her think twice about attacking him. She had no inkling as to why her breeches made him so angry, yet she had no intention of giving them back. Her small chin tilted. No, she was going to wear them, and damned if this long-legged pirate was going to say her nay!

The meal proved an exhausting affair for Sable, who was forced to endure Morgan's unnerving silence throughout.

Sitting beside him at the small table, their shoulders nearly touching, Sable was always consciously aware of him and how he towered above her, his disconcerting gaze resting from time to time upon her bent head. Try as she might she could not forget he was there, and as the evening wore on she found it increasingly difficult to smile brightly at Dr. Pierson's gallant remarks. Morgan Carey had robbed her of her peace of mind, and Sable was beginning to despair of ever getting it back.

"I believe I've had quite enough, captain," Dr. Pierson yawned some time later. His words were thick and noticeably slurred, and his hand shook when he examined his watch. "Eleven-thirty?" He blinked in confusion. "That canna be right!"

"I assure you it is," Morgan responded coolly, his lips compressed as the physician shook his watch to and fro and muttered beneath his breath. "Perhaps you've been too . . . ah . . . occupied to notice the time?" His lazy, almost insulting drawl and the brief glance he gave Sable from heavy-lidded eyes made it clear what he meant. Sable could feel the heat rush to her cheeks, but Dr. Pierson, fortified by Madeira, was oblivious to the danger signals from his brooding captain.

Rising unsteadily to his feet, he reached across the table and took Sable's small hand in his. "Aye, cap'n, I'll confess the company this evening has been most diverting. Never kenned that a lady could look so well in breeks," he added and hiccuped. "Your servant, m'dear."

"Good night, Lady Sable, captain," Jack Torance added hastily. Rising to his feet, he packed the doctor firmly by the shoulder and pulled the protesting man roughly through the door, leaving a heavy silence to fall in his wake. Sable cast a swift glance at Morgan, only to find him watching her with that unnerving scrutiny she had come to hate. She rose swiftly, tottering as she did and bringing an unpleasant tightening to Morgan's lips.

"You're not much better at holding your liquor than Pierson is," he remarked coldly. "If you're going to dress like a man, then you might as well learn to drink like one."

"Don't be ridiculous," Sable snapped. "I've no intention of altering my sex! Even you have to admit that wearing a heavy chiffon gown and lace petticoats is madness aboard a ship in this kind of weather!" She gazed at him fiercely, her slim arms akimbo, but he continued to lounge before her with his eyes on her flushed face.

"Besides, you're the only one who seems to object to my attire," she added, but her words faltered as the chair was scraped back and Morgan rose to his full height before her. Her head tilted back and she gazed at him warily, like a cornered doe that senses danger but isn't alarmed enough yet to bolt. Morgan came closer and stood looking down at her, a playful smile on his lips which alerted Sable to immediate danger. She tried to edge away but found herself trapped between his big body and the table, yet she stood her ground, her chin bravely set.

"I don't object to your attire, m'lady," Morgan said hoarsely. "In fact, I find it most . . . attractive."

As he spoke he cupped her buttocks with his big hand and pulled her toward him. Sable gasped as she found herself pressed against his muscular thighs, her breeches riding intimately against his. Morgan's steely arm was about her waist, imprisoning her, while his other hand came up under her chin, his fingers cupping its sharp point.

"You play with fire when you dress as you do, Sable St. Germain," he murmured. "Are you a born temptress or simply too innocent to realize what you do to a man when he sees you clad in pliant leather that leaves little to the imagination?"

"Please, don't," Sable whispered, her heart hammering. Her gaze was locked with the smoldering steel of Morgan's, and she found she couldn't look away, his hand still cupping her chin, his thumb resting on a pulse beating wildly in her throat.

Morgan uttered a hoarse groan and seized the back of her head, bringing her lips to his and crushing them in a kiss that sent shock waves through her. Beneath her flattened palms she could feel the wild pounding of his heart. His manhood rose taut against her and Sable uttered a panic-stricken sob, aware that her body was betraying her, insinuating itself against him so that she was engulfed by the heat of his desire.

"N-no!" she moaned.

Hearing the tears that trembled thickly in her voice, Morgan released her abruptly, his breathing harsh through clenched teeth. Sable's hands flew to her hot cheeks and she gazed at him, the stricken look in her beautiful eyes piercing Morgan to the soul.

"You promised!" she whispered raggedly. "You gave your word that you'd not touch me again! Judas, call me a guttersnipe if you will, but at least I'm not a liar!"

"Sable—"

"This opportunity was far too good to be passed up, wasn't it?" she demanded accusingly. "Having me fall into your hands is certainly more convenient than having to marry me, I warrant!"

Morgan was dumbfounded at her words. "What in the name of God are you talking about?"

"Oh, you needn't act as though I were a total idiot!" Sable cried. "I know your reason for coming to North Head, your *real* reason, not the silly excuse about Sergei Vilyusk you gave my father! I even know that you asked my parents to say nothing about it to me until you returned from Istanbul, and you may rest assured that they kept their end of the bargain! But I did learn it from someone else in the house, and even though you may have fooled my parents, I know what it is you're really after!"

Morgan seized Sable by the arms, ignoring her flailing little fists, and stared incredulously into her face. "Will you stop your babbling and explain to me what you mean?" he demanded. "What's this about marriage?"

Sable glared up at him, her flushed face only inches from his. She didn't notice that his hold on her arms was bruisingly painful and that he had lifted her nearly off of the floor. All her attention was centered on him, this monster who had wreaked such havoc in her life. She intended to prove to him once and for all that she would not be the loser in this clash of wills!

"You know exactly what I mean," she said scathingly. "You came to North Head to ask my father for my hand while in reality you just wanted—"

Morgan shocked her by throwing back his head and interrupting her tirade with a roar of laughter. Sable stared up at him in confusion, wondering if he had taken leave of his senses.

"I can't believe it!" he said when he could speak. "How in God's name did you get the idea that I'd come to North Head to beg your father for the privilege of making you my wife?"

Disconcerted by the fact that his eyes were glowing with enjoyment as he stared down at her, Sable looked away and tried to keep her voice steady as she said, "I learned it from Hannah Daniels, my mother's former governess. I overheard her telling Wyecliffe Blackburn that you'd addressed my father and that he had agreed—provided I had no objections."

Morgan's amusement vanished abruptly and a look of incredulity spread across his ruthless features. Seeing it, Sable paused uncertainly.

"Is it true?" she asked at last.

"God's blood!" Morgan exploded. "Of course not! If I were going to marry anyone, I can assure you I'd not choose a hot-tempered, ill-mannered chit the likes of you!"

Sable was stunned by his outburst. "It really isn't true?" she whispered.

"Thank the good Lord, no," Morgan responded roughly. "I don't know where your governess came by such an absurd idea, but I can assure you that it was pure fabrication."

Sable was silent. Never in her life had she felt more humiliated, but she was too proud to let him know. She bit her
lip, wanting to get away from those taunting blue eyes at all
costs.

"In that case I'm glad Danny was mistaken," she said haughtily although her voice wavered with tears of shame. "I've no
more wish to be your wife than you wish to be wed to me—
and you've made it quite c-clear how repulsive you find that
prospect!" She drew herself up, her eyes searing him with her
fury. "I will remind you, however, that you have no right to
touch me while I'm aboard your ship and . . . and that my father
will see that you pay for what you've done to me so far!"

She was gone before he could stop her, her unbound hair
falling in an untidy knot to her shoulders, her choked sobs
ending abruptly with the slamming of a door down the darkened
corridor. Morgan stood rigid for a moment grappling with his
emotions, his chest heaving. With a snarl of pure rage, he
snatched the expensive crystal decanter from the table and
dashed it with all his might against the center beam, where it
exploded in thousands of glittering fragments, staining the
planking with amber liquid.

Later, when Grayson came to clear the table, he found the
cabin deserted, the broken glass still littering the floor. Silently
he straightened up, sweeping the shards into the dust bin. It
was long after midnight when he finished and, climbing worriedly to the upper deck, he found Sir Morgan at the helm, one
muscular arm propped against the rail. It was dark and Grayson
could see nothing but the hulking silhouette against the starlight, yet it was enough to allay his fears.

It was fortunate that Grayson could not see his master's
face, for he would have been shocked to find the handsome
visage taut with anger, the full lips ominously set and the blue
eyes glittering paradoxically with desperation.

When Morgan finally retreated below several hours had
elapsed. Passing the narrow door at the end of the corridor that
led to Sable's cabin, he was startled to see a thin beam of light
shining from underneath it. It would be dawn in a few hours,
he knew. What was she still doing awake?

"Who is it?" came her soft voice in response to his knock.

"Morgan."

Sable obligingly opened the door but kept her head bent, her eyes level with his wide chest. For a moment there was silence between them, then the chest rumbled with deep, amused laughter.

"At ease, your ladyship. I don't intend to discipline you."

Sable's head tilted back and Morgan felt his heart constrict at the sight of her small face. It was obvious that she had been crying. Her beautiful eyes were red and puffy, and tears still glistened on her dusky lashes. Morgan knew a moment of remorse, well aware that he had been the cause of her weeping.

"I'm sorry, Sable," he said, feeling awkward for the first time in his life. "I didn't mean to speak so harshly with you earlier. You must understand that your disclosure was rather ... er ... startling."

Her slim shoulders rose in a shrug and she turned away from him, wiping at her eyes in an oddly childlike gesture. "It doesn't really matter."

He frowned. "Then what is it?"

For a moment he didn't think she'd answer; then she said so softly that he almost didn't hear her, "It's my parents."

"I was so unkind to them before Edward and I left for Tangier. I honestly thought they had betrayed me by—by agreeing to wed me to you without speaking to me first. Now I realize they've done no such thing and I should have known all along that they never would! What must they think of me?"

"It was an honest mistake, Sable," Morgan said softly. "You can't be blamed for believing what you overheard someone say."

She wrung her hands, refusing to be pacified. He could well understand her torment and cursed Wyecliffe Blackburn for being the inadvertent cause of it.

"Why don't you write them a letter?" he suggested. "We'll be taking on fresh stores tomorrow, and if we're lucky there may be a ship England-bound in the harbor."

Sable brightened. "Do you think I could?"

He was forced to smile. "Why not?"

She couldn't think of a better way to clear up everything between herself and her parents. Oh, the guilt that had been consuming her since she had realized her bitter treatment of her father and mother had been totally unjustified! She was doubly glad now, recalling that the first letter she had written

them lay undelivered on her dresser back at the Telleboroughs'
home in Tangier. Thank goodness no one at North Head would
be reading it now!

"I'll have Grayson bring you writing implements tomorrow,"
Morgan added, once again resuming an authoritarian tone of
voice. "It's nearly dawn and you've no business writing them
now."

He was surprised when she simply nodded her head in agreement. Her unbound hair lay in a dark, sinuous cloud across
her shoulders, and he found himself thinking idly that if he
touched it he would find it as soft between his fingers as the
beautiful creature whose name Sable bore.

"Morgan?"

"Hmm."

"Why *did* you go to North Head if not to—to—"

"If not to beg your father for your hand?"

Sable blushed and turned away, but the fact that she hadn't
lashed out at him for his mockery did not go unnoticed by the
broad-shouldered man watching her from the doorway. "Yes,"
she whispered.

Straightening, he said briskly, "It's a long tale and not for
the telling so late at night."

She sensed that he was being deliberately evasive, which
distressed her. "Will you tell me tomorrow?"

There was a pleading expression on her upturned face that
would have melted the resolve of a lesser man. Abruptly Morgan
turned away and over his broad shoulder said curtly, "Perhaps.
Sleep now, or you'll be unfit company for your admirers on
the morrow."

He heard the door slam angrily behind him and a satisfied
smile tugged at his lips. Apparently the chit had recovered her
spirits.

Chapter 9

When Sable came on deck one golden morning not long afterward, she was astonished to find that the *Defiance* had dropped anchor some time during the night and that the yards of stiff white canvas overhead had been neatly furled.

"Mr. Hayes!" she called to the redheaded officer making notes in a ledger nearby.

"Aye, Lady Sable?" he asked with a bright smile. Few things pleased him more than spending time with the *Defiance*'s charming passenger, who had grown even more beautiful since the strong Aegean sun had touched her hair with fire and turned her skin gold. By now all of the men had grown accustomed to seeing her dressed in breeches and a white muslin shirt, her glossy curls tucked beneath a wide-brimmed cap. She had enchanted them, this green-eyed, soft-spoken young girl, and Daniel Hayes, like most of them, was head over ears in love with her.

"Why have we stopped here?" Sable asked, smiling expectantly into the young seaman's face.

Daniel felt his heart turn over. "Captain Sir Morgan is waiting to receive permission to sail into the Golden Horn. It's the

Sultan's decree, m'lady," he explained when Sable gave him a puzzled look from beneath dusky lashes. "The Turkish government must grant every European ship the right to sail into Istanbul."

"Are we there, then?" Sable demanded eagerly.

Daniel gestured to starboard. "Yonder she lies, Lady Sable."

Sable hurried to the rail and gazed across the sparkling water where the seven hills of Stamboul were visible through the sunshine. The day was crystal clear and she could plainly see the deep blue Bosporus filled with ferry boats, steamers, and heavily laden cargo ships.

"The Black Sea begins beyond the Bosporus," Daniel explained. "Can you see the hills of Asia Minor?" he asked, noting Sable's absorption with the glittering panorama before her.

"I never thought to see anything like this," she said almost to herself, her eyes sparkling. Ruins of castles and temples dotted the sloping hillsides before her, and plains covered with flowers swept down to the sea.

"I've been there twice myself," Daniel informed her proudly. "I'd be happy to show you about while we're in port."

"Lady St. Germain will not be going ashore, Mr. Hayes," came the curt voice of the captain from behind them.

Both of them turned, and Sir Morgan was struck by the innocence in the two youthful faces before him. His lips tightened, for he hated to be reminded of the tenderness of Sable St. Germain's years. To his surprise Daniel reacted to his dark words by moving protectively closer to Lady Sable rather than scurrying away. The fact that the lad foresaw the need to shield Sable from him enraged Morgan.

"Back to your chores, sailor," he ordered, and Daniel, his courage faltering beneath the biting words, hurried to comply. Sable, on the other hand, straightened her shoulders when the steely gaze snapped to her.

"There's no need to bite your lip off, lass," Morgan said coldly. "I've no intention of ordering you about like a common hand, though devil knows your appearance certainly warrants it."

Sable glared at him mutinously, for Morgan of all the *Defiance*'s men had continued to ridicule her attire, his mockery hurting her though she did her best to hide it from him. "Why can't I go ashore?" she asked, glaring up at him bravely although the top of her head barely came to his chin.

"This isn't a sightseeing tour conducted for your benefit. You'll only be in the way."

"As I have been throughout the voyage," Sable finished, trying to pretend his unkind words had no effect on her whatsoever. "May I remind you that I had nothing to do with the decision to keep me aboard? You could have brought me back to Tangier, but since you didn't, I'm afraid you alone are to blame for my presence here."

"You would have died but for me, madame," Morgan reminded her softly, and the truth of his words caused Sable's gaze to falter.

From Dr. Pierson and Grayson she had gotten testimony of Morgan Carey's diligent care during her terrible illness, something she had been too proud to thank him for. That in itself was a fact that rankled constantly in her conscience, but Sable would sooner have bitten off her tongue than say a kind word to the *Defiance*'s arrogant captain.

"Need I remind you also," Morgan added smoothly, "that it was your mistaken vanity in believing I might possibly wish to marry someone like you that drove you to Morocco to begin with? I can assure you, m'lady, that the *Defiance* was not lying in wait for you in Tangier."

"That may well be," Sable admitted, turning back to him, "but don't expect me to feel grateful to you for pulling me aboard that night! You've treated me no better than your lowliest deckhand, and if that's what I was spared for I'd just as soon be dead!"

She stalked off, her head held high, and Morgan cursed savagely beneath his breath. What madness had ever led him to believe that he wanted her? She was an infuriating, ill-mannered, and thoroughly insufferable wench! No woman like that was worth possessing, and he was beginning to regret the long hours he had spent at her bedside nursing her back to health.

"I should have thrown her to the sharks long before this," he growled to himself, his gaze unconsciously following Sable's retreat from the deck, her backside tantalizingly outlined in the tight-fitting yellow breeches.

By early evening the *Defiance* had been granted permission to enter the Bosporus. At a word from their captain the waiting sailors sprang into action, leaning into the capstan to weigh the anchor. No sooner was it hove short than the headsails were loosened and the topsails came thundering down behind.

Sable, standing by the rail with the breeze stirring her hair, felt an inexplicable happiness as the cry "Anchor's aweigh, sir!" filled the air. A moment later the big ship began to heel into the wind, spray flying high above the beakhead. How she had come to love the sun-washed days aboard the rake-masted clipper, Sable reflected. It had been easy, too, to fall under the spell of the warm, golden nights when the setting sun turned the sea crimson, the breeze fragrant with the exotic smells of the Near East.

In one of the tiny seaports they had stopped at several days ago in the Dardanelles, the *Defiance* had encountered a freighter bound for England via Tangier and Rabat. Sable had been permitted to send a letter to Edward via the captain, though Sir Morgan had refused to allow her to board the other ship. Sable, having seen the leering, unkempt faces of the sailors, the filthy decks and torn sails, had not pressed him to change his mind, well aware that she had been much better treated aboard the *Defiance* than she would be on the *Harriet Clay*.

The captain, a bearded, portly gentleman with only one eye, had brought with him the reek of rum when Sir Morgan had invited him aboard, and Sable was heartily glad when he was finally gone. Sir Morgan had assured her that Captain Muldoon, though a slovenly drunkard, was a man of his word and that her letters would reach Edward and North Head without fail. Much appeased by this, Sable had come to enjoy the remainder of the *Defiance*'s voyage, her constant worry about her brother and parents finally lessened.

Now, as she leaned on the rail and watched Istanbul unfold in all its splendor, she felt her excitement growing. Never in her life had she seen anything more beautiful or exotic. The Golden Horn lay before them, the water placid beneath a cloudless sky. Kiosks and gardens covered the emerald slopes on either side of the enormous clipper, their summits dotted with cypress groves and breathtaking mosques.

"What is the name of that mountain?" Sable asked as a shadow fell across the deck beside her, thinking it might be Daniel Hayes or Dr. Pierson, who had begun spending quite a bit of his time with her of late.

"Asiatic Olympus, if you mean the one covered with snow," came Morgan's deep voice from above her.

Sable was for once far too excited to be antagonized by his nearness, and she smiled up at him briefly before turning back to the ever-changing landscape before her. In doing so she missed the faint tightening of Morgan's square jaw, her attention caught by a cluster of beautiful domes and minarets rising from an embankment before the ship's surging bow.

"Seraglio Point," Sir Morgan explained obligingly, propping his muscular arms casually on the rail beside her. "A bit farther on you'll be able to see the triple walls of old Byzantium and the summer palaces of the pashas and the Sultan's daughters."

Sable turned to look into his handsome visage, her eyes wide. "Have you been here before?"

"Many years ago," he replied, his voice soft with memories. "Long before I even knew Sergei Vilyusk had been reported killed at Sevastopol."

Sable wondered if he knew that she was aware of the nature of the *Defiance*'s voyage to Istanbul. Doubtless Grayson had informed him of their conversation days ago, but until this moment Sir Morgan had never acknowledged it.

"Do you think he's still alive?" she asked curiously.

Morgan's profile was typically ruthless, but for a moment Sable thought she saw a fleeting emotion akin to fear pass across it. "I can only hope he is," he informed her quietly.

Sable chewed her lip and turned away, more shaken by Morgan's reaction than she cared to admit. Never had she known him to display any sign of human weakness, of kindness or compassion. Aloof and insufferably arrogant, he had enraged her at times with his lack of common civility. Could it be possible, she asked herself wonderingly, that all of this was a facade to mask a man who felt deeply and cared about others?

Morgan's next words dashed her newfound hopes, convincing her that he was just as unbearable and cruel as she had always suspected. "I imagine you'd be delighted to learn he has died, wouldn't you, my heartless lady?"

"What do you mean?" Sable demanded, rounding on him. Her eyes blazed defensively, and she was oblivious of the fact that Morgan was standing so close, his broad shoulder nearly brushing hers.

The intense blue eyes bore into hers. "I'm certain it would afford you great pleasure to say 'I told you so' and tell me that my quest here was madness."

Sable gasped, recoiling as though he had struck her. "Do

you honestly believe I'd wish a man dead merely so that I could find fault with you?"

"Why not?" Morgan demanded, refusing to acknowledge that he had hurt her. "You seem to take enormous pleasure in calling me to a reckoning."

"I'm sorry you believe that of me," Sable said stiffly, and Morgan could see the trembling of her lower lip, although her face was averted.

He had been unfair, he realized, for if there was anything he had learned about Lady Sable St. Germain during his brief stay at North Head, it was that she was a gentle-hearted young woman who saw only the good in those around her. Moreover he had never taken into consideration the fact that she was little more than a child who, for the first time in her life, had been torn from the safe, sheltering arms of her family. Could one really blame her if she was hostile toward him, especially when he was responsible for putting her on the defensive in the first place?

Morgan's lips thinned. It wasn't his way to be charitable, and yet Sable St. Germain touched him oddly and forced him to examine his conscience in a way he hadn't done for years. He owed her an apology for his unkind remark, he told himself roughly.

"Captain, the wind be backin'!" came a cry from the stern, but Morgan had already noticed the nearly imperceptible movement of the deck beneath his feet. Giving Sable a brief nod, he strode aft while she lifted her eyes to the masts, where crewmen were already scurrying along the yards to reset the enormous press of canvas.

She was still smarting at Morgan's hateful remarks but told herself that she had deserved them. Had she ever given him reason to believe that she was anything other than the shrill-tongued, unfeeling woman he thought her to be? She resolved to be kinder to him, no matter how hard that might prove, for she owed him quite a bit, despite everything. Perhaps then he might even give up his attempts to take her to his bed—for that above all was what frightened Sable the most.

She could not deny that Morgan Carey held some mysterious sway over her that left her weak with longing whenever he touched her. If only she knew why he had come to North Head and what debt he owed her father! She had brought the matter up to him several times, but Morgan had been brusque with her, and she was no nearer enlightenment than before. Even Grayson had admitted ignorance, and Sable wondered how she could find out what she needed to know. With such a weapon in hand she felt certain Morgan could be persuaded to treat her as decorum demanded.

The enormous clipper was running smoothly on a new course, the sails set to make best use of the variable winds. Morgan, Sable saw with a small lurch of her heart, was at his customary place at the helm, his powerful hands sure on the brass-plated wheel. Even in the fading daylight she could see the lusty gleam in his eyes, his white teeth bared in a smile of pure enjoyment. This was what he loved most of all, she realized with a curious sense of loss. Guiding his ship through fair and foul, living a wild life on the open seas with no one but God to answer to. . . . Was there any force on earth that could ever tame him?

Abruptly Sable turned away, angry and bewildered at the sadness within her. Why should she care that Morgan Carey seemed so at home on the sea? She should be glad he called no country his own. After all, he wasn't fit to live in any decent society and belonged with the ruffians who had pledged their loyalty to him.

"Devil take him!" she whispered to herself. "I should have sailed back to Tangier on the *Harriet Clay!*"

She was still standing by the rail a half-hour later when the *Defiance* nosed into her berth between an imposing Turkish frigate-of-war and a freighter with a deckful of noisy men. The docking was smooth, the big sailing ship responding to the expert handling of well-trained men. In the setting sun the sails were tinted gold and the hills rising steeply from the quay seemed to glow with a mysterious light of their own. Sable could see crowded streets and rows of houses leading down to the waterfront, and the alien atmosphere filled her with curiosity. How dearly she would like to explore the ancient strongholds of Constantinople! Surely Morgan wouldn't forbid her one trip ashore?

"Mr. Hayes!"

"Aye, sir?"

Sable turned at the sound of Morgan's deep voice.

"Inform the men that they may leave when their watches are finished. We'll have no trouble while we're here, is that understood?"

"Aye, sir, I'll tell them, sir." Daniel hurried away, and

Morgan turned his head so that his narrowed blue eyes met Sable's green ones across the expanse of the main deck.

"Are you going ashore, too?" she asked hesitantly as he came to stand beside her.

"I've business to take up with the harbormaster," he informed her curtly, "and then perhaps I will."

She was silent a moment, trying to phrase her next question properly, unaware that Morgan had already guessed what she was thinking. Propping his big hands on the smooth wood beside hers, he said casually, "We'll be staying here until the Sultan agrees to see me. I have a letter of introduction for him penned by Disraeli himself. Your father arranged for me to see him while he was in London."

She gave him a look of utter confusion. "You saw the Prime Minister? Father never said a word about it to us! In fact, he said he'd never exchanged a single word with you before the night of the Havertys' ball," she remembered.

Morgan's lips twitched, thinking that the Earl of Monterrey must have a difficult time of it indeed with such an inquisitive daughter. "Surely you'll be able to forgive him when you understand that he was involved himself in an affair that is being conducted without Her Majesty's knowledge and one which would garner her total disapproval should she learn of it."

"Grayson told me the Queen refused to intervene in Sergei's behalf," Sable recalled.

"And so she did, which is why I turned to your father instead. He happens to be well acquainted with Mr. Disraeli, who, upon hearing my tale, promptly agreed to do what he could, without Her Majesty's knowledge, of course. His letter should gain us access into the seraglio, which I never would have been able to accomplish on my own." His eyes gleamed. "I have nothing to do now but wait to be summoned by the Sultan, which I find far less inconvenient than sneaking in under cover of darkness."

Sable shivered and looked away from his ruthless countenance. It had suddenly been made clear to her how truly dangerous his mission was. True, English ships and their personnel were welcome in Turkey, but what Morgan planned to do would place him at odds not only with the Sultan but with his own government. Her heart skipped a beat. What would happen if his plans were discovered?

"If my father agreed to help you while he was still in London,"

Sable said after a moment, "then why did you come to Cornwall?"

At first she didn't think he'd answer, but then he met her gaze directly and said softly, "Because of a man named Andrei Vilyusk."

Sable glanced up at him, startled that he had told her this when normally he was so inapproachable where she was concerned.

"Andrei Vilyusk was a high official in the Russian Embassy in Paris when your father was still considered to hold the title of Comte de Monteraux," Morgan explained. "Your father knew him well."

"Is he related to Sergei?" Sable guessed. "Or rather, was he? I suppose he's dead now, isn't he?"

Morgan nodded. "He's been dead for many years, I'm afraid. Andrei was Sergei Vilyusk's father."

To Sable's dismay, Morgan's lean cheek tightened and she recognized it as a sign that something had disturbed him. When he continued speaking, it was in a tone that was far less charitable than the one he had used a moment before. "I came to Cornwall seeking information, your ladyship, nothing more. I wanted to learn what I could about the man, and Lord Monterrey was kind enough to oblige me. Now, if you'll excuse me, I've things to do."

She watched him vanish through the companionway, her hands clenched tightly about the railing. She had been so sure he was going to tell her everything, and instead he had been so mysterious! Why had the name of Andrei Vilyusk angered him? In what way was the former Russian diplomat connected with her father?

Sable was more confused than ever before, but she knew better than to follow after Morgan and demand that he tell her. She had learned by now that he only volunteered information when he felt like it and certainly never when he was asked. He would tell her in due time, she soothed herself, but found it difficult to curb her impatience and ease the fears he had unwittingly aroused within her. The *Defiance*'s mission in Istanbul was no inconsequential matter, and Sable was beginning to fear that she would witness violence and bloodshed before it was all over.

Never had Sable known the hours to drag more slowly than they did that first night in Turkey. With the ship nearly deserted, she had no one to talk to save Grayson, but for once she felt too restless to enjoy his company. Around nine o'clock Morgan had ordered crewman Harley Gump to row him ashore, and Sable had watched from the shadows of a bulkhead as his broad-shouldered form had vanished into the night.

She had been tempted for a mad moment to follow him but had been intimidated by the dark, twisting streets and the almost sinister strangeness of a Turkish city cloaked in darkness. Her confinement to the ship also made her think twice, for though she didn't mind defying Morgan on occasion, Sable wasn't foolish enough to disobey his commands outright. Besides, she reasoned, before leaving, he had probably warned the deck watch not to let her go and to report any infraction of the rules on her part to him at once.

Sable shook her head, not caring to become the target of Morgan Carey's awesome temper. If the truth must be told she found him a despicable, arrogant, and, yes, dangerous man. On the other hand, she couldn't help worrying. How could Morgan possibly expect his rescue mission to succeed? She had seen the countless palaces and fortresses that lined the Bosporus when the *Defiance* had sailed past them earlier. Sergei Vilyusk, if he was still alive, could be imprisoned in any one of them. How was Morgan to find out without arousing suspicions?

It was still early when Sable retired after wishing Grayson a dispirited good night. Her tiny cabin seemed closer than ever, and she thought with longing of Morgan's roomy quarters as she undressed, bumping her knee on the narrow cot which served as her bed. Even the book Dr. Pierson had loaned her proved no entertainment, and Sable gave up at last, blowing out the lamp and pulling the covers up under her chin.

She lost count of how many hours she lay awake, the creaking of the beams and the occasional footsteps of the men on watch sounding mutely from above. Eventually she slept, but her rest was interrupted by fits of wakefulness, and not until dawn did she hear Morgan's footsteps in the corridor. Instantly alert, Sable slipped out of bed, peering outside, where she could see a soft golden light shining from a crack beneath Morgan's door. She heard the glass-fronted cabinet creak as he reached inside for the brandy decanter, and with a relieved sigh she tiptoed back to bed. This time when she slept, her rest was deep and without dreams.

* * *

Sable made her appearance on deck early the following morning, but Morgan, despite his late return to the ship, was there ahead of her. She was startled to find him in his customary place on the quarterdeck looking well rested, fit, and too disturbingly handsome for her own peace of mind. She hated to admit to herself that she was glad to see him and that she had been worried about him the night before. Judas, she wasn't starting to care about the evil blackguard, was she? There was nothing to recommend about him, after all, and she must never forget that he alone was responsible for kidnapping her from Tangier.

"Do you always scowl so fiercely in the mornings, m'lady?"

Sable looked about to find that Morgan had descended from the quarterdeck and was now sauntering toward her, his hands thrust casually in the pockets of his faded breeches. The wind tugged at his chestnut curls, causing them to tumble in boyish disarray across his broad forehead, and he was regarding her for once without his customary coldness.

"I do when I think of the trouble you might have gotten yourself into last night," she retorted.

Instantly a guarded look came over his handsome countenance. "You were worried about me, m'lady?"

Sable refused to acknowledge the little lurch her heart gave at his question, refusing to believe that she was beginning to feel something akin to affection for this long-legged giant who had done nothing but torment her since she'd first laid eyes on him. Surely her feelings couldn't have anything to do with the danger he was putting himself into by trying to rescue a man from the Sultan's heavily guarded palace? What utter nonsense, she told herself peevishly. Morgan Carey could take care of himself, and she strongly suspected it would take more than the Sultan's royal guards to stop him.

"It bothers me when lives are placed in jeopardy for senseless reasons," she said pointedly, "regardless of whose they may be."

Morgan's visage took on its customary ruthlessness so that Sable doubted she had seen a sign of softening there. "I see." His expression darkened even more. "Perhaps in your spoiled little mind our reason for being here is senseless, your ladyship, yet to some of us duty and friendship matter a great deal." His blue eyes bored into her and his angry words were like the lash of a whip. "What a pity your parents never raised you to care for anything more than your gowns and baubles."

Sable gasped, stung by the realization that Morgan still thought of her as being empty-headed and unkind. It was true that her original dislike of him had been justified, but of late she had been unable to fault him in his treatment of her. She had come aboard the *Defiance* with nothing but the clothes on her back, and the clipper's crew, though they owed her naught, had been kind to her and treated her as one of them. Furthermore, Sir Morgan, who had little cause to welcome a half-drowned girl aboard his ship, had patiently nursed her back to health, only to be rewarded for his kindness with haughtiness and insults.

While his attitude toward her had certainly improved, Sable realized that she had made no similar effort to bridge the yawning gap between them. Suddenly she felt deeply ashamed. She had behaved in a rude, selfish manner since her arrival here, and she knew that her parents would have been shocked to see it. Small wonder Morgan Carey thought her vain and cold-hearted.

"Morgan, wait!"

Her soft cry and the use of his Christian name startled both of them. Morgan, who had started aft toward the helm, turned to look at her, his brows raised inquiringly. Sable hurried after him, her eyes filled with pleading as she stared up into his handsome face.

"I'm sorry," she said earnestly. "It was wrong of me to ridicule you for something few men would have the courage to do. I've been behaving like an ungrateful wretch since you brought me aboard, when in fact I owe you my life. There is no justifiable reason to be rude to you especially since"—she hesitated and turned red—"especially since I'm the one who was mistaken all along about your reason for coming to North Head."

She took a deep breath, faltering for a moment beneath the intensity of his gaze, but added in a rush, "It's only that I can't help worrying that you won't find Sergei Vilyusk alive and that you'll be risking your own life for naught."

"Are you worried about me, Sable?" Morgan asked incredulously.

She tried to look away but found that she could not. Their

gazes were locked, and it was as if they were standing alone in some vast void, conscious only of each other. "I guess I am," she whispered.

Morgan startled her by throwing back his head and laughing heartily. Sable glared at him indignantly, but when he looked down at her again she felt her breath catch in her throat at the intimacy burning in his blue eyes. "Are you beginning to care for me, Sable St. Germain?"

"Perhaps a little," she confessed, a rosy stain creeping to her cheeks.

Morgan stepped nearer so that her face was only inches from his wide chest. She became aware of the exotic scent of his cologne, which mingled with the pleasant male smell of him, and she began to tremble when she felt his big hand come up under her chin, tilting back her head and forcing her to look into his eyes.

"You are a mystery to me, little one," he said thoughtfully. "At times I've wondered if that beautiful body of yours contains nothing more than the heart of a cruel little barbarian, and at other times I'm convinced we pulled Aphrodite and not some flesh-and-blood woman from the sea."

"I assure you that I'm quite real, captain," Sable responded shakily. Her pulse was racing, and Morgan, allowing his big thumb to stray over the hollow of her throat, noticed it and smiled. It was a devastating smile that made Sable grow weak, one that transformed his lean, hawkish features into those of a young and carefree man.

"Aye, I'm aware that you're no illusion," he told her softly, the intimacy in his husky voice unmistakable. For a moment he was silent as he gazed down into her exquisite face, her eyes wide with mysterious green depths a man could easily drown in.

"Cap'n! Will ye be wantin' to go now?"

Morgan cursed softly and released Sable, turning his head to address the crewman who stood bobbing respectfully behind him. "Is the launch ready?"

"Aye, cap'n, an' Mr. Torance be at the helm."

"I'll be there in a moment," Morgan said, his tone a dismissal.

"Aye, aye, sir."

"Are you going back to the city?" Sable asked fearfully.

Morgan's lips twitched. "Only for a bit of reconnoitering, nothing dangerous."

"Oh, please, may I go with you? I promise I won't get in the way. I haven't been off the ship for weeks now!"

She thought at first that he would refuse, but then he shrugged. "Why not? A bit of exercise might do you good. But Sable," he warned when she gave a delighted exclamation, "you're to stay with Daniel and follow his orders, is that understood?"

She was too happy to resent his arrogant tone. "Oh yes, I promise!"

"And get out of those britches," he growled. "The Turks have strict ideas about womenfolk and what they should be wearing."

"You'll wait for me while I change?" Sable asked, her eyes shining. "I'll only be a minute."

Morgan sighed in exasperation. "I suppose I haven't got much of a choice."

"Thank you," Sable breathed, "thank you for letting me come." Impulsively she stood on tiptoe and pressed her lips to his lean cheek. Morgan, his expression softening, slid his arm about her waist and unexpectedly turned his head so that her lips touched his own. The kiss was brief and for once devoid of passion, but Sable was scarlet-faced and her heart raced as she turned and fled toward the companionway.

Daniel Hayes was standing at attention by the launch when Sable returned, and his eyes widened appreciatively when he saw that she was wearing the gold chiffon gown she had discarded days ago in favor of his patched breeches. She had braided her dark curls and arranged them in a becoming coronet about her head. Her sloping eyes sparkled like emeralds, and Daniel flushed hotly when she smiled at him.

"You're looking very well, Lady Sable," he stammered self-consciously and reached for her hand to help her into the launch.

"That will do, Mr. Hayes," came the captain's curt voice, and Sable felt her hand being taken by a much larger one. She looked up quickly to find Morgan regarding her approvingly from his great height, the intimacy of his gaze excluding the blushing officer beside him.

"I'd forgotten how becoming that gown is," he told her as he handed her in.

"Much better than breeches?" Sable teased, delighted with the truce they seemed to have established at last. Spreading her skirts on the wooden seat, she slanted Morgan a saucy, questioning look.

"You weren't meant to traipse about like a man," he said, but she felt curiously warmed by his curt response.

"Oh, look, what are those?" she asked curiously as Daniel gave the order for the men to pick up their oars.

Morgan followed her pointing finger to a narrow boat with a turned-up prow being handled by an oarsman dressed in tight black trousers and long, flowing white sleeves. There was a flower tucked into his fez, and his black tassel blew jauntily in the breeze.

"It's called a caique," Morgan explained. "They're used to transport passengers across the Golden Horn much like the hansom cabs that take you from one end of London to the other."

Sable watched as the caique glided past, two young Turks sitting inside, their backs resting against tassled cushions. She glanced up at Morgan, who was sitting beside her, his broad shoulder nearly touching hers.

"Could we do that, too?" she asked eagerly.

Morgan's lips twitched. "This isn't a pleasure tour of Istanbul, m'lady."

"I know, but it looks like such fun," she persisted, enchanted by the picturesque oarsman and the reclining passengers.

"Perhaps on our return trip to the ship," Morgan allowed.

As the launch cut swiftly through the deep blue water, Sable's attention was caught by the numerous cargo boats moving back and forth between Stamboul and the far shore of the Golden Horn. All of them were laden with melons and figs or baskets of succulent grapes and pears. A small steamer further upriver was being disgorged of passengers who were being loaded into waiting boats by smartly attired porters. Ahead of the launch the imposing minarets and cupolas of the Yedi Mosque were visible, and Sable felt her excitement growing. Never had she seen anything so exotic, so crowded and foreign as the skyline of Istanbul! She must memorize every detail, she told herself, in order to describe everything to Liam and Edward when she returned. How they would envy her this voyage!

Casting a discreet glance at Morgan's hawkish profile, Sable found herself feeling truly happy for the first time in many days. The bitter tension between the two of them had miraculously vanished, and Morgan had agreed to let her see Istanbul.

How fortunate she was! Perhaps she might even persuade Daniel
Hayes to take her to some bustling market where she might
purchase gifts for her family.

Sable was astonished at how amenable Morgan Carey could
prove to be. Stepping ashore, he helped her from the launch
and gave several orders to his men which Sable, staring agape
about her, did not hear. They were in Old Stamboul itself with
Pera, the European quarter, lying opposite. The streets that
emptied into the dock area were crooked and rocky, but surprisingly quiet. Dogs slunk growling along the bases of patched
wooden houses, their latticed windows darkened from within.
Several donkey-drawn carts laden with goods bound for the
market rumbled past, and Sable gasped in delight when she
caught sight of a robed Turk leading a camel by a jewel-studded
halter.

"What would you like to see, m'lady?"

Morgan's deep voice roused her from her reverie. "Oh,
everything!"

One dark brow rose in mock astonishment. "Everything?
I'm afraid there isn't enough time for that."

"Then at least the Blue Mosque and the Sancta Sophia,"
Sable pleaded.

"Where did you learn about those?" Morgan asked in surprise.

"Mr. Hayes told me all about the city," Sable replied, smiling
at the young man and missing the darkening of the captain's
expression in response.

"Very well, but you'll have to walk," Morgan growled.

"I don't mind," Sable replied cheerfully, delighted to be on
solid ground once again.

"All right," Morgan agreed at last. "Mr. Hayes, I trust you
will look after the lady properly?"

"Are you not going with us?" Sable asked, crestfallen.

Morgan's reply was curt. "I've more pressing duties at the
moment, madame. Mr. Hayes, you've been given your orders."

"Aye, aye, sir," Daniel answered uncomfortably, then gave
Sable a bright smile when Morgan and the rest of his men
started off toward the city. "Where shall we go first, m'lady?"

Swallowing her disappointment, Sable returned his smile.
"Lead the way, sir. Anywhere will do."

"Righto," he responded enthusiastically. Offering Sable his

arm, he escorted her off the docks, filled with joy at the prospect of having the beautiful Lady Sable to himself for an entire morning, with Captain Sir Morgan's blessing, no less!

Clinging to Daniel's arm, Sable exclaimed over the beauty of the Turkish women in their little veils and loose silk robes and the servant girls who wore old coins of gold and silver on delicate chains around their foreheads. Men in colorful costumes lounged in the courtyards of ancient stone buildings, smoking tobacco from huge water pipes and conducting business in low, singsong dialects. Street vendors shouted from every corner, the wooden trays on their heads displaying their wares of breads, sweets, and drinks of sherbet.

"Oh, Mr. Hayes, what's that?" Sable asked when they had crossed a busy intersection, pointing to an enormous domed building from which drifted the noisy din of countless conversations. Pale sunlight filtered through openings in the cupolas of the roof, and Sable could see through the opened doors that Turks and Arabs mingled inside with European sailors and businessmen.

"The bazaar," Daniel replied obligingly. "Would you care to go inside?" he added, seeing her hopeful expression.

"I'd love to," she replied, and glanced at him shyly. "That is, if you don't mind."

Daniel shook his head, his chest swelling as he stared down at this starry-eyed slip of a girl who unwittingly held his heart in her small hands. He could deny her nothing, he knew, and suspected that the captain had found himself in a similar quandary when Sable had pleaded with him to be taken ashore.

"If m'lady wishes to do some shopping," he pronounced gallantly, "then so be it."

The bazaar was separated into alleys and dark, dusty shops opening onto the street. Merchants squatted on damask cushions and smoked their long pipes, their voices rising eagerly when they caught sight of Sable, whose elegant chiffon gown and delicate beauty proclaimed her a lady of considerable wealth.

"Oh, how my mother would love this!" Sable sighed as a bearded merchant scuttled boldly to her side and placed an intricately inlaid box of sandalwood into her hands. She shook her head sadly at his inquiring look, but he refused to take it back, unleashing a string of rhetoric and gesturing that she was to keep it.

"I can't," Sable told him in English, though she knew perfectly well that he couldn't understand her. "I haven't any money."

Even before she finished speaking she saw a copper coin fly from Daniel's hand into that of the merchant, who, quick as a ferret, tucked it into the folds of his robe and withdrew into the smoky interior of his shop. Dismayed, Sable whirled to confront her companion.

"Oh, Mr. Hayes, you shouldn't have! I've no way of paying you back!"

"Consider it a gift."

"I can't," Sable said firmly, knowing that the young man lived on a very frugal salary.

"You'd deprive Lady Monterrey of such a wonderful gift?" Daniel chided. "Truly, my lady, you're more stubborn than the captain himself!"

"Oh, all right," Sable conceded with an exasperated smile. "I'll consider it a loan until my brother pays you back."

"Done," Daniel said gaily. "Let's see if we can't find this brother of yours a silver dagger, and how about an amber pipe for Lord Monterrey?"

Sable couldn't help but be caught up in his enthusiasm. How unlike Sir Morgan this kind-natured young man was! In his presence she felt safe and happy, and he reminded her quite a bit of Edward with his shock of unruly hair and laughing eyes. An acute wave of homesickness washed over her unexpectedly, and Sable felt tears smart her eyes. North Head lay half a world away and more out of reach to her at the moment than the remotest of stars. Would she ever come to know again the peace of mind she had enjoyed there with her loved ones, or would she be a prisoner forever of the tormented longings Morgan Carey had so carelessly aroused within her?

"Are you tired, Lady Sable?" Daniel asked suddenly, noticing how pale she had grown.

"Perhaps a little," she confessed.

"Then we'd better go back to the ship."

"Oh, but that isn't necessary!" Sable protested. "There's so much left to see!"

Daniel shook his head, worried that she might plead with him, for he knew he was no match for the beguiling lure of her leaf-green eyes. "Captain Sir Morgan gave strict orders that you were to be taken back to the ship if you grew fatigued."

Sable's lips tightened mutinously. "I'm not a child, Mr. Hayes, and I feel perfectly fine. Furthermore I doubt Sir Morgan will allow me leave to come ashore again. I want to see everything now, particularly the mosques."

Daniel sighed, aware that he was lost. "Very well, m'lady."

Feeling giddy with their freedom, the pleasant young officer and the beautiful, green-eyed girl strolled arm in arm from the bazaar. At Sable's request they paused for a while to watch the crowds come and go across Galata Bridge, exclaiming over the dark-skinned Moors in their flowing gilt robes and the jeweled tack of their prancing Arab horses. Gaily dressed palace ladies in white veils rumbled by in gold-trimmed carriages, and devout pilgrims from Persia and Arabia, who had come to pray in the holy mosques, tossed coppers to the Gypsies begging along the waterfront.

Daniel bartered for a succulent orange from a bridge vendor, handing it to Sable with a flourishing bow, and tried to think when he had ever been this happy. As the son of a blacksmith in faraway Yorkshire, he had long dreamed of a better life than that spent in a dark, smoky smithy, and his mother, anxious to give her only son every chance, had scraped together enough from her meager earnings as a seamstress to send him to school. With hard work Daniel had excelled and his dream had become reality when he joined the Queen's Navy upon graduating.

Two years later the dream had been shattered. Framed by an unscrupulous rival officer for a theft he had never committed, Daniel had been tried, found guilty, and slated for imprisonment. His career all but ruined, he had been set free on the recognizance of Sir Morgan Carey, who was outfitting his ship at the time and had heard of the boy's dilemma through a close friend who also happened to be young Hayes's former senior officer. Daniel had never forgotten the faith the tall sea captain had put in him, a disgraced midshipman with the stamp of a thief upon him.

Though Daniel might fear his captain, he knew that he owed more than his life to him. Not only had Sir Morgan saved him from imprisonment, perhaps even a trip to the gallows, but he had also eventually brought the real thief to justice and cleared his own name. Yet none of that could compare at the moment with Sir Morgan's generosity in allowing Daniel to spend an entire day alone in the company of Lady Sable St. Germain. Needless to say, Daniel was head over ears in love with her,

and his happiness was complete when Sable thanked him for
the fruit he had purchased for her by smiling up at him shyly,
convincing him that paradise lurked in the shining emerald
depths of her eyes.

"I can't remember when I've enjoyed myself this much,"
Sable sighed, echoing Daniel's thoughts as they started back
to the ship hours later. They had viewed the impressively glittering facade of the Blue Mosque and the towering grandeur
of the Hagia Sophia. To Sable's disappointment neither house
of worship was open to Christians who did not possess a firman,
the special license required to obtain entry. She had nonetheless
been awed by the soaring marble columns and sparkling tile
mosaics visible from the courtyard outside. The sheer size of
the fourth-century Hagia Sophia had particularly impressed her,
especially since it had been so beautifully restored by a pair of
Swiss architects less than thirty years ago.

They could talk of little else as they started back to the
harbor, leaving the magnificent edifice behind. The afternoon
was beginning to wane, and small caravans of camels were
leaving the bazaars while shopkeepers began to make preparations to close. Boisterous children played in the alleys and
the spicy scent of cooking hung in the air.

"I imagine we'd better be getting back," Daniel said reluctantly, consulting his pocket watch.

Sable nodded, saddened that her temporary freedom was at
an end. Sir Morgan, she felt certain, would not permit her to
come ashore again. It was so unfair, she thought belligerently.
She wasn't a member of his crew and he had no right to order
her about as though she were. Besides, she wasn't involved in
his foolish scheme to find Sergei Vilyusk and therefore shouldn't
have to be forced to curtail her movements about the city.

"Look, Lady Sable." Daniel's voice interrupted her angry
thoughts. "There's a real Turkish hammam! I was hoping we'd
chance by one. Have you ever heard of them before?"

Sable turned her head to take in the ornate marble structure
on the far side of the street. To her curious eyes it looked far
less impressive than the mosques they had toured earlier that
day, and she told him so. Daniel chuckled in response.

"A hammam is valued for what's inside, m'lady, not its
exterior. It's a public bath," he explained, seeing her blank
look. "For a few coppers you can go inside and be bathed and
massaged and let the steam cure your aches and pains."

"It sounds thoroughly indecent," Sable said disapprovingly. "I've read about Roman bathhouses in history books."

Daniel blushed, thinking to himself that the delicate Lady Sable could at times speak as bluntly as a man. "They're not quite the ... er ... same. The ... ah ... sexes are kept strictly separated, and the sole purpose for being there is to cleanse the body and mind."

"Have you been in one before?" Sable asked curiously.

Daniel nodded self-consciously. "They're actually quite beautiful."

"Do you mean that foreigners are welcomed? You don't need a special license to get inside?"

If Daniel had known her better, he would have recognized and despaired of the calculating look that suddenly entered the forest-green eyes. As it was, he answered blithely, "The only special license you need, m'lady, is the proper amount of money. Just flash them a few coppers and I guarantee you'll get inside regardless of your nationality or religion."

Considering the subject closed, he offered Sable his arm and led her away, but Sable's thoughts lingered on what he had told her. During the voyage she had been forced to make do with the ewer of hot water Grayson brought to her each morning and the scratchy sponge he had managed to dig up from somewhere. Accustomed to the scented baths she had taken regularly at North Head, Sable had begun to hate these impromptu washings and had found herself wishing for a hip bath of her own. Sir Morgan possessed a bath in his quarters, she knew, but she was too stubborn to ask him if she might use it, certain that he would refuse.

Well, then, why not pay a visit to this Turkish hammam? The thought of luxuriating in the steam room that Daniel had described sounded like heaven to her. If foreigners were welcomed she ought to have nothing to fear, and surely Grayson or Daniel could be called upon to lend her the money she'd need to get inside. The only obstacle to this plan was Morgan, and Sable suspected immediately that he would refuse to let her go. Her soft lips tightened in determination, for she hated the way he controlled her life. She was Lady Sable St. Germain, after all, daughter of the Earl of Monterrey, and not one of Sir Morgan Carey's obedient deckhands. She had no more cause to answer to him than he had to order her about.

"You're very quiet, Lady Sable," Daniel observed, peering

worriedly into her small face. "Are you fatigued?"

She smiled at him brightly, causing his heart to beat faster. "Not at all, Mr. Hayes. In fact, I feel marvelous."

She did at that, Daniel thought to himself, if one could judge by her looks. A rosy stain had crept to her cheeks and her eyes sparkled like the sea on a sun-kissed morning. There was a jaunty spring to her step as she moved along the street beside him that he hadn't noticed before, and he attributed this change to the fact that she had finally been able to rid herself of the restlessness that had doubtless been plaguing her since her recovery from the fever. He resolved to speak to the captain and request permission to take her out again, perhaps on a ferry ride across the Golden Horn. Surely the captain wouldn't refuse after he saw how well this day's outing had become her.

If poor Daniel had been able to surmise the plans whirling in Sable's brain, he would have been far less confident, even horrified by what she intended to do. As it was, he remained blissfully unaware, and when he helped her back into the small rowboat that would take them back to the *Defiance*, he could scarcely wait to approach Captain Sir Morgan with his request.

Chapter 10

"Would you care for more tea, your ladyship?"

Sable looked up with a start to find Grayson hovering over her with the silver teapot in one hand, an inquiring look upon his pleasant features. Idly she stared down at her cup to find the untouched contents cold.

"Thank you, no," she said softly.

Grayson nodded and left her, inwardly enraged at Captain Sir Morgan, who was quite obviously responsible for Lady Sable's present unhappiness. It had been sunset when Daniel Hayes had finally returned Lady Sable to the ship yesterday, to be confronted near the gangway by the captain himself. Sir Morgan's black scowl had only served to make him look larger and more intimidating than ever in the young officer's eyes.

In an ominous tone Sir Morgan had pointed out to them that Lady Sable should have been brought back hours ago and that as a result Daniel was being placed on report. When Sable had attempted to speak up on Daniel's behalf, Sir Morgan had informed her coldly that he was heartily tired of her own lack of respect in following his orders and that she was confined to her quarters for the next three days. Sable had protested hotly and Grayson's original belief that the captain's anger was born from concern died when Morgan had dragged her below and personally locked her in.

Grayson had gone down to her cabin later that evening with a tray in his hands, but the sound of Sable's muffled weeping from beyond the thin door had brought him up short. His hesitation had cost Sable her supper, for Sir Morgan had appeared in the doorway of his own cabin at that moment and coldly informed his indignant steward that Lady Sable was to receive nothing to eat that night.

Bringing Sable her breakfast the following morning, Grayson had found her subdued, her beautiful eyes still reddened from the tears she had shed the night before. He had made a half-hearted attempt to excuse Sir Morgan's cruelty, but Sable had laughed at him bitterly.

"He has no heart at all and you know it, Grayson. Judas, if I didn't like you so much, I vow I'd hate you for being so loyal to him!"

She instantly regretted her unkind words, but Grayson had brushed aside her choked apology, returning a half-hour later to find her breakfast untouched. Taking the tray back to the galley, he wondered if it would help Lady Sable if he personally asked Sir Morgan to revoke his harsh punishment. Three days of confinement in that tiny cubicle? The poor lass would go mad, Grayson worried, yet he decided that it would do little good to plead with his master on her behalf. Sir Morgan had given an order and it had better not be questioned lest one cared to evoke the sea captain's terrible wrath. Furthermore the captain had gone to the Russian embassy earlier that morning, and Grayson had no idea when he planned to return.

The ship, anchored in the placid blue waters of the Golden Horn, seemed curiously empty that day without the fair Lady Sable to grace its polished decks. Those crewmen who had remained behind grumbled at the captain's unfairness and wondered why his punishment had been so severe. A demanding and difficult taskmaster Captain Sir Morgan might be, but he was never unjust, and his men saw Lady Sable's three-day confinement as an unfair sentence for the crime of being several hours late.

Sable would have heartily agreed with their sentiments if she had known of them, and when the second day rolled by in a nerve-jangling succession of monotonous hours, she began to grow angry. What right did Sir Morgan have to do this to her? Never in her life had she been locked in like a common criminal! It would serve him right if she escaped and he was forced to face her father's wrath when the Earl learned that he had lost his daughter somewhere in the crowded streets of Istanbul!

Sable's eyes lit up. Why not? she asked herself, boredom and anger at Morgan Carey firing her determination. She wouldn't actually run away, but wouldn't it be fitting if she gave him the scare of his life by slipping away for several hours while he turned the city upside down looking for her? That ought to teach the blackguard not to abuse her, she thought nastily, and just to sweeten her own revenge, she would spend the "harrowing hours" of her disappearance luxuriating in the splendor of the baths Daniel Hayes had told her about!

The idea seemed too good to abandon, and Sable set about at once plotting how she might succeed. She immediately dismissed the thought of enlisting Grayson's help, for she didn't want anyone to be punished because of her, and she still chafed when she thought of what had happened to poor Daniel. It had been at her insistence, after all, that they had lingered in the city!

A determined smile curved Sable's lips. Once she got out of her cabin she would hail a caique oarsman from the deck of the ship while the watch was being changed, and the rest would be easy. It would serve Sir Morgan bloody right if he were to believe for a few hours that he had lost her.

Grayson was pleasantly surprised when he brought Sable her luncheon several hours later and discovered that her unhappiness had all but vanished. In fact, she seemed almost cheerful as she welcomed him into her tiny cabin and watched as he set the lunch tray down on the small sea chest at the foot of her bunk.

"Don't worry, I've grown accustomed to eating like this," she remarked blithely when Grayson commented unhappily on the lack of room.

He watched as she struggled to spread her skirts about her on the narrow cot and reach for a sandwich without overturning the mug of lemonade he had set beside it. When she smiled up at him to assure him that she was all right, he felt his heart turn over. How could she remain so cheerful when Sir Morgan was treating her no better than a prisoner?

"Lady Sable, wouldn't you prefer to eat up on deck?" he

asked impulsively. "It's a lovely day, not a cloud in the sky, and I know how much you love sitting in the sun."

Sable's heart leaped, but she couldn't permit Grayson to become even an unwitting accomplice in her escape. "Oh, I couldn't. The captain would be furious."

"Sir Morgan will be gone all day," Grayson informed her with a conspiratorial grin.

It was as if a cold hand suddenly wrapped itself about her heart. What was Morgan up to? Sable wondered anxiously. Seeking information in darkened alleys from sinister-looking men, or perhaps even knocking boldly on the outer portals of the seraglio itself? She thrust these frightening thoughts from her mind, telling herself that she had other worries to deal with at the moment.

"I've been ordered to stay here until tomorrow," she persisted, unwilling to abuse Grayson's kindness.

"The captain need never know," he pointed out, wondering why she was suddenly so reluctant to disobey Sir Morgan's orders when in the past she had enjoyed defying him. "You can stay topside until his launch returns."

"What of the other men?" Sable asked skeptically.

Grayson looked affronted. "Do you think they'd turn you in, your ladyship? You underestimate the friends you have aboard."

Sable struggled with this tempting solution to her first and biggest problem, but her honesty won out. "I'm sorry, Grayson," she said in a sad voice that touched his heart. "I can't allow you to risk being at odds with Captain Sir Morgan because of me."

Grayson shrugged. "I wouldn't worry about that, your ladyship. Sir Morgan and I have been together for so many years that I'm certain he'll forgive me a trespass or two." He winked. "That's provided he ever learns of it."

Sable caught her breath, her eyes on his face. "Do you honestly think so?"

Grayson chuckled. "Even if I did incur the wrath of the Great One, as you so aptly call him, I've naught to fear. Sir Morgan would never dismiss me. I'm the only valet on earth tolerant enough to put up with him."

Sable laughed, her worry appeased. "Very well, then, I'd love to spend a few hours on deck!"

When the skeleton crew Sir Morgan had assigned the afternoon watch saw her appear, they hastened over to greet her. Sable was surprised to find that she was just as glad to see them, and she wasted a precious half-hour laughing and chatting with them before they returned to their posts. When she was finally alone, she hurried belowdecks, her heart hammering nervously as she opened the door to Morgan's quarters.

The familiar scent of him assailed her senses as soon as she stepped inside, and she tried to ignore the masculine attributes of his personal possessions that lay scattered across the spacious room. She found his desk unlocked and pulled open the drawer with trembling fingers. She had never stolen anything from anyone, and she had to force herself to tuck the handful of coins she found into her bodice. She tried telling herself that it wasn't vindictiveness that prompted her to do this, but she was feeling decidedly less sure of herself when she came back on deck.

By now intimately acquainted with the daily routine aboard the enormous clipper, Sable slipped to the port rail, knowing that Gordon Masters wouldn't round the far corner of the great cabin for at least another ten minutes. She might have abandoned her plan altogether if she hadn't spotted a caique gliding through the water not twenty feet away from the hull, the black-eyed oarsman looking up at her as though he had been waiting for her all along.

Using the few words of broken Turkish Sable had learned from Daniel Hayes, she made him understand that she wished to be taken ashore. Grinning widely, his white teeth flashing in his dark face, the oarsman watched as she negotiated the difficult ladder and then helped her down into the boat. Sable was panting and her heart hammered as she leaned against the cushions. At any moment she expected to hear a shout of alarm from the ship behind her, but the *Defiance* remained silent as the span of shimmering water between them lengthened.

Sable had expected to be the object of numerous stares when she finally came ashore and started alone up the crowded, twisting streets of Stamboul. To her relief no one paid the least bit of attention to her. It was midafternoon and all orthodox Moslems in the city had begun another set of daily prayers. The faithful sat with their eyes closed on the sun-baked walks, their prayer blankets facing Mecca, and Sable was able to hurry past them, her slippers making no sound. Only the beggar children playing in the streets grew silent as this ebony-haired young woman came by, and though they eyed her with solemn, insolent expressions, no one ventured to speak with her.

It was a simple task for Sable to retrace her steps to the entrance of the hammam Daniel had pointed out to her yesterday. Once she was standing before the carved marble portico, however, her courage failed her and she began to doubt her decision to come. Daniel had assured her the public baths were frequented by women, Turkish and European alike, and that she had nothing to fear, yet she could not force herself to go in.

As Sable hesitated, one of the doors of the bath flew open and a bowing attendant in flowing robes escorted out a pair of turbaned businessmen in long coats and proper European trousers. When they were gone, his almond eyes fell on Sable, who hovered uncertainly in the doorway, and with an encouraging hand beneath her elbow he led her inside. The abrupt change from glaring sunlight to darkness left Sable temporarily blinded. Another attendant had appeared at her side, and she could hear the soft, musical exchange of the Turkish tongue.

By the time Sable's eyes had adjusted to the weak light her fears had vanished, and when the woman attendant smiled at her shyly and beckoned her to follow, Sable did so. She was led into a small anteroom with recessed benches lined with cushions, in which light was provided by glazed glass set in arched windows. A tea service of hammered silver stood warming on a brazier in the corner, filling the air with minty fragrance.

"Camekan," the attendant said, spreading her arms wide to encompass the entire room.

"I beg your pardon?" Sable asked, beginning to feel foolish. She had no idea what was expected of her. Why had she ever decided she wanted to come here, especially if it meant provoking Morgan Carey's volatile temper?

"Dr-dressing room," the attendant qualified in heavily accented English and beamed when she saw that Sable had understood. "Please?" she added, indicating that Sable was to remove her clothes.

Sable felt herself growing self-conscious as the magnificent chiffon gown and her lace petticoats and undergarments were stripped off with the help of the Turkish woman. Yet her embarrassment faded quickly at the other's casual manner, and when she was completely naked a long, luxurious towel was deferentially wrapped about her. Offered tea, Sable accepted with a nod, not wanting to rush through what she felt certain was going to be a unique experience. Through the narrow passage beyond the dressing room she could hear the musical sound of running water and feel the warmth of the steam that hung in the air. Reclining on a cushion with her feet tucked beneath her, she closed her eyes, unable to recall when she had last known such peace.

Morgan Carey swore as he pushed his way through the crowded dining room of the Lotus Blossom, one of the few hotels that had been erected in Pera for the comfort of European travelers. *Comfort* was a bloody inappropriate word, Morgan thought irritably to himself. Even the primitive villages of the African continent had sported cleaner khans than this.

The overweight proprietor of the Lotus Blossom hurried over as Morgan seated himself in a darkened corner, sweating profusely in his shirtsleeves and soiled apron. In a foul mood, Morgan was hard put to be civil as he ordered a single ale. Though he was hungry he knew it would be wiser to wait until he had returned to the ship, where Grayson would have a wholesome meal prepared for him. No telling what form of plague he'd be risking if he ate something here.

A pair of drunken sailors eyed the silent sea captain from their nearby table, but when he turned a baleful gaze upon them they looked quickly away. Morgan's lips twitched. If trouble was what they were looking for, they'd certainly have no difficulty finding it in him. He was in a black frame of mind and wouldn't object to unleashing some of his pent-up frustrations by bashing in a few heads. Apparently the drunks had second thoughts for they left him in peace, which was just as well, Morgan decided, sipping the warm, sour ale without noticing its taste.

He had again spent the entire morning at the Russian embassy, but none of the inept attachés he had spoken to had professed any knowledge of a pair of countrymen being held prisoner in the Sultan's palace. Judging from their baffled expressions, Morgan had been forced to believe them. The information he had received from the Turkish sea captain in Dakar had been reliable, of that he was certain, and the fact that the Russian embassy was ignorant of their presence made him suspicious. Why had the Sultan hidden them away for so many years? Of what use were two young officers of the Russian army?

Morgan growled low in his throat, causing the nearby patrons to glance at him nervously. An Englishwoman in loud scarlet bombazine sitting beside her husband insisted in a frightened whisper that they move to a table farther away. Morgan smiled at them unpleasantly as they scurried past him. Let them think he was some sort of deranged individual; at least then he'd be left alone with his thoughts.

What to do to gain the information he sought? he asked himself impatiently. And how much longer would he have to wait before the Sultan deigned to receive him? He found his problems compounded at the moment by Sable St. Germain's rebellious behavior and the annoying twinge of his conscience whenever he thought of her locked in her tiny, airless cabin. How she had blossomed in the warm Asiatic sunshine, and how unfair it had been of him to place her under house arrest! Morgan growled again, telling himself irritably that he was starting to sound just like his meddlesome valet. Sable had deserved to be punished for disobeying his orders. She had to learn that the streets of Istanbul were not the safe, manicured parks of her beloved North Head.

"Captain?"

Morgan looked up to see his first mate standing by the table. The small Devonshire man's unusual eyes were glowing, and Morgan uncrossed his long legs and leaned forward.

"What've you found?"

"Probably just what we need," the grizzled officer replied smugly. "Tankard of ale, please," he told the perspiring innkeeper who huffed over to him. The din in the darkened room made it easy for him to speak frankly, but he lowered his voice nonetheless and stared straight back into his captain's glittering blue eyes.

"Ever hear of the Society of New Ottomans?"

Morgan's brows grew together. "The Young Turks? Aye. Fasir Nanak told me about them."

Both men smiled reminiscently as they thought of the colorful saber-carrying Turk who had briefly joined their ranks two years ago. After the *Defiance* had ended its short career in the American conflict, it had sailed throughout the length of Asia and the Orient in search of new diversions. It was Morgan who had saved the silver-bearded Turk from a gang of cutthroats in

Bahrain and had graciously fulfilled his request to be returned
to Ankara. Fasir, a soldier of fortune and an ardent activist,
had proven an entertaining guest aboard the clipper, especially,
as Morgan remembered, on the night Fasir had tried to rob him
of the pouch of gold coins he kept in his sea chest.

The two men had fought a panting, rousing half-hour of
hand-to-hand combat and afterward, bloodied and disheveled,
had drunk one another a toast. Morgan had been sorry to see
the lusty thief go, especially after Fasir had reluctantly turned
down the Englishman's offer to join on with the *Defiance*'s
crew. Politics, not the sea, was the bearded Turk's passion,
and Morgan had known even then that he was already deeply
embroiled in a plot against the Sultan. He had been genuinely
saddened to hear of Fasir's death a year ago in a knife brawl
over the virtue of the wife of some obscure Arab sheikh.

"For a member of a secret society, Fasir had quite a rattling
tongue," Morgan remembered with a grin.

"And that may be why he was killed," Jack mused, taking
a deep pull from his mug and making a face at the taste of the
ale. "That story about the Arab woman might've been a cover
for the more sordid truth."

Morgan made an impatient gesture. "It's still the past, Jack,
whatever the reason behind his death. I'm not planning to get
involved with Fasir's former colleagues, either. I want to find
Sergei and get him out of here."

"Then I'm afraid you've no choice but to get involved with
them," Jack said.

Morgan scowled. "The New Ottomans were trying to trans-
form the government into a constitutional monarchy when Fasir
was a member. They also had plans for bettering the treatment
of Christian subjects in the Empire."

"Aye, and as far as I know they're still working at it," Jack
informed him.

Morgan's scowl deepened. "That doesn't have much to do
with us, Jack. Exactly how much contact have you had with
these people?"

Jack spread his hands. "Just enough to learn a few interesting
facts." He sobered and regarded his captain intently. "Your
name isn't unknown in these parts, cap'n. Apparently Fasir's
rattling tongue carried it to Namik Kemal, prime motivator of
the New Ottomans, who seems not to have forgotten it. He
was curious as to what brought us to Istanbul, and the two of

us had a pleasant meeting about an hour ago." It was not Jack's
way to praise himself, but he couldn't keep the pleased grin
from his face. "Kemal was kind enough to tell me, after he
learned what you was after, that he has eyes and ears throughout
the Sultan's palace."

Morgan set his tankard aside and regarded his first mate
sharply. "Well, then, what did you find out?"

Jack flashed another of his rare smiles. "That there be two
Russians being kept at Abdülaziz's court, cap'n. One of them
was a major in the Crimean War who supposedly knew a lot
of Russian military strategy. The other is his lieutenant, Sergei
Vilyusk. As far as Namik Kemal knew, they've been held
prisoner by the Sultan since the war ended."

"Surely a pair of minor Russian officers couldn't have been
very useful to the Sultan of Turkey!" Morgan protested.

"They was originally intended to be used as pawns in case
Mother Russia didn't keep the peace accords. Afterward they
were thrown in prison and, I imagine, forgotten."

"And now?" Morgan asked impatiently.

"The Major's health is supposedly failing, and since relations with Russia have been improving, word has it the Vizier
be petitioning for their deaths, to get rid of this potential embarrassment to the Sultan's court."

"Then we haven't much time," Morgan said bluntly. His
steely eyes bored into his first mate's. "What does Kemal want
in exchange for this information?" he asked, knowing that
nothing as valuable as this ever came without a price.

Jack's grin widened. "What do all revolutionaries have in
common, cap'n, be they Turks, Indian, or Spanish scum?
They're all poor as church mice. It be money Kemal wants,
and after the payment's made we'll deal with 'em no more."

The chair scraped across the uneven floor as Morgan rose
abruptly to his feet. "Very well, Jack. You'll make the arrangements to see the debt is settled. Did Kemal know where Sergei
and the Major have been imprisoned?"

"Aye, cap'n, but that's a secret what will keep till the money
changes hands."

Morgan's lips tightened grimly. "See to it they receive it."

"Aye, aye, sir."

Out in the street the air was warm and humid. The sun was
beginning to set, and in an hour's time the gates in the wall

along the Golden Horn would be closed for the night. Morgan paused for a moment along the battlement that separated the street in front of the Lotus Blossom from the plummeting drop of the hillside upon which the hotel had been built. From here he had an uninterrupted view of the city, the minarets gleaming with a radiance of their own in the setting sun. The Golden Horn was awash with color, and his keen eyes picked out the familiar lines of the *Defiance* lying serenely at anchor below Galata Bridge.

The thought that Sable was aboard his ship right now gave him a curiously warm feeling that calmed some of the turmoil within him. Turning, he found the first mate's oddly colored eyes upon him and he wondered fleetingly if his thoughts could be read in his face.

Smiling ruefully, he slapped his first mate on the back. "Come on, man. Let's get back to the ship."

"Captain Carey, sir!"

Morgan turned, astonished to find a small delegation of men led by Nat Palmer hurrying up the slope toward them. Nat was perspiring heavily, his sandy hair clinging damply to his forehead.

"What the hell is this?" Morgan asked irritably. "You men were to return to the ship after you'd finished your business here."

"Aye, sir," Nat said hastily, wiping his face on his shirt sleeve. "But we were met by Mr. Grayson an' Harley Gump on the wharf."

Morgan propped his hands on his hips. "What in hell is Grayson doing ashore?" he demanded, thinking he'd like to keel-haul every one of his men just to show them what he thought of their slackening discipline.

"It be Lady Sable, sir," Nat panted. "She be gone!"

"Gone?" Morgan repeated softly. "What do you mean, gone?"

"Just that! Mr. Grayson said he'd let her come up for a bit of air and she just vanished. They turned the whole ship upside down and couldn't find a trace of her."

For one heart-stopping second Morgan recalled Sable's tearful threat to throw herself into the sea to escape the misery of being his prisoner, and his mind rebelled against such a terrible possibility. Sable was too strong-willed to take such a cowardly way out!

"Do you have any idea where she might have gone?" Morgan asked in a voice that caused his men to glance at one another uneasily.

"They found the caique oarsman what took her ashore," Nat replied, eager to impart some hopeful news to his captain, who was looking ready to murder every one of them with his bare hands. "He said she took off west, but that's all he knew. Mr. Grayson questioned him closely."

"We've got three parties lookin' for her now, captain," Dr. Pierson chimed in. Wan and miserable, he had just panted up the hill behind Nat Palmer's group.

Morgan glanced up at the sun which hovered like a shimmering crimson orb above the foothills of Asia. "You've got until curfew to find her," he said bluntly, but it was enough to send his men off at a run in the direction they'd come. Only Jack Torance lingered behind, watching as Morgan strode across the Lotus Blossom's weed-choked courtyard, his expression grim.

"Shall I go with you, cap'n?" he called out at last.

"No," Morgan replied without sparing him a glance. "You've been given your orders, Jack. I'll find her on my own."

It took quite a bit of searching and a small fortune in palm-greasing before Morgan finally hit upon Sable's trail. His anger mounted as he followed the directions of curious natives down one narrow alley after another. Where in God's name was the wench going? he asked himself after pausing and questioning a one-eyed beggar reclining on a filthy prayer mat.

The beggar nodded emphatically when asked if he'd seen a dark-haired Englishwoman pass this way, but his confidence faltered when Morgan suspiciously demanded that he describe her. It was obvious that the man was lying when he talked expansively of a lady clad in a gown of finest blue silk, the bodice embroidered with precious gemstones. Quelling the desire to lift the man off his feet and snap his neck in two, Morgan turned away, his mood growing even blacker. Damn the troublesome chit! Where was she?

"Perhaps I can find the woman you seek," came a sibilant whisper from a darkened doorway.

Morgan paused, his eyes searching the shadows. "Come out here," he ordered. "I'm not playing games."

He heard the rustle of robes, and then a broken-toothed old man leaning heavily on a cane emerged into the waning sunlight. "I saw this woman you asked Ramun to describe. Pah!" He spat contemptuously into the dusty street. "The man is a liar without equal!" In broken English he added craftily, "She was wearing a gown the color of spun gold and her eyes were the sloping green of a cat's."

"Where did you see her?" Morgan demanded.

The old man hesitated, and Morgan reached impatiently into his pocket.

"She went into the Kizhruk baths," the Turk said quickly, pleased by the number of coppers Morgan thrust into his gnarled hand.

Without another word Morgan started off down the street, his hawkish features set with ruthless determination.

Sable sighed deeply and opened her eyes, studying the holes in the domed marble ceiling above her. Cut in the shape of stars, they allowed the sunlight to filter into the room and illuminate the gray-veined marble columns in iridescent green light. For almost an hour Sable had been reclining on a hexagonal slab of smooth marble that was heated from below, allowing the warmth to soothe her. Her mind had drifted pleasantly, and she had been able to forget for a time the troubles that had weighed so heavily upon her shoulders since Morgan Carey had brought her aboard his ship.

The bath had been relatively empty since her arrival, which had pleased her enormously. Several Turkish women had spent a half-hour in one of the privacy alcoves earlier, but had ignored Sable completely and left soon thereafter. The attendant, sensing Sable wished to be left alone, had withdrawn to the dressing room, indicating in her heavily accented English that the young mistress should call if anything was wished.

Stretching like a cat, Sable rose at last and seated herself beside a marble basin from which water flowed through bronze taps. Using a towel and copper ladle, she washed herself, luxuriating in the splendor that surrounded her and the tingling cleanliness of her naked body. She couldn't remember when she had ever felt this sensuously warm and drowsy. Even that long-legged scoundrel Morgan Carey couldn't annoy her today, she thought to herself, and a look of sadness and yearning passed across her lovely face. In fact, she almost wished . . .

She caught at her lower lip with her small white teeth. What did she almost wish? That Morgan were here, beside her, gazing down at her with those smoldering blue eyes that always made her feel so weak? She must be mad!

"Sable!"

She shot to her feet, her silky hair flying back from her face to settle about her naked shoulders. With wide eyes she stared down the arching marble passage. That couldn't have been Morgan's angry voice, she told herself uneasily, and surely the vaulted ceiling and cloak of swirling steam must have muted and distorted the name she had heard.

"Sable, by God, I know you're here!"

But it *was* Morgan Carey storming down the passage toward her. Like a battle-crazed warrior he burst into the chamber, the frightened attendant protesting feebly behind him.

"There's no need to shout, Morgan, I can hear you."

He froze at the sound of Sable's clear voice. Like a gossamer veil the swirling mist suddenly lifted to reveal her standing there. Though she held a towel in her hands, she made no move to cover herself as her eyes locked with his across the big domed hall.

Sable St. Germain stood naked and unafraid before him, her glistening body cloaked in the mysterious light that reflected from the exotic sculpted marble about her. Droplets of silver water slid down her tapering calves to pool at her tiny feet, and her unbound hair fell to her hips, where it curled softly against her damp skin. Like a pagan goddess she tempted him with her nakedness, her beauty so wild and alluring that he could scarcely believe she was real.

Morgan caught his breath, the rage and fear that had been churning within him since he had learned of Sable's disappearance vanishing abruptly. In its stead rose an unfathomable yet undeniable certainty that he had been waiting for this moment his entire life.

Sable continued to gaze at him without speaking, her small chin lifted as she met the bold challenge beginning to burn in his eyes. She was breathless and tensed like a graceful deer ready to spring, but there was no fear within her. She was in the grip of a heady excitement, primal and without denial, that went far beyond the first kiss Morgan had ever given her on the dark balcony in London and far beyond the times he had held her to him and she had felt his manhood rising hot and ready against her silken thighs.

Her body throbbed and she found herself yearning for love

and for Morgan in a way that went beyond her innocent com-
prehension. She knew that the emotions within her were as
vital to her as the need to breathe.

"Morgan," Sable whispered, his name blending with the
musical running of the water. Her eyes had been made dark
and sultry by the radiant green of the marble surrounding her,
and in them shone the soft, unmistakable invitation of a woman.

Morgan moved closer until he was standing directly before
her, and she had to tilt back her head in order to look into his
rugged face. His finely chiseled lips were curved into a smile
that held no anger or mockery, while his eyes blazed with the
promise of what was to come. Sighing, Sable unconsciously
raised her mouth to his, her gold-dusted lashes fanning her
cheeks as she closed her eyes in anticipation.

Behind them the attendant slipped unnoticed down the passage, softly shutting the door to the dressing room. In her pocket
she could hear the satisfying clink of the coins the dark-headed
Englishman had given her when she had adamantly refused
him entry to the baths. She felt certain there would be more
forthcoming if the young couple remained undisturbed, and
with a determined little smile she slid the bolt on the outside
door and settled down to wait.

"I thought you had eluded me forever, my sweet enchantress," Morgan was murmuring huskily, gazing hungrily into
Sable's heavy-lidded eyes. When he slid his hands over her
curving hips she shivered in response. Drawing her body between his legs he covered her mouth with his, the exotic scent
of her enveloping him. He kissed her deeply, his senses swimming until the wild beating of her heart matched the throbbing
of the blood in his veins.

Morgan's hands boldly found her breasts and Sable's world
tilted alarmingly. She sank against him, her nipples taut beneath
his palms. She opened herself to his kiss while he drank deeply
of her sweetness, both of them drawn toward the ultimate union,
not only of their bodies, but of their very souls.

Gently Morgan laid Sable back against the smooth stones,
his blue eyes smoldering with unfulfilled passion. He shuddered
as she trailed her fingers in a soft, whispery caress across the
glistening expanse of his sun-bronzed chest. Her eyes were soft
and filled with the need to experience the sweet mystery she
knew lay between them. She trembled with anticipation as
Morgan's magnificent body was revealed to her, his manhood

made bold with desire for her, and she closed her eyes as he lifted her into his arms, letting her feel the hard length of him against her.

"God, how I've wanted you, my green-eyed sea witch," Morgan murmured into her ear, his lips leaving a trail of burning kisses down her throat. "But you've known that all along, haven't you? It's why you've delighted in tormenting me, strutting about my ship like a cocky young gentleman, your backside swaying provocatively in those damnably tight breeches."

"Morgan," Sable whispered, her voice breathless, the hands that caressed her making her weak with longing. She didn't know what she intended to say. All she knew was that she wanted him, was being driven half mad by his nearness and the hard maleness of his body.

His mouth claimed hers in a bruising kiss, his tongue plundering the soft recesses of her mouth. He growled low in his throat when Sable responded, her slim fingers curving through the dark curls at the nape of his neck. Although he knew her perfect body intimately by now, Morgan explored it slowly, wanting to touch and caress every silken inch of it again. Sable arched against him in response, her firm breasts brushing tantalizingly against his naked chest.

"Sweet, so sweet," Morgan breathed raggedly. Drawing back he peered down into her exquisite face, her eyes holding his, their gold-flecked depths aflame with her need for him.

"I wanted to throttle you for running away from me," he told her roughly, his brow darkening as he recalled how much she had frightened him by disappearing without a trace.

"And now?" Sable whispered, slanting him a saucy look that made his pulses race.

"Now I only want to love you," he murmured, and groaned when she touched him intimately. She had bewitched him, this green-eyed child-woman. He knew it was not the mist and the cool, dancing light touching her body so sensuously that kindled this powerful desire within him. It was Sable alone, her nearness and the scent and taste of her awakening and at the same time fulfilling the driving hunger within him that he had ravaged the earth to satisfy.

Sable knew what lay in his heart and mind. Running her hand down the sleek, muscled length of his spine to his firm buttocks, she could feel the tension within him. Her eyes, when they opened, gazed into his with such answering need that

Morgan knew he could wait no longer. Cradling her head against his arm, he slid her beneath him and, with a searing kiss upon her lips, insinuated himself against her. Sable's silken thighs opened beneath him, the silent invitation unleashing his passion with a fury he had never before experienced. With his lips upon hers Morgan drove deep inside.

Sable gasped at the unexpected pain, her small hands clenching convulsively about Morgan's broad back. He gentled her with words and touch, and as she began to relax he could feel her hips move tentatively beneath him. Morgan's restraint fell away and he thrust deeper, his heart hammering as Sable rose to meet him, her warmth and softness closing about him.

Sable found herself being driven wild by his bold, hard touch. Spreading her silken thighs wider, she met every impassioned thrust, her lips clinging to Morgan's in a searing kiss that knew no end. Fire throbbed through her veins, and she was aware of nothing but the sensations building within her and Morgan above her, his rigid manhood touching her intimately, becoming a part of her.

Morgan's kiss became more urgent and Sable clung to him breathlessly. Her feelings intensified, carrying her higher and higher until she gasped aloud as the world exploded within her head. At that same moment Morgan surged against her, catching her fiercely to him. Their bodies and souls melded as they soared together on a tide of sensation that crested in wave after wave of unbearably exquisite ecstasy.

Gradually Sable felt the dizzily spiraling world begin to steady itself. She relaxed her tight grip about Morgan's powerful neck, although she was loath to break the contact between them. The feel of his chest and muscular thighs pressed against hers was so sweet that she was content to lie beneath him without moving. She could feel his lips leaving feathery kisses across her eyelids, and the fact that their sated bodies were still joined brought a flooding surge of warmth to her heart.

"I love him," Sable thought to herself, and when she gazed at him Morgan felt his heart constrict at the tenderness suffusing the dark green depths of her eyes.

Taking her chin in his hand he allowed his big thumb to caress the curve of her cheek, entranced by the rosy blush that had crept there in response to his lovemaking. Her mouth was swollen from his kisses, and he touched it with his own, its honeyed sweetness unlike anything he had ever tasted.

"Now I know that you cannot be a mortal woman," he said huskily as his manhood stirred within her again, afterglow rekindling into passion by the soft meeting of their lips. "You have enchanted me, my beautiful sea witch, and I fear I'll be your slave forever."

"Is that so terrible a fate?" Sable asked.

"No," Morgan said roughly, surprising himself with his own vehemence. The smoky sensuality in Sable's eyes was making his pulses begin to pound anew, and he brought his hands beneath her hips, shifting her so that his manhood rose taut within her.

Sable slipped her arms about his shoulders, a soft sigh escaping her lips as Morgan pulled her roughly against him.

"My sweet, tempting Sable," he murmured into her hair, and she opened herself to him, her heart beating wildly as she lost herself in the abandon of his love.

Chapter 11

A pink pearlescent dawn stole softly across the horizon. With it came a warm, sweetly scented wind that blew from the East, whispering through the masts of the ship stirring restlessly at anchor. Fiery streaks of sunlight burst into flame upon the minarets and walls of the silent mosques and stole through the shutters of the clipper's stern windows to touch the sleeping face of the young girl lying in their path.

Sable stirred and murmured fretfully, but the fingers of sunlight were unrelenting. Opening her eyes at last, she lifted her head, not exactly sure where she was. Gradually Morgan's spacious cabin came into focus and her gaze fell on the empty bunk, its covers undisturbed. Her heart skipped a beat. It was obvious that Morgan hadn't returned from Stamboul last night. Had he stayed away because of her?

She rose to her feet, stretching her aching limbs and running a hand through her tangled curls. She had hoped to confront him when he retired, had waited patiently as the hours ticked by, and yet he had not returned to the ship at all. She paused before the mirror and peered at her face, and the tear-reddened eyes that looked back at her were those of a stranger.

She could scarcely believe that it was only yesterday that Morgan had found her in the Kizhruk baths and had shown her what it meant to be transported to the heights of ecstasy. Whatever was expected to happen between a man and a woman after they had loved so passionately was of course a mystery to her, but she knew that Morgan's treatment of her since then had not been natural. She swallowed hard, recalling how grim and silent he had grown as he had ushered her out into the deserted streets. Looking up into his hawkish profile, Sable had scarcely been able to believe that those compressed lips had claimed hers so passionately only a short while ago, and she wondered what she had done to destroy the sweet intimacy between them.

Nat Palmer and Harley Gump had been standing on guard at the wharf when they arrived, and Morgan had given Nat terse orders to row Sable back to the ship. She had cast an appealing glance at him but had seen only indifference in those hard blue eyes. Biting her lips to keep from crying, she had allowed Nat to help her into the boat and hadn't looked back as they rowed away.

Where could he have gone? Sable wondered now as she wandered about the cabin, idly touching possessions of Morgan's that lay scattered about. If only she knew the right words to say to him so that his coldness would vanish and he would once again look at her as he had the night before! Her breath caught in her throat, recalling the gentle hands and ardent lips that had left her yearning for him and how sweetly Morgan had satisfied that longing within her.

"What the devil are you doing here?"

Completely caught off guard, Sable whirled about to find Morgan on the threshold, a scowl crossing his face at the sight of her. "I-I was waiting for you to return," she stammered, "and I must have fallen asleep."

"In that chair?" Morgan asked disbelievingly, eyeing her wrinkled clothes.

"I didn't know you'd stay away all night," Sable reminded him defensively.

Morgan strode inside and pulled off his coat, tossing it unceremoniously onto the bunk. "There was business I had to attend to that took me longer than I expected. Now, what is it you wanted to talk to me about?"

Sable bit her lip as she eyed his broad back, then blurted out bravely, "What happened in the baths."

She saw Morgan's shoulders stiffen in response to her words. For a moment he didn't move, then he turned slowly and she flinched at the look on his handsome face. "It never should have happened," he told her shortly.

"But it did!" Sable burst out.

Morgan stood looking down at her with an expression of mingled mockery and annoyance. "Aye, it did," he agreed finally. "What do you want me to do about it?"

She stared at him in bewilderment. "I just want to know why you're so angry with me. What have I done to justify the way you treated me when we got back to the harbor?"

Morgan turned away and began unbuttoning his shirt with studied indifference. "Surely you didn't expect me to vow my eternal devotion or, better, offer for your hand as you thought I had done in Cornwall weeks ago?"

Sable's sharp intake of breath informed him that his words had found their mark. He turned slowly and looked down into her upturned face with a pitying air. "I'm sorry it happened, Sable," he said, "especially after I'd given my word it would not, and because I happen to think very highly of your father."

Sable's eyes widened. "Is that what troubles you?" she whispered in disbelief. "The fact that you've compromised the daughter of the Earl of Monterrey? What about me? Don't my feelings matter to you at all?"

She hated the impatience she saw in his eyes. It was as though he were trying to calm a fretful child. "In your innocence I'm afraid there's something you didn't know. Lovemaking to a man, Sable, is usually quite a casual experience, to be enjoyed for the moment and dismissed once it's over. It's certainly never to be taken as anything of significance."

Sable stifled the soft gasp that rose to her lips. For a moment he thought she would fly at him, but even as he steeled himself to ward off her tiny fists she lifted her face to his, and he was caught off guard by the look in her eyes. Instinctively he reached for her, but she recoiled as though he had struck her.

"For God's sake, Sable—"

"Good morning, sir! I've brought your breakfast, and Gilpin should be up directly with your bath water. I—oh, excuse me, your ladyship."

Sable swallowed hard. "It's all right, Grayson, I was just leaving." Lifting her skirts, she swept out, her slim shoulders stiff, and Grayson could not tell from the tone of her voice how terribly she was suffering within. He could not, however, ignore the tension that lingered in the air or the look on the captain's face as Morgan watched her go.

"Coffee, sir?" Grayson asked with as much indifference as he could muster.

"I'll help myself," Morgan growled. "Get out."

Grayson obeyed without another word, knowing it would prove unwise to linger. Closing the door softly behind him, he retreated down the corridor and paused uncertainly before Lady Sable's small cabin. Lifting his hand to knock, he froze when he heard the muffled sound of her sobs from within. He had no right to interfere in this, he knew and turned away, yet his heart was heavy as he made his way back to the galley.

Something had happened between the two of them since Lady Sable's disappearance from the ship yesterday, something that obviously had deeply affected not only Lady Sable but Sir Morgan, too. He wished there were something he could do to help, sensing that the rift between them was irreparable, but what could he do? The cards had been drawn the night the *Defiance* had pulled Sable St. Germain from the water, and he could no more change fate than alter the circumstances that had brought Sable and Morgan Carey together in the first place.

When Morgan appeared on deck an hour later, the men on watch, seeing his black expression, gave their reports in subdued tones and did their best to hide their relief when they were dismissed. The young officer at the helm snapped to attention and respectfully turned the wheel over to him, his Adam's apple bobbing nervously. Morgan took it without a word, and it was clear to all of his men that they had best avoid him lest they were willing to incur his terrible wrath. For that reason it was with hesitant steps that Daniel Hayes ascended the ladder a short time later and stood waiting stiffly for Morgan to notice him.

"What is it, Hayes?" Morgan asked at last, turning his head to regard the younger man.

Daniel's gaze slid from the glittering blue eyes. As cold as death they were, he thought with a shiver. What had set the captain off this time? He didn't think he'd ever seen him look quite this mean!

"Mr. Torance said to send word to you, sir. There's a boat coming this way that looks as if it might belong to the Sultan's fleet."

Wordlessly Morgan took the offered telescope and trained it on the small craft that was heading toward them under full sail. The royal seal on her surging bow was easily discernible through the sunlight, and the plush vermilion cushions and silk-trimmed sails were obvious signs of extravagance—a trait Sultan Abdülaziz was well known for.

"Mr. Torance thinks it might be a royal messenger," Daniel added.

"We'll soon find out," Morgan responded, closing the glass with a snap. "Give them permission to come aboard, Mr. Hayes. I'll be waiting here to receive them."

No sooner had he ascended the boarding nets than the royal messenger, flanked by two servants in turbans and pointed gold slippers, was quickly ushered into Sir Morgan's presence. In his hand the bearded Turk carried a piece of parchment rolled in the form of a scroll and tied with the same vermilion ribbon that had adorned the cushions of his boat. When Morgan had acknowledged himself as the *Defiance*'s captain, the parchment was offered with a silent, deferential bow, and it was then that Morgan realized the man was a mute. This, he knew, was not unusual, for mutes guarded the countless doors of the Sultan's palace whenever the divan and ulema met to discuss Turkish secrets of state.

Unrolling the scroll, Morgan glanced at the messenger, who folded his arms across his chest, making it obvious that he had been ordered to await an answer. There was silence as Morgan scanned the beautifully lettered missive, tension taking hold of the watching Daniel Hayes as he anticipated his captain's answer.

At last Morgan raised his head and regarded the mute with a stead gaze. "The first request I will agree to, and you may extend to His Majesty my thanks. The second, I fear, is impossible to fulfill."

The messenger shook his head to indicate that he was not satisfied with this. Morgan's brow rose inquiringly. "I take it the Sultan will withdraw his invitation if both conditions are not met?"

The messenger nodded, his dark eyes meeting the English sea captain's approvingly, pleased that he understood. Morgan turned the parchment over in his big hands as he considered for a moment what he intended to do. Then he gave the bearded Turk another piercing look.

"Inform His Majesty that I am honored to accept his invitation. We shall all three of us attend."

Greatly relieved, the messenger made a flourishing bow, touching his nose nearly to the polished deck, while the servants did the same. With a curt gesture Morgan indicated that they were to be taken back to their launch. His officers, though intensely curious, knew better than to question him, and only Jackson Torance joined him at the rail, his oddly colored eyes resting impassively on his captain's ruthless face. Morgan was silent as he watched the messenger's sleek little launch speed off across the shimmering water toward the mouth of the Bosporus. Sunlight danced on his chestnut curls as he turned to regard his first mate with twitching lips.

"Fate can sometimes play odd tricks on a man, Jack. Just when you think you've run out of ways to deceive her, she tosses a choice morsel of luck into your lap."

"Aye, cap'n?" Jack prompted.

A wolfish grin curled Morgan's lips. "Abdülaziz, Sultan of Turkey and Caliph of the Faithful, has just extended his gracious invitation to the captain and first mate of the clipper *Defiance* to spend an evening in the seraglio."

The soft-spoken Devonshireman hid his start of surprise. "You don't say." He whistled after a moment. "I take it Mr. Benjamin Disraeli himself is responsible?"

Morgan's grin widened. "Unquestionably. I never read the letter myself, but I can well imagine with what flowery embellishments upon my illustrious person the Sultan has been informed of my presence here."

"What about the second part of the invitation?" Jack asked curiously.

The amusement faded from Morgan's face. "The Sultan requested that I bring Sable with me."

"Lady Sable?" Jack was visibly startled. "How do you reckon he found out about her?"

"He didn't mention her by name—merely requested the presence of the charming beauty he knew I had aboard my ship." Morgan's expression darkened, disliking the thought that Sable had come under the Turkish ruler's scrutiny. "Apparently we were put under surveillance before Disraeli's letter arrived."

"Good thing we've been discreet," Jack added.

"And I made it clear to the Prime Minister that I wanted nothing more from him than to pull the proper strings that would get me into the palace. I'm certain the Sultan has no reason to be suspicious of us."

"Then you'll be bringing Lady Sable with us?" Jack asked.

"I had no choice," Morgan responded curtly. "The invitation would have been withdrawn without my consenting to bring her. We're expected at the palace tomorrow evening," he added thoughtfully. "That doesn't give me much time."

"Time for what, cap'n?"

Morgan's brows rose mockingly. "To find the proper attire for her, of course. Surely you wouldn't have me present the fair Lady St. Germain to the Sultan of Turkey dressed in a much-repaired gown of gold chiffon? Or worse, in breeches?"

Stepping naked from the tub that stood in the rear alcove of Captain Morgan Carey's cabin, Sable quickly dried herself with the towel Grayson had provided. With her shining curls drying in the warm breeze that wafted through the opened stern windows, she walked to Morgan's bunk and stared down at the clothes spread out for her there. Even now she could scarcely believe they were hers.

There were ruffled crinolines and a whalebone hoop to accommodate the shimmering purple petticoats. The gown itself was of watered silk of a subtle lavender color, the skirts trimmed with lacy ribbons that matched exactly the yards of rustling petticoats. Primrose kid gloves and satin slippers adorned with lavender rosettes completed the elegant outfit, and a tiny seed-pearl reticule had been supplied for her as well. Sable felt no less amazed at seeing them now than she had been when Grayson had brought them to her earlier.

"You're to wear these to the palace," he had informed her, his eyes twinkling as he laid the bursting bundle tied with jute on the bunk.

Sable, who had been despairing over the fact that she had only a faded gold gown to wear, stared at him delightedly. "Where did they come from?"

"Sir Morgan procured them for you."

"Oh." Sable's cheeks flamed. Reluctant to probe further, she had let the matter drop. No telling where Morgan had come by those things. Doubtless he had borrowed them from some former mistress tucked away in Istanbul's European quarter. Still, all that really mattered to Sable was that both she and Morgan had been invited by the Sultan to attend a feast in the seraglio. Perhaps in the exotic gardens she might be able to rekindle the magic that had flared between them in the baths, when Morgan had loved her so passionately and had looked at her with burning love in his eyes.

Sable knew she couldn't have mistaken the emotions Morgan had experienced. In that brief space of time the two of them had been united by much more than the physical joining of their bodies. If she had been able to touch some hidden part of his soul once before, then surely she could do so again! She must, or she knew her heart would break.

Sable's eyes grew hard, and she forced herself not to dwell on her misery any longer. If she didn't hurry she'd be late, and she felt certain Morgan Carey did not tolerate tardiness. As she slipped on her undergarments, however, she suddenly stopped short. How on earth was she to lace her stays without help?

"Oh, Grayson, thank goodness you've come!" she exclaimed as the cabin door opened behind her. "I need help getting dressed!"

"I can see that you do," came a deep, familiarly mocking voice from behind her.

Sable whirled about, her heart sinking, but at the sight of Morgan a tremor ran through her. He was dressed in dove-gray satin, his coat hugging his broad shoulders, his unruly curls neatly combed, and to Sable he had never seemed more commanding or ruthlessly handsome. There was an air of refinement about him, and he wore his clothes in a manner that would have filled any London dandy with envy. Yet all his raw masculinity was still there, smoldering like latent fire beneath the polished exterior. It was the same untamed quality that had overwhelmed Sable when she had first spotted him across the Havertys' crowded ballroom so long ago. She felt, as she had then, breathless and a little frightened by the magnetic blue eyes that were nailing into hers.

"I-I can't put on my gown by myself," she stammered, trying to recover her composure.

Morgan forced himself to look away from the creamy white shoulders and rounded breasts swelling above her corset. "Turn around," he commanded gruffly.

Sable obeyed, her crinolines rustling, and she held her breath as she heard him approach. As his fingers brushed her naked skin, she began to tremble and she clenched her jaw, terrified that he would notice and mock her for it. Feelings overwhelmed her, his nearness reminding her of the time he had lain hard and ready over her and had taken her with a passion that had left her breathless.

"What next?" he asked, his deep voice, so close to her ear, making her jump.

"The petticoats and gown," she instructed in a whisper.

The shimmering silk rustled softly as the skirts fell into place over her hips. Looped up with purple ribbons, they revealed the toes of Sable's slippers as she turned to thank a silent Morgan for his help. The words froze on her lips when she found herself coming face to face with him, her breasts gently brushing against his chest. Her gaze faltered and slid away, the intimacy of the dressing ritual having suddenly altered everything between them.

Morgan's eyes blazed as he looked down into her upturned face. Lavender should have been a poor choice for Sable's dramatic coloring, yet it suited her better than anything else could have that evening. The gown's full skirts were shot with silver that matched the delicate netting he had managed to find for her dark, gleaming hair. It reminded him of the mysterious highlights that had glowed in those dusky tresses in the filtered sunlight of the baths when she had stood boldly naked before him. It was obvious that she was no longer the little imp who paraded about the *Defiance*'s decks in breeches. She was Lady Sable St. Germain, well-bred daughter of the Earl and Countess of Monterrey and a woman of rare, sensual beauty.

"Do you like it?" Sable asked shyly, her cheeks glowing pink beneath Morgan's smoldering gaze.

"You look very beautiful," he murmured.

Sable found her gaze fastened to his lips, his nearness tantalizing her with a rush of memories too powerful to deny. She found she couldn't speak, and wet her dry lips with the tip of her tongue. "Thank you," she managed at last.

"I only regret that you have no jewels to adorn your throat." Without his even being aware of it, Morgan's gaze lingered between her breasts, where emeralds and diamonds should have nestled.

"It was kind of you to find the gown for me," Sable whispered. Her flesh burned where Morgan's eyes caressed it.

Morgan knew that she could have tempted the devil himself tonight and that no jewels on earth, however precious, could enhance her beauty more. This was how he had first seen her, floating around a ballroom in shimmering white, as graceful and fragile as a butterfly. He had been intrigued by her dainty features and the innocent smile that was belied by emerald eyes burning with the secret fires of womanhood. Little had he suspected then that those same fires would sweep him away in a blazing tide of passion when he finally claimed her willing body with his own.

His thoughts were following a dangerous path, he warned himself, but it was too late to break the spell. Sable St. Germain had bewitched him, and he could not turn away from her now, regardless of the danger. Her soft, kissable lips were parted as she looked up at him, and he could smell the sweet, exotic scent of her hair. Despite himself he was reminded of the feel of her naked body in his arms.

"Sable," he whispered, unaware of the husky passion in his tone.

She uttered a soft groan and fell against him, and his arms closed about her, his lips seeking hers. But the kiss was to be denied them, for a sharp rap sounded on the door at that moment, driving them apart.

"Cap'n, the jolly boat be ready for ye!"

"Stand by, Mr. Gump," Morgan responded. Reaching up, he adjusted his tie with a careless hand and regarded Sable from expressionless blue eyes. "Are you ready to go?"

She could have wept at the tone of his voice but forced herself to face him squarely. "I just have to fix my hair."

He watched as she turned to the mirror and pinned her gleaming curls into a flawless chignon before securing it with the silver netting. Engrossed in the enchanting scene before him, Morgan did not notice that Sable's hands were shaking and that her lower lip trembled dangerously as she turned to give him a hesitant smile.

"I'm ready," she said brightly.

"Then let's go. I don't want to keep the Sultan waiting."

The crewmen on watch grew tongue-tied with admiration when Sable appeared on deck at Captain Carey's side. She smiled at them shyly to acknowledge their compliments, although she was conscious only of the tall man who held her arm in an impersonal grip. She found that she ached for him, and the fact that his kiss had been thwarted filled her with despair. Would they ever find themselves in such an intimate setting again?

Morgan, whose thoughts were running a similar course, guided Sable through the press of admiring crewmen with a scowl of annoyance. As he handed her into the waiting boat, she lost her balance unexpectedly and he was forced to slide his arm about her waist to keep her from falling. His dark hand lingered on the pliant curve of her hip, and he felt her shudder in response and sink against him.

"Sit down or you'll fall," he ordered, thrusting her away and not hearing the hoarse passion in his own voice.

Pale and shaken, Sable obeyed. With her face averted she fought a private battle with her feelings, thankful that Morgan took a seat in the stern of the boat and not on the narrow bench beside her. Her chest ached, and she wondered how long she would be able to endure such pain.

Sensing the tension that hovered tangibly between his captain and the young girl, Jack Torance seated himself beside her and gave her one of his rare smiles. He had made every effort to look his best, and Sable couldn't help smiling back as she noticed his wetly slicked hair and brightly polished shoes.

"We're in for quite a treat this evening, your ladyship," he informed her, smoothing his trouser legs with a careful hand. "I warrant you'll see things tonight that'll go beyond your wildest dreams."

"Do you think so?" Sable asked, her spirits rising. It was obviously going to be a long trip across the Golden Horn, and she had been afraid that it would pass in stony silence, judging from the look on Morgan's rugged face.

Jack obliged her by launching into a tale of the seraglio's history and of the man named Abdülaziz who had ruled Turkey for the last seven years. "The Sultan's primary residence is Dolma Bagtche," he explained as the jolly boat moved with the creaking of oarlocks through the calm water. The sun was just beginning to set, giving the Golden Horn the color of its name and illuminating the magnificent mosques lining the distant shores. "I'm afraid we won't be seeing it because it's farther down the Bosporus."

"I'd rather see the seraglio," Sable exclaimed, her expression dreamy. "Mr. Hayes has told me so much about it."

"What little he knows," the first mate corrected her. He

tugged at the high collar of his shirt, feeling uncomfortable in his finery. "It's one of the most inaccessible places on earth, and few Europeans have ever been inside."

Sable shivered, thinking of Morgan's plans to rescue Sergei. She told herself not to be afraid. Even though fate had thrown her into the midst of this, Morgan's safety might very well depend on whether she lost her courage or not. "Were we invited because of the letter the Prime Minister wrote?"

"Indeed we were, your ladyship." Jack's lips twitched. "I imagine His Majesty is most eager to meet one of Great Britain's heroes of the Crimean War."

Both of them turned their eyes to Morgan, who shrugged noncommittally. Sable found herself wondering if he intended to take advantage of this visit by learning what he could about Sergei Vilyusk's imprisonment. Her heart began to beat faster. Surely Morgan wouldn't try anything foolish! He'd not risk her own safety by attempting to rescue his friend this very night, would he?

"We're paying a visit of protocol, Sable," Morgan said softly, reading her mind with uncanny accuracy. "You shouldn't worry about anything other than making a good impression on His Majesty."

"Her ladyship won't be havin' no troubles in that respect, cap'n!" Harley Gump offered, grinning broadly as he leaned into the oars. "Best keep an eye out for her or she'll be kept behind as one o' them harem ladies—no offense meant, of course," he added hastily, his eyes twinkling endearingly as he looked at Sable.

"You can rest assured that Sultan Abdülaziz will not number Lady Sable among his concubines tonight," Morgan replied casually, but when she glanced at him Sable saw something in his eyes that caused her to shiver. She looked away quickly, wishing she knew what he was thinking.

"Take a look, your ladyship," Jack Torance said, breaking the heavy silence that had fallen. "There on the cliffs is the seraglio."

Sable looked but could see nothing that remotely resembled the glittering palace of her imagination. She saw towers, minarets, and walls reaching to the quay upon which awesome-looking guns had been mounted. Irregular buildings of immense proportions were scattered in a haphazard fashion within the walls' embrace, and Sable regarded the first mate with a look of confusion.

"I see a small town, sir, not a palace!"

Jack laughed heartily in response. "That town, your lady-ship, is the seraglio itself."

"I didn't realize it was so large," Sable murmured.

"Don't be disappointed," Morgan advised, correctly reading her thoughts. "What you see now is simply fortification, a facade built for protection with nothing wasted on aesthetics. I promise you'll be quite dazzled when you step inside."

Sable had to admit that Morgan was right. They were met on the brightly painted dock by several veiled servants, who escorted them up a flight of carved marble steps that lead to a magnificent arched doorway bearing the Sultan's coat of arms. Here they were joined by other servants, and no sooner had they been permitted to enter the gates leading into the first court by a bowing, brilliantly attired attendant than Sable knew what it meant to step into a different world. They were in a low gallery supported by marble columns, the tended walkways leading to offices of breathtaking architecture, buildings that rivaled the beauty of the mosques in Stamboul.

They passed through a second gate of intricate carvings into an extensive garden with kiosks of shining marble and gold. Ancient cypresses and grove trees surrounded geometrically planted grass plots and magnificent fountains of rose-colored marble inlaid with the dark, regal blue of lapis lazuli.

A man stepped out of one of the kiosks as the three visitors arrived, his mien so noble that at first Sable thought this must be the Sultan. But as he came closer she saw that he was much younger than the man Jack Torance had described, while his robes were far too ordinary to be those worn by the ruler of Turkey.

Bowing deeply, he told them, "On behalf of His Majesty Sultan Abdülaziz, I bid you welcome. I am Ahmun Said and have the honor of being your host this evening."

His English was excellent, and the black eyes that regarded them were warm and sincere. A sense of excitement gripped Sable as she followed Ahmun Said to the kiosk. How Ned would envy her this evening, she thought. Rich carpets had been laid on the floors of the pavilion, and cloth hangings of gold, studded with precious stones, fluttered from the latticework. Sable was startled to see that the other guests reclined on tassled cushions, but Morgan and Jack seemed to have expected this.

Introductions were made, and Sable allowed her hand to be kissed by each of the three gentlemen, one Portuguese and two Frenchmen, who looked upon her with lustful eyes.

"You will sit with me, *ma belle?*" one of the Frenchmen cajoled as Ahmun Said begged them all to be seated.

Over Sable's dainty shoulder he caught sight of Morgan's warning frown and hastily released her. Yet Sable, who hadn't noticed, smiled at him winningly.

"Thank you, Monsieur Hibbert. I'd be delighted."

Morgan's intimidating scowl was all but forgotten as soon as Sable's dimples were revealed, and Jules Hibbert, feeling pleased with himself, seated the lavender-clad beauty on a cushion beside him.

"You are French, m'lady?" he inquired, gazing avidly into her small face.

"My grandfather was French," Sable explained, "but I consider myself thoroughly English."

"A pity and a great loss for our country." Pierre Duvall sighed, quite taken with the enchanting, green-eyed girl. She was a rare beauty indeed and one he'd not mind getting to know far more intimately. But there was no mistaking the fact that she belonged to the towering sea captain, who was unquestionably the sort of man who became dangerous if his possessions were tampered with.

"What part of England do you claim as your home, Lady St. Germain?" Jules Hibbert inquired curiously.

Morgan's lips tightened as he listened to Sable's description of Cornwall. Seeing the longing in her young face made him realize for the first time how homesick she was, and he wondered why he had failed to notice it before. Having been to North Head himself and having witnessed the deep love that existed in the St. Germain family, Morgan could well understand why Sable spoke so poignantly.

The fact that her sadness was entirely his fault did not sit well with him in the least. He knew perfectly well that he could have delayed his trip to Turkey by returning Sable to Tangier the morning after her accident—but he simply hadn't wanted to. He didn't need to examine his conscience to realize that he had kept her aboard his ship for selfish reasons, reasons that

had become vividly clear to him the afternoon he had held
Sable in his arms and made love to her. His loins tightened as
he recalled the passion she had unleashed within him, overwhelming him with the desire to taste of them again.

By God, he'd not allow it, he told himself fiercely. It was
foolish to remember, and dangerous to be reminded of the
forces that had driven him to do so. Sable, becoming aware
of Morgan's silence, cast an apprehensive glance in his direction. She had no inkling of his thoughts, but it seemed to her
that he was enjoying the evening immensely. Lounging against
the comfortable cushions, he acted quite at home in such exotic
surroundings. She envied him his peace of mind and wished
his nearness would not create such havoc within her. It wasn't
fair, especially since he didn't seem to reciprocate those feelings
or, for that matter, even to be aware of her presence.

A pair of servants entered the kiosk at that moment carrying
trays of golden glasses filled with a sweet concoction unlike
anything Sable had ever tasted. She sipped her drink while talk
turned in a desultory fashion to the tonnage displacement of
Morgan's ship, which all three visitors had seen and admired
as it lay anchored in the Golden Horn.

Sable scarcely listened, the opulence that surrounded her
continuing to leave her breathless. Though the palace gardens
themselves were deserted there was subdued activity going on
in most of the magnificent buildings around them. A soft,
lulling melody from some unknown instrument wafted to her
on the breeze and delicate wind chimes tinkled among the plane
trees, adding to the aura of unreality.

"You are intrigued by the palace, madame?" Ahmun Said
asked, observing her wandering gaze.

She nodded. "I suppose it's rude of me to stare so, but I
never imagined anything could be quite so beautiful."

The dark-eyed Turk looked pleased. "The seraglio stands
alone as the most magnificent palace on earth. Did you know
that over six thousand officials and servants make their home
in the Sultan's court?"

He grinned at Sable's audible gasp, his white teeth flashing
in his swarthy face. "That includes three hundred cooks and
nearly four hundred boatmen. At last count His Majesty possessed six hundred horses and almost as many coachmen and
grooms to care for them."

Sable stared down at her drink, unable to fathom such grandeur. Small wonder the Sultan was often termed extravagant! Yet Ahmun's disclosure had brought fresh worries to mind. With six thousand officials and hundreds of offices, how was Morgan expected to rescue Sergei without being detected? She sipped her drink, her mouth suddenly dry. It was madness to even contemplate finding him! Daniel Hayes had told her the Sultan possessed the ultimate power of life and death. If Morgan were to be captured . . .

"You are cold, Lady St. Germain?" It was the Portuguese businessman who sat on her right, having noticed her shudder.

Sable, suddenly finding herself the center of attention, gave him an apologetic smile. "No, I'm fine." The evening was quite warm despite the breeze that stirred the branches of the trees overhead.

"Then you are hungry," Ahmun Said put in. Clapping his hands, he sent the servants scurrying away. In a moment they returned bearing trays of sweets dipped in honey and grape leaves stuffed with rice. Ahmun Said presented the gentlemen with pipes and soon the scent of expensive Persian tobacco filled the air.

"Do you have business to discuss with the Sultan, Captain Carey?" Jules Hibbert inquired, giving the broad-shouldered Englishman an interested glance.

"Business?" Morgan asked curiously.

Monsieur Hibbert spread his hands, obviously flustered by his tone. "Of course, business. We are here in the hopes that His Majesty will graciously permit us to establish a branch of our industry here. Surely you have similar interests?"

"Captain Sir Morgan is here at the private invitation of our imperial ruler," Ahmun Said informed them. "Being that he is so highly thought of in his own country, His Majesty the Sultan was eager to welcome him to ours."

All three businessmen were visibly impressed by this, and Sable would have been amused if she hadn't known herself what Morgan's real business in Istanbul entailed. It was obvious that neither Ahmun Said nor the Sultan suspected what Morgan was up to, but she couldn't help being frightened. What Morgan contemplated was madness, and she was terrified that he'd be caught.

When Ahmun Said informed them politely that the Sultan was prepared to receive them, Sable felt her heart twist nervously in her breast. Perhaps Morgan sensed her fear, for as he bent to help her to her feet he said softly into her ear, "You need only smile, Sable. By capturing the Sultan's heart you'll have nothing to be afraid of."

She tried to remember his words as they walked side by side down a vaulting marble corridor, the ceiling high above painted with magnificent scenes of Byzantine art. Ahmun Said paused before a pair of gilded doors, and the towering guards flanking it sprang forward to open it. Sable was grateful for the hand that Morgan placed beneath her elbow, for if it hadn't been there she would surely have faltered as she stepped inside.

Stunned, she could only stare at the sight that met her eyes, unable to believe the grandeur before her. They were in an enormous gallery that could easily have engulfed the royal receiving rooms of Buckingham Palace thrice over. Murals, glittering mirrors, and priceless tapestries hung from the walls, and marble columns rose gracefully to the spiral ceiling. A fountain gurgled nearby, the sound mingling pleasantly with the exotic tunes being played by a group of musicians hovering nearby.

Sable, who had been presented to Queen Victoria at Windsor last winter, found herself dumbstruck by the difference between that staid, formal reception and this gala. Everywhere she looked she saw people clothed in outlandish costumes, all of them laughing and talking loudly in languages she did not understand. In a nearby corner a monkey with bells sewn onto its little jacket was cavorting with a black-eyed boy in burgundy brocade and jeweled slippers. Near the center of the room a bevy of beautiful women were performing sensuous dances, their faces obscured by veils but for their dark, sloping eyes.

She cast a bewildered glance at Morgan, who was looking down at her with obvious amusement.

"I don't believe a presentation at Windsor quite prepared you for this, did it?" he asked softly.

"I've never seen so many oddly dressed people!" Sable whispered back. "Who are they?"

"Palace officials, visitors, and the like," Morgan replied. "His Majesty never receives anyone without his personal bodyguard or his imam and astrologers present."

"Captain Sir Morgan Carey?"

Sable turned at the sound of the deep, heavily accented voice to find herself gazing into the florid features of a dark-skinned man wearing highly fashionable Occidental attire.

"I am Nikko Trimanos, His Majesty's steward," he went on politely, his interested gaze moving from Morgan to Sable, who stood close at Morgan's side. "His Majesty is prepared to receive you." To the rest of their party he added apologetically, "If you will wait, please?"

Jules Hibbert's expression darkened. "This is the third time we have been called to the palace, sir! Will His Majesty not receive us this evening? How much longer must we wait?"

Nikko Trimanos's smile was benevolent but his eyes were cold. "You will be summoned as the Sultan sees fit." Turning back to Morgan his smile grew noticeably warmer. "This way, if you please."

Flanked by Morgan and Jack Torance, Sable felt far less nervous than she would have if she had been forced to approach the Sultan alone. She scarcely took notice of the people they passed, many of them English like herself. Her attention was centered on the imposing throne that stood high on a pedestal at the far end of the room. A carpet liberally sprinkled with fragrant flower petals stood before it, but Sable had eyes only for the regally attired man who sat stiffly before them, an expression of acute boredom upon his dark features.

Sultan Abdülaziz, ruler of Turkey and Caliph of the Faithful, was a small man with a closely cropped beard. There was little to suggest from his nondescript countenance and close-set eyes that he ruled a mighty empire and one of the largest navies in the world. Through him passed all the decisions of life and death for the people who served him, and yet his short stature, thin lips, and long, curved nose did nothing to suggest it. Yet as Sable curtsied deeply before him, she could not help feeling awed. Priceless gems studded his cloak and plumed imperial aigrette, and the collar of diamonds he wore contained several that were larger than the robins' eggs Liam always found in North Head's parklands every spring.

Morgan had warned Sable beforehand that because she was a woman she would be considered an insignificant being by the Sultan and his court, so she was not offended when His Majesty barely acknowledged her presence before dismissing her. Speaking in flawless English, he beckoned Morgan and Jack to come nearer, meaning to engage them in a conversation that was obviously not intended to include her.

Morgan, who had watched admiringly as Sable had swept a graceful curtsy, gave her a reassuring nod as she was led away by Nikko Trimanos. She didn't think it would be proper to smile back, but her heart was warm as she allowed the Greek steward to steer her through the milling crowds.

Though Sable was intensely curious about the roles of the gloriously attired officials who had clustered about the Sultan's throne, she felt it would be impolite to ask questions. She wondered, too, how Morgan intended to learn anything about Sergei with so many people about. Surely he knew better than to arouse the Sultan's suspicions!

"You have many questions, Lady St. Germain."

She glanced up at the steward to find his dark, watchful eyes upon her. "I find all of this so fascinating," she admitted, hoping he hadn't noticed how nervous she was. "I was told the seraglio was impressive, but I never expected anything like this!"

Nikko Trimanos's lips twitched. "Your reaction is not unusual, Lady St. Germain, I assure you."

He seemed in an expansive mood and Sable was eager to encourage him. "The grounds alone seem enormous. How far beyond the gardens do they extend?"

The steward propped himself casually against one of the marble columns and regarded her indulgently. "My dear Lady St. Germain, do you realize that there are three separate courts comprising the palace grounds and that this is only a portion of the first one?" He seemed to enjoy her startled exclamation and added smoothly, "No visitors have ever been permitted beyond this one, though I doubt few even realize there are two others that stretch beyond these buildings and gardens."

"Do the other courts contain private residences?" Sable asked curiously.

"They do, and the third, the court of the royal harem, has never been seen by anyone except the Sultan himself, and of course the ladies who reside there." His dark eyes twinkled. "Even I have never been permitted inside." Taking her by the arm, he led Sable to a window where a robed servant appeared as if by magic to draw back the heavy golden drapes. Beyond the panes twilight was falling and lanterns had been lit throughout the gardens. Sable caught her breath, for it was truly a magical scene. Torches flared along the walks and lights danced in the branches of the trees. Even the fountains below her had been illuminated, the water frothing from the marble and lapis spigots in a riot of color.

"The buildings before you contain the official Departments of State," Nikko Trimanos told her, indicating the imposing structures that soared four or more stories into the night sky. Row upon row of darkened windows faced them, the offices no less imposing in appearance than those of Fleet and Bond streets in London.

"Of course Dolma Bagtche, the Sultan's primary residence, has considerably more official quarters than the seraglio," the steward continued, leaning toward her as he spoke. It pleased him to have Sable standing so close. The fragrance of her hair smelled sweet and clean to him after the cloying perfumes of the palace ladies.

"Beyond the Departments of State lies the Treasury," he added, "which contains, gold, silver and precious gemstones that are priceless. Even a single diamond collar, the sort of which His Majesty possesses dozens, could buy Captain Carey an entire new ship."

Sable's wide emerald eyes met his, and he laughed softly in response. "His Majesty possesses riches that would make your Queen seem a pauper in comparison—if you'll forgive my rather ungenerous comparison."

"And those towers there?" Sable asked, gesturing curiously toward a cluster of cream-colored minarets that were visible beyond the grove of cypress trees bordering the far gardens.

"Those contain the baths. Are you familiar with the Turkish custom, your ladyship?"

He wondered why she suddenly dropped her gaze from his and her soft cheeks flushed a pale, pretty pink. Though his curiosity was aroused, he was too polite to inquire further and chose instead to drop the subject. "Beyond the baths lies the Kafess, which in English we would call the Cages. There the Sultan keeps his heirs imprisoned, usually for the duration of their lives, so that they may not plot against him. The poor devils are kept ignorant of anything that occurs beyond their prison walls."

Sable shivered. "Are there any other prisoners kept there?"

Nikko Trimanos frowned. "Other prisoners?"

She nodded and tried to keep her voice casual. "Political prisoners, perhaps, or anyone else guilty of a crime against the state."

"Oh, indeed there are," he obliged her. "The Kafess is not designated for the heirs alone, but no one really knows how many prisoners are kept there at any given time. Do you see that man over there?"

Sable followed his pointing finger across the room to a tall individual in brilliant Oriental dress. He was richly clothed in velvet with costly jewels on his fingers, but it was his dark eyes, glowing like coals in his skeletal face, that captured Sable's attention. Deep in conversation with several other officials in a privacy alcove, he did not notice her curious stare.

"That's Mahmud Nedim Pasha, the Grand Vizier," Nikko Trimanos explained when she nodded. "He happens to be the Sultan's favorite and therefore enjoys privileges the rest of us do not. One of them includes imprisoning individuals he happens not to like, and I've no idea how many men he's clapped into irons throughout his life. Some of them are guilty of little more than committing a slight against him," he added, his eyes filled with dislike as he followed Sable's gaze across the room.

"And you say that all of his prisoners are kept in the Kafess, too?" Sable inquired.

"Oh, you'll find a few of the lucky ones there," he told her with a faint smile. "They've got it good from what I understand. Private apartments, handmaidens to serve their every whim—" He broke off, his smile becoming apologetic. "Forgive me, your ladyship, that's not a pleasant or appropriate topic to be discussing with you. You must forgive me. I tend to be indiscreet at times."

"It's all right," Sable assured him quickly. "Thank you for being so informative and interesting."

The Greek threw back his head and uttered a hearty laugh. "Believe me, that's the prettiest compliment I've received in quite some time. It was my pleasure, your ladyship, I assure you. Now, if you'll permit me I'd be most honored to escort you to dinner, though I do warn you it won't resemble anything you're accustomed to back home."

"I've been forewarned to expect anything," Sable admitted, and her candidness forced the steward to laugh again.

"Actually it will be quite conventional," he promised, "though the dishes served will be exotic enough to impress even the most indifferent palate. His Majesty the Sultan enjoys presenting the finest of our country's culinary delights to his guests. Actually I was referring to the entertainment, which I think you will find quite unusual."

Sable had to admit later that Nikko Trimanos had been right.

Never in her wildest dreams had she expected to sit down to a sumptuous feast in a hall of glittering mirrors and crystal and be entertained as she ate by a troupe of scantily clad belly dancers. She dined off gold plate and drank from glasses studded with precious gemstones, the dishes as exotic and delicious as Nikko Trimanos had promised. For a time she found she could forget the grave purpose that had brought them here as she ate and drank the heavenly choices set out for her. Though Morgan and Jack were seated far away, she was not lacking attention from those around her, most of them Europeans and Turks well schooled in the English language.

But the long night eventually began to take its toll, and Sable soon found herself wondering if the meal would ever end. Course after course was carried in by a silent army of bearers, each offering more sumptuous than the last. Sable stuffed herself on prawns braised in lemon butter, only to discover that fowl, mutton, and several varieties of stew were to follow. Rolled coconut and candied fruits were served for dessert, but by then Sable had drunk so much of the sweet, alcoholic concoction that was served in chilled glasses that she had to refuse it all.

To her embarrassment she wavered a little as she rose to her feet at the end of the meal, yet no one seemed to notice. Most of the guests had retreated to the receiving rooms, while others milled about in small groups, leaving Sable standing alone near her chair.

"Have you been abandoned, my lady fair? For shame! Who would be foolish enough to permit you to go free?"

She turned her head, relieved at the sound of Morgan's familiar voice. His lips twitched as he took in her flushed face and he reached for her arm, taking it in a firm grip.

"I believe the lady's had a bit too much to drink, Jack. What do you make of that?"

The *Defiance*'s first mate, himself exuding the essence of overindulgence, gave Sable a rare grin. "Shoulda kept a better eye on 'er, cap'n."

"Oh, believe me, I did," Morgan assured him.

"Can we go home now?" Sable asked. "My stomach hurts."

"And you told me it was your brother Liam who always overeats at parties," Morgan chided.

Feeling content now that she was with him, Sable allowed Morgan to lead her through an exchange of amenities with many of the guests. When it was time to leave, Nikko Trimanos and Ahmun Said were there to escort them through the outer chambers, and Sable vaguely recalled bidding them farewell before she found herself seated in the bow of the longboat.

The night was dark and very still. Lights from the palace docks danced across the water and rivaled the silver beams of the crescent moon that shone down from the cloudless sky. Sable tilted back her head, allowing the cool breeze to fan her hot cheeks. She was tired, her head was spinning, and she knew better than to interrupt Morgan, who was speaking in low tones with Jack on the seat behind her. Tomorrow she would ask him what he'd managed to discover, and perhaps he might even tell her. She wondered if he knew about the Cages of which Nikko Trimanos had spoken and if he suspected that Sergei Vilyusk might be imprisoned there. She shivered unexpectedly, recalling the unnerving eyes of the Grand Vizier Mahmud Nedim Pasha. Was he the man responsible for Sergei's imprisonment?

"Are you cold, Sable?"

She shook her head at Morgan's question, hiding a yawn behind her hand, and heard him chuckle softly.

"I can see that adventuring is a far too strenuous activity for you."

"Adventuring?" Sable echoed derisively. "I did naught all evening but eat and drink."

"The Sultan should be commended for his collection of spirits," Jack agreed laconically. "I've never had wines the likes of his before!"

"I can see that you haven't," Morgan observed when his first mate hiccuped appreciatively.

"Fine spy I made tonight, eh, cap'n?" Jack inquired, grinning widely.

Morgan could not help chuckling. "Indeed."

When the longboat was hoisted back aboardship Morgan was there to help Sable to the deck. She would have started immediately for the companionway but for his lingering grip on her arm. "Do you require assistance in retiring, your ladyship?" he inquired casually as she glanced up at him uncertainly.

She could see his eyes gleam in the moonlight, and a pulse in her throat leaped wildly in response. His nearness and the wine singing in her blood brought a tantalizing warmth to her being. She felt helpless, drugged by the sheer presence of this fascinating man who, she knew, needed only one word from her to sweep her off her feet and carry her below.

"I can't," she whispered, the denial torn from her before she was even aware of it. Though she yearned for Morgan with every fiber of her being, she knew it would bring her nothing but heartache to succumb to him once again. How well she remembered his cruel and spiteful behavior after he had loved her that first time, and Sable knew she would rather die than bear the pain of his rejection again.

Morgan stiffened as he gazed into her tormented eyes, and even in the darkness she could see his lean jaw clench. "Very well, your ladyship," he said coldly. "I bid you good night."

Helplessly she watched him stride around the great cabin wall. Tears welled in her eyes, but she dashed them away as she hurried below. She had done the right thing, she told herself angrily, lighting the small lamp next to her bunk and unpinning her hair. She had!

Despite her great weariness Sable found herself lying sleepless beneath the covers. It was not the splendor of the evening on which her thoughts dwelled, however, but on Morgan and the coldness in his eyes when he had walked away from her. Much as he had hurt her with his hateful taunts, she knew that she longed for him still. Would she ever be free of him? she asked herself forlornly.

There would be no sleep for her that night, Sable realized as she heard the bell strike the change of watch on the deck above. She was still wide awake though it was long after midnight, and so restless that it was a torment merely to lie still. Sighing deeply, she rose from her bunk, thinking that a few turns in the fresh air might help.

She was wearing one of Morgan's discarded shirts, which she had been sleeping in since her illness. Though it hung below her shoulders and she had to fold back the trailing cuffs, Sable was too tired to exchange it for the clothes she wore daily on deck. No one would see her dressed like this, she reasoned, tucking the long tails into her breeches.

It was cool on deck and a stiff breeze had risen that blew across the Golden Horn, whipping the placid water into whitecaps. Lights twinkled along the shore and Sable could see lanterns bobbing on the boats anchored close to Galata Bridge. There was only a small crescent moon hanging in the sky, but she welcomed the protective cloak of darkness.

She made her way forward, coming to stand beneath the towering foremast, her elbows resting on the bow rail. Why was there such a tearing pain within her? What perverse quirk of fate had caused her to fall in love with Morgan Carey when in truth she ought to hate him? He had kidnapped her, tormented her, taken her innocence, and cruelly abused her afterward. By all counts she should despise him. If only she did, how much simpler her life would be!

Try as she might, Sable found her thoughts clinging stubbornly to even more compelling memories: how Morgan had tended her during her long illness, his ministrations gentle and kind, how he had taught her the names of the many sails that graced the *Defiance*'s soaring masts, and the hours he had spent patiently tutoring her in the use of the sextant and other navigational devices.

Nor could Sable forget how his eyes had gleamed when he had seen her tonight in her lavender gown, which, she had learned from Grayson earlier, he had scoured the length and breadth of Pera to find. And his lovemaking—Sable's knees grew weak as she remembered the touch of his lips upon her, his body becoming part of hers as he took her to heights of pleasure she had never dreamed possible. How could she hate a man like that?

"What the devil are you doing out here?"

She whirled, dismayed that the very object of her torment had managed to shatter her composure once again. "I-I couldn't sleep," she confessed.

In the dim starlight she saw Morgan's hawkish features set in an expressionless mask. "Neither could I."

"I was thinking about the evening," Sable continued after a tense pause.

"It was quite an experience," Morgan agreed. "You made a considerable impression on the Sultan."

Sable glanced up at him, startled. "I did?"

Morgan threw her a mocking look. "Of course you did. He could talk of little else after you were dismissed. I warrant if he'd been any less of a civilized man, he would have asked me if he might purchase you for his harem."

"I see," Sable said softly, taken aback by the coldness of his tone.

Morgan glanced down at her as she stood silently at his side, her head barely reaching the top of his shoulder. She appeared so young and defenseless to him at the moment, swallowed up in his enormous shirt, her unbound hair falling to her waist. It was hard to believe that this innocent-looking child had wreaked such havoc in his well-ordered life. But for her he would have already made his move to free Sergei from the seraglio instead of wasting time paying his respects to a despot like the Sultan.

Indeed, Sable's presence aboard his ship had forced him to exercise uncharacteristic restraint. Morgan knew that she would make a dangerous weapon if she ever fell into the Sultan's hands. He had been greatly relieved that His Majesty had been so taken with her and seemed not to have suspected any of his guests of duplicity. Yet Morgan continued to worry. Even on his ship Sable was vulnerable, and he couldn't be sure that she'd be safe if Sergei's rescue erupted in violence.

Made curious by Morgan's long silence, Sable turned to look up at him questioningly. As she did so the wind, tugging at the collar of her shirt, parted the muslin slightly so that Morgan could see the outline of her firm breasts. Abruptly he turned away, shaken by his response to Sable's undeniable femininity. How could he possibly get her out of his life when he wanted nothing more than to seize her in his arms and kiss her until she melted against him?

"Did you wish to say something, captain?" Sable asked, puzzled by his continued silence.

"You'd better go below," he told her harshly, refusing to look at her.

"What have I done?" she asked, dismayed at the tone of his voice.

"I said go below," Morgan grated.

Seizing Sable's arms, he made as if to push her away, but it was as if a floodtide burst between them when he touched her. Groaning, he pulled her to him, wrapping his arms about her waist and lowering his mouth to hers. Sable gave a sob of relief, her lips parting beneath his.

The kiss seemed without end, growing deep with sensual arousal. Morgan's hands moved beneath Sable's shirt, and his strong, callused fingers on her naked breasts made her fall, gasping, against him. She could feel his heart thundering and she trembled with a need as fierce as his own.

Lifting her into his arms, Morgan carried her below, kicking the cabin door shut with his foot. Sable's senses reeled as he kissed her, making her aware of nothing but the taste of him and the hard-muscled arms that enveloped her. Pale moonlight streamed through the unshuttered windows, illuminating Morgan's intimidating countenance, but Sable saw nothing save the passion glittering in his eyes, a passion she knew was for her alone.

Unashamedly she slid her slender arms about his neck, drawing him down on the bunk until his lips covered hers. The heat of his body and the hardness of his enflamed manhood made her gasp, her head falling back as she awaited his bold caress.

She shivered, feeling Morgan's hot breath on her throat as he unclothed her with practiced fingers. Burning kisses were trailed over every inch of silken flesh he exposed, making her world tilt alarmingly and filling her with a yearning to please him in equal measure. When she was naked, Sable rose to her knees and unbuttoned his shirt in turn. She pressed her lips to his bronzed chest, tracing the hard ridge of muscle there while sliding her hands to his waist and boldly unfastening his breeches. Neither of them spoke, afraid to break the spell and revert again into the antagonists they could not help being.

Shrugging off his breeches, Morgan turned to face her, his powerfully muscled physique revealed to her in the pale light. Sable grew still, her eyes wide as she looked at him, thinking to herself how magnificent he was. The mere sight of his naked body caused her heart to pound with anticipation, and she closed her eyes, suddenly afraid of the depth of her emotions.

"You're beautiful," Morgan whispered raggedly, the yearning in his voice dispelling her fears. "How you tempt me to madness, my own enchanting sea-witch."

Sable opened her eyes to look at him. Starlight washed over her, giving her unbound hair mysterious highlights of silver and gold. Her skin shone silkily, and Morgan caught his breath, unable to believe that she was real and that those haunting emerald eyes were gazing back at him with bold, seductive promise. He had forgotten the vow he had made to himself never to touch her again, that the first, glorious time they had made love would also be the last. He knew only that he wanted her and that his need for her was driving him to madness.

Sable's dusky gaze and the fire in her eyes told him that she felt the same, that she knew as well as he that they had been made for each other. They were both kneeling on the rumpled covers facing one another, Sable's rosy lips parted, a look of soft, compelling need upon her lovely features. Morgan slid his hands over her smooth buttocks, pulling her toward him so that she was imprisoned between his thighs, his ready manhood nestled against her belly.

Sable lifted her face to him, her eyes closed in anticipation of his kiss. Morgan's hands cupped her breasts, inciting the nipples to rise to pink, thrusting peaks. His hands traveled lower, to the pliant curve of her hips, and he brought her firmly against his rigid chest. His kiss took her breath away and drew her soul from her body. She uttered a soft moan as Morgan's tongue thrust into her mouth, making her dizzy with desire.

Together they sank into the blankets, the length of Morgan's body fused against her own. No sooner did she feel his manhood touch her intimately than Sable spread her slim legs to accommodate him. Despite the swiftness with which he had taken her, Morgan found her moist and ready, and a whimper of pleasure escaped her lips as he thrust deep inside her.

This time there was no pain to shatter the precious moment, and Sable moved beneath him, straining her hips toward him to accept him more fully. Her hands slid over his broad shoulders, her nails digging into his flesh. Morgan's breath was ragged in her ear as he drew back and surged forward again, his big body pinning hers to the blankets. Sable clung to him, the tantalizing sensations building to dizzying heights within her.

Relentlessly Morgan worked his magic upon her until the ache within Sable's loins suddenly fanned out to consume her. She gave a cry and Morgan captured her lips with his. They shuddered together, their bodies joined as wave after wave of exquisite torment broke over them. Nothing in all creation, Sable knew then, could rival such pleasure or her love for this man.

When it was over and her ragged gasps had quieted, Sable found herself wrapped in Morgan's arms, his hard brown body covering the length of hers. His lips caressed hers lightly and his eyes were warm as he gazed down at her. She sighed deeply and tightened her hold about his neck, reluctant to let him go.

Morgan chuckled. "Would you keep me this way forever? I fear I'll crush you."

"I couldn't think of a better way to die," Sable said with a sigh.

She delighted in his throaty, masculine laugh, but protested when he loosened her arms from about his neck. "Hush, my sweet," he commanded. Sliding his arm beneath her, he pulled her body against his so that she was cradled within its protective curve, her rear end nestled against his thighs.

"Oh, Morgan," she whispered impulsively, "I'm so happy!"

The strong arms tightened about her, and she could feel his warm breath stir her hair as he pressed his lips to her temple. "I am, too."

Tears welled in her eyes at this confession, and her heart threatened to burst with the joy and pain of it. She knew at that moment that she could never allow him to risk his life for Sergei Vilyusk. How could she bear to lose him now, when he had come to mean everything to her?

The spacious cabin was silent and the rhythmic stirring of the big ship at anchor should have lulled Sable to sleep. As warm and drowsy as she might be lying against Morgan's chest, she could not close her eyes. Her mind was too full, her conscience too much at war. Morgan, she knew, was not sleeping either, and she wondered what unspoken conflicts kept him from his rest.

In a moment she knew the answer, for his manhood began to stir insistently and, with a growl, Morgan turned her to him. "By God, wench, how can I sleep with you pressed so impudently against me?"

She giggled, but her breath caught in her throat as the laughter was silenced by a kiss that left no doubts as to Morgan's reawakened passions.

"I may have hurried too much the last time," Morgan said with a glint in his eyes, "but now I intend to take my leisure."

Sable fell back against the pillows, breathless with renewed desire as his big hands roved familiarly over her body. "Oh, yes, please," she whispered, everything forgotten save the kindling fire ignited by his seeking touch. "You needn't hurry on my account!"

Chapter 12

When Sable awoke the following morning she experienced a moment of confusion. Opening her eyes, she saw not the familiar timbers of her cabin above her head but a far wall taken up with mullioned windows through which the sun was shining. She sat up quickly, the blankets falling from her naked shoulders as she recognized Morgan's spacious quarters.

She saw at once that she was alone, but the strong scent of coffee and the dishes scattered on the desktop informed her that Morgan had been there only recently. She pushed her hair from her eyes and padded barefoot across the fine Persian carpet to wash her face in the basin. Slipping into her breeches and shirt, she found herself humming and realized that for the first time in many days she was deeply happy.

Climbing up on deck, her eyes went automatically aft and her heart skipped a beat as she saw Morgan, strong and imposing, standing on the quarterdeck with his back turned toward her. Sunlight shone on his disheveled chestnut curls, and the big hands that had roved her body so passionately last night were propped on his lean hips as he spoke earnestly with his first officer and Daniel Hayes.

Sable moved to the bottom of the ladder and looked up at

him inquiringly. "Permission to join you, sir."

Morgan turned his head and his lips twitched when he saw her below him, the dimples peeping from her soft cheeks. Her breath caught in her throat as he beckoned to her, the intimacy in his gaze excluding everyone else. She felt his strong hand beneath her elbow as she ascended the ladder, and when she reached the top he did not release her but drew her forward so that she was standing directly before him.

"Did you sleep well, m'lady?" he inquired in that deep voice that had once frightened her but seemed to be caressing her now. "I fear you retired far too late last night."

He was delighted to see a shy blush creep to her cheeks. "I feel well rested, thank you, captain," she responded politely, but there was a mishievous glint in her emerald eyes as she peered up at him. She looked radiant that morning, the sunlight reflecting the deep golden highlights of her dark hair, the scent of it reminding him how the shining strands had wrapped themselves about his throat when he had brought Sable's willing lips to his the night before.

"I warrant you'll be banished from court when you return home," he told her, seeing the dusting of golden freckles across her upturned nose. "I have it on good authority that the Queen frowns upon young ladies who obviously make little use of sunbonnets and parasols."

Sable returned his smile with a saucy one of her own. "Her Majesty will simply have to understand that I was kidnapped against my will, without a single sunbonnet to my name."

"Against your will, Sable?" Morgan's expression suddenly grew serious, his blue-eyed gaze intense. "Do you still hold to that, even now?"

She felt breathless and confused by his nearness, for he had leaned down to speak to her, his breath warm against her cheek.

"Hrrmpf!"

She looked up quickly to find Jackson Torance regarding them with no small measure of interest. "Will that be all, cap'n?" the first mate inquired innocently.

Morgan straightened with a sigh. For a brief moment he had been able to forget his cares thanks to Sable's dancing eyes and alluring lips. "We'll talk later, Jack. In the meantime you've got enough to keep you busy. That goes for you as well, Mr. Hayes."

"Aye, aye, sir."

Both men hurried away, and Morgan, seeming to have forgotten Sable, bent to make an entry in the handsome buckram log that lay propped open on the binnacle. Sable regarded him in silence for a moment, then hesitantly uttered his name. As he turned to look at her, she saw the customary sternness of his countenance and knew a feeling of overwhelming despair. Whatever had happened between them, Morgan was still the commander of his ship and a man with a dangerous mission to undertake. She sensed that this would always stand like an insurmountable wall between them and that he would not tolerate any interference on her part in the matter. The fact that many facets of his life were still closed to her hurt, and she felt again the gnawing fear that had consumed her last night in the seraglio when she had seen for herself how impregnable a fortress it truly was.

"Did you find out where they're keeping Sergei?" she blurted, not expecting him to answer.

"Jack and I have known where he is even before we received the Sultan's invitation," he told her evenly.

Sable's eyes widened, but she refrained from asking him how he had found out. She had learned a great deal since joining the crew of Morgan's ship, one of them being that the captain's privacy was to be respected. She had also learned how unwise it was to meddle in his affairs, but in this, with his life perhaps riding in the balance, she could not keep silent.

"Will you tell me where he is?"

Morgan's bronzed cheek twitched as he gave her a mocking smile. "So that you can rescue him yourself, my brave, meddlesome child? No, don't protest, I wouldn't put it past you, knowing you as I do." His smile deepened, etching laugh lines into the corners of his eyes. "I have a few words to say to your parents in that respect when we return, or are they perhaps already aware that their daughter is as wild and untamable as I've found her to be?"

Sable responded to his gentle teasing with a halfhearted smile. Her love for him tore at her heart, and she couldn't find humor in his words when the gravity of their situation hung so ominously over them. Aware of her thoughts, Morgan closed the log with a snap and came to stand before her. He looked down into her face with that old mocking smile she had once despised but which she now found brought a curious weakness to her knees.

"You've nothing to fear, Sable St. Germain," he said softly.
"I don't intend to risk Sergei's freedom or the lives of anyone
aboard my ship to foolish heroics. We'll get him out, but not
before I have a plan that's totally free of complications. But
to answer your question, I do indeed know where Sergei is,
and I intend to have everything worked out within the next few
days."

"Then where is he?" Sable repeated curiously, finding it
impossible not to believe him when he stood so tall and confident before her. "Is he in the Kafess? Nikko Trimanos told
me about it yesterday. He said it was a prison where the Sultan
keeps his heirs locked up so that they can't plot intrigues against
him." She shivered, thinking what a bloodthirsty man Abdülaziz
must be.

"It would seem you were doing a bit of snooping on your
own last night," Morgan observed, not knowing whether to be
angry with her or not.

"I'm sorry," Sable whispered, her gaze faltering. "It's just
that I can't help feeling frightened knowing what it is you want
to do."

"You mustn't be," he reassured her. "Aye, Sergei's being
kept in the Kafess, and it will take some clever planning and
a bit of luck to get him out, but that's why we came to Istanbul
to begin with, isn't it?"

"I still don't—"

Morgan laid a finger on Sable's lips to silence her, and
though his touch was gentle his voice carried a warning that
she could not ignore. "I tolerate much from you, Sable St.
Germain, more so than from any other woman I've ever known,
but I will not permit your interference in this." His tone softened
as he gazed into her wide eyes. "It's for your own safety, if
nothing else. Do you understand?"

She nodded, a lump in her throat that had nothing to do
with his dire warning. He seemed on the verge of saying something else, and she stood silent as his fingers strayed to her
cheek and caressed it softly. But then he turned away and Sable
knew that she had been dismissed. Though she ached to go
after him and demand that he abandon his foolish scheme, she
forced herself to descend the ladder without another word.

Her heart was heavy as she crossed the deck and turned her
gaze to the far shore of the Golden Horn, where she knew the
seraglio lay. Last night she had sworn to herself that she would

do what she could to prevent Morgan from risking his life in that secretive, closely guarded fortress. In the light of day her resolve was by no means lessened, yet she despaired of finding a way to carry out her plan. She was naught but a helpless woman, and she didn't even know what it was Morgan intended to do. How could she find a way to protect him when he insisted on keeping her ignorant?

Morgan spent most of the morning on the quarterdeck holding counsel with his officers. Though Sable was relieved that he did not go ashore, she wished she knew what he was planning. It was obvious that the matter under discussion was serious given the grave expressions of the men who spoke with him.

"Oh, Grayson, what does he plan to do?" Sable asked when the steward brought her a small tray at lunchtime as she sat reading on the fo'c'sle.

Grayson didn't even pretend not to understand what she meant. During the past few weeks he had come to trust the beautiful young girl and had been speaking his thoughts to her in a way he had never done with anyone else. Being valet to a man as uncompromising as Morgan Carey, Grayson had often wished for a confidante, yet had respected his master far too much to bare his thoughts to anyone about him.

Lady Sable, however, had proved a willing listener to the beleaguered steward, and Grayson had come to think of her as someone with a right to hear of Sir Morgan's problems. Naturally Morgan knew nothing of the understanding between the two of them, and Grayson did not feel he was being disloyal by not mentioning it.

"I wish I knew, your ladyship," he said now, setting the tray down on the small bench beside her. His normally pleasant features were set in a mask of concern. "He's told me nothing at all since we got here, and I didn't even have a chance to question him about last night's visit with the Sultan."

"You didn't?" Sable asked, disappointed, for she had secretly hoped that Morgan might have confided something in his valet.

"As a matter of fact," Grayson added, looking extremely vexed, "he wouldn't even permit me inside with his breakfast tray this morning! Had me hand it to him through the door! I might add that I consider that the height of effrontery, though please don't be telling him I said so, your ladyship!"

Sable choked on the bite of juicy orange she had just popped into her mouth. Her cheeks grew red as she envisioned what might have happened if the steward had seen her lying fast asleep in Morgan's bed.

Grayson gestured aft, apparently unaware of Sable's self-conscious silence. "And as for all of this activity between the ship and shore, I tell you I don't like it one bit! I have every confidence in the captain and if anyone can rescue a man from the Sultan's seraglio, it's Morgan Carey, but it must be perfectly obvious even to him that no matter how carefully he plans the rescue anything can go awry."

Seeing that Sable had grown pale at his words, he added hastily, "Of course I don't expect anything will, and if it should, Sir Morgan is capable enough to overcome it."

"Do you think so?" Sable asked uncertainly, and now it was her turn to voice her doubts.

"I've been with Sir Morgan long enough to know that he can be amazingly lucky at times," Grayson assured her, assuming an air of confidence when he realized how much he had distressed her. "Furthermore, if you had been able to observe his conduct during the war, m'lady, you'd have no doubts now as to his capabilities."

"But this is different," Sable protested, unable to keep her fears to herself any longer. "How does he propose to rescue Sergei with soldiers stationed everywhere?" She shivered, recalling the awesome scimitars carried by the guards in the palace.

"I suppose I'll simply have to count on lady luck to help me," came Morgan's voice unexpectedly from behind them. The frown on his handsome countenance softened into amusement as he took in the sight of the two guilty faces before him. Grayson quickly retreated, his back stiff, while Sable averted her gaze and pretended great interest in the luncheon tray set beside her.

"What's this?" Morgan demanded, helping himself to one of the small sandwiches Grayson had prepared for her. "Curried chicken? What have you done to deserve this? Even my noon-day collations are never this ambitious."

Sable returned his smile, relieved that he hadn't chosen to comment on the fact that she and Grayson had been discussing him. And yet her fear remained, growing stronger and more ominous, as though the certainty of bloodshed had become an unshakable fact in her mind.

"Leave it to a woman to make molehills into mountains," Morgan said suddenly. Propping his booted foot on the bench beside her, he leaned down and regarded her solemnly. "Have you no faith in me, Sable?" he chided softly. "Do you trust me so little that you believe I'm doomed to fail?"

Sable shook her head, struggling to find the right words to make him understand her fears. How could she explain to Morgan that it was exactly his confidence in himself that worried her so? As captain of the *Defiance* he seemed a law unto himself, and certainly capable of driving fear into the hearts of even the most hardened men. Yet were his confidence and great strength weapons enough to defeat Turkish soldiers trained to defend their ruler's property and life at all costs?

"Never mind, Sable," Morgan said as the silence between them lengthened. "Your expression speaks volumes of disapproval, and I'd rather not hear a single unkind word about me fall from your lips. Actually," he went on with a faint smile, "I didn't come here to ask what you thought of me; I came to give you this. I purchased it the day I went to Pera to buy your lavender gown and it's been lying in my cabin ever since."

Sable reached out hesitantly to take the small bundle from him. In doing so her fingers inadvertently brushed his and she felt the shock of the warmth of his flesh travel like lightning through her.

"I suggest you open it in the privacy of your quarters," Morgan added gruffly as though he, too, had felt the jolt between them.

"What is it?" Sable asked, gazing up at him with the eager expectancy of a child.

His lips twitched. "You'll have to find out for yourself."

He was gone before she could thank him, but her eyes were shining as she hurried below, the bundle clutched to her heart. She stifled a gasp when she opened it, unable to believe that Morgan had purchased something like this for her. It was a harem costume of sheer spun silk, the pantaloons of crimson and the bolero of purple, lavishly embroidered with gold. A tiny veil and gold slippers, cunningly turned up at the toes to resemble a caique oarsman's, completed the outfit. Sable held the gossamer pantaloons against herself, wondering how Morgan could possibly have known how much she had wanted these. She had mentioned it to Daniel Hayes the day he had taken her to the bazaar in Old Stamboul, but how had Morgan learned of it?

Sable's eyes glowed as she lovingly fingered the smooth material. Dared she believe that Morgan had made her this gift because he cared for her? She shivered deliciously, recalling the light in his eyes as he had given her the package. She would wear the costume tonight, she decided, when she met Morgan and his officers in his quarters for dinner. What would he say when he saw her in it? Her expression grew dreamy as she envisioned the desire kindling in his steel blue eyes as he reached for her, caressing her flesh boldly through the gossamer thinness of the costume.

Suddenly the seraglio and the threatening fears that hovered over her were gone. All that mattered at the moment was that Sable had been presented a gift by the man she loved, a gift which she intended to use to please him as best she knew how. She spent the remainder of the afternoon preparing for dinner, taking far more care with her appearance than she had when an audience with the Sultan of Turkey had lain before her. Since Morgan was busy topside, she bathed in his quarters, Grayson obligingly providing her with hot bath water. Later she sat in the sun, her hair drying in the warm, gentle breeze so that the dark curls took on a soft, shining radiance.

There was no mirror in her tiny cabin in which she might admire herself, but Sable needed none to realize that the harem costume, once put on, enveloped her in almost mystical appeal. Never had she felt anything like this whispering caress of silk against her skin. The tiny bolero fit snugly over her slender torso and the pantaloons were gripped at the bottom to reveal the shapeliness of her ankles.

To complete the outfit Sable plaited her long hair and allowed the thick braid to dangle to her hips, where it brushed enticingly against the curve of her buttocks. She giggled as she whirled about on her toes, her arms outstretched. Would Morgan like the way she looked? Would he gaze into her eyes with smoldering fire and claim her lips with his own?

"Lady Sable?"

She halted at the sound of Grayson's voice through the thin wood. "What is it?" she asked breathlessly.

"Dinner will be served in the captain's quarters in half an hour."

"I'll be ready," she promised and Grayson, listening outside the door, wondered why she sounded so happy.

After putting the finishing touches on her costume, Sable left her cabin. Her slippers made no sound as she came to a halt before Morgan's door and lifted her hand to knock. The sound of his voice from within stayed the movement, however, and she bit her lip in disappointment. She had so wanted to find him alone!

"Tomorrow night, Jack? Are you certain?"

She froze, sensing instinctively that Morgan's question had something to do with Sergei's rescue.

"I been down to the Yedi Mosque twice to make sure," Sable heard the first mate answer firmly. "Fridays be the Sultan's day of prayer, and he'll return to Dolma Bagtche directly after the ceremonies. All of his officials and his harem travel with him when he goes, which should leave the seraglio near-deserted."

"And that usually means the slackening of discipline among remaining troops," Morgan remarked. From the tone of his voice Sable guessed that he was remembering his own days as a soldier. She frowned, pressing her ear against the wood in order to hear better. She knew that she was eavesdropping, but she didn't care. If Morgan and Jack were discussing their plan to rescue Sergei, she wanted to know everything about it!

"I got together with one of Kemal's men, too," Jack continued, his words accompanied by the creaking of the cabinet as one of them reached inside for the brandy decanter. "We went over the Kafess layouts and he had a few suggestions to make you might be wantin' to hear."

"What about the Kuzlar Achasi? Can we count on him for assistance?" Morgan's deep voice was filled with something Sable had never heard before. Tension, excitement, eagerness to begin? She couldn't tell, and she pressed her hand to her lips, grappling with the urge to burst through the door and scream at him for being such a fool.

"We've already agreed on a price," Jack responded. "It ain't much because he despises the Grand Vizier and hopes Sergei's escape will touch off some kind of incident that'll ruin any chances for peace between Turkey and Mother Russia."

"Ahem!"

Sable whirled about with a soft cry of alarm. Seeing Daniel Hayes before her, she heaved a sigh of relief. "Oh, Mr. Hayes, you gave me such a start! I-I was just about to knock."

Daniel seemed unaware of her heightened color and stammering words. In fact, nothing registered in his mind save for the startling realization that Lady Sable St. Germain seemed to have forgotten every rule of propriety a well-bred young woman should have been taught. Dressed in gossamer silk, her gleaming hair braided in an outlandish fashion, she looked shockingly improper—and more breathtakingly beautiful than Daniel had ever seen her.

"Where did you come by such a ... lovely outfit, your ladyship?" he stammered.

"Captain Sir Morgan was kind enough to purchase it for me," Sable replied, but her words were distracted and she seemed unaware of the young officer's admiring expression. Her desire to surprise Morgan and please him with the wearing of his gift was suddenly gone, replaced by the numbing certainty that he and Jack intended to set their rescue into motion tomorrow night. It was far too soon, and Sable swallowed hard to still the fearful pounding of her heart. She couldn't let them risk it, she told herself wildly, and tears sprang to her eyes as she came to realize fully how helpless she was to stop them.

"Lady Sable, are you unwell?" Daniel inquired anxiously, coming out of his lovesick stupor sufficiently to notice that she was trembling.

"I'm fine," she assured him, but in the next breath she realized that she would never be able to withstand Morgan Carey's scrutiny at the moment. He was too maddeningly perceptive and would sense immediately that something was amiss. She mustn't let him know that she had overheard his exchange with Jack Torance.

"Actually I'm feeling a little under the weather," she said with a shaky smile that convinced Daniel that she was in dire need of medical attention.

"I'll fetch Dr. Pierson," he cried immediately and would have raced down the corridor if Sable hadn't seized him by the coat, her grip surprisingly strong for one beset by illness.

"Please don't trouble him. I'm truly all right!"

"Then what is it?" Daniel asked, gazing worriedly into her upturned face. Sable St. Germain was the woman he loved, and he couldn't tolerate the thought that she was suffering some sort of discomfort.

Sensing that he'd never let her go before Dr. Pierson and perhaps even Morgan were summoned, Sable gazed at him levelly with her solemn green eyes and said unabashedly, "It's really nothing to concern yourself with, Mr. Hayes. My mother always referred to it as . . . as female trouble."

Daniel went scarlet. Having grown up in a house with four sisters he well understood what Sable was referring to. It pained him deeply to realize that his questioning had forced her to make so delicate a disclosure, and he seized her small hand in his, mortified that he had been so unthinking.

"Please, your ladyship," he begged her ardently, "you must rest. I'll inform the captain that you won't be joining us for dinner."

He was rewarded for his concern with a distracted smile, for Sable was already thinking of other things, wondering how she might prevent the man she loved with all her heart from going to his certain death. Murmuring something to Daniel, she retreated to her cabin, unaware of the endearing picture she made for him, her dark braid bobbing, as she disappeared through the door and closed it softly behind her.

What exactly did Morgan plan to do tomorrow night? she asked herself fearfully. With the Sultan away he would have a perfect opportunity of stealing into the seraglio, but how did he intend to escape detection and free Sergei Vilyusk at the same time?

"Oh, if only I knew!" she whispered to herself, wringing her hands in agitation as she paced about the tiny cabin. "There must be some way to stop him! There must be!"

The night was still and very dark. A quickening wind had driven heavy clouds in from the north, obscuring the pale light of the crescent moon. The promise of rain hung in the air but as yet the weather hadn't turned. Sable, huddled beneath the spreading branches of a plane tree, shivered in the blast of chilly air. She was thinly clad, but she scarcely noticed the cold or the dampness of the night.

Never in her young life had Sable been more afraid. The tree underneath which she found herself grew amid a protective cluster of bushes in the far corner of the grounds of the seraglio's outermost court. Only a few moments ago Sable had hidden herself there after having bravely scaled the same outer wall over which Morgan Carey and four of his men had vanished just seconds before. Now, as she huddled, panting, in the bushes, she turned her frightened eyes toward the enormous gates that separated the Cages from the rest of the outer court. A pair of imposing eunuchs stood guard without, and Sable wondered how Morgan intended to get past them.

It would never work, she thought fearfully to herself, and she strained to see beyond the fountains where Morgan and his men had vanished. Where were they? she asked herself feverishly. It was so dark and still, and the buildings around her—the offices of state which Nikko Trimanos had pointed out to her earlier—were ominously deserted.

Sable knew it had been madness to follow Morgan to the seraglio tonight. She tried not to think of the danger she had placed herself in by telling herself that she had come to help him any way she could. Hadn't he always told her that she was to thank for his current good fortune? Well, a lucky talisman was not to be left behind, was it?

She had followed Morgan's small band up the long flight of marble steps leading from the water to the imposing walls of the palace. Because it had been dark she had stumbled often and had caught her breath every time, terrified that Morgan would hear her. But he had been too intent on his own purposes, and she had managed to scramble over the wall behind him without being seen. To her dismay he and his men had vanished immediately into the impenetrable darkness, and Sable had sought shelter amid the shrubbery, unsure of what she should do.

A voice in her heart began telling her what a grave folly she had just committed and that by being here she might even jeopardize Morgan's safety. She thrust those unsettling thoughts aside, telling herself that she was beginning to lose her nerve. As a precaution she had tucked one of Morgan's pistols into the waistband of her pantaloons, and the feel of the cold metal against her skin gave her courage that she badly needed. Her father had taught her to shoot when she had been only a young girl, and she knew she wouldn't hesitate to use the pistol if need be to help Morgan tonight.

It had grown cooler, and Sable shivered in a sudden blast of wind. The boughs of the trees above her rattled ominously, and she licked her dry lips, telling herself that she had better

do something quickly, before her courage failed her altogether.
Rising to her feet, she slipped from her hiding place, but even
before she could take a step forward a hand that seemed to
come from nowhere clamped itself firmly over her mouth and
she was jerked roughly back to the ground.

"Where are you planning to go, Lady St. Germain?" a silky
voice whispered in her ear. "Not to the Kafess to aid your brave
Sir Morgan, I hope? Even dressed as you are you'd never get
away with it, and it would only result in your death, which I
would find a terrible waste."

Sable twisted her head about and her heart stopped as she
met the dark, unsmiling eyes of Nikko Trimanos. Where once
she had thought him a pleasant individual, she saw now that
his features were set in the cold, ruthless mask of a man who
knows no mercy.

"Don't struggle," he warned. "I may not have your Captain
Carey's size, but believe me when I tell you that I'm strong
enough to twist that pretty neck of yours right in two. Now,
I'm going to take my hand away from your mouth, but if you
utter so much as a single sound I'll see to it that Morgan Carey
and his loyal men die a long, painful death rather than the swift
dispatch I had in mind. Do you understand me?"

He laughed shortly as he looked into her upturned face.
"Such hatred spewing from those beautiful eyes," he lamented
with a shake of his head. Abruptly his mouth tightened and the
pressure of his fingers bit into her flesh. "Do you understand,
Sable St. Germain?"

She nodded as best she could and fell back, gasping for air,
as he released her without warning. Rubbing the back of her
neck, she gazed at him through the darkness, her voice trembling with accusation. "What are you doing here? How did you
know Morgan planned to come tonight?"

The Sultan's personal steward shrugged, but his voice was
smug as he informed her coolly, "Captain Carey may be a
clever man and adept at the art of subterfuge, but I am by far
his superior. Though His Majesty the Sultan may suspect nothing of this night's work, I, too, have eyes and ears throughout
the palace. It was a simple thing for me to learn what Morgan
Carey truly wanted here."

"And so you waited until tonight before you made your own
move," Sable whispered. "Why didn't you simply tell the Sultan
what you knew?"

"And spoil my fun?" Nikko looked offended. "His Majesty would simply have ordered Sir Morgan imprisoned, his ship impounded, and that would have been the end of it." His teeth gleamed like a predator's in the darkness. "This way if the escape is thwarted and some British blood is spilled in the process, it will only raise my esteem in the Sultan's eyes. In addition I'll be handsomely rewarded when I present him with the man who was foolish enough to break into the Kafess, and I assure you it won't matter to him if Morgan Carey is brought to him dead or alive."

Sable shivered, numbed by the realization that Morgan had walked straight into a trap devised by a bloodthirsty madman who had waited to ambush him merely for the sport. "Who else have you involved in this scheme of yours?" she asked bitterly.

"The Grand Vizier and I are the only ones who know of tonight's plan," the Greek went on smugly, "though I withheld from him the identity of the man who has instigated it—your Sir Morgan. He knows only that a group of foreigners are involved, and I prefer to keep him ignorant." He smiled broadly, enjoying the opportunity of boasting to this beautiful young woman, an added prize he hadn't originally calculated on. The spoils tonight would be rich indeed, he told himself gleefully.

"Naturally it would prove disastrous to relations with Russia should the Czar discover that we've kept two army officers prisoners for the past ten years. Poor Mahmud Nedim Pasha, who alone of all the Turks favors reconciliation with Russia, has been groveling to the Sultan for months to have Sergei Vilyusk executed to remove this potential source of embarrassment. But the Sultan is too much of a spineless, pageantry-loving buffoon to consider the consequences. Naturally our Grand Vizier understood immediately what repercussions might occur should Vilyusk be freed and take his tale back home. That's why he wholeheartedly approved of my plan to intervene in his attempted rescue. Should Sergei Vilyusk be conveniently killed tonight, it will remove a great burden from his shoulders."

"But why now?" Sable asked in confusion. "Why have you waited ten years to dispose of Sergei? Surely there were many opportunities in the past decade to plan his demise even without the Sultan's consent!"

"Sergei Vilyusk did not become a threat until recently," the

Greek informed her obligingly. "When he and Major Pyotr arrived, the young lieutenant was suffering from a head wound. There was shrapnel lodged in his skull and as a result he had total memory loss by the time he finally recovered his health. For ten years he was content to give Mahmud the information he sought, and it was only when he succumbed to the fever that ravaged the Kafess last year, taking the good Major with it, that his memory returned.

"Naturally he swore that someday he would carry his sordid tale back to his government, which would have sabotaged completely any chances the Grand Vizier has of establishing better relations with our arch enemy. His death tonight," Nikko added with a great deal of satisfaction, "will remove this thorny problem for all of us. No one will suspect that Sergei Vilyusk was ever here."

"But Morgan will know," Sable protested, her voice quivering with indignation. "He'll inform Queen Victoria and she will—"

"Dead men tell no tales," Nikko Trimanos reminded her calmly and added as she gasped, "I'm certain your British Majesty will accept the word of Turkey's Sultan Abdülaziz that Captain Morgan Carey was killed in an accident here in Istanbul—some unfortunate mishap that I plan to arrange this very night. Believe me, your ladyship, my alibi will be drumtight, and even Morgan Carey's own mother won't be suspicious enough to raise doubts concerning his death."

"You monster!" Sable cried and flew at him.

Nikko caught her flailing fists easily and jerked her roughly against him. The scent of her hair filled his senses and he ground his teeth against the responding tightness of his loins. Later, he cautioned himself. The quarry was not yet his. He'd enjoy the beautiful Lady Sable's charms later, when Morgan Carey and his friends were dead.

"Let me tell you what I intend to do," he went on, whispering sibilantly in Sable's ear. "Captain Carey has bribed the Kuzlar Achasi, the Master of the Girls and head of all the eunuchs, to smuggle him into the Kafess. By now he and one of his men, both disguised as women, will have climbed into a pair of waiting palanquins and been admitted into the Kafess as two of the Sultan's wives who have ostensibly come to visit their sons. Once inside the Kafess, Captain Carey intends to clothe Sergei Vilyusk in similar robes and smuggle him out the same way. A master plan, but," Nikko added deliciously, "a pity it will never achieve fruition. He'll never get out of the Kafess alive."

Sable shuddered at the tone of his voice, her heart hammering wildly against her ribs. She must get away and warn Morgan, but how? How?

"Why don't we go along and view the fun?" Nikko suggested. In the next moment he had wrapped the long braid of hair about his fist and wound it tight until Sable cried out in pain. "One word from you and he'll watch you die, is that understood?" he rasped.

Wordlessly Sable nodded. She felt sick with terror as he pulled her roughly across the grounds. Near the Kafess gates he was joined by several of the Sultan's personal guards, imposing men who were armed with fierce-looking scimitars. Sable's heart sank as they were admitted into the Kafess and she saw two palanquins stationed before the marble pavilions exactly as Nikko Trimanos had described.

An enormous black man was standing at the head of a small group of bearers and handmaidens who had obviously followed the conveyances inside. Only a remote flicker of surprise crossed the dark, sweat-glistening features of the Kuzlar Achasi at the sight of the Sultan's steward and his armed guard. Giving him the barest of nods, Nikko Trimanos pushed his way past the group of startled, whispering handmaidens. With Sable's wrists imprisoned in an iron grip behind her back, he propelled her up the stairs, growling in annoyance as she stumbled and nearly fell.

Sable's terror increased when they emerged in a corridor lined with row upon row of closed doors. Gas lamps shone softly, reflecting the gilded trim of the vaulted ceiling high above, and in the stillness the harshness of Nikko Trimanos's breathing was unnaturally loud. Jerking her to a halt before one of the doors halfway down the corridor, he uttered something in a harsh tone to the four soldiers who had followed them up the stairs. Positioning themselves about him, they drew their weapons and Sable moaned as she saw the bloodthirsty gleam in their dark eyes.

"I've given Ramun an order," the Greek informed her in a whisper. "Should you make one move to notify Sir Morgan of our presence, he will instantly cut your throat."

Sable struggled against the tears of futility that welled in

her eyes. In that moment she knew the certainty of Morgan's
pending death, and she railed fiercely against it. There was so
much life still to be lived and she couldn't bear the thought
that he was to die, especially now that she had tasted the
precious gift of his love.

With a low laugh Nikko Trimanos released her and casually
gestured toward the door. Grinning broadly, one of the soldiers
beat the hilt of his curved blade against the wood. There was
a moment of silence which seemed an eternity to Sable, then
the door was boldly thrown open and she found herself looking
up at Morgan's rugged profile. He was wearing flowing robes,
but the hood was thrown back and he had removed his veil so
that his dark, disheveled curls were visible as well as the ruthless set of his lean jaw.

The blue eyes showed no surprise when they met Nikko
Trimanos's dark ones. "So you've found us out, have you,
Nikko?" he inquired almost casually.

"I have." The Greek sneered contemptuously, trying to hide
his annoyance at the fact that the towering Englishman seemed
unafraid. "And we'll waste no time with foolish chitchat, eh?"

Nikko reacted with anger as Morgan had expected him to.
"Ramun!" he barked, wanting to waste no more time in dis-
patching this arrogant Englishman to hell.

Morgan tensed, but even as the Turk rushed forward with
his scimitar swinging in a deadly arc, a guttural cry was torn
from Sable's lips. She could not stand by and watch him be
killed, to witness his life's blood flowing from the terrible
wound Ramun's evil weapon intended to make. Unaware of
what she was doing, with reflexes made quick by panic, Sable
drew the pistol from her belt and fired it point blank at Ramun.

The explosion of powder blinded her and the roar the pistol
made was deafening. She heard an anguished cry and then the
sounds of a fierce struggle. Dropping the smoking weapon, she
rubbed her stinging eyes. Looking up, she stifled a scream as
Morgan, his expression terrible, ran the point of his dagger
into Nikko Trimanos's throat. Two robed men burst out of the
room behind him and had launched themselves at the remaining
guards. Steel blades flashed and the air was rent with the sounds
of mortal combat. Then, suddenly, an eerie silence fell. Sable,
who had been huddled against the wall, cried out as her arm
was taken in a powerful grip.

"Be still," she heard Morgan command in Turkish. The

familiar scent of him enveloped her, made strong by the maleness of sweat, and she ached for the chance to lay her head against his warm, comforting chest for just a moment. But Morgan, unaware of her identity, merely pulled her impersonally down the corridor.

As the buzzing in Sable's ears faded she heard Jack Torance's heavy breathing right behind her along with that of a third man. Casting a swift glance over her shoulder, she saw that he was tall and that his features were completely obscured by the hooded cloak he wore. Her heart skipped a beat. Could this be Sergei Vilyusk? Dared she hope that Morgan had found him so easily? All three men, she noticed in the next moment, were heavily armed, and she could feel the hard steel of a gun barrel that was tucked in Morgan's belt press against her as he hurried her along at his side. She swallowed hard, dismally aware that they still had a long way to go before they were safe.

At the bottom of the stairwell Morgan came to a halt, Sable's wrist still tightly imprisoned in his big hand. All was still on the landing above them, but this did not surprise him. None of the Kafess prisoners would dare leave their rooms or sound the alarm, and should they happen to have the courage to look out into the corridor, they would be greeted by five bloody corpses, a sight that would most assuredly send all of them scurrying back to the safety of their rooms.

"Jack," he said tersely, and immediately his first officer pulled a veil over his face and stole out through the foyer. Returning several moments later, he announced triumphantly that the palanquins were still waiting without.

"Walls must've been too thick for them to hear the shots," he reported with grim satisfaction. "We've still got a chance."

"I don't believe Nikko has another group of guards waiting to ambush us," Morgan added harshly. "He was far too vain to believe he could fail."

"I would still suggest we hurry, eh?" came the heavily accented voice of the tall man at his side. "I would hate to see you skewered and served to the Sultan like a piece of shish kebab."

"What about her, cap'n?" Jack asked, gesturing toward Sable. In the dim lanternlight her veiled face was pale, but none of the men noticed the fact that she was too fair-skinned to pass even for a Circassian.

"We'll take her with us," Morgan said flatly. "At least as far as the gate."

"But cap'n!" Jack protested, shocked. The last thing they needed at the moment was a girl to hinder their progress!

"I owe her my life," Morgan reminded him. "If we leave her here, she'll be put to death for aiding our escape. The least we can do is get her out of here."

Despite the urgency of their predicament Sergei Vilyusk was forced to grin, his eyes glowing in the shadows of the concealing hood. "You certainly haven't changed where the ladies are concerned, my friend! Quite the gentleman, eh?"

"I have no intention of keeping her, you bloody idiot," Morgan growled impatiently.

Sergei's grin widened, enjoying himself hugely now that he could taste freedom on his lips. "I'd think it over, tovarich. These palace beauties are trained to please a man, not to mention that from puberty on they have been instructed in all of the finer arts of sexual gratification." He smacked his lips appreciatively.

"Cap'n, please!" Jack protested, rolling his eyes at the madness of discussing the virtues of palace handmaidens while four palace guards and one high-ranking official lay dead in the corridor above them.

Despite the gravity of the situation Morgan had to laugh. "Come on," he said, hefting his sword and tightening his grip on Sable's wrist. "We'll take her as far as the gate and leave her. I want no more arguments, is that understood? We've wasted enough time already."

"I hear and obey, exalted master," Sergei intoned, and Sable wondered how he could be so flippant in the face of such terrible danger. She longed to reveal herself to Morgan, to gain comfort in the knowledge that he knew who she was and would protect her, but she was afraid to cause any more delays. Later, when they were safe, she would remove her veil and let him see her face.

Pulling the concealing hood over his face, Morgan stepped out into the darkness with Sable behind him. She caught a brief glimpse of the Kuzlar Achasi's dark features before Morgan tossed her into one of the palanquins waiting for them in the courtyard. If the enormous black man suspected what carnage they had left behind them, he gave no sign, nor did the presence of an extra handmaiden in Morgan's company seem to surprise him. Casually he took his place at the head of the procession, discreetly turning his back while the robed "ladies" settled themselves in their conveyances.

Because the palanquin had been constructed to carry only one person, Sable had to make herself very small to accommodate Morgan's immense frame. She was thrown against him as the contraption was hoisted onto the bearers' shoulders, her slim legs tangling with his so that she couldn't get free without struggling.

"Be still," Morgan ordered tersely in Turkish as they began to move toward the gates.

Sable had no intention of speaking, well aware that she'd be incurring his terrible wrath if he were to discover her identity now. Let that come later, she prayed, when they were safely aboard the *Defiance*. Once Morgan was out of danger, she'd gladly tolerate any abuse from him.

Morgan himself found the serving girl's silence curious. He knew of their loyalty to the Sultan, and it puzzled him that this one had killed a man and risked her own life to help him. He cast a glance at her small face as she sat rigidly beside him. Her eyes were wide behind the gossamer veil, and beneath the embroidered bolero her firm breasts rose and fell in rapid rhythm. She was small and slender, he noticed for the first time, and her subtle perfume lingered in the air between them.

Morgan was astonished and outraged to feel his loins begin to tighten in response to the feel of the silk-clad body pressed against his in the close confines of the palanquin. This was utter madness! How could he respond sexually to a young girl in the midst of an escape from the seraglio? He had just killed two men, for God's sake, and the lives of Sergei Vilyusk and his finest officers lay in the balance!

He shifted his weight in an effort to break the intimate contact between them. The girl turned her head to look at him then, and Morgan was struck by the brilliance of the eyes that met his. By God, perhaps the darkness was playing tricks on him, but he could swear they were green, as green as grass and as damnably alluring as those of a certain desirable woman who awaited him back aboard his ship.

Sable, who knew Morgan so well by now, recognized the sudden tightening of his lips as an expression of controlled anger. What was he thinking? she wondered. Had he seen through her veil? Quickly she turned her face away and heaved a great sigh of relief as the palanquin was lowered to the ground.

It was pitch dark and she stumbled as Morgan, who had exited first, helped her down. His hands slid about her to catch her from falling, and her breasts inadvertently brushed against him. He was shocked at the jolt that traveled through him at the contact. Clenching his teeth he set her roughly aside.

"We'll travel alone from here on," Morgan said darkly as Sergei and Jack scrambled from the other conveyance. "The Kuzlar Achasi agreed to take us only as far as the quay walls."

"What about the girl, cap'n?" Jack asked.

"Take—" Morgan began, but his words were suddenly drowned out by an explosion of musketry fire that erupted from the darkness behind them. Shot rained down through the branches of the trees overhead while one of the bearers of the palanquins dropped silently to the ground and another fell howling and clutching his shattered leg.

It was as if the night had been lit by a thousand torches. Gunshots mingled with the screams of the serving girls as they scattered in all directions. Another fusillade hit them, and Sable saw the Kuzlar Achasi spin around as a ball struck him in the chest. She screamed as he fell, blood spurting and staining his clothing crimson. With wide eyes she looked around for Morgan, but it was impossible to see anything in the thick smoke that had settled over them.

"Morgan!" she screamed, her voice breaking with the agony of her fear for him. "Morgan, where are you?"

Her voice was almost lost in the din and confusion, but Morgan heard it nonetheless. His head snapped up and the primed pistol in his hand was lowered as he gazed about him in disbelief. Was that Sable's voice, thin and shaking with fright, that he had heard? No, it was sheer insanity to think so! Sable was safe aboard the *Defiance,* and he was mad to believe she was somewhere here in this blood-soaked scrimmage!

"Morgan, where are you? Please tell me!"

The cry was nearly unintelligible, the words choked with desperate sobs, yet he could no longer doubt his instincts. Squinting against the stinging smoke, he suddenly saw her in the midst of the dead and wounded, a forlorn little figure in crimson silk which he recognized all at once as the harem costume he had purchased for her in Pera days ago. He saw that she was crying, the hopeless look on her face one that he would carry with him to the grave. Behind her the sound of furious activity warned him that the guards were nearing and that their reloaded weapons would erupt at any moment in a deadly cannonade that would cut her in two.

"No!" he shouted, the single word torn from the depths of his soul. Unmindful of the danger and the shocked exclamations of both Sergei and Jack, he dashed forward, seizing Sable about the waist. The force of impact nearly drove him to his knees, but Morgan ignored Sable's frightened scream and scooped her into his arms.

"Over the wall, quickly!" he shouted at his companions as he lifted Sable into the air. "Climb hard, my love," he urged her, his voice rough with emotion, "and don't look back!"

As a young girl Sable had climbed often along the rocks below North Head, and it was this that saved her, for she would never have made it over the ten-foot barricade otherwise. Hauling herself up, she dropped to the ground on the other side, her knees scraped and her eyes stinging from the smoke of gunpowder. The sound of exultant battle cries coming ever closer turned her blood cold, and she searched wildly for Morgan.

"Jack, signal the launch!" she heard him call through the darkness somewhere close by. "We'll have to hurry if we want to get down to the shore without being spotted!"

"Aye, aye, sir!"

Sable heard the underbrush crackle as the first mate slid down the rocky face of the cliff. She began to grope her way in the direction of Morgan's voice, but even as she opened her mouth to whisper his name she was blinded by the glaring light of torches that leaped into view along the quay wall. Faces of soldiers carrying muzzle-loaders were illuminated in nightmarish relief in the flickering light, and Sable screamed as they opened fire at random into the darkness below them.

"Sable, be still!" she heard Morgan command, and in the next moment she felt herself caught against his wide chest with his arms protectively around her. Instinctively she cowered against him, hearing the whining of musket balls slam into the earth around them. How long the cannonade lasted she couldn't tell, but it stopped as suddenly as it had begun, leaving the night so ominously still that she could hear the thundering of Morgan's heartbeat against her cheek.

"Don't move," he cautioned in a whisper, his breath stirring her hair. "They're probably trying to make sure they've killed all of us before they come down to search."

Sable huddled against him as the endless seconds ticked by, grateful for the strong arms that held her so securely. Along the wall all was still. Even the torches had vanished, but Sable felt certain the soldiers hadn't abandoned their positions. As Morgan had said, they were obviously waiting for a sign of movement from below before firing again.

"Cap'n!" It was a low, urgent whisper that came from the darkness to Sable's left. "Cap'n, we need your help!"

"What is it, Jack?" Morgan whispered back, easing Sable ever so slightly out of his arms.

"It's Sergei! I'm afraid he's been hit!"

"Oh, Judas, no!" Sable moaned. Crouching low, she followed Morgan to a small thicket where Sergei's still form lay stretched on the cold, damp ground.

"How bad is it, cap'n?" Jack asked worriedly.

"Very bad, I'm afraid." Morgan's voice was cold. "You'll have to go on alone, Jack. Take Sable with you. I'll bring Sergei down along another route."

"No!" Sable cried, ignoring the startled exclamation of the first mate as he recognized her. Her eyes were wide and beseeching as she seized the front of Morgan's robe in trembling fingers. "Morgan, don't, please don't!"

"In the name of God, Sable, do as I say!" he commanded.

"Please," she whispered, knowing it would mean their deaths if he and Sergei remained behind to face the Sultan's men.

Morgan was silent for a moment as he gazed down into her face, her pleading eyes fastened to his, all the fear and love she felt for him revealed in their haunted depths. "Take her down to the launch, Jack," he said roughly, his expression terrible to behold. "There isn't time for us to follow."

"Leave me here, you fool," Sergei implored in a whisper. "Go on back to that l-leaking scow of yours while you still have the chance."

"This is no time for heroics, my good fellow," Morgan growled. "The cliff path is too steep for you. We'll have to take an alternative route."

"Now who's being a hero?" Sergei asked, his voice growing noticeably weaker. "You'll only end up dead, you h-hard-headed idiot."

"Morgan . . ." Sable choked, aware of nothing but the fact

that she couldn't leave him here alone with a wounded man to care for.

"I told you to go with Jack!" he said harshly. Seeing her pale, tormented face he reached out his hand. "My God, Sable," he groaned softly, then caught himself abruptly. What foolish confession had he been about to make? That he loved her? That the only thing he cared about at the moment was getting her safely back to the ship?

"Jack, get her out of here!" he grated and had one last look at her wide, frightened eyes before they were gone, the underbrush crackling in their wake. Behind him along the quay wall he could hear the renewed shouts of the soldiers and knew that at any moment they would come pouring over the battlements in pursuit. Yet he could not help thinking of Sable at the moment, feeling regret that he might not survive this night. Then he cursed himself savagely. What a fool he was! No matter the outcome, nothing had changed between them, and should he return to his ship unharmed, he must remember that he had sworn to himself earlier never to succumb to her seductive powers again.

Bending down, Morgan slung Sergei's arm about his shoulder. "We'll have to run for it, old friend."

Sergei's voice was thin but steady. "Lead the way, comrade. I'm perfectly willing to follow."

The going was difficult, but both men were accustomed to hardships and the art of eluding an enemy. To Morgan's infinite relief the skies opened unexpectedly in a torrential downpour that, though it soaked them to the bone, aided greatly in concealing them from sharp, probing eyes. With their torches sputtering out, the Sultan's soldiers were handicapped by the darkness, while their quarry's skill at evasion further frustrated their attempts to capture them.

For Sable St. Germain it was a night of terror that she would remember for the rest of her life. Never had she been forced to endure such physical hardship as negotiating a treacherous cliff face in utter darkness when one false step might mean a plunge of a hundred feet or more. The path down which Jack led her was so steep that at times she felt certain the very ground would drop from beneath her feet. Sharp rocks cut the soles of her slippers, and her clothes were soon hopelessly torn. Scratches covered her arms and legs, and she clung to Jack's supporting arm with all her might.

Yet it was not the fear of falling and being dashed against the jagged rocks far below that tormented her. It was the awful awareness that Morgan had remained behind and that Sergei, badly wounded, had been left in his care.

"Jack," she panted, turning her face to him in the darkness, "what will they do?"

"Don't you worry about them," he told her firmly. "The cap'n knows this area. He'll find a way to get Sergei down to the water."

"But—"

"Mind your step now, m'lady!" Jack protested as she slipped and nearly lost her footing. "We got to think of ourselves first!"

They were halfway down the cliff when the rain began. Within seconds the path was transformed into quagmire while gushing runoffs soaked them and further threatened their tenuous footholds. Sable was thoroughly drenched and shivering uncontrollably when they finally reached the bottom. Numbly she allowed Jack to pull her along until she heard the familiar voice of Harley Gump calling to them through the darkness.

"What's to do, Jack?" he demanded gruffly as the *Defiance*'s first officer appeared, disheveled and soaking, at the water's edge.

"The cap'n's still behind. Vilyusk took a ball in the back."

Sable could hear Aaron Pierson's soft whistle from the stern of the boat. "Obviously they canna go far."

"Lady Sable!" Harley Gump burst out, seeing her shivering little form for the first time as Jack helped her into the boat. "What—"

"No time for explanations," Jack interrupted, sloshing through the waves as he pushed off. Leaping nimbly inside, he shook the wet hair from his eyes. "Look lively, mates! We'll have to put some distance between us and the palace and then wait for the cap'n's signal."

"If they make it out of there alive," one of the oarsmen remarked grimly.

"Oh, Jack!" Sable gasped.

"Never you mind, Lady Sable," the first officer said sharply. "We didn't hear any more musket fire, did we? I'm firm believing Sir Morgan lost them in the darkness."

"And what were you doing with them, your ladyship?" Dr. Pierson demanded sternly. Placing a blanket about her shaking shoulders, he handed her a brandy flask. "Did Sir Morgan find it necessary to involve hapless women in this adventure?"

Sable bristled at the censure in the doctor's voice. "Morgan had no idea I was there! I followed him tonight, and he didn't know it until later. I-I wanted to help him," she faltered, reluctant to explain further.

"Lady Sable did more than her share," Jack added gruffly. "She put a lead ball through a soldier who was just about to run a scimitar through our good captain's heart."

The listening men murmured their approval, but Sable scarcely heard them. She was bone-tired and thoroughly soaked. Even the blanket didn't help against the chills that shook her. Yet it was fear, mind-cloying fear for Morgan, that kept her staring numbly through the darkness behind them. Where was he? Had he managed to escape the soldiers, or had he and Sergei been taken prisoner?

"Wh-what are we going to do now, Jack?" Her teeth were beginning to chatter, and she clamped her jaws together to hide the fact from him.

"The captain'll pick out another spot to meet us where the path to the water won't be near as hard for Sergei to handle."

"And if he's too weak to walk at all?" Sable asked, fear lending her voice an uncharacteristic edge.

Jack hesitated a moment, then said confidently, "The captain'll find a way, m'lady. I've no fears in that quarter."

Yet Sable heard the underlying worry in his tone, and it was as if a cold hand wrapped itself about her heart. Morgan and Sergei were in dire trouble, and even Jack was forced to admit as much. Her throat ached, and she swallowed hard, determined not to behave like a foolish woman by shedding cowardly tears.

"Faster, lads," Jack ordered.

It was pitch black and ominously still on the water. The rain had finally ended and the wind had died, bringing a strange, almost menacing calm to the heavens. The lights of Istanbul were all but doused, and the only sound to be heard was the occasional creak of the oarlocks as the silent men kept the boat positioned against the current.

Sable continued to stare in the direction of the coastline until her vision began to blur, desperately searching for Morgan's signal. Where in the name of God was he? She knew she'd not be able to tolerate much more of this waiting. She thought of Morgan and how tenderly he had made love to her. How vividly she could recall the expression on his handsome face when he had cupped her chin with his strong hand and had kissed her until she melted against him.

A tear slid unnoticed down Sable's cheek. She'd not be able to go on living if anything happened to him.

"Ahoy, the boat!"

Sable jerked about, her heart stopping at the sound of the cry that came from the blackness behind them.

"It's all right, m'lady," Harley Gump soothed her. "'Tis just the other launch."

A moment later the pale face of the *Defiance*'s youngest officer materialized through the mist. "Ahoy, there," he called softly. "Can you hear me?"

"Hayes, you were to stay with the ship!" Jack exploded as the other boat shipped its oars and drifted alongside their own.

"Aye, Mr. Torance, and we've been ready to sail for the past three hours! Gilpin thought he heard shots in the direction of the palace, so I thought we'd better investigate." Daniel's jaw dropped as the light of the lantern he carried fell upon the interior of the other boat and caught the highlights of Sable's unbound hair. "My God, Lady Sable! What are you doing here?"

"There's no time for idle chitchat," Jack growled. "You'd better get back to the ship, and take Lady Sable with you."

"No!" Sable protested.

The dour Devonshireman touched her hand, his expression uncommonly gentle. "You'll be more help to the captain on the ship, lass. There's beds to be made and bandages to roll. Dr. Pierson can tell you what he'll be needing when Sergei's brought aboard."

"An excellent suggestion!" the physician chimed in. "Perpaps," he added hopefully, "I should accompany Lady St. Germain back to the ship in order to oversee the preparations myself."

Jack's oddly colored eyes became mere chips of ice. If there was anything he despised it was cowardice in another man. "You've work to do here, tending Sergei Vilyusk when we fetch him!" His soft voice was filled with menace, and Dr. Pierson instinctively shielded his face with his hands, thinking the muscular first officer intended to accompany his biting words with a physical blow.

"Quite right, quite right, I wasn't thinking!"

"Dawn'll be breakin' late," Jack added, turning his face to

the oppressively dark sky, his anger already spent. "Dan'l, keep the ship just so. I'm prayin' we'll be right behind you."

"Me, too, sir," young Hayes intoned solemnly.

Watching as Sable was assisted into the other boat, Jack found himself wishing he could find some encouraging words to say to her. How young and touchingly fragile she looked, swallowed up in the folds of the blanket Dr. Pierson had wrapped about her, her beautiful eyes pools of suffering in her small face.

"You'll have everything ready when Sir Morgan returns, your ladyship?" he called across the distance of water that was rapidly growing between them.

Startled, Sable raised her head. "What did you say?" she asked uncertainly.

"The cap'n! You'll see to it everything's put right for him, won't you?"

"Yes, Mr. Torance," she called back, her voice growing stronger. "Yes, of course! I'll do everything I can!"

"We ought to be along shortly," he added before the darkness swallowed her up, pleased that now she had something besides worrying to keep her occupied.

Despite the terrible cold and her relentless, gnawing fear, Sable dropped into an exhausted slumber as the small rowboat sped back to the *Defiance*. A loud hail from the deck high above awoke her with a start. Dazed, she rose to her feet and allowed Daniel Hayes to assist her up the boarding net. She stumbled as she reached the top and felt someone grab her, pulling her quickly through the entry port. Seconds later the solid deck of the ship was beneath her numb feet, and she was looking up into Grayson's astonished face.

"Dear God, Lady Sable! Are you hurt?" he inquired anxiously.

"No, I'm fine," she assured him hastily.

"Thank goodness!" His brisk manner quickly returned. "Come below and let me make you some hot tea."

Sable shook her head. "There isn't time, Grayson. We've got to get Morgan's cabin ready for Dr. Pierson."

Deep shock lines etched themselves into Grayson's face. "Then someone's been hurt?"

"Sergei's been badly wounded," Sable replied tremulously. "We had to leave both of them behind on Seraglio Point. They're going to try to reach the shoreline farther upriver where Mr. Torance intends to pick them up."

"We'll be ready to sail as soon as they're brought aboard," Daniel Hayes added, coming up behind them. "Now, will you please tell me, Lady Sable," he added, peering disbelievingly at her torn and muddied clothing, "what were you doing out there? Didn't you know—"

But Grayson had laid a protective arm about Sable's shoulders and turned to lead her below. "There'll be plenty of time for explanations later, Mr. Hayes," he called. Furthermore, he decided grimly, it would be to Sir Morgan that Sable should be making them and no one else.

"He'll let us know, won't he?" Sable asked, turning her wide green eyes to Grayson's face. "When the captain and Sergei return?"

"Of course. Have no fear in that quarter, m'lady!"

Morgan's cabin was pleasantly warm, thanks to the fire Grayson had laid in the small stove. Leading Sable inside, the steward reached into the dresser and drew out a thick towel. "I want you to get out of those wet things," he told her, his tone brooking no argument and reminding Sable all too well of his domineering master. "Dry yourself thoroughly and put these on." He handed her a freshly laundered shirt and a pair of breeches. Seeing Sable's uncertain look, he added sternly, "I'll have enough patients to care for without you coming down with pneumonia, madame!"

Sable was too tired to argue with him, and besides, the prospect of being warm and dry was too appealing to ignore.

"I'll bring you something hot to drink," Grayson added from the doorway. His heart went out to her when he saw her standing before him with the towel in her hands, her pantaloons and bolero soaking wet, an icy puddle forming on the floor below her feet. Her expression was that of a lost and frightened child, and for a moment he had to grapple with the urge to put his arms around her and comfort her. That would never do, he told himself sharply. Lady Sable was made of sterner stuff than that, and, besides, he could sense that she was close to the breaking point. Any show of affection on his part would only bring on the flood of tears she was obviously trying so hard to control.

When he returned he found Sable turning back the bed-clothes on the bunk and organizing the items Dr. Pierson had

requested. She was still pale, however, and Grayson set down
the tray he had carried inside. "Here, drink this," he ordered,
filling a mug with steaming coffee. "There's brandy in it, which
ought to do you a world of good."

Expecting an argument, he was surprised when she took it
obediently. Over the rim of the mug her eyes met his, and he
was shaken by the suffering he saw in their dark green depths.
Dear God, how she must love him, Grayson thought to himself,
and prayed that Sir Morgan would return unharmed.

For the next half-hour the tall, soft-spoken valet and the
silent young girl worked side by side transforming Morgan
Carey's quarters into a suitable surgery. Sable obeyed Grayson's
commands without question, relieved that she was able to keep
busy. Yet both of them worked mechanically, always listening
with half an ear to any sounds on the deck above that might
alert them to the longboat's return.

Finally, after what seemed an interminable wait, the sound
of footsteps could be heard pounding across the deck above.
At the same moment the cabin door flew open and the flushed
face of a crewman appeared.

"Captain's returned, Mr. Grayson! You're to be sure everything's ready!"

Then he was gone, leaving them gazing at one another with
jubilant expressions. A hot flush stole across Sable's cheeks.
She was bone-tired, yet inwardly her heart was singing. Morgan
was back! He was safe at last!

They had just completed the last of their tasks when the
cabin door crashed open and two crewmen came hurrying inside
bearing the unconscious form of Sergei Vilyusk between them.
Dr. Pierson, his expression grave, was right behind them. "Lay
him there, lads, gently, gently! You don't want to make it
worse, do you?" His manner was brisk and professional as he
supervised Sergei's transfer to Morgan's bunk.

"Where is the captain?" Grayson asked, voicing the question
that was foremost in Sable's mind.

"At the helm," one of the men replied. "We're making
preparations to get under way." Politely touching the front of
his watchcap in Sable's direction, he followed his companion
back out.

Sable turned her full attention to the still figure stretched
out on the bunk. She was aghast to see how pale Sergei had
grown. His eyes were closed and there was a definite bluish

cast to his lips. His shirt was damp and soaked with blood, and she gazed anxiously at the physician.

"How bad is it?"

"He's lost too much blood for my liking," Dr. Pierson replied without looking at her. "Fortunately the ball passed clean through his shoulder, but I canna vouch for his recovery. I was able to staunch the bleedin' on the trip over, but now some stitchin'll be necessary."

"I'll help him, Lady Sable," Grayson volunteered. "You go on to bed."

She shook her head. "Let me stay, Grayson. I can fetch things for you and do whatever else you need me to."

Dr. Pierson regarded her uncertainly. "It'll na be a pleasant sight, m'lady."

The stubborn look on Sable's face was not one of childish indulgence, but of the proud, determined woman Morgan had helped her become. This was Morgan's friend, the man he had risked so much to rescue, and she would do whatever lay in her power to help him survive.

"Please, I want to stay," she said softly.

"Then wash your hands, lass," Dr. Pierson commanded, aware that there was no time left for arguing. "You, too, Grayson. And I expect both of you to follow my orders to the letter, is that understood?"

There was no comparing this self-assured, competent physician with the whining, seasick coward Sable had long since come to know. She wondered if this was what Morgan had seen in the man that had prompted him to recruit his services at the onset of the voyage. Scrubbing her hands in the washbasin, she thought of Morgan, and a deep feeling of contentment trembled in her heart. Dare she feel this way with Sergei so ill? She felt almost guilty to admit it to herself but, yes, she was happy that Morgan was back where he belonged, happier than she had ever been in her entire life.

On the rain-soaked decks above, the men of the *Defiance* were going about their tasks with the speed and efficiency only long years of practice could bring. Morgan had taken his place at the helm, his narrowed eyes trained on the men working along the yards high overhead who appeared as mere shadows in the dim light of approaching dawn. It was cold, and Morgan's shirt clung damply to his skin, but he took no notice of his discomfort. Speed was what he needed now, the speed only a clipper ship and its disciplined crew could bring. Later, when they were far out to sea, he would worry about himself.

"Anchor's hove short, captain sir!" came a shout from the darkness below.

At Morgan's nearly imperceptible nod the helmsmen leaped for the enormous wheel, and Jack Torance tilted back his head to shout an order to those high above. "Loose head and tops'ls!"

A freshening wind, clammy with the recent rain, began to fill the fluttering sails while the men in the rigging worked diligently to secure them. The enormous ship tilted in response to the press of lowered canvas, the decks canting as it began to gather speed.

"Sou' by sou'west, sir!" one of the helmsmen cried. "Full an' bye!"

Morgan folded his arms across his chest, his booted legs splayed as the wind and spindrift hit his face. The *Defiance* was under way at last, and Sergei and Sable were safe below. Let the Grand Vizier do what he pleased to stop them. Morgan had accomplished what he had set out to do, and he was content.

Chapter 13

Sable St. Germain straightened with a sigh and pushed the loose strands of hair out of her eyes. Her back ached and her vision was blurred with weariness, but she didn't complain, knowing that Grayson and Dr. Pierson were just as tired as she was. Lifting a pile of bloodied bandages, she paused for a moment at the foot of the bunk to stare down at the man who held the rare distinction of being Morgan Carey's closest friend.

His was a handsome face despite the pallid hue of his skin. Dark hair fell in disarray across a wide forehead, and his neatly trimmed beard emphasized a strong chin and retroussé nose. Sable was relieved to see that the bluish tinge of his lips was gone, but she could tell from the involuntary trembling of his limbs that he was very weak and that perhaps a fever was in the making. She glanced up at Aaron Pierson and didn't even have the courage to ask him if Sergei would survive when she saw the gravity of his expression. He must! she told herself. Morgan had risked far too much for him to die now!

"I suggest you go on to bed, your ladyship."

It was Grayson reaching helpfully for the bundle of rags she held in her hands. She shook her head and gave him a weak smile.

"I will, but I'd like to go topside first and see how Mor—Captain Carey and Mr. Torance are."

"I had Gilpin bring them some coffee earlier, and they appeared to be fine," Grayson assured her kindly. "Judging from these creaking beams, we've been under way for a while." Wearily he massaged the back of his neck. The clock on Morgan's dressing table read five-thirty. Small wonder he was bleary-eyed with exhaustion. And as for Lady Sable, who had not only worked tirelessly at Dr. Pierson's side, but had followed Sir Morgan ashore—

"I'll go to bed in just a few minutes," Sable promised, reading his mind with uncanny accuracy. "That's provided Dr. Pierson doesn't need me anymore."

"Hmm?" The surgeon regarded her thoughtfully, then shook his head. "No, not at all, Lady Sable. Our patient is resting now, and we can't do any more for him."

Sable went out thankfully and stood leaning for a moment with her back against the door. She was so tired, and it seemed as if every muscle in her body ached. The events of the past night were blurred together, and she knew that her numbness was just a defense against the horrors she had witnessed. She had shot a man, she remembered, and as the terrible reality broke through, she thrust it quickly away. She must never, never think of that again! If she hadn't fired her pistol at Ramun he would have killed Morgan, and that was something far too horrible even to contemplate.

Suddenly she wanted to see Morgan so badly that her knees began to wobble. Pulling herself up the companionway, she stepped onto the deck, the chilly dawn air bracing after the stuffiness below. The *Defiance* was heeling hard into the wind, the sails above Sable's head taut, and she knew now why Morgan hadn't come down to check on Sergei's progress.

Her mouth went dry. Did he expect them to be pursued? She recalled Jack Torance telling her that Turkey possessed the third largest navy in the world. Would the Sultan see fit to dispatch a warship after them? Yet how could he when only Nikko Trimanos had known the identity of the men who had rescued Sergei Vilyusk? And Nikko Trimanos, she reminded herself with a shudder, was dead.

Sable found Morgan on the quarterdeck, a telescope in his hands as he searched the darkened waters astern. Jack Torance and Crewman Palmer were at the helm, the first mate still wearing the same filthy clothes he had come aboard in. Glancing down at herself, Sable realized she was still in her harem costume, which was torn and muddied beyond recognition. She must look a fright, she thought to herself, her hand going automatically to her tangled curls.

"Trust a woman to always think of her appearance first."

She looked up at Morgan's taunting words and gasped in dismay as she caught sight of his face. Morgan frowned, unaware of how haggard he appeared to her. Dark stubble covered his chin, and though he had stripped off his filthy shirt and exchanged it for a clean one, he still wore his badly wrinkled breeches. His eyes were red-rimmed, and there was a ruthless purpose about him that Sable had never seen before.

She hesitated on the ladder, unsure of his reception, her hands pressed against the railing behind her as though ready to bolt at a single harsh word from him. Seeing this, Morgan's brow darkened.

"Come away from there, lass. I'm not going to shout at you."

"I thought you might be angry with me," Sable admitted without moving.

The corners of Morgan's mouth lifted. "You should be soundly thrashed for what you did, Sable, and be rationed bread and water in your cabin for the duration of the voyage. But I've finally begun to learn there's no sense in trying to discipline you. If I'd succeeded, you might not have appeared when you did last night. Your intervention saved my life, Sable," he said softly, knowing the vision of her with a pistol in her hands bravely firing at Ramun would follow him to the grave.

"Then—then you're not angry?" Sable whispered.

An odd expression crossed his face. "Angry? No, Sable, not angry. I—" He broke off, as though guarding himself from revealing too much. How could he put into words what her courage had meant to him? How could he tell her what he had felt when he had seen her standing alone and unarmed in the middle of a barrage of gunfire, calling his name with tears in her eyes?

"How is Sergei, your ladyship?" Jack Torance asked into the strained silence.

"Dr. Pierson says we'll have to wait and see," Sable said softly, hating to bring them such dispiriting news. "He's lost a great deal of blood and he's very weak." Without being aware of it, she glanced at Morgan as though seeking his assurance that Sergei would not die.

Feeling her eyes upon him, he looked down at her in silence, the wind tugging at his hair. "Go to bed, Sable," he said gently.

She no longer had the will to disobey him. As she turned away, however, a cry of alarm came from the masthead lookout overhead, halting her in her tracks.

"Sails astern!"

Morgan scooped up his telescope and trained it beyond the railing. Dawn was breaking on the horizon, a sullen gray streak across the surging sea, yet it was enough for him to make out the telltale patches of white above the waterline.

For a tense moment there was silence, then came another chilling cry from the lookout. "It's a frigate, sir!"

Morgan's jaw clenched. Handing the telescope to his first officer, he stood for a moment without moving, his expression unreadable. Jack Torance's soft voice finally roused him from his thoughts.

"What'll we do, cap'n?"

"I suggest we reef those sails," Morgan responded quietly, "and see what they want."

The Devonshireman's brows rose. "Are you sure, cap'n?"

Morgan's blue eyes were cold. "This is the first time you have ever questioned my orders, Mr. Torance."

"Aye, sir." Jack was not perturbed by his captain's tone. "But it seems to me we ought to try to outrun them. I bet we could clear the headland before them."

"And if she decides to give chase? She'd blow us out of the water." Morgan's expression was hard. "Need I remind you, Jack, that Turkish frigates-of-war carry twenty times our firepower?" His lips tightened grimly. "No, we'll proceed slowly, and should we be hailed we'll put by. There's nothing yet to indicate that she was dispatched after us."

"And if she was?" Jack asked shortly. "If they request permission to come aboard?"

"That," Morgan said evenly, "is something we'll have to deal with when it happens."

Despite his indifferent manner, he was worried. Under normal circumstances he would have set the *Defiance* tearing down the enemy's throat, its great spread of sails straining from the forecourse as the bow knifed through the water. The clipper was unquestionably the faster of the two ships and could conceivably clear land before the Turkish frigate had time to fire upon them.

But Morgan wouldn't risk such odds at this time, not with Sable aboard and Sergei lying gravely wounded below. His own life mattered little to him, and he knew his loyal crew would rather fight to the death than extend docile acquiescence to the Sultan's Imperial Navy. Yet no matter his personal preference, Morgan knew that he could not afford to laugh into the face of fate this time. Far too much hung in the balance.

"I'll give the men your orders, sir," Jack said reluctantly. "Mayhap we've not seen a change in our fortunes yet."

Turning his head, Morgan suddenly caught sight of Sable, whose presence he had completely forgotten. She was standing near the ladder, her face pale, and he ground his teeth together in frustration. "Go below," he ordered, the expression on his handsome face brooking no argument.

"Are they going to attack us?" Sable asked, and despite her best efforts her voice trembled dangerously.

The fact that she was frightened enraged Morgan unexpectedly. She had endured enough, this brave, lovely woman, and he hated to think of the hardships she might still have to face before it was all over. "Go below," he repeated. "Nothing is going to happen to you, Sable, I promise."

He could not know that it was not concern for herself that troubled her, but she couldn't tell him so, not when he was glaring at her so sternly. Aware that she would only be an added burden to him if she didn't obey, Sable turned to go below. As she set foot on the top rung of the ladder, however, a deep rumble erupted like thunder from behind her. She whirled about in time to see a spout of fire belching from the other ship, now close enough that the enormous press of sails could be recognized with the naked eye.

"She's firing on us, sir!" the lookout shouted, but Morgan had already realized as much.

"Mr. Torance!" he bellowed, pushing past the gathered crewmen to the opposite railing. "Pass the order to man the action stations and load! No one is to make a move until I give the word!"

"Aye, aye, sir!"

"Shake out those reefs!" Morgan shouted to the men in the rigging, cupping his hands as he gave the order. He watched with narrowed eyes as they scrambled to obey, letting out the sails he had just ordered them to take in. The *Defiance* shuddered in response as the topgallants bellied out behind them, the bow seeming to plunge down into the water as the enormous ship began to gather speed. Turning his head, Morgan caught sight of Sable standing frozen on the ladder, her hands clenched about the railing so tight that the knuckles were white.

"I told you to go below!" he barked, but relented when he saw the fear in her wide green eyes. "For the love of God, Sable, promise me you'll stay below!" he went on less harshly. "You'll be safe there. No heroics, do you promise me? I don't want to come down to the gundeck and find you manning a cannon yourself, is that understood?"

She tried to smile but succeeded only in gazing up at him, her heart in her eyes. Still wearing the harem costume he had given her earlier, she looked too fragile to have acted as courageously as she had the night before. But Morgan knew better than to be deceived again, and he refused to allow himself to be softened by the look on her young face. Seeing Daniel Hayes hurrying across the main deck, he called out his name.

"Aye, captain?" Daniel panted as he joined them.

"Take Lady Sable below," Morgan ordered, "and inform Dr. Pierson of the circumstances. He and Grayson are to make themselves responsible for Sergei Vilyusk in the event we are attacked or boarded. They are to employ any means to keep him safe, is that understood?"

"Yes, sir. Anything else, sir?"

Morgan's tone was forbidding. "I want Lady St. Germain locked in her cabin with a sentry posted before the door."

"Morgan, please," Sable whispered, aghast.

"Higgins will do," he continued as though she hadn't spoken. "Tell him that only on my word is anyone to be permitted inside, and under no circumstances is Lady St. Germain to be released until I've given the order. See that Mr. Higgins is made clear of that, Mr. Hayes."

"Aye, aye, sir!"

Without giving Sable time to protest, Daniel hurried her away. Though the *Defiance* had seen plenty of action since he'd first signed on and he had the utmost confidence in his captain's capabilities, the fact that Lady Sable was aboard distressed Daniel greatly. She was such a delicate little creature! How would she ever endure the horrors of a naval confrontation?

"You'll be safe in here, your ladyship," he assured her, thrusting her more forcefully than was his usual way into her cabin. "Captain Sir Morgan won't allow any of us to come to harm, I promise."

She gazed up at him in mute appeal, and he found himself hopelessly lost as he looked into the pain-darkened depths of her eyes. Their haunting emerald color moved him, and he wished he had the nerve to tell her how much he loved her. But there was so little time, even less now than when he'd first delivered her back to the ship hours earlier, shocked at her behavior and at the unnecessary risks she had taken. Seeing to her welfare by following Sir Morgan's orders was all he could do for her at the moment.

"Daniel, please—"

He hesitated at the sound of his name falling for the first time from her lips, but steeled himself before it was too late. "I'm sorry, your ladyship, I have my orders."

Unable to bear the sight of her small, pleading face any longer, he shut the door and turned the key in the lock. Expecting to hear her sobbing pleas through the door, he waited for a moment, but nothing stirred beyond the thin wood. Reluctantly he pocketed the key and ran off in search of Crewman Higgins.

Up on deck the hands continued to work feverishly to secure the enormous ship. Speed was what the *Defiance* needed, and if they were to outrun the Turkish frigate, then everything depended on making the utmost use of the wind and sails. Jack Torance was at the helm, while Daniel Hayes, having just returned topside, took his position near the mast to relay Morgan's orders to the men waiting above.

Gunfire sounded again, louder this time, and a flume of water burst out of the sea a scant quarter-mile away. It was clearly a signal warning the English ship to put by, but Morgan had no intention of doing so. Should they be boarded and searched, it would prove impossible to hide Sergei without risking his life by moving him. He remembered, too, the comments made by the Sultan concerning Sable's beauty and how fitting a prize she would be for his harem. His brow darkened, wondering if Abdülaziz had given orders that the English seamen were to be killed but that Lady Sable St. Germain should be taken alive at all costs. Bloody bastard, did he honestly believe Morgan would allow Sable to submit to such a fate?

"Course sou'west by south, sir!" his helmsman informed him.

Morgan shook himself free of his dark thoughts and turned his eyes to the great sheets of canvas that were crackling like thunder in the wind. In the pale light of dawn they seemed to glow stark white against the steel-gray sky, and he could feel the strain in every spar and timber.

"Keep her just so, Mr. Torance," he called back, knowing he could not extract another ounce of speed from those sails. The *Defiance* was giving her best, and he could do nothing but pray that it was enough. With his elbow propped almost casually on the rail, he rested his telescope on the netting and settled down to wait.

The Turkish frigate, belatedly aware that the clipper was not going to heed its signal, swung in to give chase. Even without the use of his scope Morgan could see the length of its sails growing taut as the lines were made fast. Spray began to fly from the bow as the ship increased its speed, but he was already certain that its efforts would not prove good enough.

As though in agreement the frigate fired another salvo, but the shots fell hopelessly short of their mark. The *Defiance*, clearing the headland, was already beginning to make way.

"We're losing her, sir!" Daniel Hayes cried above the throbbing of the wind in the lines.

"By God, this is a fist in the Sultan's face, sir!" Jack Torance added, his normally dour face wreathed in a toothy grin.

For a moment Morgan said nothing, his blue-eyed gaze taking in each familiar smiling face below him. Then he straightened and said quietly, "I imagine we ought to let them know that we're aware of it. Mr. Hayes," he added to the young man whose grin had grown even wider at his captain's words, "give them a starboard volley. Fire when ready."

"Aye, aye, sir!" Hoarse with excitement, Daniel hurried off to relay the captain's orders. A moment later the aft cannons rumbled and the *Defiance* jerked slightly in response. Wafts of smoke whipped up from the gunports to dissipate into the sky while the watching men cheered lustily.

"Keep her so, Mr. Torance," Morgan said to his helmsman. "We may have outrun them, but I'd rather not take any chances." To the returning Daniel Hayes he added, "Send someone below to inform Dr. Pierson that we're no longer under the threat of attack. Oh, and Daniel," he added almost as an afterthought, "you can let Lady St. Germain out of her cabin now."

Daniel was already halfway down the steps when his captain's deep voice brought him up short. "Belay that order, lad."

"Sir?"

Morgan extended his hand. "Give me the keys. I'll do it myself."

"Aye, sir," Daniel said glumly, laying the key into the outstretched palm.

"Cap'n," Jack called after him and Morgan raised his brows inquiringly. "What course shall we plot, sir?"

A grin split the rugged face and it was as if his exhaustion had mysteriously vanished. "Home, Mr. Torance, where else?"

Turning the key in the lock of Sable's door, Morgan half expected her to come flying out to confront him, demanding to know exactly what had happened. To his surprise all was quiet in her quarters, and he opened the door slowly, puzzled by her odd behavior. Stepping inside, he drew up short, unable to credit the sight that met his eyes.

His bold little adventuress, despite the threat of an impending attack by a Turkish warship, had fallen asleep on her bunk. With her knees drawn up, her cheek cradled on one hand, she slept soundly, the exhaustion in her young face smoothed into the peace of repose. Morgan stood for a moment looking down at her, becoming aware for the first time since the harrowing night had begun how much it would have cost him if he had lost her.

Leaning down, he allowed his hand to softly caress the dark, glossy hair. Sable did not even stir, and her deep, regular breathing remained unchanged. Straightening, Morgan closed the door quietly behind him.

Entering his own quarters, he found Dr. Pierson bending over Sergei Vilyusk's still form. Stepping nearer, Morgan didn't need the Scotsman's smiling prognosis to see that Sergei's condition had improved. Though he was feverish and very pale, the deathly pallor that had given his face a grayish cast earlier was gone.

"I believe he's gang to be fine, cap'n," Dr. Pierson informed him happily. "There'll be fever for a wee bit an' many days before he regains his strength, but I dinna think we'll lose him now."

"I never should have expected otherwise," Morgan murmured almost to himself, sinking tiredly into the comfortable chair behind his secretary.

Dr. Pierson regarded him curiously. "I beg your pardon, sir?"

But Morgan only smiled mysteriously, for it was plain to him now that his luck had truly changed ever since the *Defiance* had taken aboard an enchanting, green-eyed sea witch.

Sable slept deeply throughout the entire day, unaware of the activity that went about on the decks above. It was only after the ship's bell rang to signal the beginning of the evening watch that she awoke. She had forgotten to wind the tiny clock Grayson had loaned her long ago, and it was stopped, which told her nothing. Peering out of the porthole, she saw that it was dark and guessed that she must have slept the day away.

"Lazy beast!" she chastised herself, though it had been nearly seven in the morning when she had at last drifted off into an exhausted slumber.

Her lavender gown lay over the chair, the muddied and still-damp harem costume beside it. Slipping into the gown, Sable brushed and plaited her hair, then carefully washed the silk costume in the corner basin. Hanging it from a brass hook on the wall to dry, she wondered if she would ever be able to wear it again without remembering the harrowing night of Sergei's rescue from the seraglio.

Sergei! Her breath caught in her throat as she thought of him. How had he been faring while she lay sleeping? And what of the Turkish frigate that had chased them down the length of the Bosporus? How could she have slept through something like that?

Opening her door, Sable peered down the corridor, only to find everything dark in Morgan's quarters. No beam of light shone from beneath the door, and she wondered if Sergei was resting there alone. Perhaps Morgan was topside, she told herself hopefully, and would be willing to answer her questions.

The moon was nearly full and silver beams danced on the water when Sable stepped out into the warm night air. A pulley slapped against one of the yards overhead, adding its rhythmic sound to the creaking of timber that had become so familiar a part of the nightly music for Sable by now. She wandered to the rail and lifted her face to the wind, glad for this chance to be alone. The thought that this might well be one of the last nights she would spend aboard the *Defiance* occurred to her suddenly, but she quickly thrust such sad musings away. This was a time for happiness, and she must remember that Morgan's mission had been a success and that none of his men had been hurt during Sergei's rescue from Istanbul.

Footsteps echoed on the planking behind her and without turning Sable knew that it was Morgan. She made no move to acknowledge his presence as he came to stand beside her, but every fiber of her being was aware of him. She felt her nerves prickle and her heartbeat quicken, conscious of an expectancy that hovered between them like the charged air before a storm.

"How is Sergei?" she asked, anxious to break the tension.

"He's going to get well, though it may take some time," Morgan's deep voice informed her softly. "I'm also pleased to report, m'lady, that we've left all Turkish vessels far behind us. I don't expect anything else to happen until we arrive safely in Tangier."

"What will happen to him when he's well?" Sable asked curiously, though deep in her heart she knew it was really Morgan's welfare that mattered to her. "Where will you take him? Does he have any family left?"

"I'm afraid not," Morgan responded regretfully. "And as for his plans, I imagine that's something he'll have to work out for himself."

Sable was silent a moment, and Morgan, looking down at her delicate profile, wondered what she was thinking.

"What about Sultan Abdülaziz?" she asked at last. "What do you think he'll do now?" She shivered, a distressing picture rising to her mind of Morgan being stripped of his knighthood and imprisoned by an angry Queen Victoria.

"Unless Sergei intends to lodge a formal complaint in his own country I have a feeling the Sultan will do nothing. It would prove best for him if none of this ever came to light."

Sable wished she had the courage to ask him what he intended to do after she had been returned to Tangier. She found she couldn't tolerate the thought of returning to North Head never knowing what had happened to either of them. It dawned on her how very little she knew about this man who owned her heart. All she had ever been told was that he had left a comfortable life in Devon to become a soldier and then a sea captain, but she was no nearer understanding the forces that drove him than before.

"Will you go home to Devon when this voyage is over?" she asked timidly, hoping he would give her something to cling to.

In the moonlight Morgan's profile was clearly defined, and she could see the cynical twisting of his lips as he said softly, "Home to Devon? I have no home save my ship."

"None at all?" she questioned disbelievingly. "Everyone has a place to live!"

"I'm not everyone," Morgan reminded her gently. "I have no house in the country, Sable, and certainly no estate as magnificent as your beloved North Head." Mocking amusement lit his eyes. "I have a small townhouse in Dartmouth where I like to stay whenever my ships needs re-outfitting, but I rent it out when I'm away. Does that satisfy your sensibilities? I'm not entirely a drifter."

Sable could not tell what emotions lay behind those casually uttered words. Bitterness, regret, indifference?

"I am what you see," Morgan added, as though trying to convince her that whatever qualities endeared him to her did not exist. "A simple sea captain and master of my own existence. Do you know," he added cynically, his blue-eyed gaze roving restlessly over the water, "once I thought I needed nothing else."

He fell silent, and Sable continued to gaze up at him questioningly, hoping he would explain to her what he meant. She had no idea how beautiful she appeared to him with the moonbeams touching her hair. Her emerald eyes were dark and haunting, eyes that a man could easily lose himself in. The lavender gown she wore hugged her supple body, her young breasts straining against the bodice, and Morgan's lips tightened. She had been nothing but a frightened child when they had first pulled her, wet and bedraggled, from the sea, but she was a woman now—and a woman made for loving.

The thought that someday another man's hands would rove her perfect body enraged him. Sable was his, for he alone was responsible for leading her across the threshold to womanhood. He had tutored her in the art of love, had taught her what it meant to express her sexuality and demand the love a man was capable of giving her.

And yet he had no right to claim Sable at all, he forced himself to remember. It would be another man who would take her to wife and plant the seeds of life within her. Yet she had given him so much, and he was haunted still by the memories of that terrible night in the seraglio when Sable had risked her life for him. No other woman would have been so courageous, yet Morgan knew that he could never claim her for his own, not even now when everything about her told him that she desired him. Her soft lips were parted, and there was a seductive light in her green eyes that he doubted she was even aware of.

"It's late, Sable, you'd better go below," he told her hoarsely, well aware that he had played out this scene with her often enough in the past. But his passion for her had risen within him in a swift, undeniable tide that left him unable to send her away. She uttered a soft sigh when he reached for her, and she came to him willingly, her dark eyes shining as she raised her lips to his.

Morgan lowered his head, aching to feel the warmth of her kiss, but it was not to be. As he folded her against his chest a cry from the quarterdeck forced them apart.

"Deck there! Sails on the larboard stern!"

Morgan raised his head, his narrowed eyes sweeping the water beyond the ship's rail. Because the moon had climbed higher in the heavens, it was bright enough for him to see the white expanse of sails without the aid of a spyglass.

"Is it a Turkish ship?" Sable asked fearfully as Morgan set her gently aside.

"I don't believe so," he said slowly. "She's coming from the wrong direction, and if the moonlight hasn't deceived me, I'd swear she's a three-master like mine."

"Shall I summon the hands to their stations, sir?" a crewman inquired, hurrying up behind them.

"Put the watch on alert as a precaution and send for Mr. Torance."

"Aye, aye, sir."

Sable waited impatiently as Morgan lifted the telescope he had been given and studied the ship that was heading toward them on a collision course.

"Her captain's in a bloody hurry," Morgan remarked, closing the glass with a snap. "I hope he sees us soon enough. Jack," he added as his first officer appeared behind him, "what do you make of her?"

Jack squinted and grunted thoughtfully. "Can't make out her colors or name in this light, and I'd say she's makin' no effort to avoid us. They've spotted us by now, for sure, but she don't seem to be changin' course."

With both ships headed toward each other at full sail, it was not long before the distance between them shortened to less than a mile. Sable, who had followed Morgan to the quarter-deck despite his insistence that she go below, was standing beside him when the *Defiance*'s forecannon boomed a warning that the other ship was to veer. An answering signal came so swiftly that no one was left in doubt that the other ship had planned all along to confront them. Turning to Jack to order evasive action, Morgan drew up short as he heard Sable whisper, "Judas, it can't be!"

"What is it, Sable?" he demanded, instantly giving her all of his attention.

"It's the *Orient Star!*" she cried. "My father's ship!"

Morgan frowned. "Are you certain?"

"Of course I am! I'd recognize that figurehead anywhere!"

"Deck there!" came a cry from aloft. "I can read her name now! She be the *Orient Star* and she's strikin' our Union Jack!"

Morgan did not acknowledge the lookout's cry, for the other ship, a scant two cable lengths away, jibbed suddenly, its timbers groaning audibly with the strain in a hair-rising show of navigational skill. As it drew alongside the *Defiance*, its sails went slack beneath hands that had even the experienced men of Sir Morgan's crew murmuring in appreciation.

Sable could see figures moving about on the far deck, and then suddenly a voice cut across the distance between them, a voice that boomed so loud that it needed no bullhorn to amplify it.

"Captain Carey, this is Dmitri Zergeyev, captain of the Earl of Monterrey's clipper *Orient Star!* I order you to turn Lady Sable St. Germain over to me at once or I will be forced to come and get her!"

Sable's startled eyes locked with Morgan's, and she saw his lips twitch in the moonlight. "I'll be damned," she heard him whisper.

The crewmen lining the *Defiance*'s railing were silent as they watched the *Orient Star*'s jollyboat approach. In the bow sat a towering man with a dark, flowing beard. Dressed in a tunic and boots with a sword at his side, he might have been a Russian nobleman preparing for war, but what impressed the spectators more was the gentleman's very size. Catching sight of Sable peering down at him as the boat drew alongside the boarding nets, he bellowed joyously to her and lifted his hand in greeting.

"By God, his arms be thick as saplings!" someone whispered.

"Hate to tangle wi' him!" another agreed.

Unaware of their comments, Sable waited impatiently by the entry port until Dmitri stepped aboard. His beard and hair, one could see now, was streaked with gray, but his black eyes twinkled with delight and vitality as he looked at her.

"Dmitri!" Sable cried.

Rushing forward, she was caught against his enormous chest in a bear hug that squeezed the very breath from her body.

"Sweet, so sweet to have you back," he sighed. "How glad I am we came after you instead of waiting for you to be returned—provided Captain Carey intended to do so."

There was a stunned silence broken only when Morgan stepped forward and asked softly, "Are you accusing me of kidnapping Lady Sable?"

"I accuse no man," Dmitri responded as he set Sable gently aside, his thick Russian accent lending an unnerving menace to his voice. "Your actions, captain, speak for themselves."

Morgan's visage darkened. That he might expect trouble from Dmitri Zergeyev had been obvious to him when Sable had first told him something of the Russian's volatile temperament. This aging lion had plenty of battle left in him, Morgan decided appraisingly, and he was tempted for a moment to accept the challenge Dmitri was obviously extending. He recognized the light glowing in the black eyes as something inherent in his own character and knew that Dmitri would enjoy thrashing him as much as he would enjoy taking on the old warrior himself.

It was then that he caught sight of Sable's pleading face. She was standing at Dmitri's side, the color high in her rose-petal cheeks. Knowing he would cause her anguish if he goaded Dmitri to anger, he merely shrugged his shoulders.

"I am unable to defend myself against your accusations, Captain Zergeyev."

Dmitri's jaw dropped. This was the last thing he had expected to hear from the arrogant young man who had been the instrument of Sable's abduction. Was he a coward? he asked himself, gazing shrewdly into the handsome features before him. No, gut instinct told him this was not the case, yet why had he suddenly backed off when Dmitri had been certain he was going to pick up the gauntlet he had so boldly flung down?

"I was terribly ill, Dmitri," came Sable's soft voice from beside him. "It would have meant my death to remove me from Sir Morgan's ship. He alone is responsible for saving my life."

Dmitri's glance snapped from Sable's pale face to Morgan's impassive one. Had this been the reason for the Englishman's sudden lack of interest in converting their verbal battle to a real one? He glanced again at Sable, and his own anger died as he saw the beauty of her mother reflected in the flawless perfection of her patrician features. A memory, long forgotten, rose unbidden to his mind of Raven intervening countless times between Charles and himself when the two of them had stood at odds. Her beautiful eyes had held his as Sable's were doing now, and Dmitri could not find it in his heart to cause her pain.

"I am sorry, little one," he said gruffly. "Your letter told us as much, but I wanted to hear the truth from Captain Carey himself."

Morgan began to grow amused by the towering Russian's quicksilver change from a maddened bull to a docile, grinning hound. That he adored Sable was obvious, and Morgan was suddenly relieved that he hadn't made an enemy of the man. "I can understand your misgivings, sir," he said cordially. "Under normal circumstances I would not have hesitated to return Lady St. Germain to Tangier immediately. Yet her health was at stake and my business in Istanbul so pressing that I could not delay it."

Mollified, Dmitri extended his hand, and the gesture seemed to ease the tension in the air. It was obvious to Morgan that the Russian didn't trust him at all despite outward appearances, yet he was not offended by the realization. He would have lost a great deal of respect for the man otherwise.

"Is Ned with you, Dmitri?" Sable asked, and the eagerness in her expression was not lost upon him.

Dmitri shook his head regretfully. "We both agreed it would be better if he remained behind in the event you returned while we were out searching for you. But you'll be happy to know," he added with a pleased grin, "that Fleur is with me."

"Fleur?" Sable cried, delighted at the prospect of seeing

Dmitri's eldest daughter and one of her closest friends again.

"Aye, little one. Jacqueline had to stay at home because she is expecting another child, so Fleur agreed to come in her stead." He assumed a mournful expression. "I am an old man, and yet I continue to produce offspring like a young bull. How many children does that make now, Sable? Six? Seven?"

"There are nine of you now, Dmitri, and another will make ten," Sable informed him, dimpling. Of course, three of those children, including Fleur, were Jacqueline's from a former marriage, but Dmitri had welcomed the dark-haired French Guianan widow's three daughters into his home and treated them as his own.

"Shall we retire to my quarters to talk?" Morgan interjected bluntly. Annoyance filled him at Sable's obvious affection for Dmitri and the look in her eyes as she spoke to him of people he knew nothing about.

Dmitri spread his big hands. "Why, there is nothing to discuss, Captain Carey," he said in genuine surprise. "I will take Lady Sable back to the *Orient Star* with me as soon as she gathers her belongings together, and you may continue on the course you originally set before she came aboard."

Unaware of the frozen silence that followed his words, he beamed happily down at Sable. "You will have your old cabin back and Ewan Fletcher to care for you. As soon as we return to Tangier, we'll pick up Edward and head home to North Head. That will please you, *nyet?*"

Sable nodded her head, but her eyes were downcast and no one, not even Dmitri who was standing so close, could see the terrible emptiness in her expression.

"Captain Carey, you will be kind enough to send someone for Lady Sable's belongings?" Dmitri continued with a scowl, wondering why all of the gathered crewmen were staring at him with such open hostility all of a sudden. The sooner he got Sable away from this ship, the better he'd feel. He didn't care at all that Edward St. Germain had insisted Morgan Carey was a man of honor who could be expected to treat Sable well, an opinion he claimed his father, Charles, would also share. Dmitri simply didn't trust the arrogant Englishman and was eager to take Sable into his custody.

"I'll have my steward pack your things for you, your ladyship," Morgan said politely, his expression inscrutable.

Sable lifted her chin and gazed at him coolly. No one, not

even Morgan, could guess at the tearing pain inside of her, for Sable had learned not only the lessons of love from him, but the meaning of courage as well. "That won't be necessary," she said clearly. "I don't have very much, and it won't take me long to collect it myself."

"As you wish," Morgan said, and with a nod to Dmitri so curt that it bordered on insult, he turned heel and strode away.

Chapter 14

The sound of a child's laughter, high and filled with delight, brought Raven St. Germain, Countess of Monterrey, to the windows of her private drawing room. Looking down into the sun-drenched garden, a smile touched her lips and her golden eyes glowed with contentment. It was Liam who had been laughing, squealing now as the two chubby puppies he had been coaxing into play leaped on him and began to bark excitedly. Raven shook her glossy head as she saw one of them latch its needle-sharp teeth onto Liam's sleeve and pull until it ripped, but Liam seemed not to mind. In fact, he seemed quite content to be tumbling in the fragrant grass as enthusiastically as the pups themselves.

Raven's expression softened as she spotted Sable sitting beneath the branches of a chestnut tree, her pale blue skirts spread about her on the grass. Her daughter's head was bowed as she stroked the silky ears of a puppy that had climbed into her lap seeking attention, but Raven could see the dimpled smile peeping from beneath the slouching brim of her straw hat.

It warmed the Countess's heart to see Sable smile. All too often she had been aware of her daughter's aching silence since her return from Tangier nearly two weeks ago. It brought a pain to her heart even now to think of the hardships Sable had endured while she and Charles had been so blissfully unaware that anything was amiss. She could well recall her own fear and Charles's towering anger when Edward had related to them on the night of their return the truth of Sable's accident.

His tone harder than Raven had ever heard it, the Earl had demanded to know why his son hadn't informed them when it had first happened. Edward had squared his shoulders proudly, and at that moment Raven had realized for the first time how like his father her older son had become. In a calm voice he had claimed that the decision had been his own and that he had considered Sable to be in capable hands, for all of them knew and trusted Sir Morgan Carey. With his father bedridden, Edward had decided against telling them anything, especially since Sable was safe aboard Sir Morgan's ship.

"You would have come after her no matter what, Father!" he had concluded gravely. "It's entirely possible, too, that you might have injured your back even worse by getting out of bed too soon!"

The Earl had been forced to concede that his son had been right, and though his expression was still stern, Raven had seen the glint of admiration in the sea-green eyes. Dmitri's presence had also soothed the Earl's anger, and Raven felt regret now that he and Fleur had returned to Barbados after only a short stay with them.

Another burst of helpless giggles from Liam brought the Countess from her reverie. She looked down to see that her youngest child was trying to fend off the swishing pink tongues of the eager pups. She saw him look up suddenly and then race with a glad cry across the lawn toward Charles and Edward, who were coming down the garden path. Dina, the mother of the puppies, detached herself from the Earl's side and began to herd her offspring back to the stables, where Sam had made a home for them in an empty stall. Only the littlest one refused to follow, unwilling to give up the attention of his new mistress, upon whose lap he lay with contentedly closed eyes, small belly exposed to the sunshine and Sable's caressing hand.

Dina sniffed at him with her long white muzzle and then turned her attention back to the others, apparently trusting Sable

enough to look after him. Raven could see Sable's lips curve
as she and her brothers laughed at the stately hound's actions.
How good it was to see Sable smile, Raven thought again. Her
eyes went to her husband, who stood between his two sons,
his head thrown back as he joined in their laughter.

Her soft lips tightened unexpectedly as she thought of how
Sable must have suffered believing that her father and mother
had betrothed her to Morgan Carey. It had been a dreadful
misunderstanding that even now continued to upset Raven terribly. If only Danny had realized the damages s᷑   had wrought
by telling such lies to Wyecliffe Blackburn! Anᴗ ᴵf only Sable
had confronted them first rather than retreat behind that stubborn St. Germain pride and follow Ned to Morocco! Raven
shivered as she thought of what her gentle daughter had endured
because of it.

"What are you thinking about, my love?"

Raven started as she felt Charles's warm breath against her
cheek. She'd been so lost in her own thoughts that she hadn't
even noticed that he'd left his children in the garden and had
come inside to join her.

"I saw you at the window," he added, running his hands in
a gentle caress over her shoulders. "You looked so pensive that
I had to hear from your own lips what's troubling you."

She turned her head to gaze into his rugged profile. "It's
Sable," she confessed with a catch in her voice. "I was thinking
of the terrible consequences that arose from the things Danny
told Wyecliffe."

"Such as the notion that we had agreed to give Morgan
Carey our daughter's hand in marriage?"

At Raven's nod the Earl's expression sobered. "If she hadn't
believed it herself, Sable might never have accompanied Ned
to Tangier," he agreed, "or met with such an unfortunate accident."

He saw the pain in Raven's golden eyes and knew she was
thinking of the *Defiance*'s voyage to Istanbul. Both of them
had known that Morgan Carey intended to free a prisoner
from the highly guarded fortress of Seraglio Point, a mission
Charles had approved of, but neither of them could have suspected that their innocent young daughter would be present!

"I'm glad Danny doesn't know what harm she did," Raven
said softly. "I'm quite certain she'd not live through the shock
of it. But, oh, Charles, I can't bear to think of Sable having

been aboard that ship while Sir Morgan risked the wrath of a man like Sultan Abdülaziz!"

"I would have done anything to have prevented that," the Earl said darkly, and the hard edge to his voice caused Raven to lay a soothing hand on his cheek.

"At least it's over now," she whispered, "and our daughter has been returned to us safely. And it was good of you not to berate Edward for his decision not to inform us. Can you imagine how he'd feel knowing his sister hadn't just accompanied a man he trusted on a simple voyage, but that she had become involved in a dangerous attempt to rescue a political prisoner from the Sultan of Turkey's most closely guarded fortress?" She shivered, for even now the horrors that might have befallen her daughter continued to haunt her.

Charles's lips brushed her forehead in a comforting caress. "Ned was right in believing there was nothing I could have done. Even if I had taken the next tide in pursuit, I'd not have been able to stop her. Nothing went wrong, the good Lord be thanked, and I agree with you that it would be wisest just to go on with our lives as though it never happened. I still don't understand, however, why Morgan didn't do us the courtesy of returning our daughter to Tangier first, where she would have been out of danger."

"Sable insisted she was too ill to be moved," the Countess reminded him, but the Earl continued to look unconvinced. "It doesn't really matter anymore," she added quickly, well aware that it would take little to fan her husband's awesome temper on the subject. "According to Sable, she was safely aboard Sir Morgan's ship the entire time. He has what he wants now, and we have our daughter back. Surely we should be content with that."

Charles's lips twitched, his smile causing his rugged, scarred features to take on the carefree looks of the young man he had been when Raven had first laid eyes on him. "As always you are the practical one, my pet," he murmured and pressed a kiss to the pulse beating in her slim wrist.

Raven returned his smile, her eyes glowing with all the depth of her feelings for him, but inwardly her heart was heavy. All should be well with the world, and yet Sable's silence and unhappiness continued to distress her. She had hoped Sable would come to her and tell her what was troubling her, but it seemed as if her daughter was determined to avoid such a confrontation.

Raven's eyes went to the window and she sighed deeply as she watched the three dark heads of her children bend over the clumsy hound pup Sable still held in her arms. She felt as if she had lost something very precious but could not explain even to herself what it might be. Yet she had decided that, until Sable came to her, she would not bring up the matter herself, nor mention her concern to Charles. It would be best to allow the unhappy affair to blow over and let the golden days of summer at North Head mend the fabric of their lives together.

"Excuse me, m'lord, m'lady."

It was one of the footmen standing stiff and proper in the doorway, embarrassed at having been forced to intrude upon the Earl and Countess in their private drawing room.

"What is it, William?" the Earl inquired, addressing the young man by his first name and thereby putting him at ease. He kept his hand on the Countess's shoulder, not at all self-conscious about displaying his affection for her before one of his servants.

"Master Wyecliffe Blackburn is downstairs," William replied, doing his best to hide his true feelings for that most obnoxious of gentlemen. "I've put him in the Red Salon."

"Oh dear." Raven sighed, glancing at the ornate clock that ticked on the mantle of the tile-inlaid fireplace across the room. "I imagine that means we'll have to invite him to eat with us."

"Wyecliffe always manages to time his visits around our meals," Charles agreed dryly. "Very well, William, we'll be down in a moment."

The footman inclined his head politely. "As you wish, m'lord. Oh, I should add that Mr. Blackburn has brought his mother with him."

The Earl and Countess exchanged startled glances.

"Letitia Blackburn?" Raven exclaimed. "I thought she'd vowed never to set foot in Cornwall again!"

"I imagine we'd better go down and see them," Charles added resignedly. Raven sighed as she glanced down into the garden, where Edward and Liam were now engaged in earnest discussion while Sable looked indulgently on.

"It's awful that Wyecliffe has to resume his courtship so soon after Sable's return!"

"Shall I send him packing?" Charles asked with a gleam in his eyes.

Raven dimpled. "Truly, m'lord, you still possess so much of a pirate's heart that I sometimes wonder how you can play the country gentleman and get away with it! Wyecliffe is our neighbor," she added with a barely perceptible warning in her soft voice, "and despite the fact that he is an unwelcome candidate for our daughter's hand, we will not be rude to him. He is a guest in our house, after all."

"Faith, madame, I wonder if anyone will ever succeed in turning you against the Blackburns! You have a far too gentle heart," Charles added, capturing her in his arms and nuzzling her neck as she tried to pass him, "and I'm beginning to believe our daughter is cursed with a similar affliction."

"Sable is wise enough to realize how unfortunate a choice Wyecliffe would be for her," Raven pointed out.

"And if not," Charles finished, "I'll simply run the fellow off the estate myself."

Raven laughed softly, aware that he would relish the chance for a bit of excitement. Despite the happy years they'd spent raising their children within North Head's warm embrace, she knew that the restless adventurer she had first fallen in love with still lurked somewhere beneath that refined exterior. Now that he was fully recovered from his accident, Charles towered handsome and fit before her, and she felt as breathless as a young girl as he lowered his lips to hers and kissed her hungrily before reluctantly accompanying her downstairs.

Sable needed no advance warning from anyone to know that Wyecliffe had come to see her. One look at Parris's glum face as the butler entered the garden to inform them that the Countess wished to see them was enough to alert her to the fact.

"I've a feeling Wyecliffe's here," Edward murmured in the same instant, as sensitive as his sister to the elderly butler's facial nuances, however slight. "Am I right, Parris?" he asked as the three St. Germain children met him at the door.

"Lord Audley?" Parris inquired formally, pretending not to understand the knowing gleam in the young Monterrey heir's green eyes.

"Cliffe Blackburn's here, isn't he?"

Parris's lips thinned. "I'm afraid so, sir. William has this moment shown him into the Red Salon."

"Which means he'll be staying for lunch," Edward groaned.

"And Danny's sick upstairs with a head cold," Liam piped in. "How are we going to chase him off without her?"

"No one is going to chase anyone away," his sister informed him firmly, but Liam was quick to hear the amusement in her voice. It pleased him, for he sensed in some little-understood way that Sable had been sad since coming home. He had tried hard to cheer her, bringing her bluebells from the woodlands and Dina's new puppies to play with, but he wasn't sure it had helped. He suspected that Wyecliffe Blackburn had been responsible for making Sable sad because he had overheard his mother and father discussing both of them a lot since his older brother and sister had sailed away to Morocco.

"You're not going to marry him, are you, Sable?" he asked now, suddenly terribly afraid that she would, recalling that betrothals and other vaguely understood concepts had accompanied his parents' discussions about Sable and Wyecliffe.

"Of course she isn't!" Ned said sternly as the three of them hurried down the long, carpeted corridor with Parris following dutifully behind them.

"I wish you'd marry Sir Morgan," Liam added, suddenly remembering that the tall sea captain had been another person his parents had mentioned often during their earnest talks in his father's study. "I liked him very much," he added firmly, unaware of the stricken expression on his sister's face.

"I'm not going to marry anyone, Liam," she said as he looked up at her expectantly. "Not now or ever." There was a hard edge to her soft voice he had never heard before, and he frowned, wondering why she had been hurt by what he'd said.

"Now go on and wash up," Sable said in the next breath, sounding enough like her old self to mollify him. "You've got mud on your face and grass in your hair. I'll be along in a moment," she added to Edward, pausing before a small wardrobe table in the elegant hallway to remove her bonnet. Catching sight of herself in the mirror above it, she bit her lip, feeling as though the haunted eyes that stared back at her were those of a stranger. Since her return she had tried desperately to hide her unhappiness from everyone, and the effort of doing so was beginning to exhaust her. It wouldn't be long before everyone began to notice. What on earth was she supposed to tell them when they started asking questions?

Sable had hoped that coming home to North Head would ease the terrible emptiness within her heart, but somehow it had only made it worse. North Head in the bloom of full summer was breathtaking to behold, the high-ceilinged rooms flooded with sunlight and the dancing reflection of the sea. Wildflowers grew everywhere in the parklands, and there were kittens, puppies, and newborn foals to admire in the stableyard. It was a rare and wondrous season that Sable had always loved, yet she found herself feeling curiously empty and alone.

Even during the past week, when North Head had echoed with the laughter Fleur and Dmitri's presence always provided, Sable had just been reminded of how heavy her heart had been since Dmitri had brought her home. She had hoped that time would diminish these feelings, but they had only grown worse. Her mother and father were worried about her, Sable knew, yet how could she tell them that she was aching for the loss of a love as deep as that which they had found in each other?

"Lady Sable?"

She looked up with a start, aware that she had been staring, lost in thought, into the mirror, her unhappiness clearly written on her face. "I'm sorry, Parris. Is everyone waiting for me?"

To her relief he chose not to comment on her odd behavior. "Yes, m'lady. They've all withdrawn to the Conservatory."

Sable quickly smoothed back the wayward curls that had worked themselves loose when she had removed her hat, and hurried to join them. The Conservatory, once used as a hothouse to cultivate the tuberoses and orchids that Sable's grandfather James Barrancourt had so prized, had become a favorite meeting place of the St. Germains. As the family had grown, room for plants had diminished, and Charles had finally decided to build a greenhouse for the Countess's beloved flowers elsewhere on the grounds.

Horticulture was a hobby that Liam, especially, had taken a fancy to, and the greenhouse had quickly become a haunt for both the Countess and her young son. An orangery had been added the following year, and to Charles's bemusement several experts had even traveled from Cambridge recently to view the St. Germains' extensive collection.

Despite the fact that the Conservatory had become the focal point of afternoon meals, Raven still cultivated many of her plants there, even though the Earl pleaded with her constantly to remove them to her greenhouse. Yet no one really minded, for it was pleasant to dine amid the fragrance of roses and to view the sparkling Atlantic through the lush green leaves of potted miniature orange trees. In summer, when the room grew too warm, the French doors were opened to permit the cooling breezes inside, and the smell of the sea would mingle with the spicy scent of the ripening fruit.

As Sable stepped inside that warm afternoon, she was greeted first by the riot of color of blooming tea roses, a sight which brought a pleased smile to her lips, and then by Wyecliffe Blackburn, who instantly caused her happiness to vanish.

"Welcome home to North Head, Lady Sable!" he greeted her, rising from his chair and taking both of her hands in his.

"Thank you," she murmured with lowered eyes. She had forgotten how pale and thin Wyecliffe was and how cold and clammy the touch of his hands.

"It's so good to have you back," Wyecliffe added huskily, oblivious to the warning glint that entered the Earl's green eyes at his intimate tone. He could scarcely credit the change in Sable St. Germain, or was it that he had merely forgotten how beautiful she was? No, he decided, scrutinizing her carefully, she had truly changed. The strong African sun had given her fair skin a golden glow, and he feasted his eyes on the bare shoulders which were revealed by the wide cut of the sprigged cotton frock she wore.

It was obvious to Wyecliffe as he looked at her that Sable was no longer the innocent young girl he remembered. She had grown sensuous, even voluptuous in her absence, and he ached to taste the sweetness of her maturing woman's body.

"Why, Mrs. Blackburn!" Sable exclaimed in surprise, catching sight of Wyecliffe's mother sitting on the small damask sofa, her hands folded demurely in her lap. "I didn't know you were back in Cornwall!"

"It's only for a visit, my dear," Letitia Blackburn assured her hastily. "I'm leaving for Devon again in the morning!"

Her passionate words reminded Sable of how much Squire Blackburn's widow had despised Cornwall, constantly complaining of the savage weather and barren coastline. No sooner had her husband died than she had packed herself off to her former home, leaving Wyecliffe alone at his stepfather's estate. Sable remembered her as a mousy, retiring sort of creature, but it seemed that she had changed much since Josiah Blackburn's death.

The severe chignon she had always worn had been replaced by carefully tonged curls, and her normally dowdy attire was no longer in evidence. Gone, too, was the nervous manner that had always beset her whenever she had visited North Head with the Squire, and Sable wondered if perhaps Josiah himself hadn't been responsible for his wife's fidgeting ways.

"It's lovely to see you again," Letitia added, giving Sable a warm smile. "I'm glad we had the chance to stop here at North Head before I left. Cliffe told me that you'd gone away to Morocco. How exciting that must have been! You must tell me everything about it!"

Sable cast a helpless glance at her father, not wishing to confide the truth to Wyecliffe or his mother. She had seen next to nothing of Tangier, and her voyage on the *Defiance* was something too painful to think about, let alone discuss with a stranger the likes of Widow Blackburn.

"My son was kind enough to represent me in Fez in a closed audience with the Sultan of Morocco," Charles said immediately, his heart going out to his daughter, feeling impotent that he had not the means to make her smile again.

"Cliffe informed me that he was responsible for the riding accident which left you unable to attend the meeting yourself," Letitia said, looking more remorseful than her son ever had.

The Earl shrugged his broad shoulders. "Fortunately no one was badly hurt, though it was a shame that one of the horses had to be put down."

"You had business to conduct in Morocco?" Wyecliffe asked Edward with an interested expression. He had come to North Head several times since the Earl's recovery but had been unable to learn anything about Sable and Edward's whereabouts.

Charles's brows drew together, recognizing the greed in the young man's sallow features. It was common knowledge that Blackburn Hall was on the verge of financial ruin, and the Earl suspected strongly that its dissolute owner would like nothing better than to get his hands on some of the St. Germain fortune.

"Barrancourt Ltd. will be opening an exhange office there before the end of next year," he informed the younger man coolly, and Wyecliffe could not miss the warning in that scarred visage this time. His thin lips tightened and he tried his best to hide his frustration. Why the devil was the Earl always so hostile with him? Didn't the man see he was doing his best to be civil and that he couldn't find a better choice for a son-in-law?

"My brother and sister were in a boating accident in Tangier," Liam added importantly, his childish voice piping loud into the silence. To him this had been the most exciting aspect of Ned and Sable's voyage.

Letitia Blackburn went pale. "Oh, dear, a boating accident?"

"It was nothing," Edward assured her quickly. "We were invited aboard a yacht to dine and had the misfortune of being struck by another one in the darkness."

"I hope no one was hurt!" Wyecliffe exclaimed, his attention centered on Sable.

"Two crewmen were killed and as a result there was an inquest," the Earl informed them evenly, coming to Edward's rescue. It was obvious to him that his son had no great wish to dredge up such a terrifying experience with anyone outside the family. "Fortunately it was ruled the fault of the skipper of the other ship, who happened to be the irresponsible son of a local dey and had taken his father's ship without permission."

"It must have been a horrible experience for you, Lady Sable," Wyecliffe murmured, wishing that she hadn't taken a seat across the room so close to her mother and father, wanting to press her hands reassuringly with his own. "I trust you weren't hurt."

"Sable almost drowned," Liam assured him before anyone could stop him, "but she was rescued by Captain Sir Morgan!"

"Morgan Carey?" Wyecliffe burst out. "What the devil was he doing in Morocco?"

Sable bowed her head as though to escape the questioning gazes of Wyecliffe and his mother. Fierce rage washed through the Earl as he saw her stricken expression, the need to protect his most vulnerable child rising strong within him.

Sensing his rising temper, Raven reached out and laid her hand over his. "Charles," she began, but the charged silence was successfully defused by the entrance of North Head's elderly butler.

"Would you be caring for luncheon now, m'lady?" he inquired politely.

"Yes, thank you, Parris," Raven responded with considerable relief.

The table had already been set, and it was a simple task for Raven to smooth over the awkward moment by ushering her family and guests to their places. Wyecliffe was annoyed that Edward St. Germain took the seat beside his sister that should have been allowed for him, but he hid his animosity for the young heir beneath a forced smile.

Because it was a sultry summer day Perry had chosen to prepare an iced cucumber soup, which was served by Parris and a footman amid appreciative sighs from Liam, who adored especially the freshly baked bread that accompanied it. It was not until the tureen had been set aside and everyone served that Letitia Blackburn spoke.

"You did say Sir Morgan Carey, didn't you?" she asked, addressing the Earl, who sat at his customary place at the head of the table. "I've been wondering why the name seemed familiar to me, and now I remember that there was a gentleman by that name residing near Totnes, some ten miles from my own home in Devon."

"I'm not exactly sure where Sir Morgan lives," Charles said politely, but it was evident from his tone that he didn't wish to pursue the subject.

Unfortunately Mrs. Blackburn had never been overly adept at interpreting the discreet hints of others and continued blithely, "This Morgan Carey was a former army officer, though I recall that he seemed extremely young at the time to have retired. I think he received a knighthood from the Queen for his services as well, but no one really knew much about him. He kept quite to himself in that big house of his—Ambling Cross, I believe it was called, because it was built at the former crossroads between Ambling Village and Totnes."

Sable listened with downcast eyes, praying no one would sense how interested she was. Was it really true that Morgan owned an estate in Devon? Was Ambling Cross the home Grayson had referred to whenever he had spoken of the comfortable country life he had led before Morgan had outfitted the *Defiance* and made him a cabin steward? She reminded herself sternly that Morgan's life meant nothing to her anymore. Both his past and future were dead to her, and she'd be better off never to think about him again.

"I believe he sold his estate several years ago," Mrs. Blackburn was saying, her brow furrowing as she strove to remember. "I wasn't surprised to hear it, being that he seemed a far too restless man for country living. Ambling is quite a modest village, too, and I do recall that his way of life raised eyebrows on more than one occasion. Of course," she added, aware that she was gossiping about a man who might be a friend of the Earl's, "all of this happened while I was still married to Josiah, and much of it was repeated to me only after I returned to Totnes."

"Sir Morgan was here visiting us at the beginning of the summer," Liam told her grandly, for it was obvious to him that Mrs. Blackburn was very impressed with him. "He was ever so nice to me, and he even rode Sable's horse Falstaff, who usually throws everyone he doesn't know."

Mrs. Blackburn smiled at him indulgently, though she wondered inwardly why the Earl and Countess tolerated the presence of their younger son at the table. Children his age should be dining upstairs in the nursery with their nanny, not joining in the grownups' conversations!

Wyecliffe had remained silent during his mother's ramblings, recalling how shocked he had been when that toothless old crone Hannah Daniels had told him that Morgan Carey had come to North Head to seek Sable St. Germain's hand in marriage. A more ill-matched couple he could not have imagined, what with Lady Sable so sweet and gentle-hearted and Morgan Carey so overpowering and ill-tempered! Since then he had learned, of course, that the old woman had been flying on the wings of fancy, but the fact that Sir Morgan had been present in Tangier at the same time as Lady Sable and her brother aroused his suspicions anew.

He had never forgotten the towering sea captain's arrogance, behaving as though he had more right to be a guest in the St. Germains' home than Wyecliffe himself. And he still chafed at the memory of how rudely Morgan Carey had ordered him from the grounds the day he had lost his head and kissed Sable in the hallway. But for Sable's presence he would have given the arrogant sod a proper setdown, Wyecliffe told himself now with thinned lips, forgetting that at the time he had been thoroughly terrified by the tall sea captain's unsettling presence.

Wyecliffe ached to learn more of the curious relationship between the Earl of Monterrey and Captain Sir Morgan Carey, but he was destined to remain ignorant. The return of Parris with the next course precluded all conversation, and he was forced to sit silently, although he burned with unanswered questions.

"Ooh, what is it?" Liam demanded eagerly as Parris set an enormous covered dish on the table. The silver lid was tightly closed so that it was impossible to see what lay within, a mystery the hungry little boy could not endure.

"It's one of your favorites, Lord Liam," Parris twinkled, unable to resist the boy's eager grin and behaving, in Mrs. Blackburn's disapproving opinion, far too familiar for a servant.

"Pickled herring!" Liam cried, his eyes round as the butler obligingly lifted the lid. Reaching out with his spoon to savor a bite, he stopped short, catching sight of his father's stern eye upon him. Liam reddened, having forgotten there were visitors present, and quickly folded his hands in his lap in a picture of propriety.

The Earl's lips twitched as he met his Countess's smiling glance across the table. Much as he disliked having his meal intruded upon by unwelcome guests who would frown on Liam's behavior, he could not help finding amusement in the antics of his young son. Yet his expression sobered as his eyes chanced to fall on his daughter, seeing the trembling of her soft lips. What was troubling the girl? he wondered with a feeling of anger born of helplessness. Despite her insistence to the contrary, he was beginning to suspect that something had happened to her on the voyage to Istanbul, something that had taken away his gentle, innocent daughter and replaced her with a sad little creature he could not seem to reach.

Damn Morgan Carey! Charles cursed silently to himself. If Sable continued to be unhappy, he would seek the man out despite Raven's entreaties to leave the matter be, and demand to know what his daughter had endured that had changed her so much.

Unaware of her father's pensive eye upon her, Sable accepted with a gentle smile the helping of herring that Parris offered her. She loved the tangy dish just as much as Liam did, but as she lifted her fork to sample it, the smell of fish, onions, and sour cream wafted to her from the plate. She choked as nausea overwhelmed her and the fork dropped with a clatter to the floor. Aghast, she saw that all eyes had turned her way, and she came unsteadily to her feet, her face flushed.

"What is it, Sable?" Raven inquired anxiously.

"I-I'm all right," Sable assured her tremulously, but she was forced to swallow hard as she stared down at the herring on her plate which moments before had seemed so appetizing.

"Are you certain?" Raven persisted. Laying down her napkin, she began to rise, but Sable put up a hand to stop her.

"I'm fine, Mother, truly I am. I just need some fresh air, that's all. Excuse me, please."

Not caring that their startled eyes were upon her, she stepped quickly through the opened door onto the terrace and hurried around the corner, where the ocean breeze blew uninterrupted from the cliffs. There she leaned for a moment on the balustrade, breathing deeply until her dizziness passed. She had no idea why she should have reacted so violently to the smell of Perry's herring. Could it be that she was just upset because everyone had been discussing Morgan?

"Curse him!" she whispered to herself, tears springing to her eyes. Would she never be free of the pain of loving him?

Her eyes followed the flight of a solitary cormorant across the whitecapped water, and she found herself suddenly yearning for the sun-washed days aboard the *Defiance* with the wind snapping in the canvas overhead and Morgan standing proud and tall at the brass-plated wheel. A lump rose in her throat but she resolutely dashed the tears away. Morgan had made his choice. He hadn't even bidden her farewell when Dmitri had come for her that night, and it served her right to suffer now for having fallen in love with a man who had considered her nothing more than passing fancy.

Yet she couldn't bear to go back into the Conservatory and meet the questioning eyes of her family. The thought of enduring Wyecliffe's solicitous attention sickened her as well, and heaven forbid if Letitia Blackburn began discussing Morgan again!

"I can't bear it anymore," Sable whispered to herself. "Judas, how I hate him!"

Swiftly she ran across the grass to one of the service entrances in the East Wing, where she startled a passing footman with her unexpected appearance.

"Yes, m'lady?" he asked as she addressed him, wondering why the Earl's normally laughing, happy daughter should seem so close to tears.

"Will you please inform my parents that I've retired to my room? Tell them I've got a headache but that they mustn't concern themselves over me."

"Very good, m'lady." He would have liked to suggest that he send for the housekeeper to bring her a powder, but Sable was already gone, her flounced skirts rustling softly as she hurried down the corridor toward the Grand Staircase.

* * *

In the carriage on the way back to Blackburn Hall a half-hour later Wyecliffe had only fierce words to say to his mother concerning their visit to North Head. Turning his back on the stately stone manor house, he glared at the woman who sat beside him in the open vehicle, his sallow cheeks a dull, mottled red.

"You promised, Mother, you promised!" he accused in a low hiss so that the driver wouldn't hear. "Why did I bother sending for you if you refused to help me?"

"I don't believe—" Letitia began stiffly, but her son silenced her with a savage gesture.

"You were supposed to bring up the subject of my marriage to Lady Sable," he accused, "and you swore before we arrived that you'd make a point to seek out Lady Monterrey! I'm certain she would have been receptive to your suggestion, and yet you couldn't wait to make your excuses! Why? Why?"

"Wyecliffe, don't shout!" his mother admonished, casting a meaningful glance at the driver's stiff back. The small carriage was swaying down the wide, tree-lined lane that led from North Head's imposing portico to the post road. It was a beautiful day, but neither mother nor son noticed the lush greenness of the stately trees or the multitude of flowers that bloomed in the park around them.

"With Lady Sable taking ill, I didn't think it was the proper time to suggest a marriage between the two of you," she added sternly, no longer the indecisive creature that Josiah Blackburn had married years ago to hide his humiliation over the fact that he had lost Raven Barrancourt to another man.

"All the more reason!" Wyecliffe contradicted. "You agreed to come to North Head with me today to speak to the Countess, and now you've thrown the perfect chance away seeing as you could have easily gotten her off alone with Sable sick upstairs!"

"I did nothing of the sort, my boy," Letitia retorted, dislike flashing in her eyes as she regarded her enraged son. He had become so like his ill-tempered stepfather that she could scarcely wait to be gone from him. "I had a perfectly good reason to leave without speaking to the Countess, and you'd do well to listen to me when I tell you what it was!"

Wyecliffe forced himself to keep a grip on his rising temper. Oh, how he had cajoled and pleaded with her to come to Cornwall when he'd heard that Lady Sable had returned, certain it would help his case if his mother were to speak up in his behalf. Now the stupid sow had failed to do anything and the entire scheme was wasted. Wasted!

"What reasons could you possibly have not to speak to Lady Monterrey?" he asked coldly, his contempt for her evident in his closed expression.

Letitia Blackburn's own temper snapped. "Dear God above, haven't you got eyes in your head, boy? Isn't it obvious to you that the St. Germain brat is breeding?"

Wyecliffe stared at her as though she had taken leave of her senses. "Oh yes, I'm perfectly sure of it, my dandy fellow," she continued smugly. "You forget I brought four babes into this world before you, though you were the only one who survived, more's the pity. It may have been years ago, but I've never forgotten how it comes on so suddenly at the sight and smell of certain foods. Mark my words, boy, that highborn bitch you're panting after is breedin' with some man's bastard child!"

"You must be mad!" Wyecliffe spluttered.

"Am I? Come spring I promise you Lord and Lady Monterrey will find themselves grandparents of a babe born without a name!" She shook her head. "None of them even aware of it, as far as I could tell, least of all little Miss Refinement herself. My advice to you, Cliffe," she added nastily, "is to look elsewhere for a fortune to restore that ruined inheritance of yours. You're too good for the likes of a girl who lets the first man she takes a fancy to plant his seed inside her belly!"

Wyecliffe made no reply, too stunned by his mother's revelation to speak. Lowering his head into his hands, he sat dumbly beside her while she savored this unexpected victory. How many times during her unhappy years of marriage to Josiah had she been forced to endure the humiliation of knowing that he still lusted after the Countess of Monterrey and that he had married her only because he could not have Raven Barrancourt? It had devastated her to learn that her son had also set his sights on the high and mighty St. Germains. Letitia knew that, much as she couldn't help liking gentle little Sable, the Earl would never allow Wyecliffe to marry her.

She had agreed to come to Cornwall and intervene in Wyecliffe's behalf only because his incessant whining had begun to wear thin on her nerves. It delighted her now to see how completely his hopes had been dashed. Spineless sod, she

thought uncharitably. What a pity he was so like his stepfather,
a man Letitia Blackburn had grown to despise over the course
of their marriage.

Well, it was over now, she thought to herself, and it was a
good thing that she hadn't let the Earl or Countess guess from
her expression what was wrong with their daughter. That was
something Letitia had no desire to involve herself in, and she
shuddered as she imagined the revenge the notorious Earl would
practice upon the man responsible. Thank goodness she hadn't
let the cat out of the bag!

As the tile roof of Blackburn Hall came into view over a
gentle rise in the moors, the occupants of the dilapidated carriage were silent. Even the driver was preoccupied with his
own thoughts, and Mrs. Blackburn would have been horrified
had she been able to read them. In her zeal to inform Wyecliffe
of the truth of Sable St. Germain's condition, she had allowed
her voice to rise to a volume that could not escape the notice
of the man holding the reins on the seat before them.

Little did Mrs. Blackburn realize that she herself would be
responsible for bringing the news of Sable's condition to North
Head the very next day, for the driver of the vehicle was none
other than Jims, Blackburn Hall's head groom and the newly
wedded husband of Lucy Walters, Lady Sable's former maid.
Though Jims did not for a moment believe the woman's vicious
words, he could not help being concerned. Someone should
notify the Earl of the lies Letitia Blackburn was capable of
spreading, and His Lordship must see to it that they went no
farther than Blackburn Hall.

It was a delicate situation, but Jims was far more loyal to
the St. Germains of North Head than to his own employer. He
knew how much his new wife adored Lady Sable St. Germain
and how horrified she would be if such a shocking tale were
to be bandied about the countryside. He'd speak to her about
it, Jims decided firmly, and Lucy would know what to do.

"Of course you're right, dear, we must go to North Head
at once," was the first thing Lucy said. "Ooh, that horrible,
horrible woman!" she added, her eyes flashing as she thought
of Letitia Blackburn. "'Tis a good thing she's gone back to
Devon or I vow I'd strangle her myself! Lady Sable expectin'
a babe, indeed! And simply on the grounds that she got a bad
stomach. Bah! The woman isn't fit to be discussin' the breedin'

habits of sows, much less human beings!"

"Lucy, please," her husband interrupted, embarrassed by his wife's tart tongue. The subject of having children was too delicate to be discussed with anyone, even one's new bride, especially when it involved the highly respected St. Germain family!

"I'll talk to Her Ladyship tomorrow," Lucy soothed. Though she had married Jims and moved to his cottage on Blackburn property, she was still employed at North Head and fiercely loyal to the St. Germains. Little Katie Pendavis had taken over many of her duties, but Lucy still insisted on caring for Lady Sable whenever she was at the great house, and she would not tolerate any criticism of her beloved young mistress.

Her eyes began to flash anew. No one would dare harm her wee darling with malicious lies while she was still alive, especially not a hateful busybody like Widow Blackburn! She'd go to North Head first thing in the morning and tell the Countess what Jims had overheard, and then, once the Earl was made aware of it, there'd be hell to pay!

Chapter 15

"Ooh, Lady Sable, ye look beautiful as a queen, ye do!" Young Katie Pendavis sighed as she tucked a wayward curl back into the strands of ribbon and flowers she had woven through her mistress's hair. Taking a step back, she sighed again as she admired Sable's pastel-yellow frock, the skirts embroidered with sky-blue ribbons. With her slim shoulders and long, graceful neck revealed by the low cut of her gown, Sable St. Germain looked exactly like a beautiful princess to her admiring maid.

"Oh, go on with you, Katie," Sable admonished good-naturedly. "You'll turn my head with such talk."

"Nay, m'lady, it's true!" Katie insisted. Reaching behind her, she took a small cut-glass perfume bottle from the dresser and extended it to her mistress. "You should be wearin' some of this," she added shyly. "I've a knowin' Master Trevennen will be likin' it."

Sable's lips curved as she gazed at the blushing maid. Katie was silly and likable with her young girl's romantic heart, and she could well imagine that Katie was already dreaming of the good things that might come of the afternoon, when the St.

Germains held a picnic on North Head's lawn for the Trevennens and Derwentwaters, close friends from nearby localities.

Sable liked Martin, the oldest of the Trevennens' four sons, but certainly not enough to encourage him! Her gaze faltered as pain filled her heart. For a moment she had almost been able to forget that she was no longer an innocent girl who might flirt as she pleased with any young man who struck her fancy. But then the memory of Morgan Carey rudely intruded upon her thoughts, filling her mind with images of his passion-glittering eyes, his strong, seeking hands and hot lips.

Would she never be free of him? she asked herself despairingly. Would she always hunger for his touch, for the lovemaking which had brought her more fulfillment than she had ever dreamed possible? It was agony to love him still and to know that he did not want her and that she must now try to fill this aching void within her as best she could alone.

"Timms says they're just about finished setting up the tables," Katie went on, imagining the colorful picture the St. Germains and their guests would make reclining under the trees, the children playing in the grass while the adults talked and laughed. Lord Edward would be dressed in shirtsleeves and cotton trousers, she decided, his dark curls tousled by the breeze, and her heart skipped a beat as she pictured the smile on his face when he joined in the afternoon's festivities.

The door to Sable's bedchamber opened at that moment to reveal the imposing figure of Lucy Walters Sullivan, a force still to be reckoned with in the St. Germain home. Katie went pale, for she had always been afraid of the dominating woman, yet she relaxed when she noticed that Lucy seemed quite pleased with the ribbons and posies she had wound through Lady Sable's dark hair.

"Faith, and ye look sweet as an angel, m'lady," Lucy said, thinking to herself that her young charge had grown into a woman equally beautiful as her mother. Yet the small face that was turned toward her wore a look of such innocence that Lucy's lips thinned with sudden anger. How dare anyone accuse this pure and lovely child of being in a family way? It was too absurd to even think about!

"Katie," she said sternly, causing the young girl to jump, "run upstairs and see if Mrs. Daniels requires anything. The guests should be arriving soon. If you're given nothing to do up there, then see if you can't keep Lord Liam clean and out of trouble until the picnic starts."

"Yes, mum," Katie whispered and fled.

"Oh, Lucy, isn't it a grand day for a picnic?" Sable asked. Rising to her feet amid a rustle of material, she wandered dreamily to the window. The ocean sparkled deep green beneath a cerulean sky in which towering cumulus clouds drifted lazily past.

"Aye, m'lady," Lucy agreed distractedly. Confronted by Sable's slim back, she found herself suddenly unable to bring up the subject which had brought her here. It would be too unkind to repeat it to anyone, true or not, especially to Lady Sable, the very object of such a malicious lie! Should she perhaps forget she had ever heard such a preposterous tale? Lucy wrung her hands, unsure of herself. What should she do? Suppose that awful Wyecliffe began to spread the story about? Shouldn't the Earl and his family be made aware of it?

"What is it, Lucy?" Sable, having grown aware of her odd silence, had looked around, and the sweet profile that was turned Lucy's way made up her mind for her. She couldn't allow Lady Sable to be hurt! She'd have to be forewarned, even if the matter in question was so very preposterous!

"I've a word or two to have with you in private, dearie," Lucy began firmly now that she had settled on her course of action. "It concerns somethin' my man Jims overheard Widow Blackburn tell that no-good son of hers on the way home to the Hall yesterday."

Sable's brows rose. "Oh?"

"Mind you, 'twas a bit of unkind gossip, but Mr. Sullivan and I be feelin' His Lordship wouldn't care to have such a story passed about."

Sable's smooth brow knitted. "You sound very grave, Lucy."

"Aye, and mad fit to burstin', too! My Jims was beside himself havin' to listen to that horrible woman and not being able to say a word to make her stop!"

"What was Mrs. Blackburn saying?" Sable asked softly.

"I'm half ashamed now to be tellin' ye, m'lady," Lucy admitted with downcast eyes.

Sable's eyes twinkled. "It couldn't be that bad, could it? And even if it is, I'm certain my father could clear the matter up with Mrs. Blackburn herself."

"I'm hopin' His Lordship'll have that pleasure," Lucy sniffed darkly. "The gossip be about ye, Lady Sable, which is why I thought I'd come to ye first and not your dear mother or father. I'd not want you to hear it from some gossipin' maid and get the shock of your young life!"

Sable was secretly amused by Lucy's fierce desire to protect her. Did everyone else still think of her as the vulnerable girl Lucy did? Oh, if only they knew the truth about her, that she wasn't an innocent child anymore! She had lain with a man, had yearned for his touch and still did so now, and she had killed another in cold blood without a moment's hesitation. Though she was not ashamed of what she had become and though she would always love the man responsible, she could not bring herself to speak the truth to her parents. Perhaps someday, when the pain was no longer so great, she might be able to stop living this lie.

"What is it, Lucy?" she asked with a glint in her leaf-green eyes. "Wyecliffe wasn't plotting with his mother to make me marry him by force, was he?"

"Oh, dearie, no, 'tis far worse!" Lucy blurted, unable to find amusement in the situation. "That overweight, pompous woman had the nerve to tell her son—and in my Jims's hearing, mind you—that you were expecting a child! There, I've said it, though I'm ashamed to have repeated such an awful thing, but don't you think it would be terrible if that she-wolf were to spread such a lie about the countryside?"

Sable's cheeks had drained of color, but Lucy, in her agitation, hadn't noticed. A hush fell over the sunny bedroom, broken only by the sound of the older woman's harsh breathing.

"Where did Mrs. Blackburn come by such information?" Sable asked at last, surprised at how calm she sounded.

Lucy threw up her hands. "From the way ye acted at luncheon yesterday, believe it or no! The fool woman said ye'd taken ill at the sight of Perry's herring, and according to her that be the way to tell—from the smell of things, I think she said. They're supposed to make ye sick without warnin'." Her voice grew louder as her anger rekindled. "I can't for the life of me imagine how she'd dare come by such an idea! Thinking ye could possibly be . . . well, in that way, just because ye couldn't stomach the sight of them fish! I vow I could strangle her myself, and if ye ask me I—"

Sable closed her eyes and willed herself to remain in control. As Lucy rattled on, she let her mind race back over the past, trying to remember when she had last been afflicted with her monthly troubles. But that was useless speculation, she told herself in the next breath, for she sensed with a woman's instinct that Letitia Blackburn's prediction was true. It would explain, for one thing, the nausea that had beset her on the voyage back to England aboard the *Orient Star*. The seas had been uncommonly rough, the clipper lashed by relentless summer squalls, and Sable had originally explained away her problem as seasickness. But illnesses of that nature had never plagued her before, and she had always prided herself on being as good a sailor as Ned and her father. Yet surely, surely there had to be some other explanation than the one Lucy had suggested!

"Dear God," she whispered to herself, knowing there wasn't, "help me!"

Not too long ago Sable would have run immediately to her mother, sobbing out her story with her face against the Countess's comforting breast. But Sable was no longer the trusting child she had been even on that dark night in March when Morgan Carey had first stepped into her life and awakened in her an awareness of her own sexuality. No, she had lived through too much since then not to turn within herself now for the strength she sought. She had already caused her parents too much heartache since Morgan had swaggered into her life and couldn't burden them with something so terrible now. Nor was she about to bring shame to the St. Germain name, and her fierce pride forbade her to carry out any action save one.

"Oh, Lucy, what utter nonsense!" she said now, and it was the strength that had become such an integral part of her character that allowed her to speak so scornfully.

"Aye, isn't it!" Lucy agreed, relieved that her young mistress had finally decided to speak instead of just standing there staring at her with such a haunted look on her face.

"There's absolutely no reason to go to my parents with it," Sable went on firmly. "You know how bad my father's temper can be, especially where the Blackburns are concerned."

"Lord Monterrey normally has the patience of a saint," Lucy nodded, "though Master Wyecliffe seems to have worn it a trifle thin lately."

"Exactly," Sable agreed. Lifting her small chin proudly, glad that Lucy was unaware of the effort it cost her, she added, "I therefore think it best that we don't say anything to him. Perchance Mrs. Blackburn has realized herself by now how ridiculous her accusations are. Furthermore, she wouldn't dare spread unfounded gossip about us," she added imperiously, for this she knew to be the undisputed truth, "and even if she did, no one would believe her."

Lucy brightened. "I hadn't thought of that." It was true, she reflected. The woman would only be digging her own grave and coming up against some hostile folks if she chose to carry tales about the St. Germains. "Oh, m'lady, can you forgive me for repeating such stuff and nonsense?"

Sable's lower lip quivered, but she forced herself to smile brightly at the older woman. "I'm ever thankful that you did, Lucy."

"Now then," the tiring woman added briskly, considering the matter closed, "we'll put a bit of rouge on your cheeks before ye go down. You're a bit pale, child, and I want ye lookin' your best."

Sable stepped away from Lucy's fussing hands. "I'll do it myself, thank you," she said softly. "Will you please tell my mother that I'll be down shortly?"

Aware that she had been dismissed, but not taking any offense from Lady Sable's gentle tone, Lucy did as she was asked. Such a dear, sweet child, she thought to herself. Made her look the fool, she had, refusing to get upset by the rumor Widow Blackburn had started. But that was Lady Sable's way, Lucy reflected with a loving smile as she hurried to the Countess's apartments in the opposite wing. Never could find a bad word to say about anyone!

For Sable the beautiful summer day had suddenly grown bleak. No sooner had the door closed behind Lucy's receding figure than she collapsed on the window seat, her face buried in her hands. Dear God, she moaned to herself, it couldn't be true that she was carrying Morgan Carey's unborn child! What was she to do now?

Lifting her tear-stained face at the sound of voices below, Sable glanced out of the window and saw her brother Liam and the youngest of the Trevennen children race into view from around the corner of the East Wing. It was obvious that they were embarking on an exploration of the cove directly below the house. At low tide the pebble-strewn beach was a place of adventure, the tidal pools teeming with aquatic life. Liam, as leader of the expedition, was marching purposefully down the path, his arms swinging at his sides. Though he still wore short pants, he carried his dark head proudly, as all the St. Germains did, and Sable felt her heart constrict with tearing pain and love as she gazed down at him.

She couldn't do this to her family, she knew in that moment. She couldn't bring such shame upon them and expect them to right the wrongs she had committed. Though the St. Germains were strong enough to weather the scandal that would surely arise once her condition was known, Sable knew that the intricate fabric of their lives would be unraveled in a way that might never be mended again. Somehow she must find her own way out of this dilemma, yet how?

Biting her lip, she considered her options. She could go to Dmitri and his family and remain on Barbados until the child was born. And then what? she asked herself contemptuously. Return to Cornwall and tell everyone that she had found the baby somewhere in the Caribbean and decided to adopt it?

She could always go to London and terminate the pregnancy, a nasty voice whispered in the dim recesses of her mind. Isn't that what Nancy Warren, the limner's daughter in the village, had done last year?

"Judas, what are you thinking of?" Sable whispered. Not only had Nancy almost died, but the thought of harming the life she and Morgan had created in a moment of love . . . never! She'd sooner die herself than commit such an unspeakable act!

"I want to keep my baby," she said aloud before the thought had even become a conscious one in her mind. As she heard her thin but sure voice repeat those words, she knew them to be true. A feeling of tenderness overwhelmed her, and her cheeks were suddenly wet with tears of happiness, not pain. She might not have the man she loved, but she would have his child, and perhaps that might be enough. . . .

But it still didn't explain how she was supposed to solve the problems the baby's birth presented. How was she to hide the fact from neighbors and friends and from those rare enemies her father had made over the years who would use the knowledge as a weapon to hurt him?

Sable's leaf-green eyes hardened, and this time it was the

fierce determination of her proud Cornish forebears that blazed in her heart. She would go to Morgan, she decided firmly, and see that he took care of her. It was Morgan's child, too, after all, and she would insist that he help her. She wouldn't beg, oh no, that was beneath her, nor would she ask for any quarter for herself. It was for the child's sake and for North Head and her family that she must not be swayed from this chosen course of action.

Morgan must marry her, Sable decided, only long enough for the child to be born. Then he could file for annulment and be free of her. It would be painless enough for him, he wouldn't even have to see her face after the ceremony, but in this way the baby would have a name and her family would be safe from ugly gossip.

"He'll have to," Sable swore to herself, ignoring the pang of uncertainty within her. No one knew better than she how impossible it was to force Morgan Carey into anything against his will, but in this she would not be dissuaded. He himself had been instrumental in changing her from the sheltered girl she had been when she'd first come to him, and his actions would now come home to roost when he found himself confronted by the determined woman he had made of her.

"You'll be foiled by your own arrogance for the first time in your life, Morgan Carey," Sable whispered, "and you will marry me and give your child a name if I have to chase you to the ends of the earth to achieve it!"

Her shoulders slumped suddenly, and the light burning in her dark green eyes was replaced by despair. Her determination was all good and fine, but how could she go to Morgan if she didn't even know where he was? She had no idea where the *Defiance* had been headed after Dmitri had taken her away, had no idea what Morgan intended to do once Sergei recovered from his injuries.

Her father would know, Sable thought to herself, pacing the elegant carpet in her agitation. Since her return she had never asked him what had brought Morgan to North Head in the first place or what mystery linked Andrei Vilyusk to the St. Germains. In truth she hadn't cared enough to ask, or at least that was what she had told herself during those first miserable days after her return to Cornwall. Now she railed against her foolishness. They had discussed Morgan at length, she, her father, and mother, when she had told them the entire story of her journey to Istanbul aboard Morgan's ship. Why had she deliberately refused to ask about him? Was the saving of a few tears worth the loss of the information she so desperately needed now?

Yet Sable knew that if she went to her father now she would only give herself away. Armed with the knowledge that she was carrying Morgan Carey's child, she would never be able to hide the truth from him.

"What shall I do?" she asked herself, tears springing to her eyes. She mustn't cry, she told herself fiercely, for that was a sign of cowardice. She must be brave now, braver than she had ever been in all her life. Yet how was she to find him?

Sable's head came up suddenly and she ceased her frantic pacing. Of course! she breathed, of course! Ambling Cross! Wasn't that where Letitia Blackburn had said Morgan used to live? It didn't matter that he no longer resided there now! It was her only lead, and the chances were good that Ambling Cross's present owners would know where Morgan had gone. And if not, there was always that rented townhouse in Dartmouth he had spoken of, whose tenants would surely be able to shed some light on their landlord's whereabouts!

Sable shook her head at the irony of it all. She had Letitia Blackburn to thank, not only for making her aware of the fact that she was carrying Morgan's child, but unwittingly supplying her with the means of finding him and making him responsible for it.

"Sable, you lazy thing! Have you fallen asleep?"

The chiding call was accompanied by the rattling of pebbles against the mullioned panes. Sable moved swiftly to the window, and her lips curved as she saw Ned standing below, a shyly grinning Martin Trevennen beside him. Her brother's upturned face was so like her handsome father's that Sable felt her heart turn over. She had decided on the right course, she told herself firmly, and she'd leave first chance she got, slipping away before anyone in the family knew she was gone. There'd be time for explanations later, but first Morgan had to be found and dealt with.

"I'll be right down," she called to them, opening the glass. She paused long enough to cast a quick glance in the mirror. Her face was pale, she saw, and her eyes were red from crying, but she didn't think anyone would find it odd, not if she tried hard to seem cheerful and free of cares.

"I *am* free of cares," Sable said sternly to herself as she started down the stairs. Squaring her slim shoulders, she gave a young footman in the hallway a sweet smile, causing him to blush furiously. Once she had found Morgan, everything would be all right, she told herself firmly.

It was fortunate that Sable had the tenacity and courage of both the Barrancourts and St. Germains flowing in her veins, for she would never have been able to convince herself thereof. The gnawing emptiness within her heart she dismissed as nerves, and if despair nibbled at the edges of her consciousness, she thrust it fiercely away. Nothing would go wrong, she told herself bravely. Nothing!

When Sable stepped down off the carriage and saw the stone chimneys and tile rooftops of Ambling Cross amid the trees, she knew at once that Morgan had not belonged here. It was far too patrician a dwelling, and the manicured lawns and carefully tended gardens were too structured for a man of his tastes. Yet it was an impressive estate nonetheless, built with its trio of wings joining the center block to form an *E* in honor of England's great Queen. In the rolling meadows behind it horned red cattle grazed peacefully, their lows carrying to her on the still air.

Sable had asked the driver of the vehicle she had hired to let her off at the end of the drive. It was a warm, overcast day, and the humid air held the promise of rain. A hot breeze stirred the branches of the towering beeches overhead, causing the leaves to rustle.

"Are you sure you're not wantin' me to drive you to the door, ma'am?" the driver asked courteously. "'Tis a long way from here and fair hot."

"I'll be fine," Sable assured him. She wanted to collect her thoughts before knocking upon the imposing door, feeling an uncharacteristic loss of nerve now that she was actually here. Tying her hat beneath her chin, she began to walk, her slim shoulders proudly carried. No one must see that she was afraid, Sable told herself firmly, otherwise she'd never get past the front door.

Bees droned in the flowerbeds she passed, and dragonflies dipped across the nearby lake where a pair of white swans glided gracefully through the lily pads. Sable found it hard to believe that Morgan had spent part of his life here, for this was

surely a place meant for raising children and entertaining friends.
What a lonely bachelor's existence he must have led! There
was so much she wished she knew about him, then reminded
herself that it really didn't matter. She wanted nothing from
Morgan Carey save the assurance that he would give their child
a name, and beyond that he could go to Hades for all she cared.

"Hey, look out there!" came an unexpected shout from the
nearby shrubbery. Startled, Sable whirled about to see a cricket
ball come hurtling toward her. She had just enough time to
step safely aside before it crashed to the ground at her feet.

The hedgerow rustled, and the round, freckled face of a boy
somewhat older than Liam appeared. His eyes were wide as
he looked at her. "So sorry! It didn't hit you, did it?"

Sable shook her head, and he grinned in relief.

"Whew! Grandfather'd have had my head if I beaned anyone! He's always telling me cricket's not my sport and that I
might as well give it up!"

Sable was forced to smile back at him. Though he was
several years older than Liam, his expression reminded her so
much of her younger brother that she couldn't help liking him.
A pang went through her at the thought of her family and she
realized that by now her absence must have been noticed. She
pictured Katie hurrying up to her room to awaken her, finding
instead an empty bed and a note explaining briefly that she had
gone to Devon for the day and should be back by nightfall.

Sable tried not to feel guilty although she knew how concerned her parents would be by her mysterious behavior. She
hoped her father wouldn't be too angry. She didn't really know
what she was going to tell her parents when she returned, but
that was something she'd have to worry about later.

"Can I help you, miss?" the boy asked politely. It was
obvious to him that she was a lady. Her speech was soft and
gentle, and the walking gown she wore with its tailored jacket
and matching hat was prettier even than the clothes his sister
Bridget ordered from London.

"I'd like very much to speak with your father," Sable replied.
"Is he at home?"

The boy shook his head and wiggled through the hedge so
that he could come stand beside her. His sleeves were rolled
up, and he carried a cricket bat in one chubby hand. "My
father's dead," he told Sable simply. "Me and Bridget have
been living with Grandfather since March."

"Your grandfather owns Ambling Cross, I take it?" Sable asked, glancing up at the house which loomed before her at the end of the tree-lined drive.

"Yes, miss. Grandfather used to live in London, but he got too old for it, he said, so he bought the house and when Papa died he had us come live with him."

"That was kind of him."

The boy made a face. "Not really. He doesn't like children very much, and we have to be ever so careful not to make any noise or bring dirt into the house. Still, I like living here better than in Brighton." He shot her a curious glance. "What did you want to see Grandfather for?"

"I want to ask him about the man who owned Ambling Cross before he bought it."

His brow furrowed. "I don't—"

"Raymond! Raymond Blair, where have you gone? Oh, you despicable boy, are you hiding from me again?"

He gave Sable a toothy grin. "That's my governess, Mrs. Ferris. She's a horrid creature, but my sister Bridget says she means well." He himself sounded unconvinced.

"Raymond! Master Raymond, if you don't come out this instant I shall be forced to tell your Grandfather when he returns!"

"Come on," Raymond whispered, grasping Sable's hand. "We'll sneak through the side entrance."

She had no choice but to follow him, lifting her skirts as she ran along beside him. Raymond led her through a small rose garden and over a low stone fence before ducking into an archway that led to a flight of stone steps. He was panting by the time they reached the top, but his grin was triumphant.

"She'll never catch us now. Come on, I'll take you to Bridget. She probably knows more about the Cross than Grandfather does since she's always reading those boring history books. Besides, I'm not sure Grandfather would tell you anything anyway."

Sable followed him hesitantly down a darkened corridor that smelled strongly of beeswax and polish. She had the feeling that Grandfather Blair was very fussy about the upkeep of his home, for none of the rooms they passed looked as if anyone had been allowed to step inside them for years. The furniture was covered to protect the upholstery, and there were runners laid over the priceless carpets. All of the windows were tightly shuttered despite the heat so that no daylight was able to filter in. It must have been a charming, rambling old edifice when Morgan had lived here, Sable decided, but now it had the gloomy air of a museum.

Raymond opened a door at the far end of the corridor and peeked inside. Sable began to relax as she heard a soft, friendly voice chide from within, "Where have you been, love? Didn't you hear Mrs. Ferris calling you?"

"I snuck through the side entrance," Raymond responded. "I didn't want her to see me."

"Doubtless you were practicing your ball playing instead of studying," the soft voice said knowingly.

"I was," Raymond admitted, "and I brought someone to see you. I don't know her name, but she seems very nice."

He stepped aside in order to let Sable enter. The parlor she found herself in was dominated by a stone fireplace lined with beautiful Delft tiles gleaming with polish. It was a relief to see some disarray at last as evidenced by the books and needlework lying on the damask sofa. Movement in the corner caught Sable's eye, and she turned her head to see a young woman come gracefully to her feet.

Bridget Blair was in her early twenties, a plain but pleasant-looking woman with dark brown hair and wide-set gray eyes. A pair of spectacles sat on the end of her nose, and it was obvious that Sable had interrupted her reading.

"Yes?" she asked politely, and Sable hurried to explain herself.

"I'm sorry to intrude on you like this, Miss Blair, but I've come from Cornwall to ask some questions about your house."

A warm smile appeared on Bridget's face. "Certainly. Won't you sit down?" Prodding her brother impatiently, she added, "Go ask Betty to fix us some tea, Raymond, quickly!"

"I don't mean to put you to trouble," Sable began, but Bridget held up a hand to silence her.

"Please, it's no trouble at all! We have so few visitors here and certainly never anyone who is curious about Ambling Cross. Now, please," she repeated kindly, "sit down. You look tired, and it's uncommonly warm today. Did you come alone?"

Sable nodded, settling herself into the armchair Bridget indicated. "I left my carriage on the roadside."

"Don't tell me you walked!" Bridget exclaimed.

"I wasn't sure of my reception, and I thought it better not

to arrive in a carriage. It seemed rather forward," Sable said, well aware that it wasn't considered proper to arrive unannounced at anyone's home, especially when you were a stranger.

"Grandfather might have thought so," Bridget conceded, "but he isn't here at the moment. Raymond and I are alone. Ah, Betty, thank you," she added as a woman in a white apron and starched cap entered with a tray. Sable watched as Bridget poured tea with graceful movements, and accepted a cup with a nod of thanks.

"What brought you to Ambling Cross?" Bridget asked, settling back against the cushions. She regarded Sable curiously over the rim of her spectacles. Such a lovely young woman, she thought to herself, and yet she seemed so full of cares. "You said you had some questions for me?"

Sable nodded, glad that Bridget Blair seemed not to think her presence here unusual.

"There isn't much I can tell you," Bridget went on. "Raymond and I have only been living here for a little over six months. My father died last year and we had nowhere else to go. Grandfather was kind enough to take us in."

Her wistful expression transformed her plain features into poignant loveliness as she spoke of her father, and Sable found her heart going out to this gentle, book-loving young woman and her playful brother. This gloomy old house was certainly no place for them! She tried not to compare the silent, loveless atmosphere of Ambling Cross with the laughter-filled warmth of North Head. It wasn't fair to Bridget and Raymond Blair, and besides, thinking of her family only weakened her own resolve to find Morgan.

"It's not really the house itself I'm interested in," Sable went on, stirring her tea. "It's the man who owned the house before your grandfather bought it. His name was Sir Morgan Carey. Have you ever heard of him?"

Bridget's gray eyes twinkled. "Indeed I have. Though he hasn't lived here for a number of years, he's still a favored parlor topic in the area. I don't believe I've ever heard so much conflicting gossip about anyone since I came here! He must have been quite a character if half the stories about him are to be believed."

How like Morgan to leave a dastardly reputation behind him, Sable thought to herself, unaware of the tenderness that softened her features as she thought of him. But what should she tell Bridget Blair her reasons were for coming here? She hadn't even given her her name!

"I wonder if you could tell me," she said, clearing her throat and plunging on determinedly, "if Sir Morgan left any forwarding address with your grandfather when he sold Ambling Cross. I need to find him, you see, and I haven't any idea where to begin looking."

Bridget was shaking her head even before Sable finished speaking. "I'm afraid I can't be of any help to you in that respect. The sale of the house was handled through a solicitor while Sir Morgan was away at sea. I don't think even Grandfather knows where you might find him. You could—"

"Bridget! Bridget, girl, where are you?"

"Oh no," Bridget whispered, growing pale at the sound of the querulous cry coming from the hallway. "It's Grandfather! He must have come home early!" Setting her teacup aside, she gave Sable an apologetic glance. "I'm afraid you're going to have to leave. He's ever so strict about having visitors in the house, and he'll probably be rude to you when he sees you."

"Would you show me out, then?" Sable suggested, hating the thought that she might have gotten this soft-spoken young woman into trouble.

"I'll take you through the back," Bridget said, relieved that her guest hadn't chosen to comment on her grandfather's eccentric behavior. It shamed her at times, but she never complained, aware of the sacrifice he had made by taking two unwanted children into his home.

But it was too late. As Bridget started for the door, it burst open and an old man with stooped shoulders and flowing white hair stood on the threshold. His eyes widened as he took in his granddaughter's pale face and the startled one of the young girl standing beside her.

"What's the meaning of this?" Benton Blair demanded incredulously. "I go away for barely half a day and what do I find? You've smuggled someone in while I've been gone! Mrs. Ferris met me at the door and told me she suspected you'd invited a friend over, but I refused to believe it. You know the policy about visitors in this house, girl!"

"I'm sorry," Bridget began, her soft lips trembling, but Sable interrupted her, outraged at the old man's behavior. How could he treat his own flesh and blood so callously?

"Please don't blame her, Mr. Blair," she said, her small

chin bravely lifted, although there was something unnerving about the madly glowing eyes glaring down at her. "I came unannounced, and your granddaughter was kind enough to let me in. I merely came to ask some questions about Ambling Cross's former owner."

Benton Blair's nostrils flared and his cheeks suffused with color. "Even worse!" he shouted. "I'll have no nosy young woman in my home bringing dust and dirt and impertinent questions! I'm afraid you'll have to leave this instant!"

"Grandfather, please!" Bridget begged.

"I'll have a word with you later, you forward creature," he railed at her. "I knew it was a mistake the day I let you and that ill-mannered brother of yours into this house!" To Sable he added harshly as she continued to gaze at him without moving, thinking to herself that he was truly mad, "Out I say! Out of this house at once, girl!"

More humiliated than she had ever been in her life, Sable pushed her way past him and ran down the corridor, her cheeks on fire. She stumbled headlong down the steps, not even caring that she had left her gloves and bonnet behind. She just wanted to get away from the gloomy old house and the madman who owned it.

To her relief the carriage was still waiting at the far end of the drive, the horses in their traces lazily batting flies with their tails. The driver, who had settled himself in the shade to wait, scrambled to his feet at the sight of her.

"Ready to go, miss?" he inquired, seeming not at all curious about the fact that she had literally escaped at a run from the house and that her skirts were covered with dust.

"Yes, please," Sable panted, wanting to put as much distance between herself and Blair as possible.

"Miss! Wait, please!"

She turned at the sound of Raymond's voice to find him running after her, his face flushed with exertion. "Bridget said I was to tell you how sorry she was," he breathed when he halted before her.

"What a horrible man your grandfather is!" Sable burst out.

A shadow passed across the young boy's freckled face. "Bridget says he wasn't always this bad. She said it was worrying about money all the time and losing Grandmother a few years ago. It's made him dislike everyone. Sometimes he can be quite nice," he added, as though trying to make himself believe that as much as her.

"Please tell your sister I'm sorry to have caused her so much trouble," Sable said regretfully. "He won't punish her, will he?" she added fearfully.

Raymond shrugged as though punishment were an accepted facet of their lives. "Maybe take her books away for a week or two. But that isn't why she sent me after you," he hurried on as Sable gave a soft gasp. "She said to tell you to go to the Howells of Glamorgan."

Sable's brow furrowed. "Glamorgan? Where is that?"

"In South Wales, I think she said. That's where Sir Morgan's people are from, and someone there should know where he is. Bridget said—"

"Master Raymond! You're to come back at once!"

It was a man's voice, and Sable turned to see a footman standing at the opposite end of the drive, his hands cupped as he shouted.

"There goes cricket for a week." Raymond sighed in resignation.

Sable's heart sank. What damage she had done by coming here! If only there were some way to make it up to the boy and his sister! But she could do nothing save voice her regrets, and as the carriage pulled away, she promised herself that someday she would help Bridget and Raymond Blair escape the living hell that was their life at Ambling Cross.

But her own thoughts soon began to trouble her more than those of two people she barely knew. She couldn't possibly travel to Wales alone, she told herself as the carriage rolled back to the village of Ambler. It was a hot, dusty trip, but Sable, leaning her head against the worn leather cushions, didn't notice. She was thinking of what Raymond had told her and wondering bleakly what she was to do. It shouldn't take long to travel to Wales and back, and she certainly had enough money to pay her way, but ought she do it? She could have a message delivered to her parents telling them where she was, but was it fair to cause them so much worry? Moreover, she didn't care for the idea of traveling alone to a rugged, mountainous region to seek out people she knew nothing about. She shivered, wondering what she'd do if the Howells of Glamorgan turned out to be as mad as Benton Blair.

"I have to go," she whispered to herself at last, even before she was aware that she had made up her mind to do so.

If she returned to North Head, she knew that she would have to tell her parents the truth about Morgan and herself, and that she couldn't do. No, she mustn't go back until she had solved her problems, even if it meant journeying to Wales.

Tears welled in Sable's eyes, but she dashed them resolutely away. What a mess she had made of everything, she thought to herself, ashamed of the heartache she had caused those she loved the most. Yet one thought continued to revolve fiercely through her pain, and that was that she wouldn't rest until Morgan Carey had paid for what he'd done!

Chapter 16

Sergei Vilyusk sat in the fresh air, his long legs propped comfortably on one of the crates stacked neatly against the *Defiance*'s great cabin wall. His eyes were half closed, and to any casual observer he seemed to be dozing in the warmth of the August sun. But Sergei was wide awake, his thoughts dwelling not only on his mending shoulder but on the freedom he was only now beginning to grow accustomed to and what he intended to do with it.

The *Defiance* was anchored at Le Havre, the sails neatly furled, her bare masts and rigging soaring into the sky. With the ship nearly deserted, an almost eerie silence had settled over the decks, broken only by the raucous cries of wheeling gulls and the slapping of a loose luff tackle against a yardarm overhead.

Along the wharf below all was still as men escaped the afternoon heat by slipping into town, to the alehouses and taprooms which were always open to welcome them. It was an uncommonly warm summer this year, and few people cared to venture out during the hottest part of the day. Thunder rumbled over the Channel, bringing with it the promise of rain, but Sergei didn't even look up, suspecting that such relief would probably not materialize.

"Excuse me, Master Sergei, would you be caring for lunch? I was going to prepare some cold chicken salad for Mr. Hayes, and I thought you might be hungry."

Sergei opened an eye and a smile curved his lips. Since his recovery he'd found himself being coddled not only by Dr. Aaron Pierson but by Grayson, who was determined to fatten his patient up by preparing the most tempting meals Sergei had eaten in a great while.

"Chicken salad would please me very much," he said promptly, well aware that the valet wouldn't cease pestering him until he'd agreed to eat something. "And a bottle of wine, too. Why don't you look and see what your knavish employer has in the cupboard? I'm heartily tired of his claret."

"Very good, sir." Grayson hesitated a moment and Sergei, who had closed his eyes again, turned his head to regard him curiously.

"Did you wish something else from me, Grayson?"

"No, sir," the steward said hastily, then, as if making up his mind, he confessed uncertainly, "Well, perhaps there is."

Sergei propped his good arm behind his head and regarded the valet indulgently. He rather liked Grayson, stuffy though he might be, and certainly had to admire him for having endured Morgan Carey's awful temper for so many years. "What is it?"

"It's about Sir Morgan. I was wondering if you might have any clues as to when he intends to return from Paris. We've been idled here for almost a week now, and I can't help suspecting that his delay is a cause for concern."

Sergei was forced to chuckle at this, his pale blue eyes crinkled with amusement. "Your captain is one man I have never concerned myself over, Grayson." He stroked his beard thoughtfully and added, "I wouldn't think a week too long considering what he had to do. I only wish I could have gone with him," he added darkly, for Morgan's refusal to let him come along had been a sore point between them. Sergei had to agree that a bone-jarring journey from Le Havre to Paris would not have done his injured shoulder and back much good, but he chafed at the restriction, especially when the information Morgan sought was so very vital to both of them.

Grayson stared off across the rooftops of the town, his

normally pleasant features set in a mask of worry and indecision. He had never pried into his master's personal affairs before, nor had he any right to do so now, yet Sir Morgan's unpredictable temper of late had given him much reason to be concerned. The slightest infraction of rules had brought severe punishment down on the heads of many hapless crewmen, and Grayson himself had all too often felt the stinging lash of Morgan's tongue. What could it mean? he had asked himself on more than one occasion.

"What are you thinking, Grayson?" Sergei asked at last. The poor man was a nervous wreck, he thought to himself, and in obvious need of a little soothing.

The loyal steward heaved a deep sigh. "Ah, Master Sergei, this ship's not been the same since Lady Sable left us. What sunny hours we enjoyed while she was here, and I vow the captain was a changed man in her presence!"

Sergei rolled his eyes, for he had heard this story often enough from every one of the crewmen who had taken him into their confidence. It was true, Morgan was an ill-tempered lout these days, but from what his men had to say, one would think Lady Sable alone had been responsible for taming him.

Sergei had to admit that he was curious about this young woman, of whom every man aboardship spoke with such respect and warmth. Morgan himself did not speak of her at all, and the merest mention of her name was enough to make him grow even more hostile than usual. Yet Sergei knew that there were other cares that weighed heavily on Morgan Carey's broad shoulders these days, cares that had driven him to Istanbul in the first place.

"I couldn't tell you whether Morgan is a changed man or not," Sergei pointed out. "I knew him ten years ago, and at the time he was suffering from a very nasty battle wound, the sort which brings out the worst in a man." His grin was disarming. "In fact, I'm inclined to believe his present behavior is a great improvement."

"I only wish I knew what was troubling him," Grayson admitted. "Surely there must be something I can do to help!"

Sergei rose to his feet and moved restlessly to the rail. The wind stirred his chestnut hair, and he squinted as he stared off across the water. Propping his injured arm with its supporting sling against the wood, he shook his head decisively.

"I'm afraid no one can help him at the moment, my friend. He is driven by demons that have possessed him long before either of us knew him."

"Won't you tell me what they are?" Grayson begged, throwing aside all restraints in his desire to look after his beloved master's welfare.

"Morgan would probably boil both of us in oil if he caught us gossiping about him," Sergei said, and held up his hand to silence Grayson's protests. "I imagine you do have a right to be told something, seeing as you've been loyal to the ill-tempered fellow for all these years. What do you know of Sir Morgan's past?"

Grayson looked startled. "His past? Why, only that he had been living in Devon for several months before he took me into his employ. He had just returned from Crimea and was nursing a war wound which fortunately left him with no permanent afflictions."

"Thanks to my excellent care," Sergei remembered, shaking his head now at the irony of it all. So many men had died or been wounded on that blood-soaked battlefield, and he had ended up taking pity on the bravest of them all. He could have turned Morgan over to his superior officer, to see him taken north as a prisoner, but instead he had been touched by the Englishman's courage and had resolved to help him as best he could. What an odd quirk of fate had been responsible for that!

"You know nothing of Morgan beyond the years he spent in Devon?" he asked now.

Grayson shook his head. "I'm afraid Sir Morgan told me very little of his past. Even now, after so many years, I know only that he was born in Wales and that some sorry affair within his family forced him to leave home at an early age. Naturally I don't care to be discussing his past," he added uncomfortably. "If Sir Morgan had wanted me to know the facts, he would have confided in me long before this."

"He couldn't confide in anyone," Sergei said gruffly, "not even me, at first. Scars of the soul never disappear, my friend, and I am only grateful that the truth I carried with me into the seraglio was important enough to prompt him to rescue me. Otherwise I'd still be rotting away there and Morgan would be no wiser than before."

"The truth concerning what?" Grayson blurted, unable to

bear these riddles any longer. What had driven Sir Morgan to risk his life in the seraglio if not a sense of duty and honor toward the man who had saved his life long ago?

"Concerning a beautiful woman by the name of Gwenna Howell," Sergei answered softly, "who fell in love with a dashing consular officer living in Paris more than thirty years ago."

"Howell was the name Morgan's mother possessed before she married Thomas Carey," Grayson remembered.

"What Morgan seeks in Paris," Sergei added, "is proof that a wedding took place between Gwenna Howell and this consular officer, proof that will change many things in his life. I understand that Lady Sable St. Germain's father helped open the doors in Paris through which Morgan must pass to obtain what he seeks."

"The Earl of Monterrey?" Grayson asked, startled.

Sergei nodded enigmatically. "Now I've said enough," he stated, straightening and turning away. "You might ask Sir Morgan yourself when he returns if his hunt was successful. If it was, perhaps he will tell you the rest of his story. Now, if you don't mind, Grayson, I'd love to have some of that excellent chicken salad of yours."

Instantly the steward's features took on the mask of servile propriety for which he was best known. "Of course, sir. I'll bring it up at once."

"Thank you." Sergei settled himself back on the bench and crossed his long legs before him. Ah, Morgan, my friend, he thought to himself, I hope that you will find what you are looking for so that you will know at last the peace that has eluded you for most of your life.

It was not until two days later that Morgan Carey returned to his ship to find his crew eager to weigh anchor. The days of inactivity had taken their toll, and there were quarrels among the men over trivial matters, a sign to their watchful captain that it was time to turn the *Defiance* seaward again.

"Aye, we'll set a new course with the tide," Morgan assured those who came to inquire of his plans the morning he returned to the ship, "but I've one stop to make along the way."

"Where might that be, cap'n?" Harley Gump, the boldest of his men, inquired curiously.

"Dartmouth. I've a few personal effects to collect there."

A gleam entered Harley's eyes. "Where will we be turnin' our bow after that, cap'n? Westward? I've a hankerin' for tropical waters, I do."

The brooding look that had been on Morgan's handsome face since he'd stepped aboard was replaced now with a glint of amusement. "As soon as I've settled my affairs and deposited Master Vilyusk wherever he may wish to go, the *Defiance* will set a course as you men see fit."

Toothy grins responded to his words, the men thinking to themselves that the cap'n was a right good fellow for all his nasty-tempered ways. Returning to their stations, they discussed the possibility of a timber run from South America or perhaps a tea race against one of the famed American clippers from China to New York.

"Mark my words, whatever the cap'n takes a fancy to, 'twill line our pockets with gold," Harley predicted.

Nat Palmer looked unconvinced. "The cap'n has me curious, he do. I can't help thinkin' the *Defiance*'ll be seein' a different sort of action before we take on any more consigned goods. I was hopin', too," he confessed self-consciously, "that he'd be swingin' by Cornwall on the way back and maybe payin' a visit to Lady Sable."

Harley Gump snorted. "That'll be the day! He'll not go changin' his mind, proud bastard that he be, and if he let her go once before, he'll not be runnin' after her again."

"Anyone can make a mistake," Nat persisted, but Harley was of a different mind.

"Maybe so, but even if he did, our cap'n's not the kind to go admittin' it. There won't be no more tanglin' with the St. Germains, I promise you that," he added, though the regret in his gruff voice was evident to all.

In the ancient seaport of Dartmouth the clipper's captain and crew was to find the summer heat laying fallow over land and sea. Though the skies were overcast, no breath of wind portended a storm and the accompanying coolness it would bring. The *Defiance* lay motionless at anchor in the mouth of the Dart River, the furled canvas lying limp against the yards, while the men grumbled ill-temperedly and sought refuge in the waterfront taprooms.

No one had seen a sign of Captain Sir Morgan since the ship had cast its mooring lines in Le Havre and slipped out into the Channel. During the short voyage to Devon, Jackson

Torance had been in command while Morgan remained sequestered below. Knowing he would be summoned should Morgan wish to tell him what, if anything, he had found in Paris, Sergei remained topside, where the hot breeze was a little easier to tolerate than the sweltering cabins belowdecks.

Yet no sooner had the lines been made fast in Dartmouth than Morgan appeared on deck. Dressed in shirtsleeves, he strode aft and conferred for several minutes with his first mate. Sergei watched him curiously from his place near the mizzenmast, and hurried forward to intercept him when Morgan descended to the main deck at last.

"Is there a reason for coming here?" he wanted to know, thinking Morgan had left him guessing long enough.

The full lips tightened. "I have some personal effects I have to collect here before we can go on."

"Go on where?" Sergei questioned. "Damn you, Morgan, you're leading all of us about by the nose and I can't blame your men for growing angry! All you can tell us after a six-day absence is that you have things to take care of before we can set a new course? What things? And where are we bound?"

Morgan's lean jaw tightened, but Sergei was not put off by such a dire warning. The search that had sent Morgan to Paris concerned him as well, and he was damned if he was going to be left in the dark!

"What did you learn in Paris?" he demanded, blocking Morgan's path as the captain of the *Defiance* attempted to step past him. Both men were roughly of the same height and build, and a confrontation between them was not something to be taken lightly.

Morgan's steel-blue eyes met the determined ones of Sergei Vilyusk, and for a moment it seemed as if he was going to push him aside. Then his lips twitched into a humorless smile and he said coldly, "Lord Monterrey's contacts were most helpful, Sergei. I have the proof I need in the form of signed church records showing that Gwenna Howell, my dear mother, did marry Andrei Vilyusk before she returned home and gave birth to me. That means I'm no longer a bastard," he added cynically, long years of bitterness in his tone, "and you, Sergei, will be pleased—or damned, I imagine—to learn that you are legally my brother."

Without another word he pushed past the startled Russian and strode toward the entry port. A moment later Sergei saw him vanish down a narrow alley flanked by Tudor houses that led from the wharf into the town center. He could only stare after him, slack-jawed with astonishment.

"You, there! I would like to see the captain of this ship."

Sergei whirled about, tensing instinctively against the underlying challenge in the steely voice that addressed him from the entry port through which Morgan had strode less than a minute ago. His eyes narrowed as he found himself confronted by a powerfully built man who had ascended the boarding plank without a sound and now stood regarding him with hostile eyes. He was not a young man, yet he carried nothing but muscle on his tall frame. His gaze was cool and appraising, and the small scar on his cheek gave him a dangerous look.

"I'm afraid he has left the ship," Sergei said warily. It was obvious to him, despite the sun-weathered features and casual attire, that this was a gentleman, and one to be reckoned with.

The bronzed brow darkened ominously. "How can that be? I've been informed you only dropped anchor fifteen minutes ago." His experienced eyes roved the decks before him, noting especially the activity about the forecastle, where the last remaining crewmen were busy at the capstan.

"Sir Morgan had business in town," Sergei explained, still watching him carefully. "Perhaps you would like to speak to the first mate?"

A humorless smile curved the full lips, causing the scar to stand out more prominently in the lean cheek. "You, I take it, are Lieutenant Sergei Vilyusk, late of Seraglio Prison in Istanbul."

Sergei's eyes narrowed, disliking to be toyed with, especially by a man who looked as though he didn't usually make it a habit of playing games. "I am," he admitted coolly, "and you, my friend, are . . . ?"

"Charles St. Germain, Earl of Monterrey."

"Your lordship," Sergei said curtly, inclining his head a fraction to acknowledge the introduction. "What brings you to Devon?"

Charles's scar whitened in his anger. No one would ever need written proof that Sergei Vilyusk and Sir Morgan Carey were half brothers. It was evident in their arrogance, a trait, Charles thought irritably, more distinguishing than their penetrating blue eyes and muscular frames. Yet he was not interested at the moment whether Morgan Carey had discovered in

Paris the papers he needed and which the Earl himself had helped him locate. One thing mattered to him now, and he wouldn't rest until he had confronted Morgan Carey with it.

"When does Captain Carey expect to return?"

"I'm afraid I cannot tell you."

Charles cursed savagely beneath his breath, his temper snapping. "I haven't time to waste waiting for him, so you may tell him this when he returns: My daughter, Sable, has been missing from home since early this morning. She left nothing save a note telling us she was going to Devon to find Sir Morgan." Ignoring Sergei's startled exclamation, he added ruthlessly, "I have no idea why she would do such a thing, but I promise you, Mr. Vilyusk, I will get her back and you may tell Captain Carey that he can expect a reckoning from me."

He started for the entry port and paused long enough to add over his shoulder, "I'm told Sir Morgan has a townhouse somewhere along the waterfront. I'm going now to find it, and should he return before I do, I suggest you persuade him not to leave."

He was gone before Sergei could respond. Watching the Earl stride with purposeful steps along the same route Morgan had taken not minutes ahead of him, Sergei pursed his lips and shook his head. Never had he come across a man quite as incensed and ready for battle as Charles St. Germain. It was obvious to him now where Lady Sable St. Germain had come by the courage to follow Morgan into the seraglio and kill a man in order to save him. Any offspring, even a female, from that snarling lion would be a terror to tangle with!

But why had the Earl's daughter come to Devon looking for Morgan? From the little he'd been told, mostly from Grayson, Lady Sable had seemed only too willing to leave the *Defiance*, and Morgan had certainly behaved as though he were glad to see her go. He shook his head. Morgan Carey had become an enigma to him where Sable St. Germain was concerned, and any attempt on his own part to learn more about her had been met by stoic silence and, at times, even a savage flaring of temper.

Emotions that ran so deep were difficult to fathom, Sergei thought to himself. The mystery of Morgan's relationship with the courageous young woman whom he had saved from drowning intrigued him, yet he had no desire to tangle with her father again.

"Kristos, I believe I was safer in the Kafess than here in

this cauldron filled with hotheads," Sergei muttered to himself. Morgan was in for an unpleasant surprise, he decided, and he hoped he'd have the chance to warn him before Charles St. Germain got to him first.

In that respect he need not have worried, for Morgan returned not ten minutes later, already alerted by gossip that the Earl of Monterrey was in town. Feeling certain that the Earl had come to confront him, Morgan had abandoned his own errands in order to meet His lordship's awesome temper head-on. Surely Sable must have told her father by now what had transpired between them, and Morgan didn't exactly relish what was to come.

As he stepped aboard his ship, his suspicions were justified when he saw Sergei hurrying toward him, his expression making it clear that he had been watching for his arrival. Morgan shook his head, still quite unable to believe that this was his half brother and the only living blood relation he had left in the world. Fate had dealt him some impossible hands when one considered how easily he might never have discovered the missing pieces of his past.

It was pure chance, after all, that had led him to discover that Sergei was imprisoned in Istanbul. And it was an even odder twist of fate that had brought him to Benjamin Disraeli, Great Britain's famed prime minister, for help—the one man who had happened to seize on the Vilyusk name and recall that another Vilyusk named Andrei had been on the staff of the Russian embassy in Paris almost three decades ago. It hadn't really interested Morgan overly until the Prime Minister had added that, among the many women the skirt-chasing Andrei had consorted with, he remembered one by the name of Howell, a reportedly lovely young thing from Wales. Morgan had been born in Wales, Disraeli had remarked with a twinkle in his eye. Had he perhaps known a family by the name of Howell?

Morgan had, but he had said nothing of the suspicions racing through his brain. Instead he had sought out Charles St. Germain at Disraeli's request, for the Earl had been a prominent member of Paris's *haut monde* in those days and might know more about the Howell woman Andrei Vilyusk had supposedly loved.

Morgan's lips tightened grimly as he recalled the shock of learning that the Earl remembered Gwenna Howell well, her beauty and intelligence having won the heart of nearly every man in Paris. One of them had been Andrei Vilyusk, and, yes,

Charles could well remember the rumors that had flown throughout the city about them. Though Morgan had known for years that Thomas Carey had been his father only in name, he couldn't accept the possibility that his true father might have been Andrei Vilyusk . . . not without proof. Only Sergei would know for sure, and Sergei was locked away in a prison cell in one of the most closely guarded fortresses in the world.

"Morgan!" Sergei called, catching sight of him. Though he was unaware of his brother's thoughts, he could see the grim determination in his cold blue eyes.

"You needn't tell me, Sergei," Morgan said darkly, stepping aboard. "I already know Monterrey is here. What does he want?" he added impatiently. "To have my head for compromising his daughter's honor? Or is he too much of a gentleman for fisticuffs? Did he demand pistols at dawn, or am I to wed the chit and make her respectable?"

"Kristos, what are you babbling about?" Sergei demanded. "Aye, St. Germain was here and he was angry, but he said nothing of dueling with you! He was looking for his daughter and seemed to think she was here."

Morgan's brow rose. "What would Sable be doing aboard my ship? Last I saw of her she was safely in the company of that bullying Zergeyev fellow His Lordship employs as his captain."

"No, my friend, you don't understand. Lady Sable has disappeared from her home in Cornwall leaving a note saying she was coming to Devon to find you."

Morgan grew still, the mocking smile fading from his handsome face. "Why on earth would she do that? She seemed heartily glad to be rid of me the night Zergeyev came for her."

"I think that's what His Lordship would like to know, too. He said he was going to your townhouse to look for you there and that you'd better stay here in the event you got back before he did."

"Grayson!" Morgan roared, catching sight of the valet over Sergei's shoulder.

"Yes sir?"

"Bring my riding boots and jacket and have Gilpin go down to the quay immediately to find me a horse. Step lively or I'll have you flayed at the mast."

"Yes sir!" Grayson called as he hurried away.

Sergei's eyes narrowed. "What are you going to do?"

"Ride to Ambling Cross, of course."

"Your old home? But why?"

Morgan mustered his brother impatiently. "If Sable has been looking for me and she isn't here in Dartmouth, it's obvious that she's gone to Ambling Cross."

"But how could she possibly know you once lived there?"

Morgan gave him a cool glance. "If you feel the need to ask that question, then you cannot know Sable St. Germain well."

"What about the Earl?" Sergei persisted as Grayson returned with the desired articles. "He said you were to wait for him."

"I don't have time," Morgan responded shortly, shrugging into his jacket, "nor do I want his help. This is between Sable and myself."

"Then let me go with you."

Morgan's ruthless visage softened a fraction as he looked into the bearded face which, for the first time he realized, was very like his own. "Thank you, Sergei, but I must go alone."

"Metyeryebets! I want to help you. Don't turn me away."

The two men eyed one another in silence, challenging blue-eyed gazes locked, and Grayson felt a prickle of apprehension down his spine. But Morgan only shrugged indifferently.

"Very well, but I intend to ride hard. If that shoulder of yours begins to pain you, I'll leave you behind."

"That won't be necessary," Sergei informed him with grim determination.

"Sir! What shall I tell His Lordship when he returns?" Grayson asked worriedly, having surmised enough of the situation to realize that Lady Sable's irate papa might appear at any moment.

"I'm sure you'll think of something, Grayson," Morgan called heartlessly over his shoulder. Then, realizing that he was being unfair to the Earl, he added, "Tell him where we've gone. I hope by the time he catches up with us, we'll have Sable in our possession."

The two men were silent as they waited for their horses to be saddled. Morgan, standing in the carriageway tapping a whip impatiently against his booted leg, seemed oblivious to the architectural beauty of the ancient coaching inn that had been host to such luminous visitors during its rich past as Sir Francis Drake, Charles II, and, more recently, Queen Victoria herself.

The expression on his face was so ominous that Sergei decided it would be better not to approach him. Only when they were galloping down the road that would take them out of town and through the green countryside did he venture to speak.

"Is it true?" he called across the distance between their racing mounts. "Did you really compromise the Lady Sable's honor?"

Morgan's face was averted, but Sergei thought he saw the carnal lips twitch. "Compromise? I made love to her, if that's what you mean." He gave a harsh laugh as he saw the look on Sergei's bearded face. "Will you condemn me, too? I did not take her by force though, by God, there were times when she almost tempted me to commit such madness."

"You're in love with her, aren't you?"

The steel-blue eyes nailed into his. "Did I say that?"

Disconcerted, Sergei fell silent as the horses swept past a wagon drawn by a drafter, a pair of laughing children riding upon his back. Primroses bloomed on the roadside, and the rolling hills lay like an immense green patchwork beneath the open sky. In the fields the threshers were bundling the sheaves, taking advantage of the hot, dry weather. To Sergei it was beautiful, this pastoral English countryside, yet he could think of nothing save the staggering revelation Morgan Carey had just made. Kristos, that explained a great deal, he thought to himself, especially Morgan's surly moods and his refusal to let anyone, even his own brother, near.

"Just tell me one thing," he said as they were forced to slow their mounts along the main thoroughfare of a tiny village. Young girls regarded them with great interest, the sight of two such broad-shouldered and handsome men a novel sight in their sleepy little hamlet. "Why did you let her go?"

Morgan's eyes narrowed. "What could I have done?" he demanded in a tone made hard by bitterness. "Kept her as my mistress? No, Sergei, not only would her father have had a word or two to say about that, but she deserves far, far better."

"Then you should have married her," Sergei retorted. "From what I've heard, Lady Sable is a rare prize indeed."

"And too good for the likes of a sailing man," Morgan grated, his big hands tightening about the reins. "Lord Monterrey might have given up the sea for his Countess, but I cannot, even for her. And she certainly doesn't deserve to spend her life waiting for me to come home from my voyages. Moreover,

I have no home as grand as her North Head to give her."

"Ah, but there you are wrong, my friend," Sergei reminded him. "You are no longer the bastard grandson of Llewelyn Howell, unworthy of claiming Penllys Wells as your own. You were born in wedlock, and Sébastien Fabois no longer has a case against you. You can go back to Wales and take what is rightfully yours, a home worthy of a woman I am convinced you love."

Morgan made no reply. They had cleared the village by now, and he had spurred his horse back into a gallop. Sergei cast a despairing glance at his broad, unyielding back and shook his head. Damn that stubborn British pride! Or was it Russian pride? he asked himself, unable to quell a grin despite the fact that his wound was beginning to bother him considerably. He was exhausted by the time Morgan slowed his mad pace but refused to acknowledge it.

"So this is Ambling Cross," he said aloud as the two lathered horses turned down a tree-lined drive which parted to reveal an impressive front facade of towering columns and numerous windows. "I'm amazed that you could afford it with your soldier's pay."

"It belonged to a distant cousin who happened to leave it to me when she died," Morgan responded shortly. "I was away with my regiment at the time, but it was a convenient place to come home to when I finally returned."

"So why didn't you keep it? It's quite impressive."

Morgan shrugged. "It didn't suit me."

"I wonder if we'll find your Sable here."

"I'm hoping we won't," Morgan responded shortly, drawing his horse to a halt before the front door. At Sergei's questioning glance he explained, "Benton Blair, the current owner, is something of an eccentric. He's fanatic in his conviction that visitors bring filth and disorder into his home. Forbes, my solicitor, wrote me after the deal had been closed and said that Blair had had the entire house scrubbed from top to bottom with lye and all remaining possessions either burned, sold, or aired before he would move in."

"With a rake like you for a former owner, I'm not sure I'd question his attitude," Sergei remarked with a grin, but a warning look from Morgan quelled him to silence, for a young boy had raced around the side yard to take the horses from them.

"Is Mr. Blair in?" Morgan asked.

"N-no, sir," the boy stammered, tilting his head back as far as he could in order to peer into that intimidating visage. "He's gone to P-Plymouth."

Morgan's answering scowl caused his knees to quake. "But Mistress Blair be in, sir."

"What's that? Blair's taken a wife?" Morgan demanded.

"No sir, it be Mistress Bridget, Master Blair's grand-daughter. She and her brother Raymond have been living here since spring."

"The poor devils," Morgan muttered, staring up at the house with its tightly drawn curtains and uninviting air. It had been so long since he himself had lived here that he could scarcely remember what it was like. Hatred had seethed in him in those days, he remembered, and an impatience to be gone that had grown unbearable as his war injuries persisted in mending so slowly.

"Is Mistress Blair in?"

"You'll have to ask at the house, sir."

Morgan took the wide steps two at a time and knocked boldly on the door. One look at his determined face, and the housekeeper thought better of sending him away. Bobbing a curtsy, she respectfully informed him that Mistress Blair was in and would he be kind enough to wait?

"I like the way you handle your inferiors," Sergei remarked, coming painfully up the steps behind him. "Did you have to practice that intimidating glower, or did it come naturally?"

Morgan's impatience was evident in the restless energy of his powerful body, but when he caught sight of Sergei's pale, sweating face, his harsh expression softened. "You should have stayed on the ship, you fool."

"And missed this?" Sergei asked with raised brows. "You forget I've been idling my life away in prison for the last decade. I've been thirsting for a bit of adventure! I only wish," he added softly as Morgan looked away, "that it didn't have to involve Lady Sable. Still, I don't believe she's gotten into trouble as Devon is only a few hours—"

"Miss Blair will see you now," the housekeeper informed them in that moment. Her back was stiff with disapproval as she led both men into the parlor. Thank God that old martinet wasn't home, she was thinking to herself. The sight of those dusty boots and the faint smell of horses that lingered on those muscular frames would have been enough to send him into an apoplectic fit!

Though the house was dark and gloomy and the air of disuse lingered in every room, Morgan found the parlor refreshingly bright and welcoming. The heavy drapes had been thrown back, and sunlight streamed unchecked onto the colorful Aubusson carpet he suddenly recognized as one he himself had purchased at auction in London years ago. In those days he had actually fooled himself into thinking a retiring country gentleman's life would satisfy him, he remembered with a cynical twist of his lips. It was only now, years later, when he finally had the truth of his past safely in hand, did he realize how haunted his youth had been. And yet he could not say that he was satisfied, for something eluded him still, something that he would not admit to himself was even more vital to him than Penllys Wells.

His thoughts were brought back to the present when the young woman who had risen from the sofa at their entrance suddenly hurried forward, her arms outstretched.

"Sir, you aren't well!"

Morgan's gaze snapped to Sergei in time to see him begin to sway forward in a faint. Moving swiftly, he was able to catch his brother before he could fall.

"Lay him down here," the young woman instructed, pushing aside the cushions that covered the sofa. "Betty!" she called to the housekeeper who had lingered in the doorway. "Bring water and a compress, quickly! What's wrong with him?" she asked, glancing into Morgan's face, though the words died on her lips as she found herself gazing into his arresting countenance. He was unlike any man she had ever seen, so tall and broad that he seemed to fill her entire field of vision.

"My . . . brother," Morgan informed her, hesitating still at the unfamiliar use of the term, "was badly injured several weeks ago. I'm afraid he hasn't fully recovered."

Bridget Blair flashed him a disapproving look, displaying far more spirit than her spinsterish airs might have led one to believe. "Then you shouldn't have brought him, sir!"

Morgan's lips twitched, liking the snapping gray eyes that flared at him from behind her spectacles. Though her dark hair was pulled in a severe chignon, it was a glossy mahogany in color and Morgan wondered how pretty she'd be if she abandoned such an unflattering style and rid herself of her dowdy clothes.

By now Betty had returned, and Bridget began to bathe Sergei's brow, her movements sure and practiced. Morgan watched her, noticing the concentration that furrowed her smooth brow. A moment later Sergei stirred and his eyelids fluttered open. Bridget, finding herself gazing into a pair of disconcerting blue eyes, blushed furiously and came to her feet.

"Are you feeling better?" Morgan asked gruffly, hiding his concern.

Sergei struggled to sit upright, wincing as pain shot through his wounded back. "Kristos, I feel as if I've been thrashed by half a dozen drunken tars," he groaned.

"Lie still until you're feeling better," Morgan commanded. "Miss Blair, do you have any brandy?"

"Vodka would be better," Sergei protested.

Bridget ignored both of them, stepping into the corridor and requesting something cold, bracing, and nonalcoholic for her patient to drink. Returning to the room, she became aware that, despite the obvious worry for his brother that was etched into his handsome features, the tall, dark-headed man before her seemed to exude a restlessness which she could sense like tension in the air. She regarded him coolly, her pointed chin raised.

"How may I help you, sir?"

Morgan's harsh expression softened. "Forgive us our untimely intrusion, Miss Blair. My name is Morgan Carey and I'm—"

"Not Captain Sir Morgan Carey who once owned this house?" Bridget interrupted disbelievingly.

Morgan's lips twitched, and she could feel hot color rush to her cheeks in response. "Indeed I am."

"How odd," Bridget murmured. "There was someone here this very morning looking for you."

Morgan's amusement vanished and Bridget nervously twisted her hands together. "She didn't tell me her name," she explained quickly. "She never had the chance before Grandfather threw her out, you see, but she left these here. Perhaps you'd be kind enough to return them to her, should you know who she is."

Opening the drawer of a low occasional table, Bridget held

up a slouch-brim hat and a pair of light summer gloves studded with tiny seed pearls. As Morgan took them he felt his heart turn over, for though he didn't recognize them, the subtle fragrance of jasmine that clung to them told him all too well whom they belonged to.

"What did she want?" he asked gruffly. "I know she was looking for me, but did she tell you why?"

Bridget shook her head. "She seemed ever so sweet," she recalled, "though I got the feeling something was troubling her." She glanced up in time to catch the ominous tightening of Sir Morgan's bronzed cheek. "She never did have the chance to tell me what it was, and I'm afraid I wasn't able to help her."

"How long ago did she leave?" Sergei asked. The lemonade he had been given, though not at all to his taste, had been cool and refreshing, and he was beginning to feel better.

"Hours ago. It was quite early when she arrived."

"She didn't tell you where she was going from here?" Morgan asked harshly.

"I am certain she's on her way home by now," Sergei said, but Bridget shook her head.

"I don't think so. I believe she went to Wales."

Morgan stood stock still, the long fingers tightening about the gloves he still held. "What makes you think she's gone to Wales?" he asked quietly.

Bridget's heart skipped a fearful beat. Never in her life had she come across a more intimidating man. She far preferred the bearded younger brother, whose blue eyes were so much less cold and frightening! "Just before she drove off, I had my brother Raymond tell her she might find a clue to your whereabouts in Glamorgan," she explained hesitantly, unsure of how he would react to this. "I knew nothing of your family, you understand, save that you were in some way connected with the Howells. I've no idea if she followed my advice," she went on, her head bowed and her voice dropping to a whisper.

Morgan could not find it in his heart to be angry with such a defenseless creature. He was silent for a moment, grappling with his emotions, and then gave Sergei a piercing look. "I'm going after her," he said curtly, "and I want you to stay here until you feel strong enough to ride back to Dartmouth. Tell Lord Monterrey where I've gone, and have Jack plot a course for Llanelly as quickly as possible."

"I'll go with you," Sergei offered, struggling to his feet.

"No!" Morgan's tone was cold. "You'll only slow me down, and I can't afford to wait for you. I'm sorry, Sergei," he added, though he refused to relent at the look on his brother's face. "You'll never withstand the ride. Penllys Wells lies in the mountains, and it's a rugged journey even for a fit man."

"But why all this haste?" Sergei demanded, hiding his disappointment behind anger. "Why not simply take the *Defiance* and intercept Sable in Glamorgan when she arrives?"

Morgan shook his head, the grim expression on his face unnerving in its intensity. "She has less than a six-hour head start, and I'm hoping to catch her before she crosses the Channel. You don't know Sébastien Fabois," he added darkly. "I can't vouch for Sable's safety should he get hold of her."

Turning heel, he vanished through the door, leaving a chill in the room behind him. Bridget's gray eyes were wide as she met Sergei's angry blue ones. Though she understood nothing of what had happened, she sensed from Sir Morgan's tone that the beautiful young woman who had been here earlier was somehow heading into danger.

"Sweet Christ, if anything happens to her it will be my fault!" she whispered, her hands flying to her lips.

"That's utter nonsense!" Sergei protested, but Bridget refused to be mollified.

"I'm the one who sent her to Wales, aren't I? Who is this Sébastien Fabois? Sir Morgan looked so grave when he spoke of him!"

"He's a Frenchman from Morgan's maternal side of the family," Sergei replied, coming to his feet and swaying as a bout of dizziness overwhelmed him. Feeling Bridget Blair's supporting hand at his elbow, he smiled down at her, causing her to blush furiously and move away. "Fabois was responsible for ousting young Morgan from his home and laying claim to his lands," he went on, sobering. "If you'll look into any history book, Miss Blair, you'll find a Fabois linked in some way with every evil deed in France's bloody history. Their wealth and power have made it impossible for anyone to stop them, though I believe," he added direly, recalling the look on Morgan's face, "that Sébastien is in for a surprise when he comes face to face with Morgan Howell Carey after fifteen years!"

Chapter 17

It was evening when Morgan arrived in Ilfracombe, his horse foam-flecked and near exhaustion. He had changed mounts several times on the way and had stopped at a roadside inn somewhere high on the lonely moors long enough to wash down a pint of cool ale. There had been no need to inquire along the way if a young woman fitting Sable's description had been seen traveling north, for he had discovered from the proprietor of the posting inn outside Totnes that she had boarded the coach there for Ilfracombe. Morgan had hoped to intercept Sable somewhere along the route, but she had been too far ahead of him, and it was nightfall before his weary mount stumbled into the courtyard of a neatly kept inn standing within sight of the gray cliffs of Bristol Channel.

Dismounting, Morgan handed the reins to the ostler, who hurried from his cozy corner chair to meet him, and strode into the taproom, ignoring the stiffness of his muscles. Never had he ridden so hard, yet his concern for Sable had grown as he imagined the den of thieves and scoundrels into which she'd fall the moment she set foot inside Penllys Wells.

"Needin' a room for the night and a bite to eat, sir?" the

comely wench behind the pockmarked counter asked. She eyed
the tall, disheveled stranger appreciatively and licked her lips.
It wasn't often they came this good-looking to Ilfracombe, she
thought to herself.

Morgan shook his head as he divested himself of his jacket.
"When does the next ferry run for Swansea?" he asked curtly.

She smiled at him saucily, displaying even white teeth of
which she was very proud. "Last steamer left two hours ago,
sir. Won't be another till mornin'."

Morgan cursed softly beneath his breath. "Is there a local
fisherman who might take me across for a proper wage?"

"You're not thinking of runnin' off so soon?" she asked
wistfully.

A muscular fellow in shirtsleeves appeared from the kitchen
in time to catch her words and pushed her roughly aside. "Go
on with ye, Prue," he said irritably. Couldn't the wench see
this was a gentleman and from the look on his hard face not
at all interested in sampling her wares? "What'll it be, sir?" he
asked politely, wiping his reddened hands on his apron front
and ignoring Prue's pouting lips as she turned away.

"I understand there are no more ships across the Channel
tonight."

The landlord shook his head. "Not till seven, sir. Would
you be carin' for a room this night?"

"I'm not sure yet." Morgan eyed the shorter man specula-
tively, then decided that he seemed trustworthy enough to give
him an honest answer. "Actually, I'm looking for a young lady
who probably arrived on this afternoon's coach from Totnes.
She was headed for Wales, and I've a feeling she might have
stopped off here before the steamer went."

The landlord brightened. "A bonnie thing with dark hair
and green eyes?" he asked promptly. "Couldn't forget those
eyes of hers, to be sure. So big and dark. Had a Cornish dialect
to her speech, though not much of one," he added helpfully
and was pleased when he saw the towering gentleman's tense
visage soften.

"Do you know which ship she took?"

"She didn't take none at all, sir. I told her she'd have to
wait about two hours for the next one, bein' as she came at
the wrong time, and she was quiet for so long I wasn't sure
she'd heard me. Then she looked at me kind of sad-like and

said it didn't matter anyway because she was going to go home."

Morgan started. "I beg your pardon?"

"Aye, sir. She said she decided she was going home, and I asked her if she cared for summat to eat first, but she thanked me proper and said she'd best be on her way."

Morgan was silent for a moment contemplating this. Could it be possible that Sable had lost her nerve or changed her mind? He didn't know whether to be relieved or disappointed at the landlord's news. Though he wouldn't admit it to himself, he had hoped Sable had been looking for him because she had wanted to be with him again. Then he shook his head, a mocking smile twisting his lips. He was a fool to think so. Sable St. Germain might have tempted him to madness often enough, but he had made the decision long ago that she deserved far better than he was capable of giving her. Though it had cost him everything to let her go, he knew that he had done right by her, and he refused to consider the possibility of a future for the both of them.

"I'll have a room and some supper brought round," Morgan said curtly, rousing himself from memories of shining emerald eyes and sweetly smiling lips. "And I do not wish to be disturbed until the first steamer puts out tomorrow morning."

The landlord nodded graciously, pleased to play host to such a distinguished-looking guest. "Of course, sir. I'll have Prue turn down your bed and bring a mite for you to eat." In the process of slipping away, he stopped as he felt iron fingers about his arm. Looking up, he saw that the steel blue eyes were glittering with warning.

"If you'd be so kind," Morgan said in a tone that was pleasant enough, "I'd prefer it if you'd send someone else up to my room. I've no wish to be distracted tonight, if you understand my meaning."

The landlord's lips curved and he sighed in relief. "Aye, sir, aye, I do. I'll serve ye myself if that's your wish."

Morgan nodded absently, his thoughts already elsewhere, and followed the landlord up the creaking flight of steps. His room was clean and pleasantly furnished, the mattress soft, but he paid no attention as he moved to the window and drew back the lace curtains. The moon was nearly full, casting silver light onto the rooftops of the little town. Bristol Channel lay beyond the whitewashed houses, and Morgan could see the masts of fishing boats moored near the shore below.

Turning away, he stripped off his boots and shirt and washed at the basin in the corner. Drying himself with the towel provided, he prowled restlessly back to the window, his hands behind his back. Though he was relieved that Sable had managed to avoid a confrontation with Sébastien Fabois, he himself didn't intend to do so. Come tomorrow evening he would be at the Wells, face to face with the man who, fifteen years before, had robbed him of his inheritance.

A muscle in Morgan's lean cheek tightened as the bitterness of long years rose like bile within him. How often had he told himself the past was dead and that Penllys Wells existed for him no longer? He had been living a colossal lie and had known it the moment Benjamin Disraeli had given him reason to believe that his real father might have been Andrei Vilyusk, Russian consular officer as well as the father of the young lieutenant who had saved his own life in Crimea years ago.

Sergei had been only too willing to talk of his father when he had finally recovered from his fever aboard the *Defiance*. Yes, it was true that Andrei had spent time in Paris, Sergei had informed him, but the Czar himself had eventually recalled him because of the scandals he had constantly been involved in. Andrei Vilyusk had had numerous lovers, Sergei also remembered, and among them, Morgan's probing had revealed, had been a Welshwoman by the name of Gwenna Howell.

Morgan could well remember the shock he had experienced hearing his mother's name fall from Sergei's lips despite the fact that he had suspected as much for so long now. Sergei had listened disbelievingly as Morgan had related his own story and added that he intended to travel to Paris to discover if Gwenna Howell and Andrei Vilyusk had actually been married.

"I refuse to believe that," Sergei had stated. "If my father did marry our mother, then why did he leave her? And how could he have returned home to marry again and bear another son? I assure you, Morgan, I am legally a Vilyusk, and that is a fact no one, not even you, can dispute."

"I don't intend to," Morgan had responded lightly, beginning to feel a great deal of affection for the pale but determined man reclining on the bunk before him, a man he had only recently come to think of as his brother. "But I do intend to prove," he had added harshly, "that Gwenna Howell was married to your father, which would clear up the stigma of my birth. My mother was not a loose woman, as one would term it, and I can't believe she would simply leave Paris and return to Wales without Andrei. I want to know, too, why she married Thomas Carey and allowed me to grow up believing he was my true father."

"Did your mother never tell you?" Sergei had asked.

Morgan shook his head bitterly. "Thomas died in a tragic house fire when I was eight, and my mother took me to Penllys Wells to live. Years later, when Sébastien Fabois appeared in Wales, she died before she was able to tell me the truth."

As he stared out across the darkened rooftops of Ilfracombe, Morgan could not help but remember the past, for it seemed as close to him tonight as the shoreline of Wales itself. He had adored his grandfather from the moment he had come to live under his roof, and Llewelyn Howell had taught him to love Penllys Wells as much as he himself did. It was obvious from the first that Llewelyn was training his grandson to take his place, and Morgan worked hard to grasp the duties involved in keeping the enormous estate in working order. There were sand and limestone mines to run, quarries that were earning enough revenue to give Penllys Wells a respected name even in the faraway London markets. Then there were tenants who had farmed Howell land since the first Norman baron had arrived with William the Conqueror to be made a Welsh Lord of the Marches. Since that day Howell chieftains had been responsible for the welfare of their people, protecting them from English overlords and battling constantly for independence.

Penllys Wells tenants raised sheep in the rugged mountains, and wool was an important part of life as well as a substantial source of income. Morgan's eyes twinkled as he recalled the endless hours he had accompanied his grandfather into the mountains, how the cold had gnawed at him while he learned the importance of proper sheep husbandry during lambing and shearing time. Aye, he had grown to love Penllys Wells with the same fierce loyalty his grandfather had and had felt enough confidence in himself to know that he could pick up the old warrior's reins when the time finally came. But that was before Sébastien Fabois had stepped into their lives.

To the weathered sea captain standing before the darkened window of a tiny English inn, time had not diminished the memory of that sharp-featured face and the piercing black eyes set below a shock of tumbling black hair. Sébastien Fabois had appeared at the Wells without warning one day, bringing with him a letter penned by Morgan's mother nearly seventeen years ago to her aunt Louise in Paris. In it she referred to her "delicate condition" and the constant fear that her father would find out. She had begged for advice, claiming that she loved the unborn child's father but that she was unwilling to burden him with its existence. Morgan had never learned where Sébastien had found the letter, yet since Louise had been his sister-in-law it was entirely possible that it had fallen into his hands quite by accident.

By accident. Even now those words caused his soul to fill with hate. Had Sébastien suspected the tragic violence the seemingly innocent-looking letter would unleash upon the inhabitants of Penllys Wells? Had he calculated on the death and destruction or had that been only an unforeseen bonus in his evil game?

"Your supper, sir." Stepping inside with a tray in his hands, the landlord drew up short as he saw the broad-shouldered man standing with his back turned in the shadows before him. "Why, sir, you should have lit the lamps!" he exclaimed, setting the tray aside and hurrying to do so. It was fortunate for him that Morgan had time to compose his features before the room was illuminated, for the expression on the sea captain's face might well have unnerved the landlord completely.

"I hope it's to your liking, sir," he stated, lifting the lid to reveal a well-roasted duckling with a savory glaze and fresh potatoes from the garden. Busily uncorking the bottle he had brought with him, he added, "I've taken the liberty of bringin' ye some of my best vintage since I had the feelin' ye appreciate good wines."

Morgan moved away from the window, causing the light to fall full on his ruthless face. The landlord shivered, thinking to himself he'd never come across a more intimidating-looking gent. Though he seemed civil enough and certainly possessed quite a bit of money, there was something about him that he didn't care too much for, a foreboding sense of purpose that to him had always spelled trouble.

"Will ye be needin' summat else?" he inquired helpfully as he filled the glass with the sparkling liquid.

Morgan folded his arms across his chest. "I don't believe so, thank you."

"Very well, sir. I'll look in later just to be sure."

"That won't be necessary," came the deep voice from behind him. "I plan to retire early and do not wish to be disturbed."

"Very good, sir. Good night, sir."

He was halfway down the landing when he heard the bolt slide home in the door behind him, and he shook his head. Odd fellow, that, and Prue should be glad he hadn't asked for her instead of carrying on the way she was. Had a cruel gleam in his eyes, that gentleman did, the kind that didn't spell good for anyone who cared to cross him.

Thinking of what the morning would bring, Morgan ignored the duckling and turned his attention instead to the wine. Draining his glass swiftly, he reached out to pour himself another. Though Sable might have decided to abandon her journey to Wales, he had not. Before he could think of the future he must lay the ghosts of the past to rest, and that included a reckoning with one certain Sébastien Fabois. His fingers tightened about the bottle, and the look in his eyes was one that even his loyal crewmen would have reacted to with uneasiness. Aye, the time had come to wash the slate clean, and he was relieved that Sable would not be present to witness it.

Sable ... The thought of her caused Morgan's scowl to deepen. He'd have a word or two with her when he saw her next! How dare she take such risks as traveling alone to Wales to confront a man she knew nothing about? Did she think her charms were sufficient to keep her safe from the likes of Sébastien Fabois? She was fortunate that she'd decided to return home, he thought blackly to himself. And as for seeing her again ... He made an impatient gesture and drained his glass a second time. No, he'd not go to Cornwall to seek her out. Not only would he be bringing her unnecessary trouble by confronting the wrath of Charles St. Germain, but he had made an irrevocable decision when he had let her go the night Dmitri had come for her.

What a pity fate could not have been called upon to treat him kindly one last time, Morgan thought cynically to himself. Though he ached to hold her in his arms again, he refused to admit as much, telling himself that Sable St. Germain had come into his life for no other purpose than to bring him fleeting pleasure. He had no right to ask for something more.

A brooding look settled on his handsome face as he reached for the bottle. It was going to be a long, lonely night, he suspected, and he might as well make free use of the landlord's generosity.

He was up before dawn the following morning, restlessly biding his time until the steamer took him across the Channel. From Swansea it was a three-hour ride through deep valleys and rugged mountains covered with blooming heather. Though the amount of industry that had sprung up between Swansea and Cardiff disheartened him, Morgan was relieved to see that the farther north he traveled, the more unchanged the land became. He crossed countless rushing streams of crystal-clear water and passed farmhouses where gentle folk came out to greet him warmly in his native tongue. He had forgotten their kind and simple ways, and his anger rose black within him when he thought of the years now wasted and lost.

His first view of Penllys Wells was something Morgan would remember for the rest of his life. It was late afternoon when he finally halted his mount on the summit of a craggy mountain and looked down into the valley spread out below. The breathtaking scene was one he had carried with him for nearly sixteen years, and he could not credit the emotions that surged through him when he spotted the battlements and walls of Penllys Wells before him. Built on the banks of a swift-moving river, the first stones of the mighty fortress had been laid by Normans and later enlarged by the English overlords who had sought control of the Welsh from their fortified castles.

Only after the Welsh House of Tudor gained the throne of England and Henry VII became king was the land and house of Penllys Wells undisputably granted to the Howells. From that time on it had reigned supreme in its mountainous domain. Over the centuries Howell lords remodeled the castle, enlarging and refortifying the imposing towers and walls, and bringing back from the Continent with them the treasures that softened its interior.

Morgan could see that Sébastien Fabois had changed little on the outside since his absence. As in Llewelyn Howells's time, there were still four circular towers standing on the corners of the thick walls and a keep, situated near the bridge which spanned the river and offered the only approach to the castle itself. The arching gate on the castle's far end was still firmly sealed as it had been in times of unrest when it had been guarded by archers stationed along the inner walkways. No advancing army had ever been able to take Penllys Wells.

But Morgan was not thinking of the castle's glorious history or of the strategic layout planned by the Norman baron Louis Jacques de Beaufort-Orléans himself. He was gazing down into the pleasant gardens visible behind the keep where he could see the hawthorns and summer flowers his mother had planted. He could remember the warm afternoons when she had strolled in the sunshine, her dark hair hidden beneath a wide-brimmed hat as she snipped flowers for the refectory table or laughed indulgently as her young son did his best to teach his unruly dogs some manners.

The soft light of remembrance in the steel-blue eyes was replaced by anger as Morgan reminded himself that Sébastien Fabois resided at Penllys Wells now and that he had doubtless taken for himself the glorious apartments that had once been Llewelyn's. It was something he hadn't dared think upon during his years of self-imposed exile, yet now, with the thirst for revenge rising within him, he knew that he would not rest until the man who had taken all that was his from him was dead. His expression far too grim for a man coming home for the first time in years, Morgan Carey turned his mount down the winding, rock-strewn path and rode boldly across the bridge that led to the iron-braced front door.

Chapter 18

Sable awoke with a start. Shivering in the chilly air, she rose from the hard mattress on which she had been dozing and hurried to the window. The wind sighed mournfully against the glass, and she could see little through the grime that covered the panes save a small section of grass below and the wide turn the river took as it passed by the castle walls.

She turned away, brushing her unbound hair from her eyes, and forced herself not to cry. She had done enough of that yesterday, and there was no sense in resuming it. She mustn't lose her nerve now or all hope would be gone.

Oh, what does it matter if I cry or not? she asked herself, sniffling as she began to pace about the bare floor of the tiny tower room. Even now she could scarcely believe that she had been imprisoned in the keep of Penllys Wells by a madman who was convinced that by taking her prisoner he would be able to lure Morgan to Wales.

Sable's tears began to flow faster as she thought again of the horrible mess she had made of everything. Though she was terribly afraid of Sébastien Fabois, she refused to believe for a moment that he would actually harm her. He couldn't! Seating

herself on the edge of the hard iron cot, she gazed without
appetite at the loaf of bread and pitcher of water that had been
brought to her by a cowering servant earlier. A bitter expression
twisted her lovely features, and she caught her breath in a
despairing sob. This wasn't the Dark Ages, she tried telling
herself fiercely. Feudal lords no longer took captives, especially
not the daughters of English earls!

But it had happened, and even now she couldn't believe the
chain of events that had brought her to this airless room. She
had arrived in Ilfracombe, exhausted and nauseated, after the
long, swaying coach ride. Upon hearing from the kindly innkeeper at the posting inn that the next ship for Swansea wouldn't
be leaving for another two hours, she had decided to go home.
It had been madness after all, she had argued with herself, to
embark on a journey without even knowing her destination!
How could she guarantee that anyone in Swansea would know
where the Howells of Glamorgan lived? And what if they treated
her as badly as Benton Blair had or, worse, refused to tell her
anything about Morgan?

No, she would go home, Sable had decided, her slim shoulders bowed in defeat. She would return to her father and hope
for the best. It no longer mattered to her that Morgan should
be forced to look after his unborn child's welfare. She would
manage on her own, and with her family behind her she would
probably be able to endure the scandals that would arise.

But fate had decreed otherwise, for no coaches bound west
for Cornwall had been scheduled to leave that day. Disheartened, Sable had wandered down to the narrow strip of sandy
beach below the village and had encountered a kindly fisherman
preparing to furl his sails for the day. Touched by her unhappy
little face, he had asked if he might help her and, upon hearing
that she had originally intended to travel to Wales, had offered
to sail her across the Channel in his sturdy little boat.

Sable had accepted his offer without hesitation, and even
now she couldn't understand what impulse had prompted her
to do so. Perhaps it was the insistent tug on her heart as she
thought of Morgan and the slim chance that he might be in
Wales. Oh, how she longed to see him despite her insistence
that she hated him!

But Morgan had not been at Penllys Wells, and Sable should
have been forewarned by the odd looks on the faces of the
kindly folk who had directed her there. From Swansea she had

traveled north to Aberdare, guided by the advice of a local
constable who had told her that the Howells' business head-
quarters were located there. Sable had cared little for the bleak
countryside surrounding Swansea and had been relieved to see
the uplands begin once the city was left behind.

In Aberdare it seemed as if everyone knew the Howell
family, and Sable had no trouble receiving directions to Penllys
Wells. Friendly and warm as the Welsh might have been, they
did not ask questions, for which Sable was grateful. She didn't
want to talk about Morgan to anyone, although she couldn't
help feeling relieved that the Howell name seemed to command
so much respect. Surely that must mean they were not the sort
of folk to turn her away when she asked for their help.

Yet Penllys Wells had been another story, Sable recalled as
she sat lonely and frightened in her tiny prison. How could she
have been foolish enough to accept Sébastien Fabois's hospitality when it had been obvious to her the moment she'd passed
through the cavernous archway that something was terribly
wrong? Oh, he had been charming enough, she reminded herself with a self-loathing sneer, and had taken her on a tour of
the castle, leaving her gasping at its size and grandeur. There
had been priceless works of oil by Dutch, German, and Italian
masters and beautiful Flemish tapestries to soften the walls.

Not until they were seated in one of the countless withdrawing rooms sipping tea served by Sébastien's pale and silent
wife had he spoken to her of Morgan. "So you have come to
the Wells seeking my nephew, have you?" he had asked unexpectedly.

Sable had been startled by this and had gazed questioningly
into the piercing black eyes. Sébastien Fabois was in his early
sixties, an enormous man with a powerful build that reminded
her of Dmitri's. His hair was as black as his eyes, and his
carefully trimmed beard was streaked with gray. His long fingers were covered with precious rings, and he wore a broadcloth
suit that had obviously been tailored in London. His subtle
French accent gave him a cultivated air that belied the savage
strength Sable sensed beneath his polished facade.

"I see I have surprised you," he remarked with a smile that
Sable had thought charming at the time. "Morgan is not really
my nephew, not directly, anyway. We are connected through
the marriage of his grandfather Llewelyn to Angélique de
Bernard, whose sister Louise was married to my older brother.

I see I have confused you, *hien?*" he laughed. "But do not worry, my dear. Ours is a long and entangled family tree, and I don't expect you to understand it fully."

"I can't believe Morgan was raised here and never mentioned it to anyone," Sable murmured, looking about her at the burnished paneling of priceless teak and the crystal chandelier that hung from the ceiling. She could scarcely believe that Penllys Wells, which appeared so medieval and imposing from the outside, could contain such an air of gentility within.

"Morgan left Penllys Wells fifteen years ago, a disgrace to the name of Howell," Sébastien Fabois informed her, his voice sharpening. Sending his wife a quelling glance as she opened her mouth to speak, he added, "I don't mean to be unkind when I speak of him, but old, bitter memories die hard."

Sable set her teacup aside and looked up into the still-handsome features, wondering why Sébastien Fabois gave her such a deep sense of foreboding. She had been welcomed into his home with little more than an introduction on her part, and he had been kind enough to show her the castle and invite her to tea. Why, then, did she feel so uncomfortable?

"What did Morgan do?" she asked now, unconsciously rising to Morgan's defense and missing the quickening interest in Sébastien's gaze at her tone.

"Do? Nothing, *ma chère*. It was more the fault of his mother, an immoral strumpet who could not resist the smiles of any good-looking man."

"Sébastien!" his wife pleaded.

"That will do," he said sharply. "You may leave us now. Lady St. Germain and I have much to discuss."

Sable remembered now the helpless look Marie Fabois had cast her way before scurrying from the room. If only she had known then that the tired little woman's fear had been for her and not her own self! If only she had never set foot in Penllys Wells to begin with!

But Sébastien Fabois had told her nothing more of Morgan's past. Instead he had asked about her own life and her relationship with Morgan. Sable had answered his questions politely enough, although she began to feel that his interest in her was unnatural. How she wished now that she had listened to her instincts and taken her leave while she still had the chance!

A timid knock on the door brought Sable to her feet with

a start. Heart pounding, she stood pressed against the cot, afraid to acknowledge her presence.

"Lady St. Germain?"

Sable swallowed as she recognized the soft voice of Marie Fabois, Sébastien's dark-haired wife. "Yes?"

"I should like to come in and talk with you. I have a key that Sébastien doesn't know about, but you must give me your word that you'll not try to escape." Her voice dropped to a whisper. "At least not while it's still light. Later, after he's gone to sleep, I'll come again for you."

Sable felt tears start in her eyes. "You'll help me?"

"Of course I will. I can't stand by and let him continue these monstrous things any longer!"

A key turned in the lock, and seconds later the ancient door creaked open. Marie Fabois blinked as her eyes adjusted to the faint light, and Sable couldn't miss the sympathy in her expression as their gazes met. Closing the door firmly behind her, Marie drew a freshly baked loaf of bread and a wedge of cheese from the pocket of her apron.

Sable shook her head at the sight of it, but Marie was firm. "You must keep up your strength, *chérie!*"

"Oh, Mrs. Fabois!" Sable burst out. "Why has he done this to me? He said it was because of the things I told him about Morgan, but I don't understand what he means!"

"Before we talk you must eat," Marie informed her. "Sébastien has gone out, and we have enough time until he returns."

Sable had no appetite at all, but to please the other woman she broke off a piece of bread. As soon as she tasted it, she realized she was ravenous. Marie watched her in silence, pleased that Sable had needed no further encouragement to eat. When the famished look began to disappear from the beautiful emerald eyes, she began to speak, her voice low and without emotion, as though she had long ago ceased to feel.

"I have been an unwilling accomplice to Sébastien's evil for the past fifteen years, Lady St. Germain. I tried to leave him once in the beginning, right after Gwenna Howell died, but he beat me until I feared for my life. Since then I have never tried to run away again. I want to tell you what he's done," she added passionately, "so that perhaps you can find someone who will stop him. You are a brave young woman, I sensed as much when I first saw you, and your heart is governed by love, which gives you the strength you'll need to see that justice is served. Sébastien must pay for the things he has done, and you must see that Morgan Carey is the one who makes him pay!"

She paused, aware of the vibrant hatred in her voice. Glancing nervously out of the filthy window, she wrung her hands. "It is hard for me to talk of this, even now, and I'm afraid there isn't time to tell you everything. You must listen to what I have to say, Lady St. Germain, and waste no time asking questions."

"Please go on," Sable breathed, the bread and cheese forgotten.

Marie Fabois cleared her throat and began to relate for the first time the secrets she had lived with for the past fifteen years. "Perhaps Sébastien didn't make clear to you his exact relationship with the Howells," she said, regarding Sable intently. "I want to explain that carefully so you'll not be confused. You did know that Morgan Carey's grandfather was Llewelyn Howell, a direct descendant of the first Howell who settled this valley?"

Sable nodded without speaking.

"Llewelyn married a de Bernard of Lyon, Angélique by name, and they had only one child, a daughter named Gwenna."

"Morgan's mother."

Marie nodded. "Angélique had a sister named Louise, who grew quite close to her niece after Angélique died. Gwenna went to Lyon often to visit her, even after Louise's late marriage to Guy Philippe Fabois."

"Sébastien's brother," Sable remembered.

"*Oui.* Guy Philippe was one of the better of the Faboises," Marie said, unable to hide her bitterness. She recalled her own marriage and how charming Sébastien had been to her. It was only later that she gradually began to understand the deep evil that was rooted in her husband's power-hungry heart. Rousing herself from her thoughts with an effort, she continued softly, "Llewelyn Howell may have loved his daughter, but his was a forceful and demanding character, so it was probably not surprising that when Gwenna fell in love with a nobleman in Paris and found herself with child, she turned to Louise for help. Louise urged her to confront the child's father, but Gwenna refused. She was a proud, willful woman and had been raised to ask for nothing from anyone."

Sable's gaze faltered at Marie's words. She felt ashamed of

her own weakness in seeking Morgan out, thinking to herself that she would never possess the courage of Gwenna Howell.

"What did Gwenna do?" she asked, her heart going out to Morgan's mother, who must have suffered a great deal of unhappiness in her life.

"Everyone believes she went home to Penllys Wells to marry Thomas Carey and eventually bear him a son. Of course Thomas knew the boy wasn't his, but he loved Gwenna enough to marry her nonetheless and claim the child as his."

"But you know otherwise?" Sable couldn't resist asking.

The Frenchwoman snorted with contained anger. "I alone of all people, Lady St. Germain, know the truth of Gwenna Howell's life, for she told me herself the day she died! She might have agreed to wed Thomas Carey, but her marriage was a sham, a heartbreaking lie to an extent that even Gwenna never fully realized, the good Lord be thanked!"

Seeing Sable's furrowed brow, she nodded emphatically. "I know I have confused you, so let me explain. I want you to hear the truth so that you can go from this place, find Morgan Carey, and see that he lays these ghosts to rest!" She paused, struggling with the emotions that surged full-blown into her heart after so many years of pent-up hatred and fear. "Sébastien only knows the half of it himself," she continued bitterly, "but it was enough for him to lay claim to Penllys Wells and see that Llewelyn Howell and his gentle daughter died in the process!"

Sable gasped, beginning to realize the terrible danger she was in as the prisoner of a possible murderer. She saw now why Marie Fabois intended to help her, and she forced herself to remain calm. For Morgan's sake she must learn what she could and then make good her escape.

"What caused Sébastien to make the decision to come here was the letter he found after Louise Fabois's death that lay forgotten in her personal effects," Marie explained. "Penned by Gwenna herself it informed her aunt of her determination to keep her unborn, illegitimate child. Though she did not name the father, the letter was weapon enough for Sébastien, who took it to Penllys Wells hoping to discredit Gwenna Howell and, through her, her son Morgan. You must understand, Lady St. Germain, that Sébastien had been wanting the Wells ever since Angélique died and left only a young girl as heir to the Howell fortune. He tried often to convince Llewelyn that he was a worthy choice to take over the quarries, the mines and lands, and he might have succeeded had Llewelyn not received and taken a fancy to a grandson.

"When Morgan came to live at the Wells the relationship between them prospered, and it soon became obvious that Morgan would someday take over as the new Howell chieftain. It galled Sébastien," Marie recalled, shivering despite the intervening years at the memory of her husband's towering rages and his hateful threats against the young boy who had usurped what he considered his. "The discovery that Morgan was in fact not Thomas Carey's son was enough for Sébastien to decide that Morgan did not deserve to inherit. He showed the letter to Llewelyn, hoping to depose Morgan as the heir, and succeeded beyond his wildest dreams."

Sable's hands had tightened into fists in her lap. "What happened?" she whispered.

"The shock was so great that Llewelyn died," Marie said simply. "He was an old man, *chérie,* though he prided himself in his strength and good health. I think his heart simply couldn't stand the pain."

"And Sébastien took Morgan's place as head of the Howell household?" Sable demanded. She had forgotten her own predicament and the fact that she was at the mercy of a madman. All that mattered to her now was Morgan, and her heart cried out for him and the pain he had suffered.

"It wasn't quite so easy," Marie said bitterly, recalling the terrible events that had followed Llewelyn Howell's death. "Morgan did his best to fight for his home, but his grandfather, believing he had years left to live, had never made a will." She spread her hands, her expression sad. "What was a fifteen-year-old boy to do? Despite the fact that he was so much like his grandfather, despite the fact that he was already more of a man than most boys his age, he wasn't able to beat Sébastien at his own game. Moreover, the death of his mother so defeated him that I think he no longer had the will to go on."

Sable swallowed hard. "How—how did she die?"

Marie Fabois's expression was bleak. "She threw herself off the keep one night, from the tower that stands directly opposite this one. Though several servants saw her fall into the water, her body was never recovered."

Sable buried her face in her hands. "Oh, Morgan!" she choked, thinking of the number of times she had been unkind to him, accused him of being heartless, insensitive, and without common decency. How could anyone blame him, knowing what he had suffered?

Marie's hard, emotionless voice roused her from her own misery. "You can see now how well Sébastien succeeded. Morgan went away, to join the army, I think, and no one dared protest the crowning of the new Howell prince. I know the servants and the people of this valley would gladly welcome the rightful heir back to his home, but how can they raise their heads in defiance when Sébastien holds them firmly beneath his thumb? He could squash them if he chose, and all of them know it."

"You said Gwenna Howell's marriage to Morgan's father was a lie," Sable remembered. "That there was more to her story than what little your husband knew."

Marie nodded. "It was not only the shock of his mother's and grandfather's deaths that drove Morgan from his home, though God knows it would have been enough. I did not know him well, but I could tell that he was fiercely proud of his birthright and the fact that he was a Howell. I think, to a man like Morgan, learning that he was illegitimate, a bastard as it were, did more to damage his self-esteem and erode his will to fight Sébastien than anything else could have done."

"You may be right," Sable agreed, recalling the cynical remarks Morgan had made to her on occasion concerning her pride in her own family and her love for North Head, her ancestral home. How it must have galled him to have once had what she did and to lose it to the likes of Sébastien Fabois!

"But the ironic truth is that Morgan is not a bastard," Marie said now, relieved to confide in someone the things Gwenna Howell had told her so many years ago. "Gwenna was married to the father of her child in Paris, secretly of course, and no one knew, not even Louise or Llewelyn."

"That seems hard to believe! Surely Morgan must have known!"

Marie shook her head sadly. "Gwenna did not tell him the truth, not even after Thomas Carey died or when Sébastien first came to Wales. She chose to tell me instead and begged me to say nothing to Morgan, knowing that proof of her marriage no longer existed and that it would be curel to send her son on a futile search. The man she had married, you see, Morgan's real father, had himself died almost immediately after the wedding ceremony—or at least that is what Gwenna had been led to believe all these years."

Marie fell silent, studying her thin, workworn hands. She couldn't bear to look into Sable St. Germain's face again, to see the pain mirrored in those beautiful eyes. It was obvious that Sable was in love with Morgan Carey, and Marie was filled with despair, wondering how such a slight young woman was going to escape Sébastien.

But she must, Marie told herself passionately. She had lived in Sébastien's evil shadow too long, afraid to confide in anyone, terrified that her every move and correspondence was carefully monitored by Sébastien and his loyal henchmen. But suddenly she found herself afraid no longer. Sable St. Germain's courage had touched her, and she was determined that, even at the risk of her own life, she would see the child got away.

"The sad truth," she said now, her voice tinged with emotion, "is that Llewelyn Howell was aware all along of his daughter's love for the man who was destined to get her with child. Though Gwenna was discreet, some gossip did reach this remote corner of the world. Not wanting his daughter to marry a lowly Russian attaché, Llewelyn schemed to drive them apart, using his power and position to have the Czar himself recall the man. But that still wasn't enough for Llewelyn, who realized that, willful as his daughter was, she would follow her lover to the ends of the earth. He therefore heartlessly arranged a plan that would separate them for all eternity. I don't know exactly what he did, but he somehow managed to convince Gwenna that her lover had been killed in a dreadful accident—and he, in turn, was led to believe the same thing of her.

"At first Gwenna refused to believe her new husband was dead, but because of the number of people willing to support Llewelyn's story, Gwenna had no choice but to accept it. In her grief she returned home, and Llewelyn never knew that she had not only been wed to the man whose death he had staged, but was expecting his child as well. If he had known," Marie concluded sadly, "I don't think he would have driven them apart and certainly wouldn't have permitted Gwenna to marry Thomas Carey. Llewelyn wasn't an evil man, Lady St. Germain. He was simply proud and couldn't bear to let his domain come into the hands of a minor Russian official who seemed naught but a dissolute womanizer."

"But this Russian wasn't really dead?"

Marie shook her head. "I don't know what ever became of him, but it does mean that Gwenna's marriage to Thomas Carey was a lie. It was after his heart attack, when Llewelyn realized he was really going to die, that he told his daughter the truth. I don't think she could accept it any more than he could the things she had kept from him, and that is why she threw herself into the river."

"And this Russian official? Is he still alive? Do you know his name?"

"That is something that never passed from Gwenna's or Llewelyn's lips," Marie informed her quietly. "She wouldn't tell me, even though she came to trust me." A bitter laugh came from her. "Can you imagine what a rare woman she was not to hate me even though I was married to the man who had succeeded in destroying everything that was precious to her?"

"If only she had told Morgan the truth!" Sable whispered. "Perhaps he might have had the will to continue fighting Sébastien!"

Marie spread her hands. "He could not, *chérie*. No one, especially not a young boy, could succeed in vanquishing the devil himself!"

"I thank you for the compliment, *ma chère* Marie," came the mocking voice of Sébastien Fabois from behind them.

Marie shrieked and Sable's hand flew to her lips as he appeared in the doorway. How long he had been standing there listening was impossible to guess, but Sable felt her heart sink as she saw the fury in his black eyes.

"Who would have suspected you of betraying your own husband?" Sébastien asked softly, shaking his head as he slowly advanced into the room. His enormous frame seemed to dwarf the two women cowering on the cot before him, and he threw back his dark head and laughed contemptuously. "I must admit I'm surprised at your courage. I would have thought the punishment you received the last time you defied me would have cured you forever."

As he spoke he seized Marie's arm and jerked her to her feet. She cried out in fear, which only seemed to amuse him more. Lifting his hand, he deliberately struck her across the face, causing her to scream in pain and leaving an angry red welt on her cheek.

"Leave her alone!" Sable cried, leaping to her feet and flying at him with small fists raised to strike.

Sébastien warded her off easily, thrusting her back so that she collapsed upon the cot. Marie was sobbing, her face buried in her hands, and he regarded her coldly. "Go to your room. I'm not through with you yet."

She fled without giving Sable another glance. Sébastien was silent for a moment, and Sable's mouth went dry as she lifted her chin and bravely tried to meet his demonic eyes.

"You," he said at last, "are almost more trouble than you're worth, Sable St. Germain. If I wasn't so certain you are the instrument I need in luring Morgan here, I'd get rid of you."

Sable tried not to let his words frighten her. Surely he wasn't mad enough to kill her? "What makes you think Morgan will come?" she demanded, trying to keep her voice from quavering. "He doesn't even know where I am!"

"Perhaps not," Sébastien conceded, "but he'll find out. For fifteen years I've waited for him to return," he added softly, his voice causing Sable to tremble. "Believe me, I've been looking forward to our confrontation. Just like his grandfather he was, even at so tender an age, and from what you've told me about him he hasn't disappointed me in becoming a man."

"He won't come here!" Sable persisted, trying to convince him as fear for Morgan made her forget her own plight. "You have what you want. Why don't you just forget him?"

Sébastien's jaw tightened. "Because he hasn't forgotten me. In all these years I've felt his hatred and known that it was only a matter of time before he would return to claim what he considers his by right. Oh, I've kept abreast of his exploits over the years, *ma chère,* and I know that he's become a favorite of your stuffy queen and received a knighthood for his bravery in Crimea. A pity he's never told anyone he also happens to be the last surviving member of a family well known and respected for its power and wealth. It would certainly have served to raise his esteem in his admirers' eyes. Yet that power," he added, tossing his head arrogantly, "is mine now, and I don't intend to give it up."

Hatred burned in Sable's eyes as she gazed up into his cold face. This was the man who had caused Morgan so much torment, who had taken away what might even have been her unborn child's by right. Though she cared neither way for Penllys Wells herself, she knew what it meant to Morgan and what it might someday mean to his child. Morgan's secret war had suddenly become her own, and Sable was determined to do what she could to see Sébastien Fabois brought to justice.

"I haven't broken any laws," he informed her, uncannily reading her thoughts in her eyes. "No court in Great Britain would dispose of me now. I've held the reins of Howell wealth too long. The only way this enmity between Morgan Carey and myself can be resolved," he added, moving to stand over her and grinning down into her frightened face, "is if one of us were to die."

"Y-you're mad!" Sable whispered, wide-eyed with terror.

He straightened and laughed. "Am I? We'll just have to see what happens when Morgan returns."

"He won't, I tell you!"

"You may be a courageous woman, Lady St. Germain," he told her bluntly, "but I'm afraid you're either a fool or a terrible liar."

As he spoke he shut the door behind her, and Sable buried her face in her hands as she heard the key turn in the lock. It was obvious that Sébastien expected Morgan to come. She knew without having to be told that their bitter hatred would flare into violence and that Morgan, perhaps caught off guard if Sébastien intended to use her as a weapon, might very well be killed.

She groaned and tried to fight against the numbing despair that filled her heart. If Morgan were killed it would be all her fault. She had come here for her own selfish reasons, to demand that he make himself responsible for their child, and instead she would be the instrument of his destruction.

"I've got to do something!" she whispered to herself. She couldn't just sit in this filthy tower room while Morgan rode to his certain death! She must get out of here somehow and find him, warn him that Sébastien Fabois was mad and intended to kill him.

She looked around wildly and suddenly her eyes fell on the bread and cheese that Marie had brought her. A cry of joy burst from her lips as she saw the small brass key lying between them, the same key with which Marie had unlocked the tower door earlier. Obviously she had laid it down on the table when she had taken the food out of her apron pocket and had forgotten it. Sébastien, in having neglected to look for it, had made his first mistake, Sable thought exultantly.

Scooping it up with trembling fingers, she searched about

for a hiding place, knowing it would be foolish to attempt to escape now. Sébastien was probably confronting his wife at the moment and might return to the tower when he failed to find her key. She must hide it from him and wait until nightfall before she used it.

A loose stone above the doorway finally caught her eye. Prying at it with her fingers, she managed to move it just enough to slide the key past the crumbling mortar. It would be safe there, Sable decided, studying it carefully, and if Sébastien returned he would never find it.

Peering out the window, she saw that the sun was beginning to sink into the westerly sky. The mountains beyond the castle's south face were already glowing gold as they caught the last dying rays. Sable shivered. Night would soon be upon them, and she must be ready to make her move then.

Chapter 19

A fire had been lit in the grate of the slate fireplace to dispel the chill of the damp mountain air. Flames danced along the timbered ceiling and were reflected with a deep red glow on the burnished paneling. Silk wall hangings and gold brocade curtains softened the decor of the imposing parlor. In a chair near the fire sat Sébastien Fabois, his legs crossed comfortably before him. His bearded profile was stern but not threatening as he watched the dancing flames, and one would have difficulty believing that this handsome, cultivated gentleman had in fact been responsible for the deaths of two innocent people years ago.

"Ah, Guillaume," Sébastien said, addressing his valet in French as he appeared in the doorway. "Put it there, will you? I'll help myself."

Guillaume inclined his head and set his tray on the inlaid table at Sébastien's elbow. He was a thin, silent man, his face horribly disfigured in a childhood carriage accident. Bowing from the waist, he retreated, his twisted features wearing their normal somber expression.

A log fell with a shower of sparks in the fireplace, and

Sébastien's movement for the wine bottle was arrested. Lifting his head, he heard soft footsteps in the hall and wondered why Guillaume had returned after he had made it specifically clear that he did not wish to be disturbed again. Surely his valet had been with him long enough to have understood that much merely from his master's tone of voice!

"Good evening, Sébastien. I trust I haven't come at a bad time."

The deep, arrogant voice was so like Llewelyn Howell's that a prickle of alarm fled down Sébastien's spine. Coming swiftly to his feet, he whirled about, and a slow smile spread across his face as he saw the tall man before him. Morgan was dressed in a leather coat and white shirt, his boots covered with dust. Dark, disheveled hair fell across his brow, and his piercing blue eyes were as cold as the sea as he stared boldly back into the bearded face of his deadliest enemy. He had grown tall and unquestionably powerful, Sébastien noticed, and carried himself as did a man accustomed to being in command of the world around him. He was not someone to be easily dismissed, but if his dangerous air unnerved some, it merely served to delight Sébastien Fabois.

"What a handsome devil you've become, my dear nephew," he remarked with a lingering smile. "I'm pleased that your Howell breeding hasn't failed you. It will make my sport all the more pleasurable for me."

"What do you intend to do?" Morgan inquired coolly. "Kill me?" His steely gaze did not waver from Sébastien's face, and the older man found himself confronted for the first time in his life by a man who showed no outward signs of fearing him.

"It has always been obvious to me that our inevitable confrontation would result in the death of one of us." Lifting his wineglass, Sébastien took a sip. "Would you care for some? Sauterne, 1863. I had it imported earlier this year and find it without equal."

Morgan said nothing. The hatred he had buried within him for so many years was slowly beginning to consume him, and he wondered why he had waited so long to return. Sébastien Fabois had not changed in the fifteen years that had passed, though his dark beard was now streaked with gray. It was obvious that none of his strength had diminished, and Morgan could feel his primal instincts for survival rise within him, knowing that this was no ordinary foe to be conquered.

"I must admit I did expect you sooner than this," Sébastien said conversationally, glancing at the cherrywood clock ticking on the wall behind him. "You didn't ride down from Breacan Hill in the dark, did you?"

"I've been at John Lloyd's cottage since early afternoon. He's been giving me an enlightening account of your activities since you became lord and master of Penllys Wells."

Sébastien's lips twitched. "Such cold fury in your tone, *mon ami!* Is it possible that you hate me even more now than you did when I ran you off fifteen years ago? What a spineless youngster you were! I wonder if you've changed?"

Morgan grappled with his temper, aware that Sébastien was goading him deliberately. To lose control now would put him at a disadvantage, and this he couldn't afford to do. Though he feared no man, he was not a fool, and despite his sixty years Sébastien Fabois was still a potentially deadly rival.

"I see you have nothing to say," Sebastien observed as the silence in the parlor lengthened. "No matter, I have much to tell you. I made many changes in the way your grandfather once administered the lands, but I'm sure Master Lloyd has told you all of this." He shook his head, thinking of the elderly tacksman who had been in Penllys Wells's employ since Llewelyn's time. "Obstinate old wretch, that Lloyd. Perhaps I'll reward his wagging tongue by turning him out."

"Will you? Are you so certain you'll still be in a position to make such decisions come morning?"

Sébastien's eyes glittered. "Is that a threat, my boy? I warn you not to goad my temper, for I can be ugly when I'm crossed, and I have a weapon at my disposal I don't believe you'd care to see me use."

"I have weapons, too, Sébastien," Morgan responded softly. "They include, among other things, inalterable proof that I am the product of a legal marriage and that the Howell blood which runs in my veins—and has never flowed in yours—gives me the right to take back what you once wrested from me."

Sébastien's handsome face contorted with anger. "Such bold words!" he sneered. "You may have enjoyed the homage of England's silly queen and the respect and admiration of your peers, but you forget that here you are nothing but the worthless bastard I threw out years ago!"

Morgan caught himself before he could lunge, knowing this was exactly what Sébastien wanted. Being as ruthless and unpredictable as a snake, he probably carried a concealed knife he'd not be hesitant to imbed in Morgan's back. Eyes glittering with suppressed emotions, Morgan made no move, his gloved hands curved in a death grip about the armchair behind which he stood.

Sébastien, his back to the fireplace, returned his gaze boldly, a knowing smile on his lips. "I must admit you've learned to control your temper exceptionally well, my boy. Discipline is a hard thing for any man to learn, but I suppose the army helped in that respect, *hien?* Knowing you no longer have the shame of your illegitimacy to live with is also excellent medicine for one's self-image. Tut, tut, don't scowl at me so. You may have intimidated many a man in the past with that fierce visage of yours, but though you may have changed, I assure you I have not. I am still the same man I was when I first came to Wales, and I can deal with you just as easily now as I did then."

"Are you certain of that?" Morgan asked silkily, unperturbed by Sébastien's tone. Regarding the older man coolly, he began casually to pull off his gloves. "You always were a boastful bastard—if you'll pardon the term."

Sébastien took another sip of wine, his movements as casual as Morgan's had been; each was signaling to the other that he was not unnerved by a simple taunt. Tossing his head arrogantly, his black eyes gleaming with enjoyment, Sébastien said smoothly, "Enough of this verbal dueling. I've grown tired of it, so let me inform you what it is I have that will take the wind out of those sails of yours." He paused, savoring the moment, and absently twirled the glass in his long-fingered hand.

"I have a young woman locked away in the keep," he announced bluntly. "Since I don't want you trying anything foolish, I have given my valet Guillaume orders to put her instantly to death should you try to harm me. Her name, in case you haven't already surmised, is Sable St. Germain."

Morgan went white as Sébastien's demonic laughter filled the room. Every nerve in his body screamed to leap on this man and break his neck in two, but he forced himself to remain calm, well aware that Sable's life hung in the balance. There was no need to ask if Sébastien was lying. One look into that grinning face was enough to convince Morgan of the truth. Deliberately he continued drawing off his gloves, but Sébastien was keen enough to see that his fingers were trembling slightly.

"I've surprised you, eh?" he asked with deep satisfaction. "I was hoping I would. *Oui,* the chit is here, and I must say you've picked yourself a pretty one. A pity there can be no future for the two of you. You're quite evenly matched in temperament, though her fairness quite outrivals your brooding looks. It really is a pity," he repeated, shaking his head regretfully.

"By God, if you harm her," Morgan whispered through clenched teeth, "I swear I'll—"

"Oh, I wouldn't dream of hurting her," Sébastien assured him. "Hers is such a flawless beauty, and it would pain me to see it marred."

Unable to control himself any longer, Morgan took a menacing step forward, and in a twinkling a pistol appeared in Sébastien's hand. Primed and ready to fire, its long barrel was aimed directly at Morgan's wide chest, and he halted immediately, knowing it would do Sable little good if he were to die before he could rescue her.

"So wise of you to respect my weapon," Sébastien almost purred, enjoying himself thoroughly. How sweet this meeting was, and far better than anything he'd ever dreamed of! Not only did he have Morgan Carey where he wanted him after all these years, but he also possessed the means of striking his most vulnerable spot—his heart.

"Let her go, Sébastien," Morgan said quietly. "It's our quarrel, not hers. She needn't be involved."

The gun barrel never wavered. "Gallant of you, my boy, but I don't intend to throw my aces in the discard pile. I intend to play them one by one, starting with your fair little Sable. I wonder how quickly I'll be able to break you," he mused, "if I were to torture her in your presence. No, no," he added warningly as Morgan tensed, "you're not to move. One step in my direction, *mon ami,* and I'll blow your—"

The unexpected roar of a pistol was so deafening in the small room that at first Morgan thought Sébastien had fired at him. By the time the smoke cleared Morgan realized not only that he wasn't bleeding, but that the cry of pain that had echoed through the room had been Sébastien's and not his. Looking up, he saw a sight he would never forget for the rest of his life: Sébastian collapsed against the wall clutching his bloodied hand and Sable standing in the doorway, the still-smoking pistol held in a white-knuckled grip. She was pale and her slim form was trembling uncontrollably, but her aim never wavered. Her muslin frock was covered with dust, and cobwebs clung to her unbound hair, but she was obviously unhurt, and to Morgan she looked indescribably dear to him.

"Sable, get out of here quickly!" he ordered, praying she would obey.

"I won't," she whispered, her eyes huge in her small face as she turned to look at him. "Not without you!"

He cursed and went to her, prying the pistol from her stiff fingers. Throwing a protective arm around her, he cast a last glance at Sébastien's inert form before pulling her from the room. Rounding a corner at the far end of the corridor, Sable screamed when their path was blocked by an enormous man with a hideously gaping mouth and an eye which hung lifeless from its socket. It was Guillaume, who was hastening to his master's rescue.

Thrusting Sable behind him, Morgan went for the startled valet, swinging the butt of his pistol upward. The cold steel caught Guillaume directly under the chin, and he crumbled without a sound. Morgan straightened and reached for Sable, only to whirl about when movement in the corridor behind them caught his eye.

It was Sébastien staggering from the parlor with the gun still in his bloodied hand. Reacting swiftly, Morgan threw himself on top of Sable to shield her with his body just as the shot rang through the air. Hearing the ball whine harmlessly over their heads, Morgan wasted no time in pulling Sable to her feet.

"Stop them!" Sébastien howled wildly, incensed that he had missed. "Stop them, I say!"

It had been fifteen years since Morgan had last set foot in Penllys Wells, but he still remembered every inch of the enormous castle's many passages and rooms. Aware that the halls would soon be swarming with servants, and not sure how many of them would be loyal to Sébastien, he ducked down a flight of steps leading to the corridor that connected the butler's pantry and the kitchens with the numerous receiving rooms at the north end of the castle. It was pitch dark on the steps, and he halted as Sable stumbled.

"Can you make it, love?"

"I think I can," she replied, but her voice shook, and he

sensed that she was dangerously close to tears. Tenderness overwhelmed him for this courageous young woman who had braved so much for him, and his heart ached knowing that he had never been worthy of the love she had so selflessly given him.

Gathering her into his arms, Morgan pulled her close, feeling her warmth and familiar fragrance envelop him in the darkness. Sable's arms wound themselves about his neck, and she pressed herself to him tightly, her shoulders shaking with silent sobs.

"Oh, Morgan, I'm sorry you had to come here! Sébastien locked me in the keep, but I had a key. I waited until dark and let myself out, but I heard voices in the passage when I reached the bottom, and when I recognized yours I couldn't let him hurt you! I found a pistol hanging in a holster near the service entrance, and I tried to stop him, Morgan, truly I did!"

He pulled her closer, closing his eyes as he buried his face in the luxuriant softness of her unbound hair. "It doesn't matter," he murmured. "You did a brave thing, and we're safe now."

He could feel her hot tears splash his shirtfront. "Are we?"

Morgan ached to assure her that it was so, yet theirs was a bleak outlook indeed. Sébastien had doubtless raised the alarm by now, and at any moment the dogs would be released. He wasn't afraid for himself, knowing he could easily escape them on the grounds of his own home, yet there was Sable to consider. She must be gotten away from the madman who had imprisoned her, safe from those demonic eyes that had glared at her with such hatred and unconcealed lust.

"This corridor leads to the storehouses," Morgan explained softly. "From there we can cross the outer ward to the stables. You'll have to hurry when we get outside because of the dogs. Can you do it, my love?"

His eyes had adjusted to the darkness sufficiently to see the emerald glitter of her eyes as she turned her face to his. She nodded wordlessly, not trusting her voice enough to speak, and Morgan felt his heart constrict with overwhelming tenderness.

"Sable—" he whispered hoarsely, but the creaking of a door behind them caused them both to break apart. Swiftly Morgan put her behind him and reached cautiously for the pistol he had tucked into his belt. Though it wasn't loaded, it was the only weapon he had. A beam of light stabbed the darkness before them, and he could feel Sable's fingers tighten about his arm.

"Master Morgan? Be you here? If so, will you come out? It's Owen Harold."

Sable heard the laughter rumble deep in Morgan's chest. "Owen, you old fool, are you still here after all these years?"

The lantern light grew brighter, and Sable, standing on tiptoe to peer over Morgan's shoulder, saw a wizened old man come toward them. He was wearing thick leather brogues and a worn apron over his simple shirt and trousers, and his face was creased into a smile as his light fell on Morgan's rugged visage.

"It be the young Howell lord himself," he cackled happily. "I knew it could be none other who could have stretched that beastie Guillaume flat out on the floor. Lookin' fit and strong, master, and the image of your grandfather." Tears welled in his rheumy eyes, and he grasped Morgan's hand in his leathery one. "Have you come home, then?"

Morgan's expression was grim. "I want to get Lady Sable out of here before I worry about anything else."

"Aye, master, aye," Owen agreed knowingly, having noticed how close the beautiful young girl kept to Morgan's side, her large green eyes never leaving his face. "I went and told Quentin to have a horse saddled when I realized you were here. Not that I expected Sébastien Fabois to run you off," he added hastily, afraid Morgan would take offense at his words, "but just in case. You can take the tunnel, too. They'll not find you there."

"You're a bloody jewel, Owen," Morgan growled, some of his tension easing. Glancing down at Sable, his hard visage softened when he saw her pale little face. "There's an underground passage connecting the outer ward to the stables. It was built in my ancestors' time, and I'm not sure even Sébastien knows about it. Are you willing to try?"

She nodded wordlessly, her heart in her eyes. Morgan grappled with the urge to put his arms around her and tell her she needn't be afraid any longer, but there wasn't time. Dimly through the thick stone walls they could hear the distant baying of the hounds. Sable gave a soft gasp, and Morgan took her hand in his.

"Come on."

Sable followed him in silence down the darkened passageway, Owen's lantern throwing their shadows against the wall. She was not afraid with Morgan there, at least not for herself, yet she despaired of the dark powers that were Sébastien's. Morgan must not be allowed to confront him again. Though he might not be willing to admit as much, Sable knew that it would take more than his solitary strength to defeat a man like Sébastien.

It was cold and damp in the passage, and Sable was relieved when they emerged at last into the warmth of the stables. Rows of loose box stalls lined the stone aisle and the smell of hay and harness dressing hung in the air. A pleasant-looking young man in breeches and a leather jacket met them as they ascended through a trapdoor, his dark eyes wide with admiration as he took in the towering Sir Morgan, who had become almost legendary to the people of Penllys Wells.

"I've saddled Damascus for you, sir. He's the master's fastest," he said at once.

"Thank you, Quentin. Bring him round and get the horse I left here earlier."

"Yes sir."

Sable was relieved to see the coal-black Arab Quentin led from a nearby stall. Surely Sébastien would never be able to catch this one! Morgan took the snorting animal by the bridle and led him to the mounting block in the small courtyard outside. Beckoning to Sable, he lifted her up into the saddle, his hands lingering for a moment about her small waist. There was no moon that night, yet he could see how pale she was as she sat looking down at him without speaking.

His hand tightened over hers. "I promise I'll get you out of here, Sable. It sounds like they're searching the inner courtyards first. We can take the horses through the south gate and follow the river instead of taking the mountain road Sébastien expects us to." His narrowed gaze took in the lights burning in the windows of the main block behind them. There was probably enough time to slip away along the mountain passes while Sébastien saw to his injuries, but Morgan intended to take no chances where Sable was concerned. In pain and thirsting for revenge, Sébastien would be more deadly than a wounded tiger.

"Morgan." Sable's slim fingers tightened about his, and he turned to look up at her questioningly. "Where will we go? Is there someone in Aberdare who won't be afraid to help us?"

"You can depend on the cooperation of the entire village for help where Sébastien is concerned. I wouldn't leave you anywhere else unless I was sure of that."

Sable went cold. "Y-you're leaving me there?" At his grim nod she moistened her dry lips. "Why?"

"I have to come back here to deal with Sébastien."

Sable stared at him in horror. "You're not thinking of killing him?"

The look in his steely eyes frightened her. "I'll see you safely to the nearest village, Sable, but then I must come back."

"You can't!" she burst out. "Oh, Morgan, it's one thing to do what you must to escape him, but to return for him . . . that's—that's cold-blooded murder!"

"Here's your horse, sir," Quentin broke in, leading a muscular gelding from the barn while Owen handed Morgan a whip. "You'd better hurry," he added worriedly. "I've a feeling they'll look here first once they realize you're not in the castle anymore."

"Morgan," Sable whispered, and all the agony of her love for him was revealed in the single utterance of his name.

She could see the struggle on his rugged face, but then he shook his head. "I'm sorry, Sable," he said curtly. "It's something I have to do."

"Is it?" she asked bitterly. "Surely you realize you might very well be throwing your life away for the sake of revenge? Isn't it enough that you have proof of your birthright? Yes, I heard what you told Sébastien, and I don't see why you can't challenge his claim to Penllys Wells through the proper channels, the courts of our country, instead of resorting to bloodshed in which you might be killed yourself!" Her voice trembled dangerously as she finished speaking, but she refused to look at him, her hands entwined in a convulsive grip about Damascus's reins.

"Sable, don't," Morgan entreated, unable to bear the sight of the tears that glittered in her eyes.

"God, how I hate you," she choked, not caring that Owen and Quentin were listening. "Nothing has ever mattered to you save your pride, has it? All right, then, go ahead and let your hatred destroy you! I can see that it doesn't matter to you how much I'll suffer by your death, but perhaps you'll think twice if you consider the welfare of your unborn child!"

The color drained from Morgan's face and his hands tightened in a death grip about the whip he carried. "In God's name, Sable—"

She jerked the Arabian's head around, causing him to stamp nervously, the iron-shod hoofs striking dangerously close to Morgan's unmoving form. "Let me go!" she cried, tears streaming down her face. "I don't care anymore what happens to you! If Penllys Wells and your bloody pride matter more to you than our child, I've nothing more to say to you! You don't have to escort me out. I can find the way myself."

Digging her heels hard into the stallion's sleek sides, she sent him galloping into the darkness. A chorus of baying hounds sounded the alarm as Damascus's hoofs clattered across the stones, but Morgan didn't wait to see if anyone responded. Springing into the saddle of the horse Quentin held, he brought his whip down hard on the unsuspecting beast's flanks.

Charging with breakneck speed into the darkness, his only intent being to find her, Morgan was drawn up short when the courtyard before him was suddenly flooded with light. Reining his mount in so hard that it reared, he gazed boldly back into the somber faces of the men revealed by the flickering torches. He saw that all of them were armed, and a mocking grin lit his dark features. It was obvious that Sable had managed to slip away, and that was all that mattered to him.

"You can call off the hounds, Sébastien, I don't intend to go anywhere," he said, catching sight of the bearded Frenchman pushing his way through the ranks of silent men. No sooner had he dismounted than three footmen rushed forward to seize him, but Morgan shook them off easily. "If your men value their lives, they'll leave me be," he warned.

Sébastien gestured and they returned to their places, their relief obvious to the dark-headed sea captain watching them arrogantly. Morgan could feel the throbbing of the blood through his veins, and a heady excitement took hold of him. Sable was free, by God, and she was carrying his child! What did all the rest matter?

"I see you've decided to cooperate," Sébastien remarked, moving closer, his eyes glowing with hatred. "Don't expect me to show you leniency for your courage, however. Not after that bitch of yours did this to me!" He thrust his bandaged hand into Morgan's face, his lips twisted. "Probably crippled me for life, she did. I imagine she's gotten away or you'd not have given up without a struggle," he added, his voice little more than a guttural hiss, "and you'd not be standing here so calmly now, *hien?* No matter, I'll simply have my pleasure with you a little at a time." Thrusting his sweating face close to Morgan's he intoned ominously, "You will die, Morgan Howell Carey, and I promise you it won't be an easy death."

Morgan's brow lifted. "Am I expected to beg for mercy?"

Sébastien hid his frustration beneath a menacing grimace. It annoyed him that the younger man showed no fear and that he seemed to make a mockery of everything that was said to him. Didn't he realize that he'd not live to see the morning? No matter, he would change his tune soon enough, and come daylight he'd send every available man into the mountains to look for Sable St. Germain. She couldn't have gotten far, not alone in the darkness, and his vengeance might yet prove supreme.

"What is it you're afraid of, Sébastien?" Morgan asked abruptly, his voice ringing with challenge. "You talk of torture and revenge, and yet where's the pleasure in watching your henchmen do your filthy work for you?"

"What are you driving at, Carey?" Sébastien demanded. "Are you bartering for extra time? I don't strike bargains with doomed men."

"If you've waited all these years to confront me, why throw the chance away?" Morgan challenged, unperturbed. "Call off your men and let's have a go at it here and now."

Sébastien began to chuckle and then threw back his head and gave a full-throated laugh. "You must be mad!" he said when he could speak. "Less than an hour ago I took a lead ball through the hand and my head's still reeling because of it! And you expect me to accept your suggestion that we duel?"

"You've always been able to use your left hand equally as well as your right," Morgan reminded him coolly. "Furthermore you can always arm yourself against me."

Sébastien could no longer tolerate the arrogance of the younger man standing calmly before him. Fifteen years ago he had sent this same pup running from home with his tail between his legs! *Mon Dieu,* he could still do so now, even with one hand hopelessly crippled!

"By God, Carey," he breathed, his face flushed with excitement, "I believe you know me better than I do myself. Yes, I would enjoy the chance to personally thrash you, and should you die in the process, all the better! Antoine!"

The watching men parted uneasily as a short, bald-headed servant hurried forward. Morgan paid no attention to this latest of vicious-looking henchmen. His steely gaze was fastened to Sébastien Fabois, the man he must kill in order to survive. He knew now that Sable had been right. His hatred and hunger for revenge had nearly destroyed him. Now he found himself wanting nothing more than to live the rest of his life with her beside him, yet he dared not think of a future for them until Sébastien was dead.

At least the driving need he had felt within was gone, and he could now face his enemy with a cold, clear mind and grim determination. He would be battling not only for his own life, but for the future of his unborn child and the woman he could finally admit to himself he loved more than anything else on this earth. Thank God Sébastien had been vain enough to accept his challenge and thereby offer him the only chance he had of surviving!

Morgan's jaw tightened as he saw the man named Antoine hand his master a small but deadly hunting knife, the blade honed and carefully oiled. Sébastien hefted it expertly in his left hand, seeming to have forgotten the pain of his right. For a brief moment Morgan experienced a flash of uncertainty, recalling Sébastien Fabois's almost inhuman strength, but the dim echo of his boyhood vanished instantly, to be replaced by the proud competence of the man he had become.

"Any time you are ready, *mon ami*," Sébastien hissed.

Morgan moved forward slowly, light on his feet for a man his size. Hoping to catch him off guard, Sébastien lunged, and Morgan had just enough time to leap aside before the glinting knife sliced an arc through the air. Whirling on his heels, Morgan threw his first punch, but Sébastien, having anticipated it, ducked, and it whistled harmlessly over his head. Holding his bandaged hand against his chest, the knife gripped loosely in the other, Sébastien feinted and lashed out at the same time with his foot. He managed to hook his boot around Morgan's calf and send him sprawling to the ground. Morgan rolled aside instinctively, and the blade of the knife slammed into the hard ground only inches from his head.

Springing upright, Morgan lashed out with his fist and had the pleasure of feeling it connect solidly with Sébastien's jaw. The older man reeled beneath the impact but recovered quickly. His breath wheezing through clenched teeth, he pounced, his knife descending in a flashing burst of speed.

Morgan grunted as he felt the cold metal slice through the

sleeve of his shirt and cut deeply into his arm. Warm, sticky blood began to pulse from the wound, and he reacted instinctively against the pain, driving his fist into Sébastien's unguarded stomach.

"Now at least we are even, *hien?*" the Frenchman panted when he staggered upright. "Each of us is wounded. Come on, my boy, I'm beginning to enjoy myself."

Morgan wasted no time in obliging him. Feigning with his good arm, knowing it would draw Sébastien's attention, he struck unexpectedly with his injured one, gritting his teeth against the white-hot pain that seared him. He felt the dull impact as his fist connected with bone and saw Sébastien's head snap backward. Morgan hit him again, and this time the knife clattered from Sébastien's grip as he howled with pain, Morgan's well-aimed blow having caught him squarely on the wrist of his bandaged hand. He went down on his knees, panting, while Morgan stood above him, his hands clenched into fists. The faces of the watching men were tense in the flickering light, but no one made a move to interfere.

"So you think you have won, do you?" Sébastien gasped, spitting blood as he squatted on his hands and knees. "A pity you are so easily fooled, my friend!"·Fumbling in the folds of his shirt, he drew out a small German-made pistol which Antoine had obviously slipped him when he'd brought him the knife.

Morgan straightened his shoulders and waited calmly for inevitable death, knowing he had gambled and lost. It was Sable of whom he thought, and he found himself worrying who would care for her child once it was born. Would she find another man to kiss those sweet lips of hers that always tempted him to madness? He groaned, unable to bear the thought of losing her, while Sébastien came unsteadily to his feet, the small pistol held in a shaky but level grip.

"I've had my fun, Morgan," he panted, "but now it's time to end the game. A pity that—"

The thunderous report of a gun exploded in the still night air. Morgan's head jerked up in time to see Sébastien pitch forward, a look of surprise on his face as he clawed at the crimson stain spreading across his chest. Of all the men watching, only Antoine leaped forward to assist him, but before he could discharge the weapon he carried, another shot came through the darkness and felled him at his master's side.

Only then did Morgan turn his head in the direction the

shots had come. Nothing could be seen along the length of the castle wall, and for a moment all was deathly still.

"I hope that teaches you not to respect your talents too much, eh?" came a clear voice through the darkness.

Morgan's lips curved in a weary smile. "You bloody fool," he murmured as Sergei Vilyusk strode into view with a pair of pistols in his gloved hands.

"Is that any way to address your rescuers?" Sergei demanded. "I rode night and day to catch up with you, and my health has suffered." His grin faded as he saw the blood staining the sleeve of Morgan's shirt. "Kristos, you're wounded!"

Morgan shrugged, refusing to acknowledge the pain.

"I'll bind it for you, sir," came a familiar voice through the darkness, and Morgan turned in surprise.

"You here, too, Jack? Who the bloody hell is in command of my ship?"

"The Earl of Monterrey," Jack responded curtly, busily cutting away Morgan's shirtsleeve. "The *Defiance* should be in Llanelly by now, especially the way he was pushin' every timber and beam fit to breaking." He whistled as he bared Morgan's arm. "It'll need some stitching, I'm afraid. Pierson's still aboardship but—"

"Bind it," Morgan interrupted curtly. "I haven't time to wait. Quentin!" he called over his shoulder. "Fetch my horse!"

"Yes sir!"

"Where are you going?" Sergei demanded, familiar enough with the look on his brother's face to know that he could not be entreated to wait until his wound had been properly cleaned and bandaged.

"I'm going after Sable," Morgan responded grimly. "She's out there on the moors alone." His cold eyes took in the men standing uncertainly about the bodies of Sébastien Fabois and his servant Antoine. "Find out from Owen which of those men can be trusted," he added in a tone that brooked no argument. "I want them armed and the rest thrown in the wine cellar until I can decide what's to be done with them. Have someone find Marie Fabois and see if she's all right. I have a feeling Sébastien's locked her away somewhere. Oh, and keep an eye out for Guillaume, Sébastien's valet. He's a nasty bloke you'll not be caring to turn your back on. Watch him closely; he's almost as vicious as his master."

Shaking off Jack's hands and tying the strip of cloth about

his arm himself, Morgan walked slowly to the spot where Sébastien lay. The servants moved respectfully aside, and he stood for a moment staring down at the man who had been responsible for so much unhappiness in his life. He felt curiously drained, and Sébastien's violent end gave him none of the satisfaction he had anticipated all these years. Instead he found himself thinking of Sable and how important it was that he find her. Was it too late to make her understand that it wasn't hatred which had spurred him to return to Penllys Wells? It had been nothing more than his desire to make a home for her here in the mountains of Wales, and he had hoped that someday she would come to love Penllys Wells as much as North Head.

"Quentin!" he roared, his expression intimidating, the wind blowing a lock of hair across his brow.

"Here's your horse, sir!" the groom exclaimed hastily, leading the trotting animal to Morgan's side.

"Let me come with you," Sergei entreated, pushing his way through the gathered men.

Morgan leaped lightly into the saddle, ignoring the twinge of pain in his arm. "I'm sorry, my friend. This is between Sable and me."

Urging the gelding into a gallop, he disappeared through the gates, clods of earth flying from beneath the pounding hoofs. His expression was grim as he turned west toward the river, knowing he had to catch Sable before it was too late. Recalling the terrible hopelessness in her eyes when she had left him, he couldn't dismiss the worry that perhaps it already was.

Damascus was limping badly. A stone had lodged itself in his shoe, and Sable had been unable to pry it out. Slowing him to a walk, she allowed him to pick his own way down the winding path that followed the river. Despite the darkness she had been able to keep her bearings by listening to the deep murmur of the swiftly flowing water. The faint graying of the sky on the distant horizon informed her that dawn was no more than a few hours off. It was cold down by the river, and Sable shivered, wishing she were wearing something warmer than the thin cotton walking frock she had left Cornwall in.

She was exhausted and her back ached, but Sable scarcely noticed her discomfort. She was thinking of Morgan, her heart emptier than it had ever been in her entire life. Lifting her face to the cool, pine-scented wind, she wept silently, and the aching certainty began to fill her that she had done wrong to leave him.

Her first intention had been to ride to Aberdare for help, but now she realized that it might take hours to get there, what with Damascus having to travel so slowly. She would have to go back, she told herself, but the despairing reality of her own helplessness numbed her. What could she possibly do to defeat a man like Sébastien Fabois?

It was then that she remembered Owen Harold and Quentin, who had seemed to be loyal to Morgan. What if there were other servants who not only hated Sébastien Fabois but were eager to see Penllys Wells's rightful heir back in command? Wheeling the Arab around, Sable urged him to a trot and patted his sleek neck apologetically.

"I'm sorry," she whispered to him. "I have to go back!"

Her anger at Morgan was gone and she burned with urgency, hoping she could rally his men in time to help him. "Oh, Morgan," she choked, "forgive me for deserting you!"

It would serve her right if she was too late, she told herself fiercely. Silent tears coursed down her cheeks, blurring her vision and making it impossible to see. It was beginning to grow lighter, and the shapes of the trees growing along the riverbank were soon distinguishable. Sable was able to keep Damascus on an even course, but the valiant Arab refused to obey when she tried to urge him into a canter. Taking one or two stumbling steps, he finally came to a halt, his proud head hanging dejectedly.

Sable slid from his back and lifted his foot. The stone had wedged itself even further between the shoe and tender frog, and she knew it would lame him if she forced him onward. Dejectedly she straightened, and a scream burst from her lungs as she suddenly found herself confronted by the hideously deformed face of Sébastien's valet, who had ridden up stealthily behind her. Guillaume's gaping mouth twisted in a triumphant grin, his lips drawn back to reveal a row of rotten teeth. He carried a pistol in one hand and the reins in the other, and Sable froze, her breast heaving.

For a long moment there was only the sound of the wind sighing through the heather, and then Sable lifted her chin and stared without flinching into that frightful visage. "Sébastien sent you, didn't he? Is Morgan dead?"

Guillaume made no reply, and Sable wondered if he spoke only French or if perhaps he understood nothing at all. She found it difficult to keep looking up into that grotesque face with its mangled eye, but she must know the truth.

"Is he dead?" she repeated. "You must tell me!"

Odd, inhuman sounds came from the black depths of Guillaume's mouth, and Sable retreated a step, her arm sliding about Damascus's sleek neck as though seeking protection. There was something terrifying about the way he was staring at her, making her feel as if she were being confronted by an evil as great as Sébastien's.

Guillaume's excitement grew as he noticed how boldly the little dark-headed Englishwoman was staring back at him. Never had he met a female who didn't turn away in horror at the sight of his mutilated face, and how long had it been since he had lain with one who could tolerate his nearness? He had her now, for Sébastien had all but thrown her away in his burning need to capture Morgan Carey. How fortunate that no one else had thought to ride after her when she had escaped! Guillaume ached to ease his terrible need within her, her sensual beauty driving him to madness.

Licking his lips, he cast a wary glance along the riverbank and back in the direction he'd come. Nothing stirred on the moors, and he knew he had plenty of time to pleasure himself with the wench before Sébastien thought to send someone looking for her.

Sable pressed herself closer to Damascus's side as the valet dismounted. The pistol in his hand never wavered, and she swallowed hard, realizing the danger of her predicament. How was she to help Morgan before it was too late? Her eyes cast about on the ground at her feet, but there were no rocks within easy reach she might have used as a weapon. Guillaume had begun walking slowly toward her, and Sable bit her lip, unable to bear the sight of his face and the drool that gathered at the corners of his mouth.

"Will you please tell me if Morgan's still alive?" she demanded loudly.

Guillaume made no reply. In the dim light his face looked even more brutal, and Sable began to feel the cold shiver of mortal dread flee down her spine. He halted a few feet away from her and indicated with a wave of his pistol that she was to step away from the stallion's side. Damascus, sensing the tension in the air, began to stir restlessly, and Sable tightened her hold about his reins. Guillaume gestured again, mouthing coarse, angry grunts, and it was then that Sable noticed the bulge in the crotch of his trousers. A cry of utter panic burst from her as his intent became clear.

"No!" she screamed shrilly. "No!"

Guillaume gave a snarl of warning, but Sable had no thought in mind save to flee before he could touch her. Without thinking, she brought her whip down hard on Damascus's hindquarters and released the reins at the same time. The startled stallion made a mad leap forward before breaking into a gallop and struck Guillaume down as he charged away. Lifting her skirts, Sable began to run, not caring where she went, knowing only that she must get away from this deformed maniac who intended to rape her. She could hear his furious grunts as he came to his feet, and a sob burst from her, for she had forgotten that he still had his horse. He need only mount and come after her, and she would be lost.

Sable screamed, the primal cry torn from her as all hope died within her. Stumbling over a tuft of gorse, she fell, her hair in her eyes, and she began to weep as she heard Guillaume's triumphant laughter. Turning her head away, she closed her eyes, not wanting to look into that twisted face. Her heart leaped into her throat when she heard a shot ring out from the rocky hills behind her. Scrambling to her feet, she gasped as she saw Guillaume stagger and then fall, his lifeless hand slipping from the reins of his terrified mount.

"Sable!"

Her head came up, and she began to sob in disbelief as she saw Morgan come charging down the slope on a bay horse, a smoking pistol in his hand. She caught her breath, seeing the blood-soaked bandage about his arm and the bruise beginning to darken above his eye where Sébastien's boot had caught him during their struggle. She wanted to run to him, to feel his strong arms close about her, but she couldn't move. Trembling uncontrollably, she gazed up at him as he approached, unable to believe that he was real.

"Sable, did he hurt you?"

She began to weep harder at the tone of his voice, knowing she need never doubt Morgan's feelings for her again. It was as if she could look into his eyes and see the depths of his soul where all of the love he felt for her in his man's heart lay clearly revealed.

"Oh, Morgan!" she gasped, stumbling forward as he leaped from his horse and held out his arms to her.

"Sable!"

Morgan, who had moved to sweep her into his arms, froze at the cry that came from the riverbed behind them. Sable turned her head and gasped when she saw the field of horses gallop into view, the muscular mount in the lead carrying none other than the Earl of Monterrey.

"Father!" She waved her arms to assure him that she was unharmed and a moment later Charles, his face reflecting his agony and relief, had his daughter crushed against his chest. Morgan watched them silently, not wishing to interrupt their reunion.

"Are you certain you're unhurt, my sweet?" Charles asked anxiously. Over Sable's bowed head he suddenly caught sight of Morgan, whose face was etched with weariness and such defeat that Charles could scarcely credit it.

"I'm fine, Papa," Sable whispered, sniffling into the handkerchief he lovingly provided. With his arms about the shaking form of his daughter, the Earl gave the silent sea captain a piercing glance.

"I trust you have a suitable explanation for all of this. I'd rather not discuss it now," he added coldly. "First I'm taking Sable to Aberdare. She needs rest and a doctor to look after her."

"I understand," Morgan said quietly.

Sable turned in the circle of her father's arms and her emerald eyes met Morgan's. She was stunned by the bleakness within those steely depths, for it was as if the proud, indomitable spirit of Morgan Carey had suddenly been snuffed out. She tried to speak, but no words would come, the emotions that filled her ravaged heart too overwhelming.

As though unable to bear looking into her little face any longer, Morgan turned wearily away, but Sable's soft voice halted him in his tracks. "Morgan, wait."

He paused unwillingly, knowing it would be madness to look at her again. Though he had turned her away so many times before, the bitter pain of having lost her forever was more than he could endure. He saw now that Penllys Wells meant nothing and that his whole life was without meaning without Sable's love to sustain him.

"I've got to get back," he told her quietly. "There's much to be done."

She looked at him defiantly, her beauty piercing him to the heart. Despite the grime on her face and the disheveled curls that tumbled down her back, she was so fragile and lovely that he ached to hold her.

"I'm going with you," she said, using the same lofty tone of voice that had annoyed him since he'd first met her, reminding him of what an arrogant little creature she was. Her sharp chin was imperiously lifted, and her clear green eyes met his with bold determination. "You can't expect to restore Penllys Wells to its former glory alone."

Morgan did not trust himself to speak, but a dawning hope began to glimmer in his eyes. "I need a wife, ma'am, not a prickly thorn in my side," he managed at last.

"I fear you'll have both if you choose me, sir," Sable warned, and it was then that Morgan noticed she was trembling, the effort of pretending costing her everything.

"Oh, God, Sable," he groaned, and she came to him, and nothing in his life had ever felt so sweet. His lips sought hers in a kiss that made meaningless the thwarted pride and pain that had marked their stormy past. There was only the promise of the future and the love that would bind them for the rest of their lives.

When it ended and Morgan raised his head to gaze tenderly into her eyes, he became aware of Charles St. Germain standing silently before him, his handsome face cold with contained fury. Reluctantly Morgan set Sable aside and steeled himself to withstand the wrath of his future father-in-law.

"Father—" Sable whispered, knowing she wouldn't be able to bear it if the Earl were to reject the man she loved.

For a moment there was tense silence as Charles's narrowed gaze traveled from his daughter's pleading face to Morgan Carey's determined visage. The full lips twitched unexpectedly and he shook his head, not really understanding what prompted him to yield. Could it be the little hand Sable slipped so trustingly into Morgan's big one or the love that blazed in the younger man's eyes as he looked down into his daughter's face?

"Your mother suspected something like this," he said gruffly.

"Naturally I refused to believe her, but I see now what a fool I've been. I should have remembered that she's never wrong."

As he spoke he extended his hand, and Sable's eyes misted with tears as Morgan reached out to clasp it warmly.

Epilogue

A gentle breeze wafted through the garden, bowing the heads of the daffodils and lifting the brim of the hat Lady Sable Carey wore on her dark curls. Closing her eyes, she tilted back her head and savored the sweet scent of pine and mountain air that she had come to love so well. Wales in springtime was a glorious blaze of hawthorn and wildflowers and the fragrance of the herb garden.

Sable's soft lips curved as she recalled the recently ended winter, her first at Penllys Wells. It had taken her a little time to get used to the amount of snow that had fallen in the mountains and on the castle grounds, but nothing had really mattered to her save the cozy intimacy she and Morgan had shared by the fire.

Sable started but did not open her eyes as she felt the touch of Morgan's lips on her cheek. His deep chuckle warmed her heart, and when she finally turned to look at him she caught her breath at the smoldering light in his steely eyes.

"Daydreaming again?" Morgan asked, seating himself beside her on the grass.

"I was thinking about how lovely it is today," Sable sighed.

"I've a feeling it's the westerly trades you're dreaming of and not Wales in the springtime," Morgan teased. It amused and delighted him that his young wife seemed to feel the calling of the sea so strongly. Studying her face with open pleasure, he missed nothing of the features he loved so well, the impudent tilt of her small nose, the sparkle in her dark green eyes, and the way the sun caught the curls peeking from beneath her hat and ignited their golden highlights.

"It's hard to wait," Sable admitted, the rosy stain on her soft cheeks revealing that she hadn't been unaware of her husband's admiring perusal. The *Defiance* was due to drop anchor in Llanelly the following morning in order to collect Captain Sir Morgan and his wife. Their first stop would be North Head, where the Earl and Countess of Monterrey were waiting eagerly to see their grandson, who had been born less than two months ago.

Charles Sergei Carey, nicknamed Chase by his parents and Penllys Wells's doting staff, had arrived in the middle of a spring blizzard, making it impossible for Raven and Charles to arrive in time for his birth. Sable had regretted such a disappointment, but it warmed her to know that Chase would be baptized at North Head with all her loved ones in attendance.

She had not begrudged the long months of pregnancy, not even when the baby had grown heavy and she had been confined indoors. With snow blanketing the valley and isolating Penllys Wells from the rest of the world, Sable had spent her time reading by the fire with a rug thrown over her knees, waiting for Morgan to return from his numerous trips to Aberdare. There had been an inquest into Sébastien's death and legal matters to be resolved as well as Marie Fabois's welfare to be thought of. Morgan had arranged for her to return home to France, and while Sable was grateful that no problems had arisen during the investigation, she wished Morgan didn't have to spend so much time away. °

She always knew whenever he hurried home to her, for he would arrive from the stables windblown and chilled, the love in his eyes warming her as nothing else could have done. Even in the final days of her pregnancy, when her moods hadn't been the best, Morgan had remained a loving husband whose patience and gentleness had brought tears to Sable's eyes. She found herself growing to love him more deeply day by day, though she never would have believed she could have felt more for him than she had on that golden September morning when they had been married in North Head's magnificent Great Hall.

Sable could scarcely believe the changes that had taken place in her life since Sébastien Fabois's death. Penllys Wells was Morgan's now, and she still experienced a sense of wonder whenever she compared the warmth of the home he had made for her with the legacy of evil that had been Sébastien's. Loyal tenants and servants, delighted to find themselves under Howell rule once again, had responded willingly to Morgan's call to restore the Wells to its former way of life. So successful had all of them been that Sable no longer thought of the horrors she had first encountered here, and she had grown to love the castle as much as Morgan did.

Of course she would always think of North Head as home, too, and it was there that she would stay whenever Morgan was gone on voyages. Or at least that was what her husband believed, Sable recalled, giving him a loving smile. She had no intention of letting him sail away without her. And as for Howell Limited, Morgan's thriving corporation, there was always Sergei to look after it whenever they were gone. If he could tear himself away from his blueprints long enough to take over, Sable told herself with a shake of her head.

It had come as a surprise to no one when Wyecliffe Blackburn's house and lands had come up for sale earlier that winter. Yet everyone, except for the Earl, who had been instrumental in closing the deal, had been astonished when the Hall, as it had since been renamed, had been sold to Morgan's half brother, Sergei. Apparently the challenge of returning the once-grand estate into working order had appealed to him tremendously, or so Sergei had claimed, but Sable wondered if perhaps Bridget Blair's gentle gray eyes hadn't been responsible for his decision not to return to Russia. Morgan had teased her for her foolish fancies, but Sable knew how pleased he had been when Sergei had formally asked for Bridget's hand and she accepted. The marriage would take place as soon as Sable and Morgan returned from Barbados, and Sable prayed that Sergei and Bridget would come to know the happiness she and Morgan shared. Nothing in life, she had come to see, was more precious than a love that filled not only the heart, but the very soul.

"I'm not sure who will be more excited about our arrival," Sable said now, allowing her slim fingers to stroke the cheek of the infant sleeping on the soft blanket beside her. "My parents or Liam and Raymond, because they're going to Barbados with us."

Unable to resist the softening of his wife's lovely features as she gazed down at their son, Morgan caught her chin in his hand and turned her face to his. His throat tightened as he gazed into the emerald depths of her eyes, which he found more alluring than the haunting mystery of the sea.

"I wish you'd reconsider and stay here this time," he told her softly. "The *Defiance* won't be gone very long."

"I can't bear for you to leave us even for a few weeks," Sable replied, but the emotions in her eyes belied the teasing tone of her voice. "Besides, I want to see Dmitri and his family, and Mrs. Pallfry's insistence that being a new mother means I have to stay in bed for the next month is total rubbish." She smiled up at him as she referred to the Careys' housekeeper, a motherly woman whose fierce protectiveness of her young mistress had increased almost to an obsession since Chase's birth.

Looking into the face of his young wife, which peeped out at him from beneath the brim of her bonnet, Morgan was inclined to agree that it would do Sable no harm to accompany him. She was achingly beautiful, the birth of their son having given her a radiance he found impossible to resist. With his big hand still cupping her chin, he allowed his thumb to stroke the silky line of her jaw and was delighted to see the blush which crept to her cheeks in response.

Bending down, he softly touched his lips to hers. Though it had meant to be a gentle caress he could not ignore the flame that leaped between them. His hand moved around the back of Sable's head, drawing her closer as the kiss grew deeper. The taste of her lips was sweet, and he could scarcely credit his desire for her as she entwined her slim arms about his neck and pressed herself closer. His hands boldly roved the curves of her body, loving the feel of her, until both of them were dangerously breathless.

"Morgan, you must stop!" he heard her whisper at last.

"How can I?" he growled, nuzzling her and refusing to allow her to slip from the circle of his arms.

"Because Jennifry will be out in a moment to fetch the baby. What will she think when she sees us like this?"

"It's nothing she isn't accustomed to," Morgan murmured,

his breath warm against her cheek. He sighed as his son awoke and drove them apart by giving a lusty cry, his tiny face turning red with the urgency of his demands. Morgan was silent as he watched Sable lift the infant into her arms and begin to suckle him at her breast. "Why is it you give him what he wants as soon as he asks, but I'm forced to wait?" he teased though he ached for her.

Sable's soft lips curved as she pressed her cheek to her son's downy head. "He'll sleep longer if he's fed," she reminded him archly, but her breath caught in her throat as she looked up and surprised the fierce love for her that blazed on Morgan's rugged face.

"Have I ever told you how much I love you?" he asked gruffly, pulling both of them into his arms.

Sable dimpled. "You don't have to," she whispered.

"Will ye be wanting me to take him now, m'lady?" Jennifry asked as she came out into the garden a few minutes later. She was not at all surprised to find Lady Carey nursing her son while leaning against Sir Morgan's shoulder, his arms wrapped securely about her. Jennifry was a fresh-faced young woman from the nearby village with three children of her own, and Sable had been delighted when Morgan had taken her into his employ to look after their son.

"Thank you, Jennifry," Sable said with a smile, handing her the infant, who had drifted off to sleep. Her hand lingered for a moment on her son's dark head, her heart constricting as she was reminded again of how much he resembled his father.

She waited until Jennifry had gone before trying to button her blouse, but her cheeks burned, aware that Morgan was watching her, and she was unaccountably clumsy with the fastenings.

"Here, let me do that," she heard him say, laughter rumbling in his chest as he captured her fingers with his.

"What is it?" she asked when he paused. Tilting back her head, she found him looking down at her with a mischievous glint in his eyes.

"I was thinking what a waste of time it would be to rebutton this when I mean to remove it anyway."

"Surely not here, sir?" Sable asked with a giggle, but the smile faded from her lips when she met his smoldering gaze.

Pulling his wife to her feet, Morgan slid his arms about her slim shoulders. "It doesn't matter where I ravish you," he murmured into her hair, "but for the sake of propriety I suppose I can curb my desire for you until we go inside."

"How good of you," Sable giggled, but she sounded breathless, and her hands tightened their hold about his neck. She looked so beautiful to him that Morgan could scarcely credit she was real. How many times had she proved her love for him in the past by courageously risking her life in the glittering passages of the seraglio and the darkened corridors of Penllys Wells? He had almost lost her through his own foolish pride, refusing to acknowledge his love for her until he had laid the shame of his birth to rest. He knew now that he had won the love of a woman of rarest courage and conviction, a woman he would give his life for if need be and one he had long since come to cherish above all others.

"What are you thinking of?" Sable inquired, aware of Morgan's silence. Tilting her head questioningly to one side, she gave him a saucy smile. "Have you already grown tired of me?"

Morgan's steel-blue eyes gleamed with kindling passion, and his arms tightened possessively about her. "Faith, madame, that will never happen. More likely than not it will be you who will tire of me first."

Sable's leaf-green eyes glowed with love as she peered up into his rugged face. "Then I suggest that you try very hard to please me lest I begin to look elsewhere for diversion."

She gasped as Morgan caressed her naked breast boldly beneath the ruffled blouse she wore, the desire for her he saw burning in the depths of his eyes making her breathless.

"I couldn't have chosen a better occupation than this," Morgan murmured huskily as his mouth found hers in a kiss that all but drew the soul from her body. "Keeping you satisfied, Sable Carey, will be a task I intend to enjoy for the rest of my life."

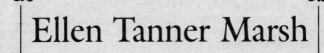

Turn back the pages of history...
and discover

Romance

as it once was!